THE WAGES OF SIN

THE WAGES OF SIN

A DS Matt Arnold Mystery

Sarah Cox

Severn House

This first world edition published 2009
in Great Britain and in the USA by
SEVERN HOUSE PUBLISHERS LTD of
9–15 High Street, Sutton, Surrey, England, SM1 1DF.

British Library Cataloguing in Publication Data

Cox, Sarah
  The Wages Of Sin
  1. Police – England – London – Fiction 2. Serial murder
  investigation – England – Fiction 3. Detective and mystery
  stories
  I. Title
  823.9'2[F]

ISBN-13: 978-0-7278-6764-3   (cased)

All Severn House titles are printed on acid-free paper.

Typeset by Palimpsest Book Production Ltd.,
Grangemouth, Stirlingshire, Scotland.
Printed and bound in Great Britain by
MPG Books Ltd., Bodmin, Cornwall.

PRELUDE

I t was the answer she had always dreaded but it was also the answer she had known would be delivered to her one day. She was still shocked by the starkness of the words though; by the way they had opened a door into oblivion and catapulted her head first towards death and deep, deep blackness. She gulped in the sterile air, hoping for the words to be lost but they remained, hanging above her head, like a guillotine, razor sharp and poised to sever her life.

The date was Thursday 26th April 2003 and the young prostitute sat in a white examination room in a white clinic at St Thomas's Hospital, London. She was dirty, felt dirty, silhouetted against the white brightness of the walls and the words had served to make the distinction between her and her surroundings even greater.

'I'm very sorry to have to give you this news, but your tests are positive,' the doctor said. 'You are carrying HIV . . .'

The rest of the sentence had disappeared in the blur of the shock, swallowed into the darkness of the chasm into which she had been pushed. She had always teetered on the edge, her lifestyle forcing her on to the very brink of life itself, but now there was no way back. She was falling towards her death and nothing and no one was going to stop her. She could hear the middle-aged, female doctor continuing to speak but her lips were just mouthing sentiments. Her eyes looked kindly enough and she had placed a well-manicured hand on her shoulder but it was just a facade, just like the sympathetic expression she had plastered across her face. The girl knew what she was really thinking. She knew the score. She had seen it on display on the faces of some of her punters, before they had unzipped themselves and waited for her teenage flesh. It was what the great and good thought. Prostitutes were the scum of society and she was getting her just reward. There to be used, abused and legislated against in a vain bid to stop the same great and good tarnishing their good names when caught in the act. Where were all the high morals and pronouncements then?

Men, in her opinion, were all the same. Sex was a commodity like everything else and she provided the goods, but now, one of them had sentenced her to death.

She glanced down at her body and didn't like what she saw. Her bony arms and legs were infected with sores and scabs, her mane of matted blonde hair fell down limply across her face, her thin torso and empty breasts were devoid of any real pleasure. She imagined the virus spreading through her limbs and body and up to her brain, like a black plague gradually taking over every part of her and dragging her inexorably towards the grave. She would be unable to fight it successfully; she knew that as a certainty. Her thin, unhealthy body was already ravished by the crack cocaine that had been her master since her first teenage experiments and she had been its slave from the moment her 'friends' had encouraged her to try some. 'It'll make you forget all your problems,' they'd prompted and like a hapless quarry enticed by a siren song she'd followed their instructions and been ensnared. The small creamy rock and crack pipe had become her new companions, chosen in preference to the needle and the reason she knew the disease had been passed through sex rather than injection.

She unfolded her bare legs and stood up, gripping tightly to the edge of the desk. Her mind was still spinning and she fought to regain her balance and composure, conscious that the doctor had also risen to her feet in front of her.

'Please sit down. I need to speak to you about your future and the drugs that are now available,' the doctor was saying. 'There's so much we can do these days.'

But she wasn't interested. There was nothing the older woman could say or do for her now and she wouldn't give her the satisfaction of knowing another whore was getting her just desserts.

'I need to get out of here,' she said, with more strength than she was feeling. 'I'll come back when I'm ready.'

The doctor stepped to one side, gathering up the thin file in her hands.

She stumbled past and lurched through the door, her thin heels clicking against the polished floor. Several other patients turned to stare in her direction. She was suddenly angry at their curiosity, shouting out words of abuse at them. Their heads shot downwards immediately, their eyes averted, obviously fearful of her aggressive reaction. She smiled in triumph, launching herself out through the double doors into the noise and bustle of London.

She knew, though, that she would never return.

Dr Trearchy watched her totter down the steps of the hospital and knew too that she would never see the young girl again.

Just twenty-four years of age, she would be lucky to reach thirty without proper medication. It hadn't been hard to comprehend the sense of hopelessness and despair in her expression and the primitive fear that was immediately evident in her tortured eyes when the word HIV was uttered. She had seen it many times before and though she could never understand the compulsions of the drug addict for herself, she couldn't help but sympathize with their dilemma. The girls in particular were vulnerable to the vice trade and the plentiful supply of punters ensured an easy means for the cash needed for their habits.

Dr Trearchy was genuinely not judgemental but she recognized that her inability to prove it sufficiently to her young client had caused her sudden departure. Now as she watched her disappearing into the background, it was all she could do to stand by and do nothing further. It had to be the patient's decision however to stay and learn. She couldn't force treatment on any single person.

This girl was different though. Most came back, but she knew without doubt that this one wouldn't. The despair was too great; the sense of inevitability had not been lost on her. This girl had expected to be given this news. She had already determined she was to die young and nothing could be said to stop her.

The question was: how many other people would now be at risk because of her infection? The doctor sighed heavily and turned her back as the girl finally disappeared and indicated for the next patient.

The prostitute turned left when she got outside and found herself on Westminster Bridge staring down into the turbulent waters of the Thames. For a brief moment she wondered whether she should end her life now and throw herself at the mercy of the currents, before the disease overwhelmed her but anger prevented the thought taking grip. Tears of frustration fell in abundance down her hollow cheeks, streaking their paleness with thick black rivers of mascara. She rubbed her eyes, smudging what little make-up that remained around her bloodshot eyes. She didn't care though. Pity was being replaced by rage with each step she took. Life was a bitch and its unfairness made her blood boil.

She came to the Houses of Parliament and stared at its entrance, guarded by uniformed, armed police and security officers. Life was going on as usual all around, although pomp and pageantry masked the day-to-day movements. Tourists took countless photos, delivery vans were checked and allowed access, visitors were patted down and their belongings scanned. She had a sudden compulsion to break through the barriers and scream her anger at the politicians, none of whom had the slightest knowledge of the kind of life in which she was trapped. She had things to do though, so instead, throwing her head back, she spat at the building, letting loose her contempt for its never-ending new laws and hypocrisy.

Walking on, she crossed Parliament Square and saw the twin towers of Westminster Abbey looming up in her sights. The age of the building drew her to it, hundreds of years of history, hundreds of thousands of prayers sent up to the God of Justness and Retribution. He was her sort of God. She didn't need his love, only his justice. He would forgive her sins, but the men who had perpetrated their evil on her would have to be punished. *Vengeance is mine, sayeth the Lord.* How she loved those words.

She entered; pausing beneath the ten martyrs positioned in niches above the door and felt the power and stillness surround her. The rage still seethed within her but she knew what she had to do. With each step her confidence grew, walking with her head straight ahead and her expression confrontational. She didn't care about the pensioner who tutted her disapproval and gave the sign of the cross as she strode past or the whisperings of a group of school children who giggled at her bare legs and low-cut top. She ignored the curious expression of a dark-haired man with lipgloss and painted nails and when asked quietly to cover her modesty by a church deacon, stuffy in religious drapes, she just as quietly sat down and ignored his beseeching.

He left her then and she closed her eyes and prayed for help to carry out her desires. She prayed with her eyes closed for over an hour, gradually feeling the rage dissipating, flowing out, to be replaced by overwhelming calm. By the time she paced silently out into the late afternoon, past the four voiceless figures symbolizing mercy, truth, righteousness and peace beside the Great West door, her prayers had been answered and the fuse lit.

ONE

It was 0603 hours on Monday 11th June 2008 and his shift was nearly over. Less than an hour and he'd be on his way home to his bed, the end of another gruelling week of night shifts completed. It had been a very quiet Sunday night, with few calls to disturb his thoughts. The less work he did, the less he wanted to do. A small amber light pulsed on the terminal in front of him indicating a call for help. He tried to ignore it, hoping one of the other operators would answer the nagging wink, but when none did so, a sleepy, rather irritated Gary Fitz-Gerald flicked the button on the switchboard and spoke automatically.

'Good morning, police at Lambeth. How can I help you?'

There was a pause, a strained silence and it sounded as if the caller had changed their mind. He hoped they would. Eventually a young woman's voice answered.

'I don't know what to do,' she said falteringly. 'I think my husband is missing.'

He sighed. Another bloody waste of time. 'What makes you think that?'

'He didn't come home last night.'

'But why do you think he's gone missing, as opposed to other options?' He couldn't avoid the hint of sarcasm. The woman went quiet again.

'I'm sorry to bother you. It's just so unusual. He's never done this before. He always phones if he's going to be late. I'm sure something must have happened.' She was talking too fast, trying to justify her need to be heard and he had difficulty understanding her. He ignored the rather breathy panic in her speech, wishing instead that she would just go away and leave him in peace.

'Have you tried any of the hospitals?'

'No, should I?' the voice raised an octave. 'I presumed I would have been told if he'd been taken in.' He could tell that he'd made her panic more. 'I'm sure something awful must have happened. I don't know what I'll do if something has.

I won't be able to cope without him. He does everything for me. I'm not very good . . .'

He cut across her ramblings, trying to reassure her, to put her mind at rest and delay the inevitable report. The woman sounded young and inadequate, more unbalanced than stable and obviously blessed with a vivid imagination.

'I shouldn't worry yourself too much. You probably would have been told. It's just another option to consider.'

'What should I do then?'

He sighed again, a little too loud. 'It's still only just six a.m., madam. I would give it a few more hours. I'm sure he'll phone when it's a reasonable time. He's probably lost his keys, or broken down, or met someone he hasn't seen for a while and got talking.'

'But he would have contacted me. And I've tried to phone him and it just keeps going straight to answer phone. He always lets me know what he's doing.'

She was starting to really annoy him now.

'Was he depressed about anything that you know of, or on any daily medication?'

'No.'

'Had you had an argument or fight or anything like that?'

'No.'

'In that case, call back later and make an official report if he still hasn't appeared.' There was nothing to make the man's disappearance suspicious and nothing to make the report that urgent. No point wasting his time any further. Her old man was obviously as fed up with her as he was.

'But don't you want his details or his description or anything?'

He didn't but guessed that he wouldn't get rid of her unless he at least humoured the bitch. He yawned and scrolled down to the free text box. She was babbling on again.

'I just know something's happened. I keep thinking he's dead. Ray knows how much I worry. He was only supposed to be going for a quick drink. And I've been so tired and stressed recently. I can't seem to sleep.'

Christ. He could almost imagine the tears. He smiled as she proved him right. A sob followed by several sniffs sounded through the ear piece and he knew he had to keep her concentration on his questions before she started crying properly. Then he'd never get rid of her.

'What's his name?' he interrupted.
'Raymond Arthur Barnes.'
'Date of birth?'
'3rd June 1974. He was 34 last week. We all went out for a picnic.'
He wasn't interested.
'Address?'
'68 Eastleigh Street, SE19 2DB.'
'And you are?'
'His wife, Vanessa.'
'Is there a number we can contact you on?'
'You'd better have my mobile.' She reeled off the number. 'Contact me if you get any information, won't you?'
'Phone us when he returns.'
'Look, I know you think I'm making this up but I'm not going until I've given you his description?' She sounded cross. 'I've had enough of being treated like a headcase. Right.' She didn't give him a chance to answer. 'He's 34 years old, about 5ft 8", slim build, with thick dark hair about collar length.' She paused briefly. 'I think he was wearing a blue and white checked shirt. I bought it for him for Christmas last year and smartish, blue jeans. He was starting to grow a beard although I wasn't too keen on the idea. Have you got all that?'
'Yep.'
'Right. I'll expect a call back later to tell me how you're getting on with the investigation.'
The phone clicked and went dead.
He flicked the switch and lent back in his chair, speechless for a few seconds. That was some lady, all simpering and weak at the beginning but icy and demanding at the end. He sure as hell was glad he wasn't married to her. You'd never know what mood she was in. He tabbed down to the bottom of the page and smiled.
'Awaits scheduled appointment at 1000 hours if husband has not arrived back home,' he typed.
At least he'd be finished and tucked snugly up in his bed by then. Someone else could deal with the mad bitch.

Alfred O'Brien was a man of habit and it was his habit to get up early and take his old Labrador Molly out on the common each morning. She'd been his only company since his wife's

death two years previously and the two had become inseparable. She was the reason he carried on, the motivation for rising
each morning, washing, shaving and dressing in his favourite
grey flannel trousers, shirt and braces. She was also the reason
he was fitter and healthier than men half his age. He was proud
of his constitution and physique and was always quick to compli-
ment the army and his military service for the discipline and
routine that had served him well throughout the many years
since. Lack of self-control was the cause, in his opinion, that
society was going down the pan. Not enough discipline. Not
enough structure. The younger generation needed to learn from
the old soldiers.

He pulled a tie around his neck, tying it effortlessly and
folding the collar back over the top. Molly shifted from her
basket and shook, arching her back and breathing out noisily
through jaws locked open with the effort. Her tail started to
wag in anticipation of the expected walk and Alfred bent down
to stroke the golden fur of his old companion around the scruff
of her neck.

'Are you ready, old girl?' he asked, smiling down as the tail
flicked against him harder and faster. 'It's a lovely day out
there.'

Molly answered with a high-pitched whine, buffeting him
against the door in her eagerness to escape the confines of the
orderly house. He hooked a lead on to her collar and opened
the door. Rays of sunlight shone down across the patio, casting
oval and round shadows on to the slabs from randomly sited
plant pots, like balloons against a bright sky. He looked across
at the trees on the common and breathed in the heady scent of
the pine and wild grasses. Pollen hung in the air, not yet taken
skywards by the warmer wind currents and thermals of the hot
midday sun. He loved this time of the morning. It was an hour
in which the traffic had not yet built up to the constant drone
of the rush hour and only infrequent joggers and dog walkers
were yet out and about.

He crossed the road and skirted around the outside of the
common until he got to the track that cut across the centre. It
was his usual route and the dog knew it well, zigzagging between
the outer trunks, sniffing, squatting, following scents without
ever raising her head. The ground was firm but not yet brown
and arid. His feet followed the track, keeping to the centre of

the dried ruts, taking care at the points at which the deeper gashes veered off into the undergrowth. The common was used by lovers and strangers alike, a fact that Alfred found both immoral and debauched. His had been a marriage that had stood the test of time, a pairing not marred by disloyalty or infidelity even through the war and lean years that followed.

He stopped at his usual bench and sat down, listening to the quietness. He liked this spot. It was almost at the centre of the common, surrounded by trees and shrubs and the viewpoint from every angle was one of lush, green woodland. The distant, indistinct hum of the traffic was the only clue to the closeness of the city and he closed his eyes briefly to try to forget its proximity. It was comforting to imagine the world as it had been in his childhood, without the constantly growing population.

The dog was acting strangely. Alfred could hear her rushing about in a sort of frenzy, panting and whining, in and out of a small copse. He called her name but she didn't come. He stood up and shouted her name loudly, the authority still obvious despite the breathiness of his voice. He saw her emerge from behind a bush and start towards him, but then she turned, as if unsure of what she should do and barked. He called her name again and she turned in his direction, this time making straight for him. She was clearly agitated and he didn't know why.

As she neared him, he saw the reason. Her front paws and snout were dark with blood. She had obviously cut herself, probably on a broken bottle carelessly discarded by one of the night-time visitors. He pulled a handkerchief from his trouser pocket and opened it wide, at the same time clipping the lead back to her collar.

'Blasted yobs,' he muttered out loud. 'Why don't they think before they throw their rubbish out? Come on, girl. Let's sort you out.'

He rubbed the hanky across the dog's snout, checking for any small cuts on her nose or round her mouth. The blood was dark and thick, smeared across her teeth and gums but most came away without too much trouble. The examination proved fruitless, so he lifted each foot in turn, wiping and checking each pad for lacerations. The dog remained calm, not yelping in pain or pulling away at each stroke. He could find no reason for the blood to be there and no apparent cause. He tied the lead to the bench and stood shakily, a cold dread filtering into his imagination. He looked around for assistance, knowing he had to find the source of the blood and hoping the job could be shared with another passer-by. There was no one in sight.

Gingerly he started to walk towards the copse, scanning each step ahead to check for any more spots of the same dark red fluid. The area seemed to have descended into an eerie stillness, what noise there was subsiding and even the gentle wind ceasing to rustle the leaves. No bird song broke the silence and he strained to hear cries or sobs or even heavy breathing coming from the bushes ahead. Muggings occurred on a fairly regular basis and it wouldn't be unknown for a person to lie unconscious for a short time until found by the next walker.

The wheel ruts petered out by the side of a large tree. He pushed at some twigs that spread out across his path and stepped through into an unimaginable nightmare. He saw the large pool of blood first, spreading out to where he now stood, deep and congealed on the dry ground. His eyes followed in horror to where it appeared to have emanated from and he took a step back, gagging at the sight of the man's body. It was as bad a sight as he could ever remember seeing and one that would remain with him for the rest of his life.

He stumbled out from the bushes, his hand reaching up to his mouth to stop the bile rising in his throat. The dog was whining again, straining at the lead. He looked at the blood staining his handkerchief, the dried remnants on his pet's snout and the smears on his own fingers and retched violently on to the grass in front of him.

Matt Arnold was just finishing in the shower when the phone rang. He tied a towel around his waist and ventured out on to the landing. He'd taken to running first thing in the morning, enjoying the rush of warm summer air on his sleepy skin. It woke him up, got rid of some of the tension that was ever present between him and his wife Jo and allowed him to start the day's work invigorated and ready for anything. Things had not improved since their son Ben's accident and the subsequent recriminations. Communication, as a result, was non-existent between them.

He wished with all his heart he could turn the clocks back and change the events that had culminated in the accident, but it couldn't be done. His boy was brain-damaged and although the improvement in his condition was, by all accounts, remarkable, his small child would never return to the carefree days prior to his injury.

He could hear Jo on the phone downstairs and knew immediately by her clipped tones that she was speaking to someone from his work. She had no time for the police force anymore. Any mention of it had become a battle of wills. His police commitments and work colleagues were her personal rivals and she had adopted an aggressive stance whenever he was called in. Gradually, over the last few months, however, she had capitulated to its demands, not caring whether he was at home with her or at work. Matt didn't know which was worse, the aggression or the apathy.

She climbed up the stairs towards him holding the phone in her hand. As she strained her neck upwards to look at him he realized how much he still loved her. He longed to reach out and touch her slender neck, kiss the mouth upturned towards him and run his fingers through her hair.

'It's work. For you. For a change.'

The moment was gone in the last sarcastic syllable. Irritation at the way she chose to demean his job and his commitment replaced any tender thoughts.

He took the handset and responded, watching as she spun away from him and disappeared into the kitchen.

'DS Arnold.'

'Matt.' It was his boss, Detective Inspector Roger Blandford on the other end of the phone.

'What's up?'

'I need you in as soon as possible. A body's just been found in the middle of Streatham Common. The local uniforms have got the scene cordoned off but, by all accounts, it's a good one. Mutilated and hanged. The press have somehow been given the nod by someone and have started turning up. I don't know how they get to find out so bloody quick. I'm going straight down to stop them crawling all over any evidence. Can you meet me there ASAP?'

'Will do, guv. I can be there in about half an hour if that's OK?'

'Yeah, that's fine. It'll take me that long anyway. I've got to give the management a ring and fill them in on the details as far as I know. It's got potential to get big. There are similarities in the MO with another one last week up in Tewkesbury. As soon as the press make the connection they'll go crazy. Before we know it they'll have a serial killer on the loose, terrorizing the streets of London, whipping up hysteria. You know what it's like? Everyone loves a serial killer!'

Matt laughed, despite himself, and promised his haste, but he knew it was true. The media did love mass murderers in a macabre sort of way. Before the enquiry could even get started there'd be journalists camped out on the doorsteps of any friends and families of the victims, trying to interview potential witnesses, and God help anyone when they got a sniff of a potential suspect. Every person who'd ever spoken to them, been to school with them or looked in their direction would have their own story to tell, of evil looks, twisted words or a premonition that one day that person was destined to become another celebrity slayer. It amused the hell out of him but it did, however, make their job a hell of a lot harder. The pressure for a quick result would intensify and their every movement and every decision would be scrutinized by a baying, petrified public.

As he dressed and ran from the house he couldn't help the excitement creasing his face into a grin. He knew only too well the scourge of blame and hurt that spread out, like a plague, contaminating and polluting any person affected by a killing but, from a police point of view, there was nothing like a good murder to sink your teeth into.

TWO

A small group of reporters were huddled by the cordon tape, notepads in hands, when Matt arrived at the scene. Various uniformed and plain-clothed police officers were also bunched together discussing the case, far enough from the reporters so as not to be overheard. The murder had obviously attracted a lot of interest as, within just over an hour of its discovery, there were already senior officers up to the rank of detective superintendent gathered. DI Blandford was already there and he turned towards Matt as he joined them.

'Thanks for coming so quickly,' he said out loud. He gave a sly smile in his direction, cocking his eyebrows at the group of senior officers behind him. 'It's amazing how many chiefs come out of the woodwork when there's a chance to appear on the box.'

'I don't know what you mean,' Matt replied, with mock incredulity.

They smiled knowingly at each other before turning back to the group and being formally introduced.

'This is Detective Sergeant Matt Arnold,' his boss said. 'He's on my team at Lambeth HQ. He'll be doing all the legwork with me and the squad.' A few mumbled their greetings but he guessed they weren't really interested in him. He had nothing further to offer.

'If you'll excuse us, we'd better head up to the scene.'

Matt and DI Blandford peeled away, donning the obligatory white forensic overalls and shoe coverings. Pulling the hoods up over their hair and picking up the face masks, they started a slow walk along the designated footpath towards the inner cordon.

Matt glanced towards his boss and stifled a snigger. No matter how grave the circumstances and how many times they wore the overalls, he still found it amusing to watch the slightly rotund figure of his DI squeezed into the unflattering suit. He liked Roger Blandford. They hadn't always seen eye to eye on things, but more recently his boss seemed to have mellowed.

He thought it was a combination of things. The fact that Blandford had accepted that he wasn't going any further on up the promotion ladder was probably the main reason. He'd made a few ill-judged decisions whilst going through a bitter, drink-fuelled divorce and these had ensured his card was marked. Screwing the chief super's missus was never going to be a good career move and the ensuing bouts of drunkenness on duty and screaming rows at the police station had sealed his fate. It was a fate that he had now accepted and he'd relaxed into his rank, supporting his underlings rather than competing with them. Over time he'd become a good laugh, frequently taking the piss out of the stuffiness of seniority and making small asides that had Matt in stitches.

More recently, since Ben's accident, he had become something of a marriage guidance councillor, dispensing gems of wisdom to Matt about how to make amends with Jo. Matt did appreciate his boss's concern but didn't allow his remarks too much credence; after all, Roger Blandford was no shining role model.

'I haven't seen the body myself as yet but by all accounts it's quite a picture,' Roger Blandford remarked. 'It's a male, although now you wouldn't be so sure.' He smiled grimly. 'His genitals have been cut off and sliced up. Whoever the sick bastard is who did this he then laid them neatly on a plate next to the body with a text from the Bible cut out and stuck above.'

'Christ,' Matt mumbled.

'That's why this murder has been linked with the one in Tewkesbury. Similar locations, both out of the way and both woodland. Both males and both believed killed by the same method. But most importantly, both victims have been mutilated and displayed in the same way. The details of the mutilation haven't been released to the press yet. They'd have a bloody field day if they got hold of that. They'd certainly have their headlines then.'

'And that body also had a text from the Bible next to it?'

'I believe so, although I don't know what that one said.'

'What's the Bible text for this one?'

'It's something about the "wages of sin is death" although I'm told that's only part of the verse. I don't know the full details as yet. We'll have to look into that later.'

'What's the cause of death, apart from his sinful wages?'

DI Blandford glanced at him and grinned. 'Thank God for your sense of humour, Matt. Keeps us all sane. I don't suppose this guy saw the funny side though. A doctor's been and pronounced life extinct, so that bit's done. He's given an initial opinion but he's at pains to say that's all it is at the moment. An opinion. He seems to think it's probably asphyxiation. The victim's got a noose around his neck but he's not suspended from the tree and he's not hanging as such. The doctor thinks that the poor bastard had his balls sliced off first and bled out so much that he gradually lost consciousness. Once unconscious he then slumped against the noose which cut off his breathing, effectively throttling him.'

'Bloody hell! What on earth did he do to deserve that?'

'That's what we've got to find out. At this stage the killing appears to be sexually motivated, but whether this is the over-riding motive, I don't know.'

'Could it be some sort of sadomasochistic ritual that went wrong?'

'I don't know at the moment. It could be. Certainly there are people that are willing to go to all sorts of extremes for their pleasure, but this far . . .' He tailed off as they both lapsed into thought.

'Have we got an identity for the victim as yet?' Matt asked at last.

'We've an idea of one, but it's yet to be confirmed. The victim's a white male, aged about 30 to 35 years, slim build, not particularly tall with dark, almost black hair. It looks as if he's got a wallet in his back pocket but his body weight is against it and it's too difficult to get to. Until the photographers and forensics have done their bit I don't really want the body moved. A male fitting that description has been reported missing this morning by his wife. It could be ident but we don't know for definite. We'll have to follow that up very soon before news starts getting out. I don't want her hearing about the body when she switches on the TV. I'll probably get you to go and speak with her when we've finished here.'

Matt nodded. He always seemed to get that job, maybe because he knew what it was like to receive a knock at the door. His father, also a serving police constable, had been murdered whilst on duty and the horror of having a policeman, full of sympathetic words and expressions, on your doorstep had never left him. He guessed it never would. Matt now knew, however, that the job also brought with it certain responsibilities. It was a task he dreaded, possibly the worst thing he ever had to do, but it was also a job that had to be done correctly and with due consideration. It was vitally important the situation be dealt with sensitively, not just from the relative's point of view but also evidentially. Important facts could be learned or lost by the way the victim's family and friends perceived their treatment. Not to mention the fact that they might eventually turn out to be the prime suspects and vital clues might be gleaned in the way in which they reacted.

The blue and white plastic tape denoting the inner cordon flapped gently in the breeze just in front of them as they approached the crime scene. They paused.

'The body's been here for quite a few hours and rigor mortis has begun to set in,' DI Blandford commented, taking a deep breath and pulling the tapes of his face mask tight. 'Right let's go.'

There was an allocated path through to the actual site of the murder, designated in order that only one small area of the crime scene should be trampled. They gave their names again to the officer in charge of the scene log and nervously stepped forward into the copse. Although still open to the elements, the small cluster of trees seemed enclosed and silent, as if endeavouring to hide its grisly secret from prying eyes. The air was calm, not even the smallest traces of breeze filtering through the ring of shrubs, and Matt could almost hear the hammering of his heart against his ribcage in the stillness.

The grass underneath the largest tree was stained red and a large pool of congealed scarlet liquid spread outwards from the trunk, against which the man's body was slumped. His eyes were open but dull; fixed and expressionless they failed to show any signs of the anguish he must have suffered. His head and body were slumped over to the side, with the noose tight against his windpipe. The rope was little more than a thick garden flex, dark green against his skin, which in turn was mottled mauve and black against the twine. He was wearing a blue and white checked shirt, open at the collar and his jeans were undone from the waist. The zip of his trousers was covered in dried blood and the skin around his groin area was raw and exposed where his genitals had once been. His legs lay along the ground, apart, and the pool of blood filled the space between them.

Small round circles of blood were dotted about the outskirts of the main pool, filtering through towards a path on the opposite side of the copse.

Matt pointed down at them. 'What are those?'

The answer was not immediate and he glanced round at his boss to await a response. DI Blandford's gaze was locked on an object at the side of the body, his horror clearly displayed. Matt followed his stare to where a white plate lay on the stained grass. Laid out neatly round the plate were small circular rings of flesh, overlapping and still, like raw meat lying out to dry in the fresh air. Above the remains was an oblong piece of text, cut from a large print Bible. It read:

> 20. When you were slaves to sin, you were free from the control of righteousness. 21. What benefit did you reap at that time from the things you are now ashamed of? Those things result in death! 22. But now that you have been set free from sin and have become slaves to God, the benefit you reap leads to holiness, and the result is eternal life. 23. For the wages of sin is death

The paper was cut untidily around the last word of the verse preventing the finish of the sentence. Whatever the missing words were they were clearly unimportant and undesirable to the murderer.

Verses 20, 21 and 23 were highlighted in a bright pink fluorescent marker pen and verse 22 was scored through with a black biro. Underneath in a thick black felt pen was the place from where it was found, Romans 6, v 20-23, followed by the words, scrawled in untidy capital letters:

THE WAGES OF SIN IS DEATH!!

At the top of the paper, also written in black felt pen were the words:

3. ONE FOR EVERY YEAR OF SUFFERING!

Matt glanced back at DI Blandford's face, which appeared to have whitened considerably, and pointed towards the plate.

'Is that what I think it is?'

His boss nodded his reply. 'I had been warned his genitals had been removed but there's nothing that can actually prepare you for the sight of them laid out on display, like at a dinner party. Christ, I don't know what this guy did to deserve this, but I sure as hell hope I've never done anything similar.'

'Nor me,' Matt agreed, a little too seriously. 'Still it makes me think I'd better work a bit harder at getting back into Jo's good books, just in case.'

The older man's expression broke into a wide grin and he suppressed a laugh. 'Hey, you don't suppose shagging the chief superintendent's wife might bring this on me, do you?'

'I don't know, but you'd better take care. I heard a rumour the guvnor was after your balls when he found out. Maybe he's having a practise on this poor bugger.'

The tension of the moment caused them to laugh a bit too long and a bit too hard, but the moment was swiftly ended by another glance down at the plate and its contents. A twig cracked behind them and Matt turned to see the first of many forensics officers edging their way forward. He wiped his eyes carefully and again noticed the small circles of blood filtering back from the main pool.

'What are those?' He repeated the question he'd asked earlier.

DI Blandford straightened. 'I would hazard a guess those are the paw prints of the informant's dog. The poor old boy who phoned kept saying that his dog was covered in the man's blood. It seems to have shaken him up more than anything.' He paused. 'I'd like you to speak to him when you've finished with the victim's wife. There's no mad rush. He's still in shock. The paramedics wanted him to go to hospital because of the state he was in but he refused. Said he needed to get home and sit down. And there was no one to look after the dog if he'd gone. There's a uniform officer with him for the time being, making sure he's OK, but when he's calmed down we'll get him into the station to make a statement.' He paused, suppressing another laugh. 'And we'll have to get the dog swabbed as well and checked over. I just hope the animal hasn't eaten any of the evidence.'

Matt smiled at his boss as they turned to leave.

'It certainly brings a new meaning to being "done up like a dog's dinner", doesn't it?'

By the time he and a colleague were en route to the suspected victim's address all thoughts of humour were gone.

Matt checked the details on his clipboard. Raymond Arthur Barnes, date of birth 03/06/1973, male, white. Not previously known to police. No criminal record. No reason at the moment to be a victim. He looked down to confirm the address he was on his way to. 68 Eastleigh Street, SE19. Nearly there, but the traffic was tedious at this time on a Monday morning.

He thought of the woman he was about to visit. Vanessa Barnes sounded intriguing. Her swings from pathos to assertiveness in her dealings with Gary Fitz-Gerald were interesting. After a shaky start she had got her message across clearly and succinctly. She wanted to report her husband's absence and appeared sure that he was missing. Too sure. He checked his watch and saw the time was only just gone 9.30 a.m., three and a half hours after she'd been positive he wasn't coming back. Even now it would still not be unreasonable for him to return, quite unaware of the worry he had caused. All they had was a description, even though the wife had been quite certain. They could be wrong!

He turned to his female companion, Alison Richards, who was sitting pensively in the seat next to him, staring blankly out of the window. He was glad she was there, at least between them they could deal with any forthcoming reactions. They had worked together previously and understood each other. He valued her advice both professionally and personally and had even shared some of his marital problems with her. Alison's home life mirrored his own, with a relationship suffering from the demands of the job.

'What do you reckon then? Is it or isn't it him?'

She appeared to start, disturbed from her thoughts. 'Sorry, what's that?'

'I was just debating whether the body on the common is her husband's. All we have really is her call and the description she gave.'

'It sounds very similar.'

Matt paused. 'It's a bit strange, though, isn't it? If Colin didn't return one night, would you phone the police up at 6 a.m. to report him missing?'

'No, I wouldn't unless I was absolutely sure that something had happened and certainly not as early as that. Anyway,' she said, with a small, sad shrug, 'I'd probably be quite glad.'

He smiled back sympathetically as his memory returned momentarily to Jo's frosty last words. She'd probably be glad too. It was a thought he pushed to the back of his mind.

'What do you make of this woman, Vanessa Barnes? No previous convictions as far as I'm aware and no previous dealings with police, but not afraid to speak quite forcefully to get what she wants.'

'Yes she sounds interesting. A bit erratic maybe but then maybe their relationship is much more intense than yours or mine. Our partners have to get used to us being away for long periods of time and often overnight. I know some people who do everything together and have never been away from each other for a single night.'

'God help them.' Matt winced.

She laughed. 'I suppose if they had that sort of relationship she would know immediately that something was wrong. Colin is so placid and accepting that he probably wouldn't notice if I'd been away for a week.' She paused and looked straight at Matt, smiling sadly. 'Maybe that's why I'd be glad if he disappeared. No passion.'

Their eyes met briefly and he smiled back. He knew exactly what she meant.

The lights in front changed to green and the moment was forgotten as he turned down the hill and a panoramic view opened up before them. Sunlight reflected off sky scrapers stretching upwards in front of the horizon, great glass mirrors of hope, shining beacons against a blue, cloudless backdrop. The City of London spread out from their vantage point, like a huge, pulsing armoured creature.

'I'd die for a view like this, every morning,' Matt said, changing the subject.

They turned into Eastleigh Street. Number 68 appeared on their left, a small red-bricked terrace, with peeling red paint on the front door and a tiny, shingled front patio area. Sash windows with large concrete ledges were the only decoration to the frontage, with the exception of a mottled beige and brown plant pot with a stringy, mauve clematis struggling to reach and hang on to a decaying wooden trellis.

He pulled up outside and saw the silhouette of a woman appear at the window.

'Well, here goes. She's either the periphery victim of a horribly brutal murder or an intriguing suspect. Let me do the talking. I want you to watch her reactions and listen closely. I'll be interested to see which one you think, when we've finished.'

By the time they'd climbed out of the vehicle, the front door was open. The woman who stood on the doorstep gripping the frame, didn't seem to fit either profile on first appearance. She was dressed comfortably in jeans and a T-shirt bearing the motif of a pair of hands holding up a planet with no words of explanation. On her feet she wore a pair of soft brown sandals, through which gold painted toenails peeped. She was slim, about 5ft 6" in height and her blonde hair was pulled up at the back of her neck, twisted round and pinned up loosely with a large, purple hairgrip. Her face was worn, with lines running out from the edge of pale blue irises and small frown lines at the centre of her brows. It appeared to be a fascinating mix of worry and anger, surrender and resolve, and he was intrigued by the watery paleness of her eyes.

As they walked up the path towards her, Matt saw her tighten her grip, desperate to stop the slight swaying of her body.

'I presume you're police,' the woman said. 'I've been expecting you.'

Matt held out his warrant card and nodded.

'I'm DS Matt Arnold and this is DC Alison Richards. You must be Vanessa Barnes. Can we come in?'

'Have you found him, or are *you* going to tell me I'm mistaken too?' She looked directly at him and her stare made Matt feel immediately uncomfortable. He didn't like being interrogated and he had the distinct impression she was assessing him just as much as he was passing judgement on her.

He didn't answer her explicitly.

'We need to ask you some more questions.'

She appeared satisfied with the answer. 'You'd better come in then.'

She stepped back and indicated they should follow, walking directly to a dining table and sitting down opposite them. She motioned for them to take a seat. Matt cleared his throat, holding the pause to allow him to take control.

'You reported your husband Raymond Barnes missing this morning. Have you heard from him yet?'

'No I haven't. Have you found him then?'

'We're not sure as yet.'

'What does that mean? Either you have or you haven't.' She was very direct.

He decided to come straight to the point. 'A body has been found on Streatham Common. It fits the description you gave of your husband when you phoned this morning. Do you have a photograph of him?'

Her face paled and she nodded, getting shakily to her feet. From the top of the mantelpiece she took several photo frames, passing them silently across the table. Matt stared at an image of the same face he had seen earlier, at once pleased for the identification but apprehensive about the reaction. He searched for the words to say but didn't need to. Vanessa Barnes had obviously read his expression. She sank to her knees, the room filling with the most hideous noise, like an animal in the jaws of its predator, letting out its death cry, even as it struggled to be freed. Strangulated and in panic.

He bent down to touch her shoulder, but she recoiled instantly, turning her head up to show wild eyes, bitter and challenging.

'Don't touch me. None of you believed me but I knew. Straight away, I knew. I saw his face dead and white in my dream. You lot wanted to laugh at me, but you were wrong and I was right. He is dead. He's never coming back.' She started to laugh and sob together, the noises sounding unnatural together.

Matt didn't know what to do, so he stood motionless while she vented her anger. Alison too, stood stock still. Vanessa Barnes looked quite mad in her appearance now. There was a manic quality in her eyes, fixed and wide, staring but not seeing. He waited until her reaction had run its course and she had pulled herself up on to a sofa and sat, head in hands with tears coursing down her cheeks.

'I'm very sorry.' He knew he had to placate. 'Is there anyone we can call for you?'

'There is no one,' she said starkly. 'I have no family or friends.'

'There must be someone . . .' The look she shot at him silenced him mid-sentence.

'There is no one else. It was just Ray and me. And now there's just me. I don't know what I will do without him.'

She closed her eyes and started to rock backwards and forwards, slowly, deliberately. Alison sat down next to her, placing a hand on her shoulder. This time she didn't move it.

Matt dropped his voice. 'We need to ask you some questions about Ray although it's up to you whether you want to talk to us now.'

She nodded almost imperceptibly, clearly willing to tell them about her husband.

'What was he like?'

'He was a quiet, gentle man but incredibly strong. We've been together for almost six years and he has always been there for me, even through the black times.' She opened her eyes and concentrated on a spot above Matt's head. 'He was so patient, so ready to wait when I worried about things.' She slid her watery eyes down so she was looking directly into his. 'We were trying for a baby, but nothing was happening. It's my fault. I'm not well, but he was willing to wait. He kept saying it didn't matter, that we had time but I was so worried we'd run out of time. He would have made a great father. He loves children. That's why he went into teaching.'

'Where does he teach?'

'At Westbourne Junior School, in Crystal Palace . . .' She paused. 'What happened to him? Did he kill himself?'

Matt shook his head. 'We don't know exactly what the cause of death is at the moment but it definitely isn't suicide. We think he was attacked and he died as a result of his injuries.'

'He was murdered. Are you saying he was murdered?'

He couldn't catch the fleeting expression that crossed her face. A hint of shock, horror and something else, like resignation, caught in a sigh, the tightening of her lips, almost invisible, but still there.

'It appears likely at the moment.' He paused. 'Did he drive?'

She frowned. 'Wasn't he in his car?'

Matt shook his head. 'No. What car does he have?'

He jotted down the answer. The question had opened up a range of enquiries.

'Did he say where he was going last night? Or whether he was meeting anyone?'

'He said he was going to a colleague's house, Evelyn

Johnson's, to discuss a teaching plan for next term. He told me not to wait up. He's been there before and it sometimes ends up going on quite late. Sometimes he has a few glasses of wine with his colleague and her husband.'

'I'm sorry to have to ask you this but is there any possibility Ray might have been having an affair?'

She stared straight at him, her expression fierce. 'He wouldn't. I know he wouldn't. He knows what it would do to me.' She gabbled the answer, her voice rising, becoming slightly hysterical again.

Matt decided to change the subject. They could pursue that line of enquiry later but it was interesting to see her immediate response. 'Could he be having money troubles?'

She calmed again.

'Not that I'm aware of. We don't have much to spare each month but neither of us are extravagant. We live within our means.'

'Is there any reason that you know of, why anyone would want to harm Ray?'

'Nothing that I can think of. He was a good man.'

'Is there anything that you know about in his past that might have come back to haunt him?'

'Not that I know about.'

He was almost finished for now. 'Vanessa, we will need someone to identify the body. Is there someone you can think of that can do that, or do you think you'll be up to it?'

'I will,' she said immediately. 'I want to take one last look at him before he's gone forever.'

Matt nodded and stood. Alison was already in the process of summoning a family liaison officer; still he didn't like to leave her on her own. He watched as she rummaged in her handbag and popped out a tablet from a small pill box, swallowing it easily.

'They keep me going,' she murmured vacantly.

'Someone will be along very soon to be with you. Once Ray's body is ready for identification I'll be in touch. Will you be alright?'

They moved to leave, turning back towards her at the front door.

She nodded, her lips turning up into a small twisted smile. 'Was he in pain when he died? Or would it have been instantaneous?'

Matt thought of the sight that was now ingrained in his memory, the amount of blood, the mutilation, the noose, the drying flesh set to one side on the plate.

'Like I said, we don't know yet the exact cause of death.' He paused, trying to erase the memory and make the answer more bearable. 'But I'm sure the last thing he would have thought about would be you.'

She caught his eye. 'I'd like to think it would have been, too.'

THREE

Lambeth HQ was buzzing with energy by the time he returned to his office. A growing hub of reporters, with cameras, large fluffy mikes and clipboards were camped out on the pavement, eagerly awaiting the drizzle of further information from within.

Matt drove round to the car park at the rear, keeping the window firmly shut. He scaled the rear fire escape stairs quickly, leaving Alison lagging a flight of steps behind, and found his boss standing on the flat roof at the top, sucking hard at the end of a cigarette. He stubbed it out on the ground as he saw Matt and Alison approach and waited for the pair of them to join him.

'Christ,' Matt exclaimed as he drew close. 'We seem to be popular.'

DI Blandford grimaced. 'It's going to be a bleedin' nightmare with all the speculation already.' He changed the subject. 'How'd it go then? I gather it's a positive ID?'

'Yes, no doubt about it. The guy's photos are everywhere. It's definitely the same poor sod as we saw earlier.'

'We'll need a DNA sample just to confirm that and as a control sample against any others we might find, but I'll arrange that with the family liaison officer. What did you make of the wife?'

Matt glanced at Alison and smiled. 'We've been discussing her all the way back and we both agree that there's something not right about her. She just seems to know what's happening before we've even said anything. And her emotions are so extreme . . .'

'Well, she has just found out her husband's been murdered,' DI Blandford cut in.

'I know, but even taking that into account she's still weird. Angry when we first got there, then distraught when she heard the news. She literally screamed at the top of her voice in this awful, crazy way. A bit over the top, if you ask me. But then when I went to try to comfort her, she rounded on me, angry again. Finally, she appeared almost resigned to the news, accepting it, as if she knew it was going to happen.'

'And she reported him missing so early, earlier than most people would,' Alison pitched in. 'I think she knew something had happened to him.'

'There were a few things she said that will definitely need following up. She says he went out in their car last night to a "friend's" house,' Matt continued, emphasizing the word. 'Obviously we'll need to speak to this "friend", find out whether anything was going on between them.'

'And try to track down the car.' DI Blandford rubbed his chin, stroking the spot where, until recently, a small goatee beard had adorned. 'I wonder whether there'll be any CCTV available of it. And we'll also need to establish how the hell he came to be up on the common without his motor, unless it's parked nearby.'

'I want to dig a lot more into her background as well,' Matt added. 'I've a feeling there'll be a few skeletons in her cupboard.'

'What makes you say that?'

'She did hint that she'd had problems in the past. "Black times" she called them, but she clearly didn't want to go into detail. And she said they had no friends or family. That's unusual. Most people have at least some friends or work colleagues or neighbours, even if there is no family. And she's still popping pills. She took one just before we left, said it "kept her going". My guess is she's had some sort of psychiatric problems in the past. Probably still has. She's well worth going into further.'

'Do you think she could have done it then?'

'It wouldn't be beyond the realm of possibility. She's very volatile, almost manic and she's certainly got a temper. If he'd done something too awful for her to cope with, like having an affair, I wouldn't put it past her and that would certainly account for his injuries. Some kind of warped revenge.'

'And the Bible passage would fit; punishment for some real or imagined sin.' DI Blandford shrugged. 'It's a pretty extreme punishment though.'

'Not if you're mentally unbalanced. Maybe in some situations she can't control herself.'

His boss raised his eyebrows. 'Look into it, Matt. See if you can somehow obtain her medical records and the circumstances surrounding any mental health issues.'

Matt nodded.

'It's almost certainly linked with the other one up in Tewkesbury. I've spoken to the DCI in charge of that one and the injuries are almost identical. Genitals removed and sliced up on a similarly described white plate with a Bible passage. It would be nice if we could solve our one with a crazy, knife-wielding wife but I think we'd have an awful job finding out why she would travel to Gloucestershire to cut the balls off some total stranger in another wooded area.'

'True, but she's a strange lady. Maybe there's a connection somewhere, in her past. We'll have to see.' He paused. 'Do the press know the full details?'

'No, thank God. Tewkesbury have kept back details of the particular injuries. They're a bit too gruesome for public consumption. Imagine the panic if it got out that there was some crazy going around doing unwanted castrations.'

DI Blandford pulled open the fire escape door, grinning back at Matt and Alison as he disappeared. 'Well, I suppose it might solve some of our Vice problems!'

Alfred O'Brien was waiting for Matt. At a sprightly eighty-two years of age and of previous good character he would make a very believable, although slightly vulnerable witness, Matt thought.

As Matt pulled up outside the address, he glanced across towards the common. The crime scene was not actually visible from where he stood but the area was busy with police and press vehicles circulating the perimeter. He walked up the pathway, noticing the orderliness of the garden, and knocked at the door. A dog barked from somewhere towards the rear of the premises and he could hear the sound of footsteps coming towards him. The door opened and Alfred O'Brien introduced himself and ushered him in. The first thing he noticed was the old man's stature, the dignified way in which he held himself tall and upright and the manner of his dress, very formal, suit and tie for every occasion.

He followed him through to a small, neat front room and waited while Alfred made tea. While his host was gone Matt wandered around the room, taking in the stiff, dark wood dining chairs, the glass cabinet containing the 'best' crockery and cutlery sets and the polished wooden floorboards adorned with a small maroon patterned rug in the centre. He could well imagine the character of the pensioner by the tidiness and order of his surroundings. As if to confirm his thoughts his gaze came to rest on several old photos in prime position on top of the glass cabinet, showing the man in army uniform, standing tall and dignified. His youthful good looks shone through the discoloured photo paper and had obviously been enough to entice the young, dark-haired beauty pictured next to him in an adjacent photo.

'That was my wife, Audrey,' Alfred commented, catching him still standing in front of the images, as he entered the room bearing their refreshments. 'We were married sixty-one years, until she died two years ago.' He placed the tray down and moved across to where Matt was still standing.

'She was a very special lady,' he said simply. 'I'm glad she hasn't had to witness what I saw this morning. It was a terrible sight. As bad as anything I saw in the war. She would have been utterly shocked and mortified if she'd seen something like that. You see, we always went for our early morning stroll together when she was still alive.'

He moved back to the tray and lifted the teapot pouring the steaming liquid into one of the cups. The dog barked several times from the back garden and the ensuing whine sounded loud and pitiful. All of a sudden the pot started to shake and fell from the old man's hand, spilling scalding tea across the table.

'I'm so sorry,' he mumbled, his voice breaking slightly. 'Molly, our old dog, found the body. She had the man's blood all over her nose and mouth and paws. Goodness knows where she'd put her muzzle.' He sat down heavily on a chair and put both hands up over his face, his voice thick with emotion.

'I don't know what I'm going to do. I brought her back but now I can't bear to look at her. I've shut her in the back garden for now. I keep seeing the man's blood all over her and imagining what she was doing to the body. She's been with me all her life. She's what keeps me going each day, but I don't know whether I can keep her now, not after this.'

Matt watched impotently as the dignified old soldier broke down and sobbed into his hands inconsolably. Not for the first time it struck him how the ripples of crime spread out to affect so many others caught on the periphery.

'I'm Detective Superintendent Graves and this is Detective Chief Inspector Huggins.' The assembled unit of detectives sat up and cast their eyes over the small group of suited men who were standing at the front of the room. DI Blandford was at the end of the line and raised his eyebrows, smiling carefully in Matt's direction as he took his place at the side of the room.

The man speaking was well built with a shock of wild, auburn hair, ruddy cheeks and a pockmarked complexion. His suit was fashioned from creamy beige linen and had all the hallmarks of having been worn almost continuously for the last month. Standing next to him was a slick, well-groomed individual.

'I'll be overseeing the investigation and making sure every detail gets covered. Obviously, as you've heard, this enquiry has been provisionally linked with another murder up in Tewkesbury. We don't have the forensics yet to positively connect them but the fact that both victims are male, the locations are similar and most importantly the methodology and presentation of the severed genitals are too similar to be ignored. It would be highly unlikely that there would be two or more unrelated suspects committing identical murders at the same time. We have therefore assessed that the two cases are the work of one individual or group of individuals and this has inevitably raised the profile of both incidents and led to the press frenzy. Like Tewkesbury, I do not intend to release all the details of the method and I would remind you all to be very careful to whom you speak, even casually. I don't want the full details getting out in the papers for fear of mass panic.

'The public will want a quick result and so do I, or else it'll be my balls on the line, so in view of that I'm now handing you all over to your DI who will start coordinating the enquiries.'

Without stopping for any questions or further conversation the two men then turned and strode towards the door, pausing just prior to leaving the hushed group. 'I will of course be liaising with the press regularly and giving interviews where required. Give me something good to tell them and do it fast.'

As the door closed DI Blandford stepped forward, his face serious and his voice steady. 'You've had your orders, ladies and gentlemen. So let's see if we can get a result quick, if for no other reason than to save the poor make-up artist several hours hard work every time he steps up to the camera.'

The group broke into laughter, glad of the chance to vent

their amusement at the stuffy soliloquy. DI Blandford held his hands up after a short time and the laughter dissolved. 'DS Matt Arnold will brief you all now on some of the enquiries to be started. You know the form, complete each action as thoroughly as possible and hand every statement or result to the analysts who'll input every word on to the computer. Seriously, I don't want anything missed.'

Matt was now in charge. This was what he enjoyed the most about his job. The ability to take the lead, make a real difference, pit his wits against that of his suspects. It was a battle that he seldom lost.

The assembled detectives were to be split into three groups, with DI Blandford in overall charge of the strategies to be followed and decisions made.

The first group, Group A led by DS Mark Lewis, was to concentrate on the victim Ray Barnes and everything about him. Matt needed to know all about his background: financial, personal, sexual or professional. They needed to know of any tiny detail, however minuscule or seemingly unimportant, that might provide a motive for his murder.

The second group, Group B led by DS Colin Edridge, was to be in charge of all the physical evidence and enquiries around the scene. Forensic exhibits needed to be logged, CCTV gathered, enquiries with regards to the post-mortem and identification carried out and the full circumstances of the crime checked and double checked. Mobile phone records needed to be analysed, along with questions about the religious implications of the Biblical passage. Every possible clue from the scene had to be explored and every physical detail investigated.

The third and final group, Group C led by DS Ernie Watling, was to be in charge of any suspects. They were to liaise with Tewkesbury, research any names that might be thrown up and assist in the arrest and identification of suspects. And the first suspect to be researched was Vanessa Barnes. Every detail of her life and background needed to be known just as surely as her husband's and any resentments or secrets festering in the background unearthed.

The atmosphere was charged as Matt finished the briefing. Every detective knew what to do and every one of them knew that time was of the essence if they were to catch the killer before they struck again. As one body they rose when Matt concluded and within seconds the squad had swung into action. There was work to be done. They had a serial killer to catch and they were determined that it would be their team to get the murderer banged up.

FOUR

'Is that Matt Arnold?' the voice on the end of the phone asked.

He looked down at the name displayed, realizing immediately the number was shown as coming from the unit in which his son was now living.

'Yes it is. Is that Mary? What's up?'

'It's Ben. He's had some sort of seizure. We've had to send him back to St George's Accident and Emergency.'

He'd known Mary, the team leader, for some months now and was full of admiration for her ceaseless enthusiasm. She was determined to get the best from the children in her care. She ran a unit for those kids born severely handicapped or left brain-damaged as a result of accidents. Ben had been in her care for almost six months and his improvement had been steady. From a two-week coma he had emerged to fight adversity, gradually becoming able to breathe on his own, and learning slowly how to sit up, and the beginnings of walking and speech. He was still a long way from normality and both Matt and Jo had been forced to realize that he would probably never be able to function totally independently again, but they had to try. Sometimes a look or a smile or a word was all they needed to provide the encouragement, but other times Matt would look at his son still trapped in a body that wouldn't respond and wondered if it would have been better had he died of his injuries at the time.

'Do you know what's caused it?'

'He's been running a temperature for the last few hours and it's made him quite listless. We were trying to get it down but it was still higher than we were happy with. We phoned your wife a short time ago and she was on her way but she hasn't arrived as yet and then when Ben fitted we thought we ought to phone again but we couldn't get through to her.'

He was shocked into silence.

'Didn't your wife phone you? I'm sorry; I thought she was going to let you know.'

'I was in a meeting,' he stuttered eventually. 'She probably tried. I'll make my way to St George's straight away. Is he going to be OK?'

The pause was too long. 'I don't know, Matt. He's unconscious. I think you need to get there as soon as possible.'

He clicked the receiver and stood stock still, taking in the words. There'd been other times like this when he'd received phone calls from the hospital, times when Ben had suffered a setback in his recovery, but this time it sounded serious. Mary was not one to exaggerate; on the contrary, she normally played down bad news, suffusing her words with apologies for worrying them unnecessarily and telling them time and time again it was just a precaution.

He checked his phone. There were no missed calls from Jo. She obviously thought it unnecessary to let him know about their son's temperature, but two could play at that game. He explained the phone call to his boss and rushed out of the office, forgetting about the waiting hoards of reporters and running headlong into them. His worried frown was immediately interpreted as concern over the murder case and the ensuing scrum prevented his easy escape. Cameras and microphones were thrust forward towards his face as he attempted to push his way through. A reporter, already reading a statement from an autocue above a lens, swung around towards him.

'Are there any developments in the case?' he shouted.

Matt, taken temporarily by surprise at the melee, could only mumble. 'No, no. It's my son. He's been taken seriously ill.'

The crowd parted on hearing the words, the reporter went straight back to the prepared statement and Matt was free to continue.

By the time he got to the hospital the evening was coming to a close and a tired sun was disappearing beneath the horizon. The entrance to A and E was bathed in light, bright against the grey blanket of the remaining day. Matt strode towards its main doors, a faint fear taking grip of his stomach. He was fighting the urge to panic.

The receptionist took his name and told him to wait while she spoke with the doctor assigned to Ben. For nearly ten minutes he struggled to suppress his fear, pacing the waiting room and watching the last remnants of the sun finally disappear. As the dark shadow of night crept up the sky he was called through.

Ben lay on a trolley in the resuscitation area surrounded by tubes and monitors. His chest was bare and his shrunken limbs, still not fully mobile, were lying beside his body, contorted at strange angles. The sight of his young son, so seriously ill again, sent his mind spinning back to the night of the accident. He remembered his panic vividly and the knowledge there was nothing he could do to make things better. Ben had been left for dead by a hit-and-run driver, neither licensed or insured. The driver, a Russian national by the name of Andrei Kachan, had been driving at speed, down the wrong side of the road and was still to be brought to justice. It had been Matt who had caught him, bringing him back from the brink of death himself, to face the courts. He now had to believe that when the driver's punishment was finally meted out, their family, torn apart by the tragedy, would finally receive justice.

Looking down at Ben again now Matt hated his inability to act. He was powerless.

He bent down and kissed him on the forehead, immediately realizing how hot he still was and wiping gently at the thin layer of sweat that covered his brow.

A doctor sidled up to him.

'He's on temperature suppressants. They should bring his temperature down soon and prevent any further seizures.'

He nodded. 'Will he regain consciousness then?'

The doctor paused and looked down at the chart, appearing to study the report. When he looked back up at Matt his face was serious.

'He won't ever regain consciousness, I'm afraid. His temperature set off a chain of events that meant he may well never recover any further. Apparently he had recently been taken off anticonvulsants as he'd been recovering well but this temperature came on so quickly and was so high it caused his body to fit. Because he is still weak, he was unable to cope with the pressures this put on him and he had a massive heart attack. When he arrived here he was still in cardiac arrest. We were able to resuscitate him but he is not able to survive without help from the machine.'

He heard the sound of footsteps from behind.

'I'm afraid his brain was starved of oxygen for too long.

We've run some tests but have been unable to detect any brain activity. He appears to be brain dead.'

'*No.*' The noise came from behind him, a long drawn out wail of desperation that forced the tears from his own eyes. He turned to see Jo almost collapse against the trolley. He caught her by the arm and held her while she sobbed on to his shoulder.

'He can't die now. Not after all this time. Not after all the hours we've spent with him.'

Matt couldn't trust himself to speak. His mind was so full of anger and grief, the two emotions forever linked together. He couldn't bear to see two of the people he loved the most like this and he couldn't do anything to stop it. He felt the drumming in his head get louder. He felt Jo's body against his and was glad. He wanted her next to him like this forever, but he couldn't bear the fact that he couldn't help his son. His only son, who had effectively been killed by Andrei Kachan, the man he himself had pulled from his burning car, the man due to stand trial for the accident the following week. He hated the man, now more than ever before.

'There must be something you can do,' he asked eventually. 'He's battled against so much. You can't just give up.'

The doctor shifted position. 'We did everything we could to save him, but it was just too late. His brain had been starved of oxygen for too long. We will be doing some further tests to confirm this, but I don't expect them to be any different from the first set. I'm really sorry.'

He walked away and pulled the curtains around them, leaving them alone with the shell of their beloved son, still warm, yet so still.

Bambi sat alone with her thoughts. She liked this particular room, enjoyed being there and revelled in its anonymity. It wasn't her actual place of abode but it felt like home to her. It was where she had been accepted, it was where the clients had been brought in the past, it was where she had found peace within herself at least for a few years. It was now the place, however, where she was carrying out the plan.

The room itself was small, barely large enough to house a double bed, a small kitchenette and a settee. It had been decorated many years before and nothing much had been done since, consequently the wallpaper was ripped in places and the paintwork stained. A tired bedspread lay across the bed on which she was stretched, and a few vases of dried flowers brought faded colour to the blandness. Several pictures hung precariously on the walls, cheap prints from cheap shops, nothing special beside the large gold crucifix that hung above the bed. Solid and bare, it was devoid of any imagery of the Son of God. The God of the Old Testament was preferable. Almighty and avenging, He was ready to cover the earth with water, or raze a city to the ground rather than deal in forgiveness.

The single window in the room was flung open and wafts of curry floated in from the flat opposite. A grey net curtain prevented the sight of occupants from across the way but their noise, scents and speech were regular visitors to the bedsit, shattering her solace. She didn't mind too much though. It was good just to be there.

She stood up and stretched out aching limbs. Ray had been heavier than she thought and it had taken all her strength to manoeuvre his dead weight to the copse. He had deserved it though. Deserved every second of the agony his expression had borne. For the pain he had brought. She smiled to herself as she remembered how his blood had flowed out and she'd watched as his eyes glazed over. She recalled the way his head had slumped against the cord that would restrict his airway and take his life from him, just as he had effectively taken hers. It was too quick really though. Too easy.

She stepped across the rug, not knowing whether to break the silence but wanting to see the results of her actions.

Her fingers twitched slightly as she pressed the button on the television. She looked down at the slender wrists, the soft papery texture of her hands and the long, slim fingers rounded off with brightly painted nails. One of them was broken now, bent back and split when the surgical gloves had been removed. She stared down at it, picking at the loose ends to make them smooth. She didn't like to have broken nails; she didn't like anything broken anymore. She'd had enough of pain and destruction. She traced the lifeline on the palm of her left hand with the broken nail concentrating on the point at which it fractured. The fission made her stop briefly, thinking, remembering, fighting not to fall into the yawning chasm that was opening up within her brain. She forced the memories from her mind before continuing along the remaining thread of lifeline.

It resumed weakly before petering out altogether. It was short, too short, but it didn't matter now.

The television flicked into life, with a reporter mouthing silently from within his boxed prison. His appearance was one of comfortable confidence, affluence even, and she hated him, as much for his poise and self-assurance as for the knowledge, that she herself would never have the ability to fit in. Never had. She had been shunned by society's prejudice and judgements and was forced to live on the sidelines, pitied for her lifestyle.

Her friends had been the ones to nickname her Bambi, although she couldn't really call them friends and rarely saw them these days. They weren't there when she needed help and they weren't interested in her distress, her fears or her pain. They had their own. They had been her drinking buddies, meeting in parks and graveyards to consume enough alcohol to erase the painful childhood and adolescent memories. Alcohol for the most part had replaced the crack, from which she'd successfully weaned herself some years before, after the news. She liked the name Bambi because it conjured up a picture of grace and beauty, like the young deer in the cartoon. Loveable, sad, a bit gawky but determined. She had bought the film when the nickname had caught on, and on nights when she felt particularly alone she would watch it, time and again, replaying the moment when the shot ran out across the forest and Bambi's mother lay dead, like her own mother. Her own mother had however chosen death, swallowing mouthfuls of tablets and catapulting Bambi into a care system that cared little for a mixed-up orphan and did even less to support her needs.

Bambi turned the volume up and listened to the end of the report. A reporter was speaking live when his attention was drawn to a man running from the building. The man appeared distressed, but the camera quickly panned back to the original statement when the man's words revealed he was worried about his own child and nothing to do with the case. The reporter apologized for the interruption and continued. 'Police were hoping for public assistance in catching the brutal murderer or murderers.' She smiled. They obviously did not have much to go on if they didn't even know how many persons were committing the crimes. 'Anybody who thinks they have seen anything suspicious should phone the incident room or Crimestoppers.'

She had done the job well, researched her victims and bided her time, waiting for the trigger. There would be nothing suspicious to see. She was too well organized.

Soon she would phone her next victim and prime him for their meeting. He wouldn't resist the offer, they never did. They were too vain and greedy. She just had to pick the right temptation. Smiling, she went to her bedside table and took out her Bible, leafing through the well thumbed pages and pausing briefly to read the comments written down the edges, her own comments, highlighting the omnipotence of God and her desire to seek retribution. The last few years had been a waiting game, designed to test her, full of moments of intense joy and times of almost unimaginable trauma. Now the blackness was surrounding her again and it was time to act.

She picked up a pair of scissors and donned another pair of surgical gloves, going to a small cupboard below the sink. Opening the door she removed a black bucket, covered over with a tea towel. Inside were the items she needed. Two plain white plates wrapped carefully in brown paper, a quantity of twine, a gag, several small vials, some syringes, a hunting knife and the new larger print Bible.

Pulling the Bible from the bucket, she leafed carefully to Galatians chapter 6, verse 7. It wouldn't hurt to get the next page prepared early. There were already three pages missing. She didn't care. They all deserved it and so would the next. In less than a week, the next parasite would die.

FIVE

The night hours disappeared in a single tick of the clock as Matt and Jo sat beside Ben's motionless body. He'd been moved to a single room off the ITU, a small space that at least afforded them a degree of privacy. Whichever position they held him or spoke to him in made no difference. There was no response, just the monotonous bleeping of the machines and the regular rise and fall of his small, pale chest as the air was pumped in and sucked back out. His eyes stayed still, with no movement behind the lids to signal any awareness. They tried to talk the life back into him but to no avail. By the time dawn was blinking its first rays of light into the world outside Matt knew there was no hope. He felt as if the machine had sucked the life out of him too and failed to replace the vacuum with anything but deep, deep grief. The pain was as physical as it was mental and he was exhausted beyond anything he had known before. Even at the time of the accident there'd been hope, a glimmer of life on which he could feed and replenish his energy. This time there was nothing.

The doctor had said the tests would be carried out in the morning but Matt knew they would show that his son had gone. He had already sensed the difference. The figure that lay on the bed in front of him was flesh and blood, but the spirit was no longer there. Ben had left them, never to return, and although he couldn't bear the knowledge he would never see him again, he had reconciled himself to the fact that this just might be the better end result. The battle for the life in which he had been trapped had been hard and there had been no guarantee he would have progressed to any kind of normal way of life.

He was much more pragmatic than Jo was. She would do anything to keep him alive whatever his quality of life. For her, his presence was all she needed, whether any form of recovery was forthcoming. She would stop at nothing to keep him there but Matt knew he was already gone and there was nothing he could do to bring him back.

'Do you think we should get another opinion?' Jo said

suddenly. Her voice sounded hopeful and its tone just served to make him guilty at his acceptance of the inevitable.

'I think that's what the other tests are for,' he replied carefully. They had taken a shaky step towards mending their relationship in their reaction to the news and he didn't want to undo the only good to have come from it.

'But I still think we should get another. You hear all the time about people who make miraculous recoveries. Maybe Ben will be one of them.'

'Jo, Ben was seriously damaged before this happened. It would have been miraculous if he'd recovered from those injuries, never mind what's happened now. Maybe we should just face the fact that this time, there's no going back.' He dropped his voice almost to a whisper. 'I don't believe he's still with us.'

She shot him a despairing look.

'I do and I can't believe you can say that. He hasn't even had the next lot of tests yet and you're giving up.'

'I'm not giving up on him, Jo, because I just can't believe he's still there. Can't you sense the difference? Somehow last time, it was if he was listening to us but was unable to respond until the time was right. This time I don't feel that at all. This time I think he's already gone. Maybe he's decided that enough is enough. Maybe he's tired of always having to fight for every tiny bit of progress he makes.'

'Ben wouldn't give up.'

She turned away and stood up, walking across to a window and staring out abjectly. 'I thought maybe you'd changed after earlier and you wanted the same as I do, but you haven't. I can see that having a disabled son is too difficult for you. It doesn't fit in with your idea of happy families.'

'That's not fair and you know it's not. I was up at the hospital just as much as you after the accident.'

'Only when you weren't rushing around trying to catch the driver single-handedly and solving every other case at the station. Why couldn't you have left that to someone else?'

'You know why. Because I just had to do something. Because I couldn't sit back and let the bastard escape and because I have a job to do, in case you hadn't noticed. Someone's got to earn the cash to pay the mortgage and bills and I didn't hear you moaning about the fact that my wages provided the money required to keep Ben in that unit.' He turned away and in that moment knew that the barrier, broken down temporarily at the start of the night, was now firmly back in place. 'Why do you always think I put my job before my family? It's important, I agree, but my family comes first and it always will.'

'I wish I could agree with you, but I can't. You seem to have this thing in your head that says you have to be more dedicated to the job than your father was, more brave and courageous than him. He died for the job and you could have too when you pulled that bloke from his burning car a few months ago. And for what?'

He was exasperated. She just couldn't seem to grasp his need for justice and now it was happening to him all over again. His father had been killed in the line of duty, murdered as he tried to save a woman from being stabbed to death. Even as a young boy it'd been important for him to know that the perpetrator had got his just desserts. It had been necessary to appease the keen sense of right and wrong instilled in him by his strict upbringing. It was what made him tick and one of the main reasons for following his father into the police service. He hadn't changed but Jo now seemed to be treating it as a flaw in his personality. Now he craved justice for his son too, and the knowledge that the driver had not yet been punished for his actions was constantly in his thoughts. He tried to quell the anger from showing in his words.

'You ask me for what?' He dropped his voice. 'For the chance to see the bastard who did this to Ben get sent to prison for a few years. So no other parent will have to go through what we've suffered at his hands. At least it means we'll get justice for Ben.'

'But we'll have lost him in the process.'

She turned away, her eyes glistening and he could see her shoulders start to shake gently. He took a few steps towards her but stopped, desperate to say something to make things right again.

'Next week, when he gets to court you'll be glad, I promise you. People need to see the guilty punished.'

She swung round towards him, tears coursing down her flushed cheeks. 'Next week, we'll probably be burying our son.'

The test results brought the news they had been expecting and although he had anticipated the answer it was still a suffocating blow. Jo no longer expressed a desire to have any further tests, appearing to accept the inevitable. Her face however was etched in distress, dark shadows around her eyes mirroring the despair that had settled on them both.

At eleven o'clock a different doctor came into their small busy space. He was older than the others, with greying hair, glasses propped on the end of his nose and a bow tie. He carried a clipboard, in which several printed sheets were bundled together, and had a pen tucked over his ear. He explained the severity of Ben's condition, how there was nothing further they could do for him and how they should let him go. He spoke sympathetically and practically but had no comprehension of that which he asked. He told them they should allow the medical staff to switch off the machine keeping their young son still functioning and allow him to slip away. That it was for the best. That they should not keep him alive for the sake of not having the strength to let him die. He said he would leave them alone to discuss their decision but would return again soon for their written consent. He gave them no real choice.

They asked whether they could have time to allow their youngest daughter and parents to visit and say their goodbyes. They asked whether there was even the remotest hope of recovery. They asked whether Ben could hear them and if they could hold him in their arms when he slipped away.

He said there was no particular rush but it would get harder, with more time. He said there was no chance of hearing and no feasible chance of recovery. He said of course they could hold him. He then left them to consider what he'd said.

Chloe arrived with her grandparents. At only just four years of age she didn't understand what was happening. Her older brother Ben was lying asleep in bed. She had seen him like this before, at Christmas time. He had woken up just after Christmas and he would wake up again soon. She didn't realize that when she said goodbye to him this time she wouldn't ever be saying it again. She did however sense that something was different. Her gran and grandad were crying and her mummy was crying and even her daddy hid his face from her.

She climbed on to the bed next to Ben and put her cheek against his. She ran her finger over the tube that held his mouth open and felt the dryness of his lips. She asked whether she could wet his lips to stop them looking so sore and gently rubbed a small sponge across them, smiling as she did so. He was her brother and he would wake up and play with her again soon, just as he had before the accident. Her actions seemed to make the adults cry more.

Matt picked her up and held her against him. She wriggled in his arms, desperate to be given the freedom to move around as she wished. He let her down and she climbed back up on to the bed, squirming back towards Ben carefully. Kissing him on the cheek she turned to her gran, Jo's mother.

'Can we go now? We'll come and see Ben again in the morning.'

'He won't be here in the morning. He'll be gone,' she replied gently. 'He's going up to heaven later today.'

'If he's going to heaven, I want to go too,' she responded indignantly.

'You can't go with him now.' Matt scooped her back up and stepped away from the bed. 'Because I need you to stay and help me.' He put on a sad expression and she threw her arms around his neck, nuzzling down into the space between his shoulder blades and chin. Her warm breath tickled his skin and her hair smelt fresh and strawberry scented. She raised her thumb to her mouth and sucked on it softly, a habit she had never quite beaten. 'Don't worry, I'll stay with you,' she murmured and he closed his eyes and wished Ben could have made the same promise.

Jo's parents slipped out of the room, taking over the care of Chloe, their faces looking stricken and older than their years. Her father took his arm as they left and squeezed it, the gesture almost moving him to tears. Chloe lifted her head from its new position on her grandad's shoulder and waved her hand through the gap in the door.

'Bye, bye, Ben,' she called.

Then she was gone. The words hung in the air, heavy with emotion, both him and Jo knowing they too would soon be saying the same words for the last time.

The paperwork was signed and he watched the older doctor move away from them. They had effectively put their names on Ben's death warrant and would soon be watching the consequences of their signatures take effect.

Matt knew only pain.

An army of doctors and nurses entered, stepping silently to their posts, their eyes cast downwards, obviously unwilling to face the parents' grief. Most were young, too young to know the joy of childbirth and much too youthful to know the abject misery of outliving an offspring. They worked quietly and respectfully unhooking tubes and removing drips, allowing the closeness he craved with his young son. Ben slept on, oblivious to the movement all around, unaware that these were to be his last few minutes.

When the switch on the machine was flicked the growing silence became unbearable. They sat on either side of the bed and watched as the oxygen pump ceased moving and the breathing tube was removed. Ben's mouth relaxed and his face was serene. Matt held his breath, hoping for the slight spasm that would show that Ben was not ready to die. It never came. Matt watched as his small chest remained still and the rosy hue disappeared from his cheeks. He listened as the regular electronic beep of the machine gave way to a single note and then to nothing and inside he wanted to scream. He felt Ben's small hand cool slightly and wanted at that moment to reverse the decision and allow the warmth to return to his tiny limbs. He wished that he could take his place and go to where his son was going but his body wouldn't release him. It remained motionless, watching, listening and touching but unable to prevent the awful scenario that was happening before him.

After what seemed like only a few seconds the doctor pronounced death. It seemed too soon. He heard the words but couldn't relate them to his own son. They were words he'd heard many times before but on those occasions he'd been more concerned with recording the details than thinking of the implications. Ben was dead. Official. His life had been pronounced extinct. He was no longer living. His six-year-old son killed by the man he himself had saved from death. It was a cruel irony.

Jo was sobbing and he glanced across at her, the noise sounding loud in the stillness of the room. Her face mirrored his pain and he ached to hold her but as strong as the need was, so too was the knowledge that she wouldn't accept the gesture. Her arms were thrown around herself and she was hugging her body tightly and rocking, cocooned in a bubble of grief. The knowledge roused an anger in him that flared uncontrollably. In little over six months their previously happy life had been torn apart. Six months in which not only had they had to deal with the death of their first born son but now also the possibility that their relationship had been damaged beyond repair by the finger of blame.

He didn't know how to deal with it or retrieve the situation.

Jo was leaning forward now, cradling Ben's head to her body, her tears splashing unhindered on to his pale skin. Matt couldn't watch.

He stood shakily and strode across to the door, needing to be far away. A nurse nodded towards him.

'Are you OK?'

He returned the nod, thinking immediately how obtuse the question sounded. He recognized in his head what she had meant but the returned nod was as far from the truth as was possible. He wasn't OK, the scene was not OK and he would probably never be OK again in his life.

By the time he reached the fresh air outside the building his rage was in danger of consuming him. A few faceless people wandered aimlessly by the exits, having a break from the vigils they were keeping. He hardly acknowledged their presence. Clenching his fists he punched the wall of the building hard, not once but twice, three times, again and again until he felt the blood flowing down the back of his hands and his wrists and the pain in his hands ran parallel to the pain in his head. Tears of anger and grief flowed and he didn't care who saw them. The unfairness and injustices of his life, losing his father and now his son to crime, threatened to engulf him but as his blood flowed the rage gradually subsided and an overwhelming tiredness took its place.

He let himself be led back into the hospital and sat wordlessly while his injured hands were dressed, refusing with a shake of the head for them to be X-rayed.

By the time he walked back into the small room, Jo had gone. Ben remained, lying peacefully on the bed, a white sheet drawn up, covering his naked, still chest. His eyes were closed and his blond hair brushed neatly against his head. His mouth was motionless, turned slightly at the corners, giving the appearance of a small smile. Matt walked across and ran his fingers gently across his forehead, tracing down to his eyelids and the contours of his nose. He tucked his arms under his neck and lay down on the bed next to him cradling his son's small body to his. His smell was still the same and he breathed in deeply of the scent, never wanting the memory to leave. His skin was cooler now and whiter than it should be but it didn't matter for that moment in time.

He pulled the small body against his and cupped his head in his hand, drawing his face towards his and kissing him gently on the forehead.

'Goodbye, Ben,' he whispered. 'Goodbye. You'll always be in my heart in everything I do.'

He closed his eyes then and let the darkness engulf him.

SIX

The office was quiet when Matt entered three days later, even quieter when those at work saw him step into the room unannounced.

'Where is everyone?' he asked, knowing instinctively it was he who needed to break the ice first.

Alison Richards and Tom Berwick were standing to one side, deep in conversation. Tom was the one who spoke out. He was one of Matt's oldest friends having joined the police force at the same time and emerged from their initial training to be posted to the same station. Even now their career paths and interests were still remarkably similar, although Tom had chosen to remain a detective constable rather than take promotion like Matt, and they had continued their friendship out of work, socializing as a couple with Tom and his wife Sue.

'Some are still out on enquiries and the others are around somewhere.' He paused. 'Matt, we're all so sorry to hear your news. I told the guys the other day when I first heard. If there's anything anyone can do you only have to ask.'

'Thanks. I appreciate the offer.' He smiled at his colleagues, anxious to show them he wasn't about to break down at the mere mention of his bereavement. 'At the moment we're getting along a day at a time. Jo's doing most of the funeral arrangements, so I was a bit redundant. I thought I'd have a break and pop in to see how the case was going. I've been following it on TV but you don't know how much of what you see is for real.'

'What date is the funeral set for?' Alison asked quietly.

'Next Wednesday the 20th. Only a couple of days before Kachan's case is due at court. Which reminds me, I need to make a phone call and then I'll come and find out what's been happening.'

He turned smartly and strode out of the office and along the corridor to his own small room, shutting the door behind him. He was glad to get over the initial sentiments and guessed they would be too. His father's face stared out from its wooden photo frame situated directly in front of him on his desk, neither stern nor sympathetic, neither proud nor guilty. He picked the frame up and looked at the uniformed figure, dressed as he was in the old style police uniform, smart belted tunic, shiny whistle chain and high beat helmet. His face was matter of fact. He was doing a job that had to be done, fulfilling his belief in the law and its judgements, working to ensure that criminals were safely locked behind bars. From a young age Matt could still vaguely remember his father's lectures on always doing what was right and honourable. That was before they'd received the knock on the door informing them of his father's death during the course of the Job.

He sighed heavily and replaced the photo on the desk, glancing across at the corresponding frame containing his favourite picture of Ben. Everything had changed since his father had walked the beat. The law had turned full circle, in his opinion, to protect the suspect in preference to the victim and uphold the rights of the aggressor over the needs of the aggrieved. His father would have turned in his grave to know how blurred right and wrong had become in the eyes of magistrates and politicians. He gazed at his son's smiling face, frowning at the memory of his small lifeless body and his fight for justice. It made him cross to think of justice these days. Ben's five-year-old expression radiated optimism, hopefulness and the sheer joy of living. He knew no different and never would now.

Matt picked up the phone and keyed in the number of the investigating officer with whom he had dealt following Ben's accident. The phone was answered promptly.

'Hi. Gary Fellowes speaking.'

'Gary, its Matt Arnold here. How're things?'

'Fine, fine. Keeping quite busy at the moment.' He paused. 'I suppose you're ringing about Andrei Kachan's court case on 22nd June. I presume you and Jo will both be attending and Ben's condition is pretty much the same as before?'

'Ben died on Tuesday evening.' Matt blurted out the words in reply, knowing no other way to make them sound less harsh. 'He caught an infection which made his temperature too high and that caused him to have a heart attack. He never regained consciousness.'

'Oh my God, Matt. I'm so sorry. I didn't realize.'

Matt heard the shock in his voice. They'd worked well together in the initial investigation and he guessed the fact that the traffic officer's kids were only slightly older than his own, made the impact of his rather blunt statement more poignant.

'That's what I'm ringing you about,' Matt continued. 'I know Kachan was charged with dangerous driving at the time, as well as failing to stop after an accident and the other bits and pieces. Can he now be charged with causing death by dangerous driving? We're well within the one-year time limit and the charge is that much more serious. At least then when the case comes up at court, it'll enable the judge to have a much wider range of options. He'll hopefully be given a punishment, more likely to fit the crime.'

'That sounds feasible to me. I've got a meeting with the Crown Prosecution reps next week. I'll give them a ring right away and ask whether this could be done and see if I can have any necessary statements ready for then. I'll probably need permission from you or Jo to access Ben's hospital records.'

'You already have it. I filled out the form some time ago when you needed details of his immediate injuries. It should still cover his further treatment.'

'That's true, but I will still need to get statements from the doctors concerned. You realize that it might mean the case being put back again if we do get the chance to have the further charge put. If the defence aren't satisfied with the further evidence, it could be a good few months before the case is ready to be heard.'

'I know that Gary, but I'd rather wait and get Kachan banged up for a decent time than see him walk.'

'Me too, Matt. I've always thought the lesser charge was totally insufficient. We need a sentencing policy that recognizes when an accident results in serious injuries. It's a loophole that needs plugging.' He paused as if trying to gather his thoughts. 'I'm so sorry to hear about Ben's death. Let's hope we've got time to at least get you a proper result. I suppose the only good thing about Ben's death now is that at least the case hasn't gone to court yet.'

Matt closed his eyes and tried to think of a single good thing that had come of the accident. 'I suppose so,' he said remotely. 'Although I wish to God I'd never set eyes on Andrei Kachan.'

*   *   *

Tom was hanging about in the corridor outside his office when he replaced the receiver. He opened the door and beckoned him in, glad not to have to face the group again.

'You look awful,' Tom said as he entered.

'Thanks.'

'Nobody was expecting you back so soon.'

'I couldn't stay in the house any longer, Tom. It was doing my head in. Everywhere you look there are reminders of Ben and Jo has been in a kind of frenzy, getting everything ready for the funeral. She's determined to give him the best send-off she can. Her parents are looking after Chloe and I feel like I've been sidelined. Of course she runs her ideas past me because she has to, but apart from that, I may as well not be there.'

'Things are no better then?'

'Worse if anything. I thought for a while at the hospital that we'd turned things around but then she accused me of being pleased that he was dying because I didn't like the idea of having a disabled son. Do you know what? She didn't even bother to let me know when the unit originally called to say Ben was running a temperature and it looked serious. As it turned out it didn't matter, because he was unconscious by the time either of us got there but supposing she'd got to see him and I hadn't. I would never have forgiven her for robbing me of the last chance to see him conscious.'

He didn't mention that he had neglected to let Jo know that he'd received the second call from the unit with further information. Her decision to withhold his phone call was of more relevance, as far as he was concerned.

Tom shrugged. 'But at least that wasn't the case, so try to forget it. It's not worth thinking about something that might have happened.'

'It shows me how little she cares about what I think though. And she accuses me of not caring and giving up.' He turned away from his friend bitterly. 'Tom. I haven't changed. I've always been like I am now. My family have always come first, but I couldn't just sit back and see the bastard who did this to Ben get away without at least trying to catch him.'

'I know but in Jo's mind, you weren't there when she needed you and –' he took a deep breath – 'you're not there now.'

Matt spun round, picking up on the accusation immediately.

'I'm not there now because she doesn't want me there.

She only wants me to rubber stamp what decisions she makes. She doesn't ask me what I want. I don't matter, as far as she is concerned.'

'OK, sorry mate. I didn't mean to upset you.' Tom held his hands up in placation. 'Don't forget I hear a different story from Sue, who talks to Jo. As far as Sue's aware, Jo doesn't want it to be like this either. The two of you just need to talk but neither of you will make the first move and you both think you're right. You really need each other now, more than at any other time in your lives.'

'I know, but I've tried and I just seem to be met with a brick wall. It feels like she hates me and everything I stand for at the moment.'

He pulled a pack of cigarettes from his pocket and took two out, throwing one in Tom's direction.

Tom caught it and popped it into the corner of his mouth, a small smile of embarrassment flickering on his lips. 'Just don't give up on her yet. Otherwise you might realize too late what you had.'

Matt stared at his friend in amazement. They had never really spoken about such personal things before and he was touched by Tom's concern, although still slightly uncomfortable with this kind of discussion. He saw Alison walking towards them and decided to change the subject.

'Thanks. I'll bear in mind what you've said. And now –' he clapped Tom on the back and nodded towards Alison – 'let's have a fag outside and you can fill me in on what's been happening.'

They both followed Matt out on to the roof space, squinting at the brightness as the light hit their eyes.

'So how's the investigation going, then?' Matt asked as soon as they'd lit up. 'Have we got any nearer identifying a suspect?'

Tom shook his head. 'Apart from Vanessa Barnes, no. It's quite slow going unfortunately. So far most of the stuff is background info. Ernie Watling is off to Tewkesbury tomorrow to see first hand what they've got so far. I'm sure he wouldn't mind a few passengers if you were interested. I'm off to visit Evelyn Johnson later if you want to join me. I've spoken to her on the phone and she sounded quite nervous about meeting. She even asked if she could speak to me without her husband being present. I've a feeling she might come up with something interesting.'

'What's the betting she's been having an affair with Ray Barnes?'

'I tend to agree and Alison and I both think that Vanessa Barnes might also suspect that to be the case, even if she was not a hundred per cent sure.' Alison nodded her agreement.

'So what other background information has been dug up about Ray Barnes?'

'Well, from what we can gather, he's quite a regular sort of guy. His father is dead but his mother is still alive, living in Cambridgeshire. I don't think they communicate much, in fact they don't appear to have been in contact much since he married Vanessa. I'm not sure if there's a reason for that but a visit has been arranged to speak to her. Apart from that he has one sister, Margaret, who is married with two teenage daughters and who again he rarely sees. Rob spoke to her and she seemed a bit reticent about talking too much about the family. I don't know whether there have been any particular reasons for a rift but we're looking into it.'

'What about his schooling and education history? Any misrepresentations or lies in his CV?'

Tom shook his head again. 'Not that we could find. He attended Huntingdon primary and junior schools, before going on to Ramsey Abbey Secondary School, Huntingdon. He left there with good qualifications before going on to Kingston University in London where he got an English degree and did his teacher training courses. He appears to have passed through all his education without rousing too much attention. He gained adequate grades and seemed to be a quiet, studious pupil. All in all, he's not the sort of man to rouse passions or seemingly give anyone a reason to want him dead, at least, not then.'

Matt ran his hands through his hair. 'What about when he met Vanessa and more recently?'

'This bit gets more interesting.' Alison spoke now. 'Ray appears to have met Vanessa about six years ago and they got married pretty quickly. I've been assisting the family liaison officers but Vanessa doesn't really like talking about that time in her life. I find that quite strange especially as most people have the best memories of their partners at the start of their relationships and more forgettable ones a few years into it.'

Matt caught Alison's eye and they nodded almost imperceptibly.

'And she's not keen on us checking her medical records. She doesn't mind us having Ray's and has signed the form but she doesn't see why we need hers.'

'I'll have a think about how to get around her on that one. It would be so much easier if she volunteered them, rather than having to get a warrant. I'm sure she'll come to see my point of view.' Matt took a long draw on his cigarette. 'Anything come up on the post-mortem or forensics as yet?'

'The post-mortem was done the day before yesterday,' Tom took over. 'I can't remember all the technical terms but basically it was as we thought. Death was due to asphyxiation from the ligature around his neck. That has now been sent off for forensics to match it against the cord on the Tewkesbury body. It also confirms he died at that scene and his genitals were cut off there too. It appears from the amount of blood that he went unconscious either from blood loss or shock or a combination of them both and then slumped against the ligature. His body weight was against the cord and there were deep lacerations and bruising around his neck consistent with that. There were also restraint marks around his wrists where they were tied behind his back and bruising around his mouth consistent with him being gagged.'

'I didn't notice a gag when I saw the body.'

'No, there wasn't one. The suspect obviously removed it at some point before they left, although we're not sure whether it was before or after the victim went unconscious. Maybe the killer wanted to hear him speak, we don't know.'

'What about any trace of drugs or alcohol? Has anything shown up?'

'Again we don't know as yet. The samples have been sent off and the guvnor's pushing for a quick analysis. We should get the results later today or tomorrow at the latest.'

'Are there any other forensics from the scene?'

'Yes,' Alison chipped in. 'There are tyre marks where a vehicle was backed right up to the tree. They're not very good prints though as the grass was too dry, but it does show where the vehicle stops. There are also drag marks from the edge of the tyre tracks to the tree. It appears that the victim was either unconscious when he was removed from the vehicle or certainly bound tight enough not to be able to struggle free. They're pretty sure he was probably unconscious as the marks are so regular. If he had struggled they think there would be more movement in the marks, but they can't discount the idea completely.'

'So that rules out Ray going of his own accord then. That's interesting.' Matt ran his hands through his hair again. 'Were there any other significant injuries on his body? Could he have been hit or knocked unconscious prior to being brought there?'

'Not that I'm aware of.' Alison looked towards Tom who shook his head. 'There were no head injuries and nothing else serious enough to cause him to black out, only minor scratches and abrasions from the bushes and woodland probably from where he was dragged. It's possible he was partially asphyxiated, of course, enough to cause him to lapse into unconsciousness. Any injuries would have been obscured by the later ligature marks.'

'So it would be reasonable to assume that there was some sort of drug used. It'll be interesting to see whether our suspect has access to street drugs or prescription drugs.'

Tom checked his watch. 'I've arranged to be at Evelyn Johnson's house in about an hour. Why don't I fill you in on the rest as we drive?'

'Sounds good to me and it gets me out and about. I got the feeling it was a bit awkward when I came in.'

Alison smiled sympathetically. 'We're so used to dealing with other people's tragedies, but when it comes to one of our own it's so different. None of us really know what to say, in case we sound like we're just talking job.' She put her hand on his arm lightly. 'It's hit all of us hard though. Ever since Ben's accident, it was as if he was one of our own. We knew all his ups and downs and realized how hard you both fought for him. It seems so unfair for this to happen now and there weren't many dry eyes when we heard. Quite a few of the team have started a collection for you and Jo.'

Matt swallowed hard, fighting back his emotion. He couldn't explain it but ever since his father had died he'd always felt he belonged in the police. Jo couldn't understand it. Ben, too, had belonged and his accident had affected everyone. Now, with his death, it was as if his family unit was being drawn into the larger extended group and giving him the support that Jo had rejected. He was touched by the sentiment.

'Thanks,' he replied finally. 'I'll speak to Jo and see what she wants to do.'

'So, what else has been happening?' asked Matt as they came to rest in a long queue of traffic on the way to Evelyn Johnson's house.

'Nothing much,' Tom replied. 'We just don't seem to be getting any positive leads at the moment.'

'In what way?'

'Well, house-to-house enquiries are almost complete and no one seems to have heard or seen a thing. There is no CCTV on the common and none nearby that was working so we have no idea what vehicle the suspect was using. We do know it's not Ray Barnes' vehicle though. The tyre tracks don't match his car.'

'Has his Renault Laguna been found then?'

'Yep, that was found in a street search on Wednesday parked up all legally, but again no one seems to have heard or seen a thing and there was no CCTV anywhere nearby. It's been lifted for full forensics of course.'

'But that's not going to be much use if Vanessa Barnes is our killer. Her DNA and dabs are going to be all over it anyway. Any evidence of a struggle?'

'No, nothing obvious. No blood or damage or anything.'

'It might mean that Ray Barnes knew the suspect. If nothing else is found by forensics, I suppose we could conclude that he left his car and got into the killer's.'

They continued in silence, both men considering the implications of the suggestion. Matt didn't know quite what to think. If Vanessa Barnes was the murderer, why had she gone to such elaborate lengths to kill her husband? He was intrigued by her but needed to find out a good deal more before she could be taken seriously as a suspect. Her background, motive and means were still quite vague. Did she have access to another vehicle? Had Ray gone with her quite willingly as now seemed possible? But why such brutality? It all pointed to the suspect being very well prepared and the murder having been executed to a precise plan. And what could possibly link it to the Tewkesbury murder? He was still deep in thought as the traffic thinned and their car moved off again.

Their route took them into the Vice area of Brixton, busy

with the everyday activities of the local residents. By day the area was comprised of tree-lined residential streets with nothing to mark them out as anything but normal, but by night the area would be left to the street workers and dwellers, and the middle-class residents, hidden away within their fortresses, would try to block from their minds and vision the seedy goings-on outside their doors. Even now at midday the odd hooker would be out, plying for the lunchtime trade.

They stopped opposite a lone prostitute and waited for her approach. She was a light-skinned black girl, in her early thirties, unhealthily thin, with streaked hair tied up in a ponytail and clothing that barely covered her bony frame. Sauntering over from the corner, she leant low into the vehicle exposing what cleavage she had in their direction. Her breath smelt of stale cigarettes and her eyes were wild and staring, the need for drugs in her fixed pupils obvious. Known better by her street name of 'Tricks', Carol Pritchard was well known to the local police, having worked the same streets since she was a teenager. Now fifteen years on, her face and voice had suffered the ravages of the weather, drugs and assaults and she appeared way older than her years.

As her eyes became focused, she recognized them as police and made to walk off. Matt recognized her from a previous murder enquiry and called her back.

'Carol, we need to speak before you go.'

She rounded on them, her expression hostile. 'Why aren't you lot out catching the fucking sick bastard who's taking my customers rather than harassing me?' she screeched, through blackened front teeth.

'That's why we want to talk to you. We're not interested in what you're up to today,' Matt replied testily. 'Any word on the street about who it might be? As you've no doubt seen, it happened up on Streatham Common. Any of you girls had any trouble with any of your punters up there, in the past?'

Carol Pritchard stopped her attack and straightened, smiling apologetically. 'Sorry, I thought you was going to take me in again. I didn't recognize you. I've been up in court twice already this bleedin' week and I'm hardly making enough cash to pay the fines, never mind anything else.' She scratched at a scab on her arm and frowned. 'I haven't heard of no bother up there before with punters. We don't take our customers to that common so much though. It's mainly used by the queers and nonces. I do know a few of the rent boys though. I'll see if I can have a word.'

'Cheers, Carol. Have a word with any of the other girls as well, will you. Just because it's been two male victims at the moment, doesn't mean it will stay that way. Give me a ring if you come up with anyone.'

'Will do, sarge.'

She nodded, grinning the same blackened toothy grin as previously, before saluting shakily and tottering away on her stilettos back to her corner.

Evelyn Johnson could not be more different to Carol Pritchard.

Small and round, she wore sensible clothes, sensible shoes and had a short, mousy sensible hair cut. Her face was a contradiction to the middle-aged maturity of her clothing, however, and was almost childlike in appearance, with rounded, slightly plump cheeks, a snub nose, unplucked eyebrows and no make-up. She looked like a mischievous daughter, experimenting with her mother's wardrobe.

They saw her first, peeping round the curtain, before listening as the locks were slid across and the door opened. She ushered them into her small house and closed the door swiftly behind them, bolting it carefully. Tom cast Matt a curious expression but said nothing.

'Thank you for seeing us,' Tom started, squeezing into the dining-room chair he was offered and laying his folder out across the pine veneered table in front of him.

She grimaced. 'To be honest it's been difficult. My husband didn't really want me to talk to you, certainly not without him being present, but I've arranged an afternoon off from school, without his knowledge.'

'Can I ask why he didn't want you to speak to us?' Matt jumped in.

She turned to face him. 'Because he's afraid.'

'But what's he got to be afraid of?'

'He's frightened he might become the next victim.'

'Why?'

'Because of Vanessa, Ray's wife. She's mad and she's always hated both of us. Now Ray's dead he's got this idea in his head that one of us is going to be next.'

Matt leaned forward and watched as Evelyn sat down opposite them. Her hands were clearly shaking and she immediately
began to fiddle nervously with her wedding ring.

'Is that why you're so safety conscious?' Tom asked.

She nodded. 'I'm frightened too.'

'I think you'd better tell us everything you know about Vanessa
and Ray,' Matt said. 'And we need to know everything.'

Evelyn sighed. 'I don't know where to begin really. I've
known Ray for ages, since he finished his teacher training.
We've been working at the same school for about eight years
now and from the start, we always got on well. We started
dating for a while at the beginning but it didn't work out.' She
smiled awkwardly. 'We weren't ready to commit, or at least I
wasn't, so we both decided to split. It was quite amicable and
we've remained firm friends ever since.

'Anyway, then I met my husband, Ian. He worked at a
different school but we met at council training days and got
chatting and I suppose we gradually fell in love. We were
married quite quickly and Ray and Ian became friends. We
used to socialize together. Ray had various girlfriends and he
would bring his date along for us to meet. Some were better
than others, I must admit, but none ever really lasted that long.
He just couldn't seem to settle.

'By that time I had started helping Ian out at a domestic
violence centre where he did voluntary work. I really enjoyed
the challenge. Some of the women and children were so badly
abused and it actually felt as if we were able to help. We would
chat to them and offer them practical help with rehousing and
benefits etc. I even did a counselling course to learn how to
deal with their emotional problems better.'

She glanced up at Matt and he could see from her expression the importance of her work at the centre. 'One day Ian
invited Ray to come along. It was good for the women to learn
to trust men again and realize that not all men are bastards.'
She grinned apologetically. 'Sorry, but that's what all the
women there thought and I can't say I blame them, looking
at the way they were treated.' She stopped suddenly and got
up, pacing across the room and rearranging the cushions on
her sofa.

'Ray seemed to take to it too. We used to go for a drink
when we finished each week and he would tell us how much

he enjoyed working with the women and especially the kids. Of course the men always had their fair share of come-ons from the women. It always made me laugh how some of them would be vitriolic about men one moment, but as soon as one showed them a bit of attention they would literally throw themselves at them. I think Ian and Ray enjoyed that bit too, although there was always an unwritten rule that any kind of relationship between the helpers and the women was off limits and of course Ian and I were married. Ray wasn't though and was still quite young and good-looking and rich, by their standards. He certainly got enough attention.'

She came back across the room and sat down again, rubbing her hands together and pulling her ring on and off her finger.

'I presume that's how he met Vanessa?' Matt surmised out loud.

She nodded. 'Yes, she turned up one day out of the blue, but having said that, they seemed to know each other because there seemed to be an immediate bond between them. We warned him not to get involved but he wouldn't listen. There was something about her that just took control of him. She had lovely long blonde hair and large eyes, but she also seemed to be so vulnerable. It was like she hypnotized him. When she first arrived she played the victim and played it very well. She would break down and cry whenever she spoke of how she was treated and he was taken in completely. He denied anything was going on but we could see they were getting close. Too close. Then we started hearing rumours about her background and tried to warn him off, but I think it was too late by then.'

She stared straight up at him and Matt could see tears forming in her eyes. A droplet escaped from the corner and slid down her cheek and she brushed it quickly away.

'What did you find out?' he asked.

'We weren't allowed to see any official records. It's all tied up in patient confidentiality, but we found out that she'd been admitted to a psychiatric unit. I believe she'd been sectioned under the mental health act after problems with a previous partner. Of course, we never found out the full facts and we only heard her side of the story which was that she was beaten continuously until she had a breakdown. I personally think there was more to it but we only had her word. She said that she'd caught him out having an affair and when she'd confronted him with the evidence he'd tried to force her out of the house and then tried to strangle her. She did let slip that she'd got her revenge by cutting up all his favourite clothes and that was what seemed odd to me. Why would you then stay in the house and cut up all his clothes if you'd just been frightened for your life?

'Anyway, as a result, I believe she was then admitted to a psychiatric ward for treatment. I'm not sure how long she was in the mental hospital but she hadn't long been out when she was referred to our unit. I think she was still receiving treatment as an out patient at the beginning.' Evelyn dabbed at her eyes with a tissue.

'Ray seemed to lap up her story though and wouldn't listen to either of us. I must admit she could certainly make herself look and sound very appealing and vulnerable when she wanted something, all tears and dramatics, but underneath I thought she was cold and calculating and hard as nails. I don't know any more of her history but she was certainly very disturbed. I tried to tell her to leave Ray alone several times and that he wasn't allowed to get involved but she turned quite nasty towards me. Told me to mind my own fucking business and keep my nose out of her affairs. Ian tried too, but she was even more threatening towards him. He told her she would have to leave the unit if her and Ray didn't cool it, but she said he didn't have the balls to chuck her out. Then she said if he did do anything to come between her and Ray she would personally guarantee he paid for his troubles and that he'd lose what balls he did have in the process.'

'That's an interesting turn of phrase,' Matt said with a grimace.

'It was more the way she said it than anything,' Evelyn continued. 'One minute she'd be all calm, the next she'd be absolutely manic. She would come right up so she was face-to-face and stare you right in the eyes as she made her threats. Then she'd be calm again. It makes my blood run cold just to think of it.'

'And I take it Ray didn't listen to your warnings?'

'No, he wouldn't believe a word of what we said. Thought I was just overreacting. Even accused me of being jealous at one point.' She smiled sadly. 'He might have been a little right on that score but anyway, there was nothing either of us could do to stop them at the time. She moved in with him and they got married pretty quickly. The service was a very quiet one from what I can gather. Neither of us was invited. She didn't like us, after we'd tried to put Ray off the relationship and she made sure she did everything in her power to stop Ray socializing with us, or anyone else for that matter.'

'Do you know what happened between Ray and his family? They appear to have fallen out.'

'Not exactly, but she didn't like anyone who was close to Ray. She was extremely jealous. Gradually, as time went on they lost contact with virtually all their friends and family. She would manufacture reasons why he should stay away from them and create hell if she found he had gone against her wishes. Of course he did see me through work, but he was quite distant and cold and I know she hated the fact that we both worked together. Sometimes she would turn up at the school out of the blue to speak to him or at home time. I'm sure she was just doing it to keep an eye on what he was doing and make sure she didn't catch him talking to me.'

'But obviously you did talk,' Matt encouraged with a smile.

'What makes you say that?' she looked at him curiously.

'Because Vanessa says Ray was at your house the night he was murdered.'

The colour drained from her face as she took in what he'd just said. 'Oh my God. I didn't realize she knew. He told me that he'd persuaded her he had to be at the school late for a parents' meeting and then to speak to the headmaster.'

Matt was puzzled. 'She told us that Ray had said he was visiting you and your husband to discuss a work plan and to expect him home late.'

'He would never have said that to her. She would have gone mad.'

'Was your husband there?'

He knew the answer from her expression before she answered. She threw her hands to her face and groaned. When she let her hands fall slightly he could see the panic in her eyes.

'That explains things,' she exclaimed, her face still pale.

'What things?'

'Well, I had a phone call that night but no one spoke, although I could hear breathing. I put it down to a crank call but in hindsight, it was probably her. Also one of my neighbours said they saw a strange car parked up just down the road on a couple of occasions. I wonder now whether it was her watching for any signs of Ray coming or going.' She paused and looked down at the table.

'Do you know what car your neighbour saw?'

'I don't know, but I can check. I think he said it was a dark coloured Renault.' She looked back up at him. 'I didn't realize she'd claimed he was here. I thought you were only coming to speak to me because Ray was an old friend. I thought you were speaking to anyone who knew him.'

'We are speaking to everyone we can find that knows Ray, but from what she said, Vanessa sort of hinted that something more might have been going on. So were you and Ray having an affair?'

She hesitated before straightening up and facing him. 'Yes, but it had only just begun. I was going to tell you. That's why I didn't want my husband present. I thought you ought to know, but I didn't realize you already knew and I certainly didn't realize that she knew.' She let her hands slip to the table and looked up at him fearfully. 'Over the last year or so Ray has been talking to me a lot more, in break-times and lunch hours at school. He'd realized what a mistake he'd made when they got together. He used to tell me how she would go mad if they were out and he so much as glanced at another woman. He wasn't allowed out without her permission and she wanted him there all the time. He was always complaining about how needy she was and how she would swing from crying to violence within seconds if she didn't get her own way. I think it had got worse recently. She was trying to conceive but for some reason she couldn't. She never appeared to be very healthy. She was very thin, almost anorexic. He was worried that she might be suffering from extra stress as a result but she wouldn't go and seek help for it. She kept telling him that he was all she needed and she didn't know what she would do without him.

'We spoke more and more and gradually realized we still loved each other. All the feelings from before returned but this time I think it would have been different. He told me he wanted to leave her but was worried about what she might do. She'd always said that she'd never be able to handle him having an affair because she'd been let down before. On a few occasions she threatened to kill him and then take her own life.'

'Did he think she might be capable of doing that?'

'Yes I think he was genuinely worried about what she might do if she found out. He never told me her full background or what had happened before they met but I know she was very unstable. I suppose he'd just had enough. Five years of marriage to such a possessive woman was enough for any man. He just didn't know how to deal with the problem. He kept saying that everything would sort itself out with time. The trouble was, the more jealous she got, the more it was driving him away.'

'Straight into your arms?' Matt couldn't quite credit the rather plain, dumpy woman in front of him as being capable of enticing any man away from his wife, let alone her slim, blonde opposite.

'I suppose so,' she said miserably. 'And I might just have been the reason for his death.'

SEVEN

Tewkesbury town was a mixture of the old and the new. Nestling in between the angle created by the meeting of the M5 and the M50, it struggled to retain its ancient heritage whilst embracing new shops, cinemas and a thriving nearby country golf course and hotel. Situated on the outskirts of the picturesque Cotswold area of Gloucestershire, it played host to buses of tourists who stopped to admire the imposing stained glass splendour of the abbey, before heading on to the quintessentially English thatched cottages and old stonewalled gardens of small, strikingly named country villages such as Stow-on-the-Wold, Stratford-upon-Avon and Chipping Camden.

A river meandered to one end of the town with a small marina cocooning an attractive selection of small sailing boats and colourful long boats, resting from their travels along the waterways of the West Country.

Matt watched the passing countryside from the rear of an unmarked police Mondeo and wished he lived and worked somewhere less grey than his own streets and neighbourhood. Somehow the colours and energy spread by the multi-canopied evergreens, sparkling canal water and summer blooms contrived to make his own life seem dull and dreary, a thought made worse by the loss of Ben.

Jo had merely turned over in bed and ignored him as he'd tried to explain that he wanted, for the sake of the investigation, to see the scene of the other linked murder. He'd guessed her response before it came, but it still depressed him. Luckily he was with the people most likely to take his morose mood away.

Ernie Watling was their driver, a ruddy faced, career detective who Matt had selected to lead one of his teams. Not always the most dynamic, his steady, down-to-earth approach ensured that he rarely left any stone unturned in his quest for justice. Tom and Alison were the other two.

They stopped at a newsagent and Matt jumped out, brushing himself down and picking up a copy of the local newspaper.

'Tewkesbury murderer claims new victim' screamed the head-lines on the one he'd selected. He paid for a couple of others and threw them towards Tom and Alison in the rear of the car.

'Take a look at these before we get to the scene,' he said. 'They'll probably tell us what the locals make of it all.'

Matt scanned the first few pages as Ernie drove slowly past the Tudor houses and the stone frontage of the abbey. It didn't tell him anything he didn't already know.

The Tewkesbury victim, Jeffrey Bamfo was a forty-four-year-old black defence lawyer specializing in crime. He had been brought up in South London by immigrant parents, both of whom were determined he wouldn't follow the fate of other young West Indian boys and end up on the wrong side of the law. Instead they had persuaded him to put his energies into sport and his studies and he had graduated to law school where he had excelled in his exams and shown a natural propensity to argue his case in a reasoned and irrefutable way.

He and his family had continued to live in the same area of London and from that base he had gradually established himself in his Central London law chambers, slowly building his repu-tation with each case he defended, until he became known as a formidable rival in the many crown courts around the metrop-olis. Gazing at the face in the paper, Matt briefly wondered whether they had ever been adversaries in any of his previous court appearances, and if so, who had won.

He carried on reading. In 1991 Jeffrey met and married another barrister from his chambers by the name of Letitia Clements and between them they had commanded a large and extremely healthy salary. The property market beckoned and they climbed the ladder fast, trading each residence for another of larger and more elegant proportions than the previous.

Two children followed; a boy and a girl, raised for the majority of the time by Jeffrey's parents while Letitia sought to continue her career. Their bank balance continued to grow, prompting their decision to move from London and set up their own law firm based in Tewkesbury, catering not only for the affluent area around Avon and the Cotswolds but also for the more troubled areas within Bristol and Swindon.

The move had taken place at the beginning of the previous autumn and the children, by now aged twelve and ten had taken their places at the start of the new school term eager to make new friends and build a solid educational base, as had their parents.

Their new residence was a sprawling country estate house with outdoor swimming pool, games room and stables attached. It was an idyll Jeffrey and Letitia had worked hard for and one that, by all accounts, he was justifiably proud.

The law firm expanded as their reputation became known around the area and they soon found themselves pursued by clients of all social rankings, anxious to be exonerated from a vast selection of remarkable and unremarkable crimes.

The murder therefore had come as a total shock to all who knew them or knew of them and the papers were full of rumours of what might have been the cause. Speculation about money lending, drugs, guns and blackmail abounded from interviews with 'friends and acquaintances of the couple'. The overriding belief in the print was that he had been slaughtered by a disgruntled client and it was a suggestion that Matt knew the local constabulary were taking seriously. There appeared at that stage to be no other motive or certainly none of which the papers were interested.

Matt had only just finished reading when Ernie indicated they had arrived at the murder scene in the grounds of Tewkesbury Park Hotel, Golf and Country Club. It was rather ironically the golf course to which the victim belonged and his whole family regularly attended the luxurious spa area to play tennis or swim. A detective from the Tewkesbury murder squad was to meet them at the entrance and guide them to the exact site. As they turned into the lane leading to the hotel, the grandeur of the estate became clear. Rolling hills surrounded the magnificent, creamy building and its small conical turrets stood out against the brilliance of the morning sky. The golf course spread out all around the building, its grasses still a bright, well-watered green, its fairways sprinkled with trees and shrubs and small dots of yellow shimmering sand.

A large mound of flowers adorned the hotel entrance, tied to the gates or set down in orderly rows on the gravel below. Some were still fresh but others were showing their age, browning slightly at the edges and losing the brightness of colour that the newer ones still exhibited. Carefully written messages on small cards bore witness to the family's popularity.

The gates stood open and there appeared to be a small CCTV

camera trained on the entrance from a tree opposite, next to
which a tall suited man was standing. The man waved towards
them and indicated for them to park to the side of the gates.

Walking up he leant down to Ernie's open window and
peered in.

'You look like job, are you the Met team?'

'Good guess,' Ernie replied amicably.

'We might as well walk to the scene. It'll give you a chance
to have a good look around and I can explain anything you
want to know.'

He waited while the group climbed out and then held his
hand out towards them.

'DI Greg Northborough,' he said, shaking each one by the
hand. 'With the exception of the detective superintendent, who
likes to put his two pennyworths in, I'm basically in charge up
here. I thought I'd take the chance of an hour or two out of
the office and come and meet you. Hopefully you can help us
as much as we can help you.'

'It's good to meet you in person,' Matt commented straightaway. 'Ernie here has been bringing us up to speed on your
enquiries so far. I gather you've a few good leads.'

They started to walk along a track that ran around the
periphery of the grounds. It was large enough for a vehicle and
was obviously used by the groundsmen and gardeners to gain
access to the further extremities of the golf course.

'I wouldn't call them good leads. We have several useful bits
of evidence,' Greg said. 'But not nearly as much as we would
have hoped for at this stage. I don't know whether the press
interest is helping or hindering us. We've had literally hundreds
of phone calls based on press appeals, but the majority of what's
come in has been irrelevant. My squad seem to be running
around like headless chickens trying to follow up each and
every tip, most of which are turning out to be useless.'

Matt pulled a sympathetic face and nodded. 'Our team is
the same. We'll just have to hope that, with so much coming
in, we don't miss the most crucial evidence. Any luck with
forensics?'

'No, I can't believe there's nothing of use. No fingerprints,
no DNA, nothing. There are fibres and tread marks from vehicles and plenty of bits that we can no doubt use in the future
when we have our suspect, but nothing to actually identify

them. It's a shame the body's not in a building – at least you'd usually find plenty of human samples. But out here –' he swept his hand out across the landscape – 'the scene's a lot more sterile.'

'We've the same problem,' Matt agreed. 'We've got enquiries running on the cord, the paper the text was written on and anything that might have DNA attached, but so far, nothing. The suspect's good. Everything is clean. They must be wearing gloves.'

'Same with ours.'

The group lapsed into silence for a few seconds as they negotiated the rough terrain. Matt ran his hands through his hair, stopping to scratch a small itch at the hairline.

'Have you a credible suspect yet?' he asked eventually.

'We do have a picture of the suspect courtesy of the CCTV camera just above the gates.'

'I saw that on the way in and wondered whether that was working.'

'Well, the camera was working fine, but unfortunately the street lamp was out, so the images it shows are very grainy and dark. We do have a few stills taken from it, although they're poor quality. You can see a vehicle enter the gates at approximately 2330 hours with two figures in the front seats. It leaves after about forty-five minutes and there is only one person in the driver's seat. The passenger has disappeared. We've checked through the hotel records and CCTV and the car never got up as far as the car park and no one entered reception. It must be the suspect's car.'

'Can you see what the driver looked like?'

'Not really. All you can see is that they have a mass of light-coloured, possibly blonde hair, it's difficult to see anything else.'

'Male, female, black or white?'

'The suspect looks to be lighter skinned than the victim, but even that is difficult to see for sure. I would say, looking at the hair, that our suspect is a white female.'

'Can you see anything at all further, such as age, height or build?'

'You can't get anything on the face so it's impossible to put an age on her, likewise with her build, but she seems to be a reasonable height for a female. By the way she's positioned

in the vehicle, she's been estimated at being around 5ft 5" to
5ft 8".'

'I'd be interested in taking a look. We have a female suspect
for ours with long blonde hair and about the same height. There
might be something in her mannerism or profile that's familiar.
What about the car? Have you got a make or model or registration number?'

'Again, the images are not good but it appears to be a small
dark car, probably a Golf or Polo or something similar. The
registration number is unreadable but it looks like it starts with
an L. We've sent the film off to see if the lab can enhance any
of the images. That's due back at any time. You're more than
welcome to see the copy, although I'd be surprised if you can
make anything further out on it.' He paused and turned towards
Matt. 'The pressure's on and it's frustrating how little we've
got after all this time. It's in both our interests to wind this up
as soon as possible.'

The track ran downhill before bearing round to the right.
Another smaller path veered off, leading directly back uphill
to the golf course and they turned into it. The trees were closer
together here, with branches hanging low over the path, making
a green-tinted corridor of wooden guardsmen to usher them
forward.

The sound became muted, just as it had been at their murder.
They walked on until they could see the grass of the course
peeping through at the end of the shaded tunnel. The path had
been well trampled by police and forensic officers and the last
remnants of cordon tape could still be seen tied to nearby trees,
fluttering gently. Matt expected at any moment to be shown
into a small hidden clearing in which to be told the body had
been found.

'It's just up here now,' Greg Northborough said, continuing
up the path. 'The suspect drove her vehicle up this way and
stopped about here. There were tyre marks found about here.'
He pointed to an area just off to the left, only a matter of yards
from the end of the track.

'She seems to know exactly where she was heading,' Matt
commented.

'We're not sure. There's not enough space to turn here and
it's almost impossible to reverse in the darkness back along the
track. She would have had to drive out on to the course to turn

round and therefore run the risk of being seen; unless she wanted to be, of course. We think the car was stopped here and Bamfo was then dragged the short distance to the edge of the trees.' He pointed out towards the course.

'So his body wasn't hidden?'

'No, it was quite visible. In fact it was found by one of the golfers quite early the next morning.' He continued, 'Once she'd finished she must have gone back to the car and driven it out on to the course to turn round before heading back along the track and out. There were recent tyre marks on the course, running round in a circle. Just before she disappeared she put the full beam on. One of the hotel security guards reported seeing car headlights in this area but just thought it was a courting couple. It wasn't until the body was found that he put two and two together.'

'Why did she switch the lights on then, I wonder, and risk being stopped, back at the gate?'

'We don't really know. There were no other reports of any lights or activity being seen until then and the moon was almost full so there would have been a reasonable amount of light to see by. We think she must have wanted a last look at her handiwork before she left.'

'Or else to maybe make sure anyone who saw the light would come down to investigate and find the body.'

They walked out from the track into the bright glare of the sunlight. There were few remnants of the murder left, most having been taken away for forensic examination and the scene had been sanitized. The usual mound of flowers and messages were laid round a large tree the roots of which burrowed outwards towards the fifth tee of the course.

'He was sitting against the tree with his arms pulled back around the trunk and tied from behind. There was also another cord, slung over that low hanging branch and tied around his neck. His genitals had been removed. When he went unconscious, the cord tightened and he effectively hanged.'

'Exactly like our one, except that ours was more secluded.'

'But still easily found,' Greg Northborough commented. 'Up in London, a body wouldn't remain hidden for long, what with all the people using a common. Out here, if it hadn't been obvious, the body could have stayed hidden for weeks, if not months.'

Matt looked out at the view from the tree. Hills rolled into the distance, each successive mound bathed in a patchwork of green and yellow squares. Trees sprung up in clumps, dotted about randomly, attracting the attention of large black crows who sat precariously on the very highest branches casting their beady black eyes on all around. The air was full of insects flitting silently from leaf to flower to tree trunk. The setting was beautiful, but macabre at the same time.

At night, with the mist low on the swathes of grassy undulations and a clear, moonlit sky the scene must have looked just as stunning. That was, he realized, unless you were Jeffrey Bamfo and it was the last view you were ever to see.

The office in which the Tewkesbury murder squad was working was much the same as theirs. White boards covered much of the available wall space with various names, locations and facts joined by wobbly lines. Strategies for dealing with every conceivable eventuality were written in bold black marker pen at the top of the boards, only to be covered by the mass of new leads yet to be followed. Graphic photographs adorned one of the boards and newspaper cuttings were pinned up in any remaining gaps. Desks groaned under the weight of files, computers and a multitude of empty mugs and the Met team immediately felt at home.

Ernie was introduced to the detective with whom he had been liaising and fell straight into a detailed discussion of the information so far unearthed.

Matt, Tom and Alison were left to wander about the office, while Greg Northborough attended to an urgent delivery. Matt's eyes were immediately drawn to the photographs. He glanced at the family picture showing the victim with his wife and two children, not allowing his eyes to come to rest on it for any great length of time. It brought with it too many painful thoughts of his own fragmented family and the guilt at not being there even now hung heavily on his mind. He concentrated instead on the crime scene. The murder site was equally as gruesome as their one; although almost identical. Next to photographs of the corpse were close-ups of the plate, laden with the sliced body parts and the Bible passage. He peered closely at the picture showing the writing. It too was composed in the same

way as in their scene. At the top, in the suspect's own handwriting, were the words:

ONE FOR EVERY YEAR OF SUFFERING!

The Bible passage chosen for Jeffrey Bamfo was cut from
a large print Bible and the words 'sin' and 'death' were highlighted in pink marker pen.

For when we were controlled by the sinful nature, the
sinful passions aroused by the law were at work in our
bodies, so that we bore fruit for death
Romans Ch 7, v 5

Finally, scrawled in black felt pen at the bottom were
the same words as on the Streatham victim. Large and prominent it read:

THE WAGES OF SIN IS DEATH!!

'Same sort of message as ours,' Matt turned to Tom. 'She obviously believes that both victims have sinned. Both Bible passages
suggest she is punishing them for their wrong doing but how
the hell are the two victims linked? We've a good reason for
Vanessa Barnes to want to punish her husband having just found
out he was having an affair, although her choice of punishment
was pretty extreme, even if it was appropriate. But why Jeffrey
Bamfo? What possible link could there be between them?'

The two were deep in thought when Greg Northborough sauntered back into the room, taking up a position just behind them.
His eyes followed Matt's to the photograph of the Bible verse.
      'We still can't work out what our victim has done wrong.
It's pretty obvious the suspect believes that Bamfo has sinned,'
he commented.
      'Our victim had. He was having an affair with a work
colleague. Have you uncovered anything in Bamfo's past? I
gather you are checking through a list of his previous clients.
Have you found any yet that might feel that he's sinned against
them, or done them a wrong?'
      'Plenty. He might have quite a reputation for winning his

cases but he still lost a fair few or got his clients to plead to a lesser offence in return for dropping the more serious charge. Any one of them could be aggrieved that he lost their case or plea-bargained away a possible not guilty verdict. It's time consuming though, trying to make enquiries and track down some of the scum that he's dealt with. Some have moved from the addresses we know about and others are inside and, of course as we've gradually worked our way down the list, we're now coming to a large number that he represented in London where his previous law firm was. They're even harder to try to track down.'

'How far back are you going?'

'I don't know yet. We've started at the present and are going backwards through them. At some point we'll have to stop, but until that decision is made, we'll continue.

'Can you check our suspect, Vanessa Barnes?'

'I can check it now for you,' he said. He bent down and tapped on a keyboard, watching as the Holmes message board sprang into life. Quickly typing in a password, the screen changed to reveal a search engine. He entered her name and waited, while the computer scanned its memory.

'All the names of guilty clients for the last ten years have been entered. We're only at the beginning of that list as far as the enquiries go though. Ah, here we are.' He squinted at the screen and read out the words.

'No trace, sorry. She doesn't appear on the list and I think ten years is far enough back to look.'

'Damn, that's a shame,' Matt couldn't help showing his disappointment. He turned away moodily from the screen and looked back at the photo of the Bible passage.

'There's something different about your writing to ours. I can't make out what it is though.'

Tom stared at the photo. 'This one doesn't have a number on it. Our one has the number three.'

'That's right,' Matt smiled. 'I remember now asking what the significance of the number was. We weren't sure whether it related to the number of victims or something to do with the number of weeks or months or even years of suffering, the suspect mentions. Let's now presume it does relate to the number of victims, as we thought. Ray Barnes is then the third victim which means Jeffrey Bamfo could be victim one or two. My guess is that he is the second one and number one still hasn't been discovered as yet. This time the killer wanted to make absolutely sure Bamfo was found, by placing him in a prominent place and even spotlighting him on main beam before she left. She's trying to publicly accuse him of leading a sinful life and obviously wants to ruin his reputation.'

He paused, running his hands through his hair.

'She's written the number three on our body to make absolutely sure we know she has struck before and how many she's killed.' He turned back to the photo, gazing at the written passage, 'Shit! So who is the other victim and where on earth has he been hidden?'

EIGHT

Sunday 17th June 2008 dawned bright and clear and Matt was up early. Jo watched him as he pulled on a pair of shorts and prepared to go out for a morning run. He had his back to her so she was safe to steal a look without being discovered. He'd lost weight since Ben's accident and having recently taken up running, was fitter now than he had been for a long while.

As she watched, she realized how much she still fancied him. It had been months since they had embraced or had sex. Even the merest of touches now made her jump and recoil but even the merest of touches also sent a thrill of excitement racing through her body that each time she had to fight to control. It didn't make sense to her. How could she still be attracted to him while so angry and hurt at everything he did.

She realized she was staring at him but couldn't stop. His body was still good, not muscular but toned and firm and his shoulders were broad. At thirty-five years of age his waist was slightly thicker than when they had first met but the increase had just served to make him appear stocky, not fat. He was not overly tall but his upright posture gave height to his otherwise average stature. She watched as he turned slightly, stretching his torso and pulling a running vest down over the thin covering of dark curls on his chest. He rubbed his hands over his eyes and up across his forehead, stifling a yawn as he brought them back to cover his mouth. His dark hair was even more unruly than ever, spiked upwards in sleep mounds which refused to bow to his constant attempts to flatten and subdue them. She'd loved him for his hair and the way it went its own way. It mirrored his personality. Independent, untamed, defiant. She'd loved his drive and resolve not to allow events from his past to mould his future.

She watched as he crept quietly from the room, unaware that he'd been watched as he creaked over the loose floorboards on the steps. She heard the front door open and shut and listened to the sound of his footsteps on the concrete, until they retreated into the distance.

Rolling over, she pulled open the top drawer of her bedside cabinet and lifted out the letter that had arrived in the post the day before. It had been addressed to them both and she had opened it, curious as to what a letter from the Home Office might bring, but presuming at the same time that it would be connected to Ben's accident and death. Matt had not been there to read it, in any case.

What she read had shocked her and she knew it would astonish and anger her husband. It was only a few lines long and was formal and abrupt. She read the words again.

> Dear Mr and Mrs Arnold
> This letter is to inform you that the parole hearing of William Mortimer was heard on 30th May 2008 and at the conclusion, the panel ruled to uphold his application for parole.
> His release date has therefore been set for Friday 22nd June 2008.

It was signed by a faceless official from the Home Office and gave no other information.

She folded the letter and tucked it back into the envelope, placing it carefully back underneath a book out of sight. William Mortimer was a name that would provoke instant nightmares for Matt. William Mortimer was the name of the man who had murdered his father. William Mortimer was supposed to be incarcerated for life and she knew in Matt's mind, life meant life. To think that he had been granted parole without their knowledge and without any chance to lodge an appeal was a fact that would disturb and anger him beyond reason. While William Mortimer was locked away, she knew that Matt could cling on to the vestiges of a justice system that he already had his doubts about. Now his father's murderer was to be released imminently the knowledge would fester within him like a malignant tumour, growing and growing until, finally, the vitriol it produced would have to find a route out. Whether that would now be directed towards her she didn't know. He already blamed her for Ben's accident. She knew that, although he had tried to back track. She blamed herself for it too although she knew deep down she wasn't really to blame. Neither could voice their anger and hurt, so they didn't speak, or at least not properly.

She climbed out of bed and walked across to the window, throwing the curtains open and squinting out through the brightness of the new day. The sun was low on the horizon, peeping out over the roofs of a thousand families who knew nothing of their anguish. Whatever she did, she couldn't win. Tell him now and she risked Ben's funeral becoming secondary to his rage, tell him later and she knew she would receive the blame, not just for the delay in appraising him of the imminent release but also, unfairly, for the fact that he was to be released at all.

She opened the window, allowing the first warm, timid rays of sunlight to pierce the stagnancy of the bedroom and realized with a mild shock that Matt was now running back up the road towards the house. Thirty minutes had elapsed since he'd crept out and she'd been swamped with indecision. She watched as he sprinted the last few yards, his head down, his arms and legs powering his body towards her. She felt her heart beat quicken briefly at the sight and her mind became clearer.

Matt would have to be shown the contents at some stage but she would wait until she was ready to deliver the letter. She didn't want to have the predictable discussion about unfairness with the prospect of burying their small son looming. There was no greater injustice than burying your child and she wanted all their energies spent putting his last service before anything else. If there was fallout to come, she would deal with it after the funeral.

She stepped back from the window and pulled a thin dressing gown over her shoulders. She would try and make more of an effort to stop the recriminations and accept her husband's burning desire for justice, however much that was at odds with her own priorities. After all that was a major part of the man with whom she had fallen in love.

Running down the stairs she almost knocked him flying. He was breathing hard and his hair was even more tousled, the wind having thrown it up into waves of rolling spikes. His face was flushed and sweat glistened in beads along his forehead and nose.

'I'm sorry,' he gasped, jumping backwards to try to avoid the collision.

She brushed against him, powerless to avoid their skin meeting and quite liking the clammy hardness of his biceps.

'Don't worry, it was my fault,' she said with a smile, unable to stop the slight guilt at his reaction to their accidental touch. 'I thought I'd get down to the kitchen before you returned and cook you some breakfast, seeing as I haven't seen much of you for the last few days.' She tried to keep her voice light, anxious to avoid an accusatory tone detracting from her attempt at reconciliation. 'I was going to ask if there was anything in particular you wanted at Ben's funeral. A special hymn or poem or anything . . .'

Her voice tailed off and she gulped the hurt away, closing her eyes to stop the tears from starting.

'There is something.' Firm hands took hold of her shoulders and she was swivelled round. When she reopened her eyes, Matt was in front of her, his face close and his breath warm against her cheek. She closed her eyes again, almost willing the moment when their lips would touch but the pause was too long and the moment never arrived. She couldn't help the small wave of disappointment that washed over her as she heard him speak.

'I've been thinking about it while I ran and was going to mention it to you anyway when I got back. I want to carry Ben's coffin into the church. I think it would be the proper thing to do. I remember my father's friends and colleagues carrying him at his funeral and how right that seemed.'

She paused, trying to swallow the hurt that had bubbled up on hearing his words. He seemed to sense her reticence but was obviously determined. 'Don't you think that would be fitting?' he persisted. 'For his father to carry him on his last journey.'

She knew that the thought was said and made in the right spirit but still couldn't help the slight resentment and jealousy it had provoked within her.

'I was rather hoping you might stay with me, in case I need you.'

'But I'll come straight over when I've laid him at the front of the church. I just think it's my duty to do that for him.'

The word hit her hard and she was suddenly aware of his hands still at rest on her shoulders. The two were incompatible. To him, duty was the priority. He wanted to carry his son because it was his duty, not for the reasons she herself would have wanted. Everything was duty, he always had to do what was right and proper and never mind what she wanted.

The familiar bitterness rose up and she tried to summon the previous conciliatory thoughts.

'What do you think then?' Matt persisted. 'I was going to ask Tom if he'd be willing to help when I go into work later. I expect it would need two to carry the coffin.'

She noticed the excitement flicker across his features and recognized it was something that he really wanted to do. But her mouth was already speaking.

'I didn't realize you were going in today. It's Sunday. What's so urgent that you can't leave it until tomorrow?'

She turned away and felt his hands drop, immediately regretting the loss of his touch but unwilling to take any action to restore them to their previous position. A cold blanket of resentment wrapped itself around her.

'There are some enquiries that need to be completed as a matter of necessity. We're under pressure from the management and the press to get a quick result and we've already had a week, two if you count the time between the first body being found. And we think there might be a third out there somewhere too.' He paused. 'What do you think of my idea? You haven't answered it yet. I'd be honoured to carry Ben, if you were happy with that, and I'm sure Tom would too.'

She didn't turn back towards him. She couldn't risk letting him see her pain. 'Do what you want,' she said carefully. 'You always do anyway.' She stepped away from him in the direction of the door and spun round. 'Oh, and you need to get your hair cut before the funeral. It looks a right mess.'

'Are we any closer to making any arrests?' DI Blandford's voice caught him off guard as Matt walked past his office. He was in a bad mood, confused by Jo's treatment. He'd thought she'd be pleased at his idea. To carry their son's coffin would be the fitting conclusion to his young life. It was his duty as a father. It was right, but more than that, it was what he wanted to do for his beloved son, the last act he could perform for the small boy he loved with all his heart. And he would do it for Ben, whether she liked it or not.

He nodded to himself and switched his attention to his boss's question.

'I'm going to visit Vanessa Barnes today and persuade her to allow me access to her medical records. I'm sure she won't refuse me and if she does I'll just have to threaten her with getting a section 9 warrant. There's a lot more to her than meets the eye. The Tewkesbury team have identified a female suspect with long blonde hair from CCTV that fits her down to a tee. God only knows what the link is between the two bodies but there must be something we haven't as yet found. She'll definitely be worth speaking to.'

DI Blandford frowned slightly. 'Anyone else?'

Matt shook his head. 'No one other than her. We've both got plenty of ancillary forensic stuff for when we get our suspect, but nothing to actually identify them in the first place.'

'And this possible third victim?'

'Nothing yet. A message has been sent to all the other forces with a request for them to search missing person records for any possible victims that fit the bill and then to make urgent enquiries. I've asked for them to report back with anything significant ASAP.'

'Let's hope we're both wrong! But then, like you said, why number our body?'

'To make it absolutely clear we've missed one. The thing that worries me though is the threat: "One for every year of suffering." We haven't a clue what the suspect's talking about. What suffering? Is it physical, mental, have they been locked away for a crime they haven't committed or married to an abusive partner? It could be anything. And how many years could it add up to? It could be just the three years, like we think we've victims for at present, or it could be five years, ten years, or a lifetime, who knows?'

DI Blandford opened his window, lit himself a cigarette and inhaled deeply. 'Christ Matt, I'll be dead from cancer if this carries on. Two victims already, possibly another and the threatened prospect of God knows how many more.' He blew out the smoke and watched as it drifted slowly away, quickening as it was taken on a gust of wind out over the roof tops. He glanced down at the entrance. 'Look at those vultures out there, just waiting for a kill. If we don't get a charge soon they'll be sharpening the knives.' He thrust his hands deep into his trouser pockets.

'Oh, by the way. I've got the toxicology report back. It arrived yesterday while you were gone. It appears that there were traces of ketamine found. It's a Class C drug fairly widely available both legally and illegally.'

'That's the same with the Tewkesbury body as well then. I was chatting to Greg Northborough about it. It's the drug used by vets to sedate horses and also in cases of date rape. It can be injected intravenously or intramuscularly or else inhaled, smoked or taken orally. It works better and quicker when injected though.'

Matt sauntered over to the window.

'Apparently in small doses it can induce hallucinations and out-of-body experiences but in large enough doses it can be used as a general anaesthetic, without necessarily affecting the breathing like some other drugs. It can also be used recreationally and is particularly liked by homosexuals as it's a stimulant and can heighten pleasure, especially if mixed with other drugs.'

'How long does it take to act?'

'It depends how it's taken. The quickest way is intravenously when it takes only about ten to fifteen seconds, but it would be pretty much impossible for our suspect to have used this method. It's too precise. Inhaling it or taking it orally would last longer overall but does not take effect so quickly. Greg reckons that the amount found in his victim indicates the drug was injected into muscle. That way, it could be easily done, needing to be less precise than finding a vein, and by the time the victim realizes what's happening, it would be too late.'

DI Blandford nodded. 'That makes sense. There was no evidence of a struggle but there were drag marks. If our suspect is a woman, like it appears from the Tewkesbury CCTV, injecting ketamine would be a good way of subduing her victim physically. Plus if she'd merely threatened him with a weapon there wouldn't have been the drag marks.'

'That's exactly what Greg Northborough thinks.'

'I'll get some enquiries set up at hospitals and veterinary surgeries in London to see whether there have been any thefts or losses of ketamine. It's not readily available over the counter. It's a bit of a long shot because it is fairly easy to obtain on the streets but you never know.'

'Thanks, guv. Anything else found on the tox report?'

'No, not of any note. A small amount of alcohol consistent with the amount Evelyn Johnson states Ray drank at her house before leaving. It was below the legal limit for driving and certainly not enough to cause any physical problems. His stomach contents too have been analysed and they seem to be consistent with the small meal she said they shared together.'

'Any idea of how much ketamine was present? Apparently they reckon Jeffrey Bamfo would have been conscious when he had his dick removed, poor bastard!' Matt winced as he spoke.

'Same with Ray Barnes. I asked about this. Apparently the drug is absorbed into the body at a set rate and in an operation the anaesthetist would have to keep topping up the amount to ensure the patient remained unconscious. If Ray Barnes had died while still unconscious, the level of ketamine found would have been much higher as absorption would stop. According to the report, the quantity found was consistent with the victim having been fully conscious for at least a while before death.'

'So the killer would have watched him squirm or even talked to him while he bled out. Christ! What sort of sick bitch have we got here?'

The two men fell silent. When Matt looked up, his boss's face was still screwed up as if in pain himself.

'Guv, do you think we should just bring Vanessa Barnes in now, on suspicion? She's certainly got the motive and I think she's mad enough.'

'I'd like just a little more, if possible.' DI Blandford shook his head and grimaced. 'We've got nothing physical at the moment to link her. I know she's got a motive, but lots of men have affairs without their wives taking a knife to their balls. The public's sympathy will be with her at the moment. Her husband's been brutally killed and she's been left alone and vulnerable. If we then drag her in just because she's a blonde-haired female and have no other credible evidence, they'll accuse us of clutching at straws. We need a bit more. If it's her I want enough to keep her in. Get round to Vanessa Barnes' house this afternoon. Keep it very short but get her authority to disclose her medical history by whatever way you can. We'll get that tomorrow morning and if that reveals anything of note, we'll haul her in straight away.'

He threw the glowing end of his cigarette out of the window and watched as it bounced off the wall and dropped down to the street below.

'I want a suspect that we can end up with a realistic prospect of charging. Not one that will make us look like idiots if we've jumped to the wrong conclusion.'

Vanessa Barnes was asleep when they rang on the doorbell. Matt and Tom peered through the window when no one answered and on seeing her lying prostrate on the sofa were on the verge of kicking the door down when her body twitched. Further hard banging on the window eventually brought her around and she stood unsteadily on her feet and shuffled slowly to the door. Matt was shocked at how her appearance had changed so radically in such a short space of time. Her face, always lined, was now thinner and gaunter, surrounded by blonde hair that was not only untied, but unkempt. Gone was the easy way in which it had been twisted and pinned. Now it hung in limp tangles, knotted and lifeless. Her clothes too were grubby and creased, appearing to have been unchanged for several days. It was, however, her eyes that struck Matt the most forcefully; the pale watery quality of the iris having been replaced with a startled, startling blue. She looked like a rabbit caught in the headlights, exhibiting a mix of fear and madness that was unsettling at best, frightening at worst.

'What do you want?' she demanded.

'Can we come in?' Matt asked gently, showing his warrant card. 'I came to see you the day you reported Ray missing. Do you remember?'

She grimaced. 'That seems like a lifetime ago. I do remember you though. You listened to me. You were the only one.' She cast bleary eyes over them and repeated her initial question. 'What do you want?'

'We need to speak to you. It's nothing to worry about.'

She glared at them. 'That's what the others keep saying, especially that bitch Alison. Why can't you just leave me alone? All you want to do is harass me.'

'We just want to talk,' Matt said again. 'This is Tom Berwick. We won't keep you long.'

She stared up at Tom's bulky frame suspiciously before slowly opening the door and beckoning them through. The house wore a similar lack of care. Dirty dishes lay across the floor amongst newspapers opened to reveal the same grim story-line. The television flickered in the corner, its surface dusty, its top littered with discarded empty mugs. A chair had been pulled up opposite the TV to seat the occupant of the room with a direct view of its contents.

She motioned for them to sit down on the sofa and sat in the chair, swivelling it slightly to enable her to observe her visitors. Her fingers drummed against the fabric of the arms and she pursed her lips tightly.

'So, what do you want to talk about?'

The question was direct and Matt had to think quickly.

'We came to see how you were. We were told that you were not too good and were having trouble sleeping.'

'How did you expect me to be?' she almost shouted. 'Dancing about with joy?'

'I'm not saying that,' Matt said defensively. 'I was concerned about your health.'

'Don't lie!' she spat out. 'You're not *concerned* about me. You're *interested* in me because you think I killed my husband. You're interested in whether I'm some mad psycho bitch that goes round slaughtering people. Well, what do you think? Do you think I'm mad?'

She stood up quickly from her chair and faced them, her eyes flashing dangerously. 'Do you think I'm going to produce a machete or something and attack you both?'

'No,' Matt answered carefully. 'I think you need help. I think Ray's death has hit you harder than you realize and you might need to see a doctor.'

She laughed suddenly. 'That's what the others kept saying. You're all the same. They wanted my medical records but I wouldn't let them have them. Why should I? It's nothing to do with you what illnesses I've had.'

'But it would help us to help you. You said before that Ray helped you through your "black" times. I'm guessing that you've suffered from depression. There's no shame in that. Thousands of other people suffer from it. I've suffered from it myself.'

She turned and stared him straight in the eyes and he saw again the deep intensity of the blue. He couldn't read her and it disturbed him. He was normally able to sense a person's guilt but she was unfathomable. He did however get the distinct impression she could see his weaknesses and knew he had just lied. He was the first to shift his gaze and she smiled at his discomfiture.

'They won't let me see his body.' Her statement was directed at Matt. 'Why won't they let me visit him?'

'But you have been and identified him, haven't you?'

'That's not visiting him properly. He was laid out in a coffin, all covered up when I went in. They would only let me see his face for a few seconds when they rolled back the sheet and I wasn't allowed to touch him or stay with him. I want to be able to see him and touch him and talk to him.' She fixed him with another stare. 'I want to be able to ask him things about what he was thinking at the end and why.'

'But won't that just make things harder for you to deal with?' Matt tried to smile sympathetically but she still unnerved him. 'He can never give you the answers you want.'

'I already know the answers. I know what he was doing. I know he was visiting that bitch, Evelyn Johnson.' She turned away. 'They went out before, when they were younger but he split up with her. She was too dull. He liked a bit of life in his women. I was what he wanted but she could never accept that. She kept trying to poison him against me all the time.' She swung round and stared directly at Tom. 'Men are weak. They can't help themselves. They can be manipulated and she was good at the art. She was trying to entice him away from me. I couldn't let that happen.'

She turned and walked away from them, leaving the room and heading towards the kitchen. Matt felt suddenly unsure what to do. Conflicting thoughts were running through his head. She'd almost got to the point of an admission, but the words of his boss kept drowning out his desire to place the woman under arrest. She was a possible suspect and as such none of their conversation was likely to be admissible, should it come to court. She should have been cautioned and given access to legal advice. They should have got her words recorded properly on tape and that would only happen after arrest. And arrest had been pencilled in for when they had obtained her medical history whether or not it yielded anything of note. DI Blandford wanted a final chance to gather more evidence before the constraints of prisoner detention kicked in. Matt jumped up from the sofa and followed her.

She was leaning over the sink when he entered, drinking directly from the tap. A small plastic container lay on its side on the draining board, its top unscrewed and several oblong shaped tablets spread out across its opening. At the sound of his footsteps she straightened and wiped the drips from around her mouth, keeping her back towards him.

'What's the matter? Did you think I was going to run away from you or something? You are suspicious, aren't you? Why can't you accept that I'm a victim in all this, just as much as my husband?' She laughed suddenly, spinning round to face him. Her lips still glistened with excess water and her eyes were alight. Leaning across, she picked up a knife from the sink and ran her finger along its serrated blade. Matt bristled automatically taking a step back. She laughed again. 'Don't worry. I won't hurt you. I would be more likely to hurt myself. What life is there left for me now? My husband has been murdered, I'm not even permitted a visit and I have no idea when I will be allowed to bury him. On top of that, I'm treated as the suspect, not the victim.' She threw the knife angrily down on to the floor, so that it clattered across the lino and disappeared underneath the table. 'Do you get some sort of sick pleasure doing this to me? Haven't I been through enough?'

She pushed herself away from the sink and strode past a speechless Matt into the hallway, stopping by the front door.

'I tell you what,' she said suddenly, 'I will allow you access to my medical records, but only if you will allow me to see my husband. Give me the form and I'll sign it for you now but you must promise me the visit. Then I want you out of here. Is that a deal?'

Matt paused while he weighed up the question. Nothing would be lost by allowing her a visit and potentially everything could be gained.

'Is that a deal, or not?' Her voice was raised and had taken on the slightly manic quality he remembered from his previous visit. She opened the door wide and stared at him.

'OK, Vanessa,' he said. 'It's a deal. I'll make arrangements for you to have some time alone with Ray. In return . . .' He pulled the form from his clipboard and offered her a pen.

'How do I know you'll keep your side of the bargain?' she asked, her tone low and hesitant for the first time since their arrival.

'You'll just have to trust me.' He passed the clipboard across and watched while she signed her name with hands that shook almost uncontrollably. 'And like I said before, I'll speak to your doctor and if you need help I promise you I'll find you some, you only have to ask.'

The phrase seemed to inflame her already fragile demeanour and she thrust the board back, glaring at him furiously.

'If I need help, I'll get it myself . . . this time.' The pause was only for a split second but enough for him to notice. 'Now get out and don't come back until you've caught my husband's murderer.'

As the door slammed behind them Matt wondered whether he would be back sooner than Vanessa Barnes realized.

NINE

The bells in the church tower rang out across the roof tops, as Bambi lay on the bed. The rhythmic peal soothed her nerves and helped to quell the pleasure and anticipation of the ensuing hunt.

The tension was good. It made her remember the reasons for her actions and the reasons were noble and upright. These men had done wrong. They had been the cause of all her pain and suffering. They had spread death and now they would receive their just reward. 'Vengeance is mine,' God himself said. 'And their doom comes swiftly.' Well she was God's instrument to do his bidding and tonight she would carry out His wishes. Another sinner would die. Another contemptuous, conceited man would reap what he had sown. But their death would not be swift. It would be agonizing and absolute. No question of leniency. They deserved to experience the same suffering and agony that they were guilty of spreading. When they had used her flesh and left the seeds of death within her they had not cared. They hadn't even bothered to find out the reason she had finally disappeared. They thought only of themselves and their own sordid requirements.

The bells pealed on, their deep resonance remaining in the air, even as the next peal began, the call to worship so distinct. The ringing became untidy, the bells, for a few minutes were dissonant and she shifted her position, rolling over and pulling out the Bible from her bedside cabinet. She laid it on her pillow and leant back towards the drawer, removing a small black book from a pile of five stacked on top of each other. It was a well-thumbed diary started on Friday 27th April 2003, a day after the death sentence had been pronounced. AIDS was to be the executor and every minute from that moment had been borrowed time, every month, every day, every hour counting down to the inevitable conclusion. It had been hard, bloody hard, and at times she'd wished it could be over but it had also yielded moments of exquisite joy and laughter. She had found acceptance and love for who she was, not who society wanted her to be.

She continued reading, letting the memories wash over her. Memories of the time when she had conquered her addiction and had walked from the tiny rented bedsit and started to live. Started to live until the time she would die.

Bambi put the diary down and swallowed the sob that had crept up her throat. She closed her eyes and let the injustice of it all wash over her. Why, when she had been so brave in beating the cravings, did she have to die? Salty tears ran from blackened eyes, heavy with mascara and shadow and mingled with the gloss on her lips. She licked the drops away, tasting the bitterness of her hate, and ran her finger over the small gold chain and crucifix swinging at her neck. It had been the best present she had ever received and she would always treasure it.

She rolled off the bed and stood up, walking slowly over to the window. The crucifix glinted in the quivering beams of evening light thrown in from the window and she fingered its shape remembering back to when she'd realized the guillotine, still poised unsteadily above her head, was about to fall. It wasn't much, just an annoying cough but it wouldn't go and as it took control of her lungs, she had known it was the beginning of the end.

The fuse, for the last few years lying dormant, had been reignited and was starting to burn. Her life had become a ticking time bomb, which would detonate an orgy of violent revenge. Justice required it. God required it. She required it. Someone had to pay for the casual way in which she had been infected with AIDS and that someone would be her most regular punters. Old, young, professional or unemployed, she had become convinced it was one of them and they would all have to be punished.

The first had yet to be found. She'd been too careful to avoid capture, knowing she still had a job to do. His body had carried with it a warning of things to come, which she'd wanted publicized. The final one would carry the reason for the deaths. The world would then make their judgement on who was the greatest sinner, the man who spread death or the prostitute who unwittingly and innocently catered for his desires.

She turned away from the window and strode over to the cupboard, pulling some surgical gloves on as she did so. Several more pairs would be required as the evening wore on but it didn't bother her. They felt clean and tight and sterile against her skin and she could touch her victims as much as she wanted without risk of being identified. That was important. She needed to touch them in the places they had desired to be touched, for those places were the cause of the evil. They carried the seeds of death and it was they too that drove the immoral desires. They had to be removed and served up as the cause, the reason for the punishment, the motive on a plate for the world to consider. It was they that had brought her so much pain and suffering.

Opening the cupboard she extricated the black bucket and selected the items she would need, carefully placing them in a black plastic sack. One white plate, the green garden twine, a strip of material to be used as a gag and the hunting knife, cleaned from its last use and wrapped carefully in a new tea towel. The ketamine she placed in a small handbag. It would need to be easily accessible, along with the syringes. Lastly she picked up the large print Bible and opened it up taking from within it the piece of paper carefully prepared.

The Bible passage she had selected this time spoke for itself:

> Do not be deceived: God cannot be mocked. A man reaps
> what he sows.
> Galatians 6, v 7

Highlighted in pink marker pen were the words 'reaps' and 'sows' and at the bottom in black felt pen she had written the same as on the others, THE WAGES OF SIN IS DEATH!! She read through it, nodding contentedly and then, taking a black felt pen from her handbag, wrote out the last part across the top:

4. ONE FOR EVERY YEAR OF SUFFERING!

Bambi tucked it back inside the Bible and placed the holy book reverently inside the sack, wrapping the plastic around it so that the whole package was bound tightly together. She put the plastic sack into a small holdall on a table next to her handbag, her car keys and her phone. Her preparations were almost done. The victim had already been primed for their meeting. She had phoned him from a public call box earlier in the week and the fool had fallen for her story like all the others.

This time, he had been informed that his dalliances had produced a child, whose existence had been kept secret from him. A one-off payment was required for the upkeep of the child and to prevent his exposure to his new wife as a man who had frequently associated with prostitutes. She'd only requested one thousand pounds in cash this time but the grasping victim had been only too happy to part with the relatively small amount of cash as a payment for her silence. Bambi snorted at the thought. She wasn't interested in the money. It was blood money and it showed her how little it took to buy redemption.

The bells were nearly finished now and it would soon be time to make her way to the church. She slung the holdall over her shoulder and picked up the other items. Walking over to the mirror, she checked her reflection, touching up the foundation powder and replenishing the layer of mascara. She wanted to look good when she came face to face with Tunde Oshodi.

TEN

Tunde Oshodi was just beginning to realize the seriousness of the situation in which he found himself. It had never occurred to him that the rather gentle, lilting voice might be the last he heard. There was no menace in it, just a determination that he should do as requested. The instructions had been clear, precise, beyond dispute.

One thousand pounds to provide for the child and no further commitment, ever. He would never be contacted again. One thousand pounds to buy her silence and keep his new life. It was a small price to pay, almost too small and he hoped the promise would be honoured. He was worried that it would be the start of more demands, more cash which would gradually bleed him of all his assets and strip him of his ability to keep his past indiscretions secret.

He had tried to remember her character, what she was like as a person, but all he could remember was her thin, emaciated body, her ribs that showed through the pale, transparency of her flesh and her hollow breasts emptied of healthiness and well-being. Her face was unforgettable. The mass of unruly blonde hair that fell forward over her face when she bent down to him, the pale, watery eyes that disappeared almost to a dot into her skull, framed by long, long black lashes, the high cheekbones that could have bestowed beauty on her if the drugs hadn't robbed her skin of its elasticity and colour. He saw too her mouth, open, accommodating, even though her lips were dry, her teeth yellow and her breath acetone. He remembered their first encounter and how her stocky, brutal partner had arranged it, a fact that he could never understand, but it was obvious the man liked the cash.

He tried to forget the occasional guilt as he screwed her, but it had never been enough to stop his need. Sometimes he had wondered what made her do what she did, but he knew the answer, in the desperate flicking of her sunken eyes, the rainbow colours of her bruised and stained skin and the needles and foil left discarded about her bedsit. He had known only too well and he hadn't cared. All he'd wanted was the release she gave him and a chance to fuck without consequences.

It had come as a huge shock that there had been consequences and that he was the father of a child he had never met, a baby born into the poverty and squalid conditions in which she'd lived. He wondered whether the words he had heard were the truth, whether he really was the biological father but he couldn't risk the implications of asking. His life had moved on and he was not willing to allow the memory of a filthy prostitute to hold him to ransom. A filthy prostitute and her child, whose existence was now being dangled before him, lives he could neither claim nor ignore. Life for him had changed beyond all recognition since he had uprooted from his home country of Nigeria and flown to England for a better quality of life. He now supported an obedient and devoutly religious wife who doted on his every need and had followed him trustingly a few years later to cater for his desire to have a good wife. She had provided him with a young daughter; a curly-haired bundle of energy who he hoped would be the first of many.

The guilt had returned after the phone call, but so too had his memory of the pleasures. Even now as he waited to meet the voice on the other end of the phone, he revelled in the tremor of pure lust that shot straight from his head to his groin and took root in the nerves and muscles that fed his growing erection. He shifted in his seat, wondering if there might be the offer of more thrills, in return for the cash.

The time was edging towards eleven thirty. It was still warm, but not hot enough for the amount of perspiration that was prickling across his body. His adrenalin was fired up and his body twitched with anticipation. The traffic was dying down but was still regular. The night was relaxed, in marked contrast to his own taut nerves. A gentle breeze stirred the leaves, a discarded newspaper vibrated lazily along the pavement and a fat city fox stood stock still in the centre of the road, sniffing languidly at the scents of the night. Everything seemed normal, except that it wasn't, at least for him.

He checked the envelope in his pocket, counting the notes out yet again as he had so many times. Used notes, wrapped in bundles of £100, as requested. He replaced them and wiped his brow with a handkerchief initialled at the corner, a gift from his own daughter at Christmas. He wondered idly whether this forgotten child was a girl or a boy. He hadn't thought to ask. Would there be a photo given, in exchange for the cash? He was curious. Would the child be dark skinned like himself or white like its mother? Would it be full of energy or listless and unhappy, a creature warped by its surroundings. He wanted to know, yet didn't at the same time.

A car pulled up next to him. It made him jump. The window wound slowly downwards and he caught a glimpse of straggly, blonde hair, falling forward. He strained to see into the shadow of the vehicle and was relieved to see there was only the one occupant. He relaxed slightly and at the same time a flutter of anticipation returned to his groin. It hit him then, the familiar thrill of danger, the knowledge that he was doing something that would be frowned upon, the promise of pleasure.

'We need to talk,' the lilting voice said. It was high and sing-song and he wasn't worried by it. The flutter of anticipation was stronger now. She was near him, alone, needy. His mouth turned up into a grin at the thought.

'Get into my car and I'll take you some place a little less crowded.'

He interpreted the instruction as an offer and his brain switched off all thoughts of danger and concentrated only on the pleasure to come. His fingers fumbled at the window winder, desperate to do as he was bid, while his excitement was still rising. He slammed the door, listening as the locks clicked into place and walked the few steps across to her car. Pulling the handle, he baulked at the smell. It was a stale, rancid, musty smell, which propelled him backwards in time to her bedsit. He lowered himself down on to the passenger seat and waited for the next instructions. The engine was running. He turned to pull his seat belt across and felt a sharp scratch on the top of his right arm. It took him by surprise and he wheeled round to see what it was.

A cold sensation was running down the length of his arm to his fingers and back up to his shoulder. He winced as it travelled through into his neck and torso. He saw the syringe suspended above him in surgical yellow gloves. A small droplet of liquid dripped from the needle and he wondered what it was. It didn't make sense. The coldness was seeping through his body. It made him feel so tired and he wanted to close his eyes.

He was so sleepy and his body was exhausted. He couldn't raise his arm. It was too tired. It wouldn't move. The coldness was filling him now, spreading down his legs to his feet. He thought he'd better leave but his hand wouldn't lift, his leg wouldn't move. His head was against the head rest and it was heavy. He could see what was around but he couldn't change a thing. The sing-song voice was chanting but he couldn't make out the words.

The car was moving forward now, slowly, building momentum. He watched the façade of the buildings change, as they flicked past on either side. Tall, two-storey Victorian houses, smaller shops squeezed between them, a block of flats, with lights chinking out from random windows, reflections of headlights glinting crazily as they passed. He wanted to ask where they were going but he couldn't. A set of traffic lights were in front of them. The red light shone into his pupils. He stared at the light and it penetrated his head, turning everything a blood red. Straight ahead he could see the road bisecting a common. There were no cars in front and none behind and only a few street lights. Trees reared up on either side, their boughs heavy with summer foliage, switching the light from the moon off and leaving the surroundings basted in a dull red glow. The redness was filling his body and as he gave up the struggle to keep his eyes open, he could still hear the sing-song voice chanting next to him.

His senses were the first to wake. The smell of the forest was all around, warm and moist and welcoming and the noises of city traffic had faded to little more than a background murmur.

Darkness enveloped him and he waited while his eyes acclimatized. He tried to speak, but his mouth wouldn't move. He tried to turn his body to see if he had company, but it wouldn't turn. He swivelled his pupils round, and gradually focused on a mass of unruly, blonde hair which pulsed backwards and forwards, building momentum. The sing-song voice started again. It was singing a hymn.

He was frightened now, more frightened than he had ever been in his life. He couldn't move but he could hear and see and smell and feel. He could hear the rustling of the woods, small movements of night animals curious at the disturbance of their habitat; feel his heart beating hard against his rib cage, see the torch light coming to rest at a spot nearby and smell his own fear, pungent and cloying and desperate.

The blonde hair was moving back towards him now. He struggled to stand but his arms were pulled backwards, with wrists bound tightly behind the tree on which he had been leant. He couldn't move. He tried to call out to the figure but his mouth wouldn't move against the thick wad of material tied securely around his head. His voice came out in pathetic grunts of exertion as he tried to petition his captor. A noose was tied loosely around his neck, attached to a branch above, hanging slack while his body remained upright. He was trapped.

He felt a hand against his chest unbuttoning his shirt, rifling around inside his jacket. It moved downwards undoing his belt and the zip of his jeans, pulling, opening, exposing. The hair was in his face and he could hear her breath coming fast and urgent.

'Is this what you want?' the sing-song voice was asking. 'Is this all that you've ever wanted?'

He relaxed slightly. Maybe his fears were unnecessary. Maybe this was her way of getting back at him. To give him what he had always taken from her but only when she was in control.

The hand moved upwards and he felt the envelope being extricated from his pocket. In the gloom he saw the gloved hand open it and take out the cash, counting each bundle. He thought it was strange that she should be wearing surgical gloves but the thought was quickly forgotten. He waited for his reward. The warmth of the night air stirred him, stimulating nerve endings and caressing his nakedness.

He watched as the blonde hair got closer, transfixed by its sheer volume. She knelt down in front of him, head bent, face obscured in the shadows. Then the rocking started, to and fro, to and fro, mesmerizing, hypnotizing. The sing-song voice started up again, low and quiet, woeful, tragic, a mournful lament and the disquiet in his body reared up. His eyes darted this way and that, looking about, searching for help but there was none. As the moon shifted out from the cloud cover, he saw the glint of a blade on a white plate just to the side of the tree to which he was tied. He couldn't take his eyes from it. He tried again to move but his body wouldn't respond.

The chanting stopped and he caught a glimpse of black eyes and white sunken cheeks. The surgical gloves folded themselves around the knife and he felt white hot pain rush through his groin. His body convulsed upwards against the pain and his scream was muted into the wad of fabric.

He was just aware of the figure in front of him. The gloves were wrapped around a glass of wine now, lifting it upwards into the hair until it was empty. The sing-song voice was angry. It was speaking loudly next to him.

'So you think you can buy me off, do you? You think you can behave like you do and not suffer the consequences? Well, you won't have to worry. There is no child. There never was.'

He watched as the cash was scattered in front of him, down on to the grass, on to the dried dirt. He watched as some of the notes turned red. The pain shot through him in waves of white, searing heat. He wanted to scream but couldn't. He wanted to fight back but he was impotent to do anything. He saw only the injustice of the situation. He didn't deserve this. He'd been willing to pay.

As the pain rolled over and over him, a thought came into his head. It made no sense that he should find it funny, but if he'd been able, he would have smiled at the inappropriateness. Ever since he'd received the phone call, he'd been worried that this would be the first of many requests for cash and that the demands would bleed him and his family dry. He'd fretted that his bank accounts would gradually be stripped and all his assets taken from him.

Now he was actually, physically, being bled dry and he could do nothing to stop it. Nothing, except watch helplessly as his life congealed on the grass beneath him.

His throat filled with waves of nausea and he knew only an overwhelming desire to sleep, but he forced himself to focus. The hair was coming forward towards him and he felt the gag being removed. He swallowed the bile down and tried to speak but his lips were dry and his jaw stiff.

'Say you're sorry,' the sing-song voice was instructing. 'Say you're sorry for your sins. Beg for your life.'

He couldn't think what he had to be sorry for. He had been willing to pay, he always had.

'I'm sorry,' he croaked. 'I'm so sorry for whatever I've done. Please let me go. I have a young daughter.'

The figure in front of him laughed a small tortured laugh that cut through the haze. 'You took away life and yet you have created a child. Your daughter will learn what you have done. You're not sorry. You never will be. You're a liar and you will die for it.'

And as his eyesight began to blur and his head go muzzy, he felt the kick pushing him sideways against the noose. He saw images of his wife and daughter dancing in front of his eyes and he heard the sing-song voice chanting; it wasn't cross or angry any more, but satisfied, matter-of-fact. And this time he could hear the words clearly.

'The wages of sin is death; the wages of sin is death, the wages of sin . . .'

ELEVEN

'I'm sorry. There's nothing else,' the receptionist muttered. 'All her records are on computer for the five years she's been with us. We don't appear to have been sent any previous medical history either on computer or on paper. Only what you have.'

The doctor's surgery had been heaving when Matt had arrived. Monday morning and all the woes and ills of the weekend had been queued in front of the reception desk.

It hadn't taken too long however before he had been allowed access to Vanessa Barnes' medical history.

Matt turned back through the records, reading the list of ailments that had been recorded from past visits: flu, holiday inoculations, insomnia; nothing more to catch his attention. He was deflated. He'd been sure there would be something further to explain her demeanour. He ran his eye back over the first screen, noticing for the first time a small entry at the bottom of the page which read: 'cross reference Vanessa Barrington'.

'What's this?' he asked excitedly. 'There's another name here.'

The woman peered across at where he was indicating and returned to the paper files, quickly pulling a brown envelope from the shelf.

'Here we are,' she said. She pulled the notes out, scanned them swiftly and smiled towards Matt. 'I think you might find this more interesting.'

'For fuck's sake! How did we miss this?' DI Blandford's voice contained barely restrained annoyance.

'How could we have known?' Matt replied, slightly aggrieved. 'She wasn't exactly sharing her secrets. We checked her maiden name and married name and both are clear. How were we supposed to know she'd had another relationship and taken another name in between?'

He threw the file down angrily on his boss's desk.

'Maybe if we'd bitten the bullet and arrested her we'd have

found out. Her fingerprints would have thrown up her linked file.'

DI Blandford flipped the file open and read silently, his brows furrowed in disbelief. After a few minutes he shook his head. 'OK Matt, you're right. Maybe we should have brought her in earlier. I couldn't face the idea of her walking.' He looked down at the pages. 'I just can't believe she has a history of mental illness, culminating in a violent attack on her ex-partner, and we knew nothing about it.'

'And she spent quite a long time in a psychiatric hospital by order of the court,' Matt chipped in, looking round at Alison who had been in the DI's office when he'd arrived.

'No wonder Evelyn and Ian Johnson were worried,' she commented. 'We both thought there was something strange about Vanessa and they'd obviously heard rumours about her past too. They were probably frightened for their lives, especially after her threats.'

'It's a wonder Ray hadn't told Evelyn,' DI Blandford mused.

'Maybe Vanessa thought he was about to tell her. Maybe that's another reason why he had to go.' Matt turned to Alison. 'Alison, I need you to check out our records for Vanessa Barrington. If she's been sectioned by the court, we should have a record of the charge and circumstances. Find out what hospital she received her treatment in and contact them. We need to know what the specific mental illness was and whether the treatment she received worked. Is it an illness that occurs regularly and if it is, is she likely to have become violent again?'

Alison nodded and scurried out of the office. 'I'll do the initial checks and let you know straight away.'

DI Blandford motioned for Matt to sit down.

'Well done, Matt. That's good work. As soon as Alison does those checks I think we'll pay Vanessa Barnes a visit. She's got a bit of explaining to do now.' He paused. 'The only thing that concerns me is what, if anything, links her to Jeffrey Bamfo? She's well in the frame for ours now but why a barrister in Tewkesbury? It doesn't make sense.'

Matt nodded his agreement, pulling out his phone and tapping in a number.

The phone was answered promptly.

'Greg. It's Matt Arnold from Lambeth HQ. Could you run

the name Vanessa Barrington through your indexes of Jeffrey Bamfo's clients?'

'Hold on Matt, I'll do it now'

He found himself tapping nervously on the table top as he waited for the result to come back. The wait seemed never ending.

'She's there.' The voice held the same note of excitement that he recognized from his own. 'Who is she?'

'She's the suspect that I told you about before, the wife of Ray Barnes, our victim. We've just found out today that she's used this other name in the past. I only found it by chance going through her medical records. What does your report say?'

'Well,' he read slowly. 'It appears that she was his client about six years ago. She was due to appear in court for GBH and criminal damage but was pleading not guilty on the grounds of self-defence. Bamfo apparently argued that she had been the subject of documented domestic violence for the whole time she'd been with her partner and that he had attacked her first. He claimed that she was just defending herself. He also used the fact that, as a result of the prolonged abuse, she had developed serious mental health issues and this should be taken into consideration, should they refuse to believe her assertion that it was self-defence.' He paused.

'So basically he gave the court a choice of self-defence or diminished responsibility. Apparently he then tried to get the prosecution to agree to drop the case but they would only consent to the arrangement in part. They agreed to reduce the more substantive GBH offence to a lesser charge of common assault but they refused to drop the case completely. That way it allowed the court the chance to impose an order requiring her to receive compulsory mental health treatment.'

'So she was sent to hospital against her will?'

'It appears so. It doesn't say how long the order was made for or how long she was actually treated, but she was definitely sectioned, under the Mental Health Act.'

'So she might still hold a grudge about the fact she was sent off to a mental hospital because of his plea bargaining.'

'She could well do. Those are exactly the sort of circumstances we were searching for in the list. It looks like you've hit the jackpot.'

Matt smiled broadly at the thought. It did indeed feel as if he'd finally found the missing piece of the jigsaw that would link the two murders. One suspect known to both victims and so far she was the only one that fitted the bill. He thanked Greg Northborough for his assistance and put the handset down, turning towards his own boss and explaining with relish the facts that he'd just heard.

As he was finishing the explanation Alison burst back in and threw a wad of paper on the table.

'Good news, Matt.' She smiled at him warmly. 'Vanessa Barrington is known to police on several occasions for domestic related incidents. She has convictions for common assault, criminal damage, possession of drugs and a couple of deceptions. All the reports stem from a five-year period just before she met Ray Barnes. That's why we didn't find anything.'

'Good stuff,' Matt said smiling back with equal warmth. 'Do we know any details of the offences?'

'From what I can gather from the reports, Vanessa was living with this guy called Dave Barrington. The relationship appears to have been pretty volatile. Police were called several times to fights between them and there were allegations of abuse. She alleged that he beat her regularly and forced her to do things she didn't want to do—'

'What kind of things?' DI Blandford interrupted.

'It's not that specific, but it does say there was evidence of drug taking in the premises and the two other convictions she had were for credit card fraud. The picture I get is that Dave Barrington was the driving force and seemed to dominate her. Whether they were both on drugs or it was just one of them I don't know but they certainly seemed to need cash for their habit.'

'So it looks like he could have forced her into crime? Or maybe to do things of a sexual nature against her will?'

'It looks like it. Especially if they had a habit to feed.'

Matt thought for a moment. 'So what happened in the end?'

'She cut up his clothes and stabbed him, almost to death.'

'Bloody hell, that's a bit extreme.'

Alison picked up the top sheet of the paper and scrutinized the notes she'd jotted down.

'I've only got the potted version of events but it appears that on the night of the stabbing, both Vanessa and Dave Barrington had been drinking and taking substances. An argument blew

up, it says here, because Vanessa had found out that he was
sleeping with a neighbour. The argument got more violent
and she alleged that he tried to strangle her. She then goes on
to say that she picked up a pair of scissors that were lying
nearby and stabbed him several times in the chest and neck in
order to force him to release his grip.'

'I'm a little surprised she was charged then. You know what
the CPS is like, particularly with their history of violence and
the imminent threat to her life,' DI Blandford commented.

'Exactly, but the CPS decided to go ahead with a charge
this time, apparently because after the stabbing, she then went
upstairs and calmly cut up all his clothes before going to a
neighbour's and calling for the police and ambulance.'

'Not quite the actions of someone who has nearly been throt-
tled. You'd think she would have got out straight away,' DI
Blandford agreed. 'I suppose that's why Jeffrey Bamfo had to
go down the line of diminished responsibility as well as self-
defence.'

'Yes, he persuaded the prosecution that a person in their right
mind would have run for help immediately and that because
of her actions and various medical and mental health assess-
ments, she must have been disturbed and unable to make
reasoned decisions. The prosecution agreed with him but stipu-
lated immediate hospitalization, saying she needed psychiatric
help. Vanessa Barrington then effectively disappeared into the
hospital for good. When she finished her treatment she came
out reinvented and using her maiden name again until she
bumped into Ray Barnes.'

'She seems to be very good at portraying herself as the poor
victim! That's what Evelyn Johnson said too. I wonder if she
really is though.' Matt ran his hands through his hair.

'What do you mean?' DI Blandford grimaced.

'Well, I wonder if she could have planned it all along, especially when she found out her ex was cheating on her. Maybe
she isn't as mad as we think. It wouldn't have been difficult to
make up the whole story that she was attacked first, bearing in
mind their history. Maybe she was as cold blooded then as she
appears to be now with Ray. Ray needed to be punished as he
had betrayed her and Jeffrey Bamfo had to be punished for failing
to get the charge dropped. Maybe that's what she's doing now.'
He paused and ran his hands through his hair again, frowning

thoughtfully. 'For all we know she might be trying to make us think she's crazy to get off Ray's murder.'

They all fell silent. DI Blandford finally spoke. 'I think we need to get her now, in case she's got other targets. How soon can you be ready?'

The phone rang as Matt was about to answer. He picked up the receiver and felt the colour drain from his face.

'Not soon enough,' he said to his boss. 'Shit, not nearly soon enough.'

TWELVE

Tunde Oshodi's body bore the same grotesque mutilations as the previous two. He was younger than the others, only twenty-four according to the driving licence that was hanging out from the wallet lying in the foreground. Money was spread out on the grass, ten- and twenty-pound notes weighted down by the stickiness of the crimson, clotted blood. The inference wasn't lost on the two detectives. The killer wasn't bothered with the money. Tunde Oshodi had paid with his life.

Matt Arnold and Roger Blandford were deadly serious this time. There was no time for the frivolous banter that had masked their nervousness at witnessing the first mutilated body. The death toll had grown and they were wondering whether their inaction had been the cause of the death of the young man spread out in front of them.

Matt peered towards the plate from where he stood, trying not to let his gaze remain too long on the sliced, bloody genitals. Instead he concentrated on reading out loud the contents of the now familiar attached note.

'"4. One for every year of suffering",' he recited. '"Do not be deceived: God cannot be mocked. A man reaps what he sows. Galatians 6 verse 7." Same as before then, murdered for his past sins, whatever they were. She's made that quite obvious again.'

'It's also quite obvious that we're missing a body,' DI Blandford muttered. 'This one's numbered four and we've still only found three. Let's just hope the missing one doesn't turn up on our patch too.'

Matt nodded. 'With any luck she might have wanted to get the ones further afield like Bamfo sorted out first before concentrating on this area.'

He thought of Vanessa Barnes and her imminent arrest. How he hoped they had the right suspect. There seemed so many things to connect her, too many coincidences even, but yet there was still a niggle playing at the back of his mind. The Barnes' car was different to the vehicle used by the suspect at Tewkesbury. Theirs was a Blue Renault Laguna bearing the registration number LF51FPII and the vehicle seen on the CCTV was an L reg VW Golf. The tyre tracks found at both scenes did not match their car either. But had she the use of another vehicle that was kept hidden, even from her husband? She was certainly capable of keeping secrets; that was clear. The questions were intriguing.

They turned away and started walking back along the specified route and out from the cordons. The sun was high in the sky and cast tiny shadows down amongst the trees. The copse chosen this time was tucked away in the far corner of Brockwell Park, on the border of Streatham and Brixton. The park was a hilly, sprawling mix of play areas, well-trodden footways, cut-grass fields and areas where the grass was left to grow wild. Most of the vehicular entrances to the park were closed at night with the exception of one. The CCTV camera aimed down at this particular point had already been seized from the local council for examination and Matt hoped it would yield a complete registration number and even an image of its driver. The copse was in the wilderness area of the park, far away from the more common walking routes. This had enabled it to hide its grisly secret for a few hours before being discovered by a park ranger following the tracks left by the vehicle through the long grass.

He looked around as he neared the edge of the outer cordon and saw a multitude of onlookers, poised with camera phones at the ready to capture any opportune occurrence. The press were congregated in larger than ever numbers too and TV and newspaper helicopters buzzed overhead periodically. This would be big news. The papers would be full of victim profiles and criticism of the perceived lack of progress on the part of the police investigation. A twinge of frustration shot through him. With the lack of positive forensic identification the public hadn't a clue how difficult it was to sift through the thousands of snippets of information and pick out the most relevant.

The arrest of Vanessa Barnes would be reported, but the victory of Matt's breakthrough would be downgraded against the fevered body count. He let his disappointment wash over him wishing that he had been at work the previous week to coordinate the investigation more closely. As quickly as the thought dawned on him, however, the guilt followed. Ben's

death had shattered his world and had obviously taken prece-
dence over every thing. He just wished with all his heart he
could have prevented it. His son's funeral was less than two
days away and he couldn't bear to dwell on the moment he
would have to say a final goodbye. Work was the only way of
blotting out the pain. It hurt to walk out of the house each
morning and leave Jo and Chloe, but it hurt even more to stay.
He just hoped Jo could understand but he feared she couldn't.

DI Blandford was entering a small tent hastily erected to
hold the variety of paperwork and exhibits required. Matt
followed, pulling off the white paper forensic suit and shoes
and folding them carefully into an evidence bag.

'We won't be answering any questions from the press now,'
his boss said. 'They can speak to the press liaison officer if they
need to know anything.'

He smiled grimly and strode out towards their car. Matt
followed closely, climbing into the driver's seat and aiming the
car towards the exit. A crowd of reporters jostled towards them,
thrusting microphones at the windows and shouting questions
through the glass.

'Why hasn't anyone been arrested?' he heard one of them
shout. 'Haven't you got any suspects yet?'

Matt drove carefully through the group, windows remaining
tightly shut, slowly forcing a path through the heaving melee.
He swung the vehicle out from the park on to the road and
pushed his foot down hard on the accelerator eager to get to
the Barnes' house in time to witness their only suspect's arrest.
He just hoped, in the rapidly growing profile of this series of
killings, that they had the right suspect

Tom Berwick glanced round at the clutter. The state of 68
Eastleigh Street appeared to have worsened even within the last
twenty-four hours and the stale smell of its interior wafted up
into his nostrils as he entered. The appearance of Vanessa Barnes
had also deteriorated. As well as the dishevelled, dirty clothes,
unbrushed hair and manic expression in her eyes, her limbs
now shook noticeably. She'd appeared at the door as he and
Alison Richards had been reaching for the bell, startling him
momentarily. She had then stood fidgeting on the doorstep, her
pupils swivelling nervously and her hands shaking against
her sides before gesturing for them to enter.

'I was waiting for you,' she said simply. 'I knew you'd be back.'

'Vanessa Barnes,' Tom said immediately, 'I'm arresting you on suspicion of the murder of your husband, Ray Barnes, and also on suspicion of the murder of Jeffrey Bamfo. You do not have to say anything, but it may harm your defence if you do not mention, when questioned, something you later rely on in court. Anything you do say will be given in evidence.'

She made no direct reply, merely raising an eyebrow at the mention of Jeffrey Bamfo and rubbing the palms of her hands together continually, as if trying to stop them shaking.

'I'm ready to go,' she commented dully, with as little emotion as if she was going shopping. 'I've even packed an overnight bag.'

She peered up at him, staring into his face, her eyes unblinking, and held her arms out while Tom placed handcuffs around her wrists and started to lead her back down the path towards his car.

An army of scenes-of-crime officers were awaiting their exit in preparation for the meticulous fingertip search that would be required at the house. Uniformed officers were in the process of tying cordon tape around the outskirts of the premises and a small group of neighbours were beginning to emerge from nearby houses to watch the unfolding drama. Tom couldn't resist a slight smile. He could guess exactly what they'd be saying to each other. The press was starting to appear as well and Tom was anxious to leave before they got too close. He glanced up the road and saw DI Blandford and Matt sitting watching from their vehicle, unable to be directly involved in Vanessa's arrest for fear of any cross-contamination from the new murder scene. He guessed Matt would be itching to get started on the interviews but until all the clothing and swabs had been taken he would have to wait.

As she reached Tom's police vehicle, Vanessa glanced up the road and saw their unmarked car, stopping to squint towards its occupants.

'You've got your side of the bargain,' she screamed, raising her manacled arms towards them. 'When do I get to visit Ray? I want to see him. I want to see him.'

Her voice came out in a shrill screech, silencing the watching neighbours and press alike. They watched in excited horror as

Tom guided her head under the door sill and eased her into the back of the car.

'I want to visit my husband one last time,' she screamed as the door was slammed firmly, muffling any further outbursts. She pressed her face to the window as she was driven from her house and the silent crowd watched as tears slid from her wild eyes and wetted the steamy condensation of her breath on the glass.

The interview with Vanessa Barnes was postponed several times much to Matt's irritation. By the time she'd been booked in, her clothing seized and a full examination carried out, hours had already passed and the custody officer, in conjunction with senior officers from the murder enquiry, had decided that it wasn't fair for her to be interviewed without a full mental health assessment being conducted. This was likely to prevent any questioning until at least the following morning and he was increasingly frustrated by the delay, however necessary. Any evidence gleaned from an interview with somebody suspected of suffering from mental problems, without the proper safeguards, would be deemed inadmissible and that would hinder, rather than assist, the investigation.

All in all he had no choice. He would have to return in the morning if he wished to be the investigating officer. Jo would not be happy with this prospect but, having made the breakthrough, he wanted to be there to get started. He would speak to Vanessa Barnes initially to see what she had to say and then leave any further interviews with DI Blandford, Tom or Alison. That decided he made his way to the Borough Intelligence Unit where they were viewing the CCTV of the entrance into the park where Oshodi's body was found.

Tom and Alison were already there, staring intently at the screen. He watched the time ticking onwards, awaiting the moment they would get a proper look at their murderer. It didn't take too long. At 0012 hours a small dark car slowed at the gates and inched forward into the park. The driver didn't bother to turn the lights off and the registration plate showed up in its own small light.

'This is it,' Matt exclaimed. 'It's a black Golf, just like at Tewkesbury. This must be her.'

He slowed the recording down, peering closely at the images. The view of the occupants was only momentary, the angle of the camera only showing the rear of the car as it entered the park. There was barely enough time to see the back of two heads as it passed through.

'Damn,' Tom muttered. 'I couldn't see the driver at all. Hopefully we'll get a better view as the vehicle leaves.'

Matt grunted his agreement, pausing the recording at a view of the rear of the vehicle. The number plate was clear.

'Brilliant, at least we've got the number this time,' he almost shouted. 'L889EGB.'

They fast forwarded to almost 0114 hours before the vehicle came back into view.

'She certainly likes to take her time with her victims,' commented Alison. 'She seems to like the process as much as the end result.'

They scanned the footage closely but the headlights had been set to main beam as the vehicle approached the gates and the view was of glaring light and nothing much else. For a second, as the car passed directly underneath the camera, there was the briefest of views of the driver. The image was of blonde hair, with head bent down and the facial features obscured. They could just see a hand on top of the steering wheel directing it outwards on to the road.

'Damn,' Tom muttered again. 'I can't see her face at all. We'll be lucky to get anything usable from that image.'

'I'll get it sent up to the lab to see if they can enhance what image we do have,' Matt agreed. 'But I think we'll be lucky. She's quite careful not to let us see her face.'

'At least we have the registration number,' Alison chipped in. 'Maybe there'll be CCTV from nearby.'

Tom sighed. 'It'll take forever to scan through the hours and hours of tapes and there's no reason to presume that there'll be a better image of her face anyway. Most of the cameras are only set to read the number plates.'

'I know, but we've got to give it a try,' Matt said. 'If for no other reason than to log her movements. Tom, get a check on the number plate straight away. We've got to find that car. If necessary arrange a street search of every street south of the river. When we find that car we'll have our charge.'

THIRTEEN

It was half an hour into their encounter when Vanessa Barnes' mental fragility kicked in. Assessed as mentally unstable but fit to be interviewed, she was to be dealt with gently but firmly and was fully supported by a raft of solicitors, mental health workers and appropriate adults. It was a high profile and interesting case.

The interview had started well with Matt gently explaining the procedure and taking time to ensure she was settled and happy. She spoke then of a childhood, blighted by the deaths of both her parents in circumstances she refused to embellish upon. She spoke of school, the area in which she lived and the friendships that had been forged. Her voice was steady and she refused to be drawn into any aspect of her past that she herself did not wish to reveal. He was surprised at the calmness of her tone and the easy way in which she recounted her memories.

Only when he'd delved into her more recent history did the calm exterior start to crumble. His attempt to probe the relationship she'd endured with Dave Barrington brought with it a sullen silence. He'd tried again from a different angle.

'Police were called to fights between you and Dave quite regularly and you said then that he forced you to do things that you didn't want to. What sort of things were those?'

'I don't want to talk about it.'

'But I'm just trying to find out more about you. It must have been hard living with a man like that?'

'I wasn't living. I was existing.'

'Were you on drugs then?'

'Yeah, he had me hooked on heroin. He mixed it with the weed I was smoking without me knowing to start with until he'd got me where he wanted me. Then he forced me to do stuff.'

'But what kind of things?'

'I don't want to talk about it.'

'Did he make you go out and commit crime? You have convictions for deception in the name Barrington.'

'Yeah, that kind of stuff.'

'Did he make you do sexual favours for him?'

'I don't want to talk about it.'

'What about for others? Did he make you do sexual favours for others?'

She looked down at the table top.

'Did he make you work the streets?'

She blanched at the words, closing her eyes and tilting her head down. There was silence, long and pronounced, and he waited for her to break it. When at last she looked up the mania was back in her expression.

'He tried to,' she replied, her voice rising. 'He tried to make me work the streets like a dirty whore but I wouldn't let him. I wouldn't go out there. So what did he do? Do you know what he made me do? He brought men in to my place and he made me spread my legs there on my own bed for them and for him. And he watched them sometimes and laughed. And if I tried to get away, he beat me.' She was almost screaming at him, her eyes wild and her fists clenched, pounding on the table. 'And that's why I don't want to talk about it. That's why.'

Matt leant forward, keeping his voice so soft that she had to concentrate to hear him. 'And is that the reason why you fought on the day you stabbed him?'

'Yes that's part of it. But I did it for him because I loved him, even though he treated me so bad. But then he betrayed me, with the slag across the road. He fucked her right in front of my eyes and he didn't care what I felt, the bastard. I caught him in the act and all he could do was laugh in my face.' Her expression was blank now, her voice almost inaudible. 'I wanted him to die. He deserved to for what he did to me.' She lifted her head and her eyes were dead and glassy. 'Of course he attacked me first, like I said before. I had to defend myself. I was suffering from clinical depression and a form of continuing post-traumatic stress, that's what they said. I didn't know what I was doing properly after so long being beaten.'

'I've read your mental assessment. They thought you had quite a complex personality.'

She laughed suddenly, loudly and the shock of the noise reverberating around the small room made him jump slightly. She wore an expression of amusement now and a dangerous spark glinted in her eyes.

'They would, wouldn't they? They don't know me any more than you do.'

He caught the edge in her tone and the slight challenge in her words and changed his tack slightly.

'Why didn't you tell us you used a different name?'

'Why should I? It's irrelevant. Besides I wanted to see how long it took for you to find out. You were a bit slow, but you got there in the end.'

Matt blushed slightly at the criticism.

'And,' she continued, smiling decisively, 'I knew you'd jump to the wrong conclusion.'

'And what conclusion might that be?'

'That just because I nearly killed a previous partner in self-defence while mentally unbalanced I obviously had to have killed Ray.'

'Well did you?'

She looked stunned at the directness of the question.

'Did you kill him Vanessa, when you found out he too was having sex with another woman? And another woman you knew.'

She shook her head.

'We've got photographs of a blonde-haired woman with two of the victims just before they were killed. Was that you?'

She shook her head again.

'Why do you keep shaking your head? Ray did you wrong, didn't he? Just like Dave had, just like Jeffrey Bamfo, your barrister had when he got you locked up in a mental hospital, just like all the men you've met have.'

She shook her head again, but this time a slight smile played across her lips.

'You've got me all wrong,' she said. 'I thought you might be different. You seemed to listen but you're just the same. You policemen are all the same. You just want your pound of flesh like all the others.' She jumped up on to her feet, her voice rising to a crescendo and tears coursing down her cheeks.

'Can't you get it into your fucking heads that I'm the victim in all this? The victim! You decide who needs to be punished.'

Several times on the journey home Matt found himself being forced to brake or swerve to avoid the crass manoeuvres of other drivers. He was frustrated; frustrated with the fact that Vanessa Barnes' outburst had now given her the excuse to hide behind the shield of mental instability; frustrated that a check on the vehicle registration number had shown it to be a Red Hyundai coupe and not a Black Golf, and frustrated that a visit to the address of the registered owner had revealed nothing. A Hyundai car bearing the same registration number was parked on the owner's driveway and all the documentation was correct. The killer had obviously changed the plate and the number of combinations possible was too many to consider owner enquiries on every single one.

He punched the steering wheel in anger. Everything they tried seemed to be failing. Every time they appeared to have a lead, it turned out to be a dead end. Every time they got a new piece of information, it was not enough and to make matters worse, every failure was exacerbated by the increasingly hysterical headlines and equally hysterical outbursts of senior officers anxious to stop the body count rising any further.

They had three corpses so far, two of them in Lambeth, one in Tewkesbury. There was almost certainly one yet to be found. All three known victims had left their own vehicles in quiet side streets and appeared to have moved willingly into the suspect's car. There was no reported disturbance at the swap-over points, few witnesses with any worthwhile evidence, no CCTV and more exasperatingly, no DNA or fingerprints to identify the suspect. It pointed to the theory that all the victims were deliberately chosen by the suspect and the suspect was known to them. Two could be possibly attributed to Vanessa Barnes but what of the third?

Tunde Oshodi lived in the same area but they hadn't as yet found anything to tie him to Vanessa Barnes or indeed to connect the three known victims together.

Something obviously did link them, though, and it was Matt's priority to find out what.

Enquiries had also been made to isolate any unusual calls coming to the victims' phones. Each had received two phone calls from public boxes in the week leading up to their deaths. The telephone boxes had been located but weren't covered by CCTV. A small group of his detectives were now scanning through CCTV of nearby roads at the time of the calls to try to locate their murderer's vehicle and obtain a better view of its driver, but it was like trying to find a needle in a haystack.

They needed to find the car and its treasure chest of forensic identification evidence, but where it was being hidden he didn't

know. The number had been circulated Met wide but so far
nothing had turned up. It was so frustrating.

The fact that ketamine was illegal had stopped its users talking
freely, even with promises of immunity from prosecution and
none had been reported stolen or misplaced from vets or hospitals.

Even enquiries on the plate and cord found at the murder scenes
had drawn a blank. The plates had been bought from a common
high street retail outlet but the batch numbers were such that they
allowed only the generalization that they were sold from one of
the south-east England area shops. The cord was an even more
common brand, on sale in many different DIY stores in London.

Every lead seemed to go so far but then hit a brick wall.

His house was in sight by the time he'd finished thinking.
The tiny rectangular front garden had been neatened in readiness for the family and guests that would even now be
descending on them. Tomorrow was the day of Ben's funeral
and he wasn't ready for it. He would be burying his son and
losing him forever. On a whim, he spun the car round and drove
to the funeral directors.

The atmosphere was tranquil when he entered, at complete
odds with the pounding inside his chest. The air was fragranced
with sweet smelling oils which added to the sense of peacefulness. He was greeted by a softly spoken female receptionist and
asked to wait for a few minutes while they prepared a room.

The wait did nothing to calm his nerves. He hadn't seen Ben
since the night he'd died, when the nurses had gently roused him
and lifted his son's lifeless body from his arms. He hadn't really
wanted to see him again until now when the finality of his burial
was only hours away. He'd wanted to remember the warmth his
small body had still retained in his arms and the way his skin felt
soft to the touch, but he suddenly needed a last visit.

The receptionist was back, guiding him to the room. The
lighting was soft as the door slid noiselessly shut, locking him
together with the small wooden casket. He stepped forward
towards it peering down at the familiar features. Ben was
sleeping with his eyes closed. He wore his favourite football
shirt and an expression of absolute beauty. Matt knew immediately that now was the right time to say goodbye. Not
tomorrow, when the eyes of all the others mourners would be
upon him and journalists from the local paper would no doubt
be hovering in the background trying to give words to his grief.

Now while there was just him and his son and no one else he would say the things that needed to be said. His son was to be lain next to his father, a fact that gave Matt comfort while at the same time highlighting the age gap. Matt remained alive, the missing middle generation. It wasn't right. It wasn't the proper order.

He spoke softly to him, as if afraid to wake the sleeping child but hoping he would still be able to listen to the words. The sentiments slipped out easily, with just the two of them together. He loved him. He always would. He would never forget his special boy and he was so proud to have had him as his son. He would do anything to trade places with him and allow him a few more years to sample the joys of study, travel, marriage and fatherhood. Ben was sure to have made a great dad, better than he. After all where had he been when the car had swept his young son off his feet and sent him flying, half-dead through the air. Where had he been as he'd fought to recover, only to succumb to fever and heart failure? He'd been present at his birth and death but in between? Now more than anything he wished he'd been around more.

He leant forward, reaching down to stroke the pale cheek. It was cold, so cold and his skin was hard and stiff. He recoiled at the touch, stepping backwards. It didn't feel like Ben at all and his peaceful appearance didn't correspond with the waxy texture of his flesh.

Ben was gone forever. Even though he'd known it from the moment he'd held his son's lifeless body at the hospital and been aware of his spirit leaving, it hadn't really hit him, until now. Now, all signs of life had been eliminated totally and even his warmth and liveliness had disappeared. His son was lost to him for good. The reality hit him hard.

He wanted to run away from the room, from the body that didn't feel like Ben's but he couldn't leave without a final goodbye. He walked back across the carpet and gazed down at his son, glad that he'd come but at the same time wishing he hadn't. He couldn't shake off the coldness of his pale skin and the chill had replaced the warmth of his memories.

Bending down he stroked the blonde hair, relieved at its texture and smell which had not changed. He kissed the small head, turned and was gone.

FOURTEEN

His black suit and tie were hanging on the back of the door when Matt woke the next morning. It was still early but he could hear Jo busying herself downstairs. The bed next to him was cool and she had obviously been up for some time. There was one thing he needed to do before he gave himself over entirely to the day's events. He dialled Tom's number and waited impatiently for a rather sleepy voice to answer.

'Tom, it's Matt. Just a quick one. I've promised Jo not to talk job today. How did it go with Vanessa Barnes after I left yesterday?'

'Not much further I'm afraid, Matt. She refused to say anything more. She just kept crying.'

'Did you think it was put on?'

'Couldn't really say. It seemed quite genuine but I don't know. Suffice to say, we weren't able to interview her again. She's been admitted to the South Western secure unit for a full mental health assessment. They're worried she might try to harm herself or others.'

'I'm not worried about her. It's the "others" I'm more concerned about. How long is she there for?'

'Up to twenty-eight days and then they have to make a further order or release her. She's been bailed straight into their custody. I've asked them to let me know if they're about to let her go and we can decide on our course of action. Bloody frustrating though, not to be able to get going properly.'

'Quite useful though. At least it gives us more time for forensics to go through her house and have a really good dig around. There must be something there to tie her down.'

'Let's hope so! It would be nice to talk to her at the same time though. If the gear's not at her house it'll be somewhere else. I'm sure we'd be able to get her talking, given a proper chance.'

Matt shook his head in frustration. 'I know, mate, but she's off the streets and that's got to be a step in the right direction. I have a feeling she wouldn't have given us much anyway.'

'I think you're probably right.' He paused. 'You all set for later?'

'Yeah, thanks. As much as I'm ever going to be. On that note, I'd better go. I'm supposed to be looking after Chloe. I'll see you at the church.'

He ended the call and padded from the room, stripping off as he entered the bathroom and throwing his boxers on to the floor. They had up to a month to get everything together. Surely there'd be something more tangible by then, some physical link to incriminate her. Whatever happened, he'd make sure they found the missing link; but until then . . .

He shut himself into the shower and turned the water up to full power allowing a jet of cold water to bring his thoughts back to the forthcoming events.

The service was not until twelve noon at the church in which Ben had been christened just a few short years before. It was their local parish church, not particularly picturesque but large and functional, with a high domed ceiling and cream walls. He allowed himself a small smile at the memory of Ben's enthusiastic visits to the church and the rows of flickering naked candles at the front of each altar which seemed to draw him and other children to stand bathed in their glow. He remembered how Ben wouldn't budge until he'd lit a candle for Grandpa and would watch mesmerized as the wick struggled to burn, even though the pungent smell of the incense made him wrinkle his nose.

Matt would be lighting two candles today.

Downstairs the sound of voices was becoming louder and more distinct. He listened to the arrival of his parents-in-law, their speech hushed, and knew that he ought to be with them helping to ensure the day ran smoothly. Jo had taken care of that, though, and apart from a few tasks, his presence was barely needed, at least by her. He could do as much or as little as he wanted, so long as he did his allotted jobs.

His main function was to babysit Chloe and ensure she got to nursery fed, watered and dressed on time. He finished his shower and dressed, running swiftly into the kitchen to find most of that job already near to completion. Chloe sat, fully dressed, eating a bowl of cereal and chatting animatedly to Jo's mother.

'I thought I was supposed to be—'

Jo cut him off mid sentence. 'Well, you were still in bed.'
The edge to her voice was so obvious even her mother spun
round towards her.

'Sorry, Matt,' she said, stepping into the fray. 'It's my fault.
I needed something to do. I didn't realize you were sorting her
out.'

*And Jo wouldn't have told you of course. Anything to exclude
me.* He bit back the words as they formed, unwilling to start
an argument on this day of all days. It rankled with him more
than he cared to admit though and he didn't know why such a
small thing should cause him so much irritation. It was going
to be a hard enough day without all the extra crap.

The journey to nursery was only short but he didn't want it
to end. He left the house early, hastened by the uncomfortable
atmosphere and took the long route, taking in the play area at
the nearby recreation ground. Chloe was delighted, throwing
herself enthusiastically at the colourful climbing frame and
empty swings. She had no real idea of the awful gnawing pain
of loss, a pain that Matt knew only too well. He watched her
leap from the top of a small ladder, blissfully unaware, knowing
only the added excitement of an early visit from Granny and
Grandpa, an extra session at the playground and the promise
of lunch at the home of her best friend from nursery. If only
his life were this simple.

When the time came to say goodbye to her at the nursery,
he didn't want to. Hanging back, he waited for the other parents
to leave, turning away from the expressions of sympathy. He
knew they were genuine and that many of those same parents
would be at the church, but he was not yet ready to deal with
them.

Chloe kicked against his all-consuming hug desperate to be
allowed to follow her compatriots into the brightly painted
building. She didn't understand his sudden need to hold on to
his one surviving offspring, to keep her safe in his arms away
from every danger or risk and never, ever let go.

'Daddy, I'll see you later,' she pleaded, planting a kiss on
his cheek and nuzzling her warm skin into his neck. He didn't
want to put her down. Hadn't Ben said exactly the same thing
before the accident?

A nursery teacher was standing by the gate, ready to lock
her young charges safely inside. She didn't say anything.

She just stood quietly waiting and Matt felt inordinately grateful for her patience and understanding.

'I love you, poppet,' he smiled, setting his little girl down eventually.

She made to run off but stopped briefly, as if sensing his disquiet and turned back towards him. 'I love you too, Daddy,' she shouted, kissing her hand and blowing it towards him. He pretended to catch it and she giggled gleefully. Then she was gone and he vaguely heard her laughter turned to squeals of delight as the gate was shut behind her and she entered her domain.

He walked back through the park, stopping to sit on a bench to delay his return. The day was warm, with a stillness that saturated the air. Horse chestnut and oak trees stood serene, ignoring the languid pursuits of a pair of sleepy squirrels, not yet roused from the cool inactivity of the night. A few sounds penetrated the tranquillity. Dogs frolicked together across the barren brown grass, joyous in their early morning release; toddlers, en route back from the school run, already missing the company of older siblings screamed to be permitted liberation from harnesses: the sounds of a city stirring from its rest. The sounds of normality. Matt stayed cocooned in a bubble of grief and fear, not wanting the hours and minutes to advance any further, oblivious to the pulse of life that surrounded him.

He remained in his own world even when his body rose and returned to the hubbub of last-minute arrangements, completing each allotted job robotically and thoroughly until the protective skin around him was burst at eleven forty-five by the arrival of the funeral cortège.

Ben's small white coffin was floating on a sea of colour, its passage to the church carried on a tidal wave of emotion. Matt climbed into the following car and sat next to, but not close to Jo. He kept his eyes firmly focussed on the hearse, not wanting to let his son's body leave his sight for even a few seconds.

As they pulled up at the church he saw Tom waiting, his tall, bulky figure standing out above a small collection of gathered colleagues. He bowed his head almost imperceptibly as the funeral cortège stopped and the group dispersed towards the door of the church.

Then it was just he and Tom and the unspoken task and Matt

led the way, hoisting the small casket up on to his shoulder, at once surprised and saddened at its size, knowing the weight of his son's death would burden him for the rest of his life. He waited for a few moments summoning the courage to proceed, his mind concentrated on the coffin, large enough to show the first timid stirrings of childhood but too small by far for the experiences and complexities of longevity.

When he was prepared, he nodded his readiness and they carried Ben through the gates and along a path lined un-expectedly by a guard of silent colleagues wordlessly formed, as if in respect to a fallen comrade; his son as much a part of the assumed family as the father. And Matt was glad he'd done this for Ben, glad for this last act of love, glad of the support of his friends and glad that Jo, following behind, might somehow see and recognize the strength that he drew from the job that he performed.

The church was full to capacity as they entered, its aisles obliterated by a realm of standing, hushed observers. Matt and Tom walked slowly, deliberately as 'All things bright and beauti-ful' rang out. Jo had chosen it as a hymn that appealed to children, a hymn that spoke about birds and flowers and mountains and rivers and everything that Ben had previously scrutinized with a child's fascination for wildlife. It seemed to Matt as if all the brightness and beauty was being removed from his life. They placed the coffin gently down on the trestles and moved to their seats, his next to Jo, Tom's the row behind next to Sue, his wife.

Jo turned and smiled at him as he sat, her fingers brushing his knee fleetingly.

'Thanks,' she whispered.

He grasped her hand and held it tightly squeezing it in time with the last few chords. Somehow it seemed smaller, more fragile than he remembered. She didn't try to remove it from his.

The priest was speaking of love and loss and of Ben having been God's child. The words hung in the air, mingling with the scent of incense and candles. They made no sense to him. Ben was his child and God had no right to take him so prematurely.

The service passed with not a dry eye remaining as Sue read out a eulogy composed by Jo and encompassing the tender-ness, poignancy and sense of loss only a grieving parent could express. Matt listened to his son's life compressed into a few wordy pages. It was beautiful. It encapsulated his very being but it was inadequate.

And then it was over and Matt and Tom rose wordlessly and moved towards the coffin. They lifted it as the CD player clicked on and the words of Michael Jackson's song 'Ben', clear and vibrant soared out over the congregation.

It was the song he and Jo had sung to their young son as they'd carried him to his room at bedtime, their own lullaby that was guaranteed to nudge him gently towards sleep. He knew it was corny, that the song was about a pet, but it was their song and they'd just changed the words to fit.

The sound swelled as they paced down the centre aisle towards the waiting graveyard. Matt held his head high, his pride in his son's courage on display, determined to complete the final journey with quiet dignity. He cast around the congregation as he walked and saw familiar faces: Jo and her parents, family, parents from the school, teachers, senior officers from his borough, work colleagues, neighbours, so many others. He saw Alison and for the briefest of moments their eyes connected and he smiled his gratitude. So many people.

The coffin was being borne, not just by him and Tom, but by each and every person present and he took comfort in the thought that Ben's small cold body would be surrounded with that same strong everlasting love, even when the first spade of soil rained down upon it.

It was late evening by the time he was able to return to the church. The emotion of the day had left him drained and empty but he was determined to do this one last task. He thought of the flame in the reception lobby at Scotland Yard, burning brightly, steadfastly, a constant never-ending reminder of those fallen colleagues whose deaths would never be forgotten. It burned for his father.

Now in his own small way he would start a flame of remembrance burning for Ben. It wouldn't be constant at the church, he knew that, but it would forever be a symbol to him of the life that had burned brightly for a few short years before being extinguished at the hands of a drunk driver. He thought of Andrei Kachan and the court case that was to follow in just a few days. He thought of William Mortimer, the man who had killed his father. One man had ruined his childhood and the other had ruined his adulthood.

He walked to a side altar and lifted two candles from a box. They were only tea lights and wouldn't last long but it was the sentiment that was important. He stooped down holding the clean wicks in the flames of another already burning candle and then held them up in his fingers until the heat got too much.

Carefully he placed them in two empty casings and stepped back, staring down at his two candles. One burnt strongly, the orange glow bright against the shadowy background. It belonged to his father, John Arnold, whose killer was locked up for life. To Matt it was the flame of justice burning bright.

The other candle was still twitching weakly, sucking at the surrounding air. The process of obtaining justice for Ben was still in its early stages, just like the candle's first feeble attempts. Matt watched it gradually take hold, burning weakly with a concentrated intensity. He would return after the court case and light another candle and next time it would flare with right-eous justice.

He heard a slight movement at the rear of the church. An elderly man was shifting prayer books as if to fill in time. He turned and walked towards the exit nodding his thanks to the man for waiting, before stopping to take one last look back. The old man was shuffling towards the alcove now. Leaning down he held a blackened, metallic candle snuffer over the tea lights, extinguishing each small flame and watching the small plume of black smoke that wove upwards into the gloom.

Matt blinked hard as tears sprung unbidden behind his lids at the finality of the movement. He couldn't help a slight unease, that he was witnessing something symbolic but he didn't know what precisely. The flames were gone, extinguished, even quicker than he'd anticipated.

The tears were flowing down his cheeks now. He spun round, pushing at the door and stumbled out into the growing darkness.

FIFTEEN

D awn broke eventually. Spindly rays of light filtering through the gap in the curtains danced in time with the growing chorus of bird song. Matt lay wide awake watching the time pass slowly, each minute bringing him nearer the time when he could justifiably rise without appearing either mad or sad. Jo lay next to him, her breathing deep and even, her body warm against his. Yesterday had seen a thaw in her attitude towards him, starting at the beginning of the funeral service and continuing throughout the day until at last he had returned from the church and explained his final mission. It had been a day in which all his concentration had been centred on his family and he had consciously tried to set aside his thoughts on the triple murder investigation. He heard snippets of conversation from some of his men, hushed voices whispering about up-to-date news but he hadn't allowed himself to participate. Yesterday had been about Ben.

Jo shifted in her sleep, reaching out and laying her arm across his chest. He'd badly wanted to make love to her last night but they had both been mentally and physically drained and in any case it wouldn't have felt right having just buried their son. Now was too early, although he was sorely tempted. The digital clock next to the bed blinked over to 04.42. He savoured the touch of her fingers against his skin and hoped that his early start wouldn't be the catalyst for a refreezing of relations. Yesterday as he had lit the candles for his own two loved ones it had also brought home to him that there were three other families at least who would also be burying their dead. He owed it to them to get justice for their loss. His own justice he hoped would be meted out at the court hearing the next day. He made a mental note to give Gary Fellowes a ring to check on the further charge.

As the clock clicked another minute forward he decided he could wait no longer. There were too many things to be done. Carefully he removed Jo's hand and slipped out, showering and shaving silently and leaving a note next to the kettle explaining his absence. If it hadn't been for the high profile of the case he wouldn't have bothered but there was too much to be done and he felt responsible. With Vanessa Barnes safely locked up inside a secure unit he didn't want the squad to rest on their laurels. They had to be completely ready for her release.

Lambeth HQ was quiet when he arrived. He made for the confines of his own office; passing DI Blandford's along the way he was surprised to see his boss, slumped over his desk, with his head resting on a pile of files, apparently asleep.

'Are you alright, guv?' he offered cautiously, pushing the door open.

An empty bottle of scotch lay alongside a tumbler on the floor to his side and remnants of its distinctive aroma still hung in the air. His boss stirred at the noise and lifted red-rimmed eyes towards him.

'Oh, it's you, Matt.' He glanced blearily towards the clock. 'What are you doing in so early?'

'I thought I'd come in and try to pull everything together.'

'I was trying to do the same,' his boss agreed, nodding towards the empty bottle and grinning sheepishly. 'Only I got a little waylaid.'

'Have you been here all night?'

DI Blandford nodded again. 'I came straight from Ben's funeral yesterday to sort a few things out. Bumped into the DCI when I got here. Bloody tosser! I was probably a little worse for wear, I must admit, but he gave me a right bollocking. Said we weren't doing enough and that the press were having a field day with our lack of progress.'

'What about the arrest of Vanessa Barnes?'

'Oh, that,' he imitated in mock derision. 'Apparently we shouldn't have let her be carted off to the hospital. Apparently we should have insisted she stay and be interviewed.'

'Yeah right and see everything she says disallowed in court. Great idea!'

'I know. Anyway, you know what they're like! I'd like to see him dealing with the menagerie of bleeding advisers, solicitors and doctors on hand to uphold all her human rights. I don't suppose he's been in a custody office for years.'

'Tom told me all about it. It's a shame she's not still with us but at least she's off the streets. Hopefully the body count won't go up any further.'

'How sure are you that she's the one?'

Matt frowned at the question. His boss was staring at him intently. He pulled up a chair. 'Well, as sure as I can be. What are the odds on another person having links with two of the victims and fitting the description of the suspect on CCTV? Vanessa's got the motive for two of the murders, a background history of violence towards men and is unstable. She's also withheld information.'

'I just don't want to discount any other theories. I've been burned before in one case when I was sure my suspect was the one. Three years later he walked free when the real suspect got nicked for a similar offence and confessed everything. Talk about miscarriage of justice. I was made to look a complete and utter idiot in court. Why do you think I'm still a DI? I should have been at least two ranks higher by my stage of service. Things like that don't get forgotten.'

'I thought that was because you were shagging your boss's wife!'

'Yeah that didn't help either.' He grinned momentarily. 'But seriously. We've been through her house with a fine toothcomb and found nothing. We don't yet have any forensic evidence that ties her to the two murders and nothing as yet to connect her with the last one. I've left a file of details on your desk about the last one, Tunde Oshodi. Don't discount other suspects though. You just never know what else might crop up.'

Matt stood up. 'I won't, guv. But the odds are stacked against it being anyone else. We just need a bit of luck. She must have somewhere she keeps all her gear and while she's inside we need to find it. Don't worry! We'll have the case sewn up before you know it.' He pushed his chair in and glanced at his boss. DI Blandford was wiping at his forehead with a handkerchief, his brows furrowed, his cheeks flushed. Matt frowned. It wasn't like his boss to fret so much over a job. He was normally so laid-back. It certainly wasn't like him to down a bottle of booze and fall asleep over his desk. But then it wasn't every day a serial killer came to roost on your patch.

The conversation left Matt feeling strangely disquieted.

When he got to his office he flipped open the file that his boss had mentioned and skimmed through the details, trying to keep an open mind.

Same method. Same type of location. Same religious

connotations. Same approximate time of death. Same mutilations. Plate and twine of the same type but awaiting forensic results. Drugged with the same substance. Same day of the week.

He'd noticed this before but now with the third suspect it had become even more obvious. Each victim had been enticed to meet their killer on a Sunday evening. Each body had been found on a Monday morning. Bearing in mind the religious passages, it was fairly sensible to assume that Sunday was their day of choice for killing.

He jotted down another set of actions to be completed. Check out local churches for anyone fitting the suspect's description and in particular churches local to Vanessa Barnes.

In essence the rest of the report was depressingly familiar.

He read through a precis of Tunde Oshodi's life, looking for the snippet of information that would lead to a link between the victims. This victim appeared totally different to the other two. The others were both older, professional men, working in academic occupations with decent salaries.

Tunde, on the other hand, was only twenty-four years of age and only fairly recently married. He had emigrated from Nigeria when he was twelve and moved around, living with a variety of aunts and uncles. He attended the local comprehensive school, with only a timid grasp of English, failed to thrive in academic subjects, was barely able to read and write, but became determined with the help of a strong work ethic, to make something of himself.

He'd left school at sixteen years of age and been fortunate to win an apprenticeship from a local carpenter using the initial skills gleaned from his woodwork classes. Day and night he'd striven to learn the craft until he was able to set his work to good use and take on jobs of his own.

As his earnings had grown he'd travelled to and fro from England to Nigeria visiting family and providing a percentage of his income towards improving their lives. It was from one of these home visits that he gained a wife. He was married at twenty and brought his new wife, Jumoke, to England two years later where they settled, initially in rather grim council accommodation in Lambeth. A baby girl, Bayo, now fourteen months had been born within a year and the young family had recently moved to a rented semi-detached house in Norbury. By all accounts, Tunde was extremely hard-working and motivated and it was through his efforts that the family were now able to better themselves.

There was nothing of note in the background information. Tunde Oshodi appeared to be a poor boy made good, or at least in the process of making good.

Matt skimmed through the wife's account of the events leading up to his death. Jumoke stated that her husband's behaviour had changed slightly in the preceding week but that she was unaware of any particular problems and he had refused to expand on his worries. He had, according to his wife, been slightly more irritable and had snapped irrationally when questioned why he had their bank books with him on a trip out. She was not however unduly worried by this as the recent move had caused him a few financial headaches that he'd preferred to work through without bothering her.

On the night of his death he had left the house at about ten stating he was going to visit an old friend. Jumoke had no knowledge of who the friend might be as she knew little of his life in England before they had married. She had thought it strange but had not questioned it at the time, allowing him to leave with a promise he would return later. When he did not arrive back, she had gone to bed and when he was still not back in the middle of the night when the baby had woken, she had worried but presumed he would arrive home in the morning. She had been unsure of what to do the next day when he was still not back, due to her lack of knowledge of the English police and procedures. The first she had known of his death was the arrival on her doorstep of several uniformed and non-uniformed police officers who had explained their suspicions that her husband was the body found in the park.

There was no more information than that.

Matt checked a further sheet containing a record of all the calls made and received by Tunde over the last three months. In the previous week his phone records showed that he too had received two phone calls made from public call boxes. The locations of the call boxes were, as usual, in non-CCTV areas and enquiries in the locality had unsurprisingly been negative. There was nothing to suggest the contents of the calls but Matt knew without doubt they had been made by Tunde's killer making the arrangements for his murder.

The Bible passage showed the same motive, punishment for sins committed. 'A man reaps what he sows.' The murderer was doling out the punishment they deemed appropriate to his crime. But death! He wondered what sin Tunde Oshodi had committed to warrant death in his killer's warped mind.

More puzzling, though, was what could link it with Vanessa Barnes.

He hadn't gone to the same school and didn't appear to socialize with the same class or nationality of people. He could think of little that would have brought the two of them together. There was a chance that he may have been employed by her or Ray in the past, maybe some sort of relationship could have occurred, but the latter was unlikely and the former difficult to prove with both the employee and one half of the employer dead.

He checked his watch. The lab would be open shortly and he needed results from there as soon as possible. Taking hold of the phone he swiftly pressed the number of his contact at the lab. The phone was answered almost immediately and the gruff voice of Rob Wallace answered.

'Rob, it's Matt Arnold.'

'Bloody hell, Matt. I was just about to phone your office. We've managed to get some fingerprints off the plate in your last murder. They were very scuffed and faint, which is why it's taken a few days, but they're better than nothing.'

'Rob, that's fantastic. Have you got an ID for them?'

'Not yet Matt. That's what I was about to ring you for. The prints are not of a high enough quality to be fed into the LiveScan machine. They'll have to be examined manually. If we arrange it, it'll take several hours before the dispatch rider even gets to us and then there's no guarantee they'll be the first on the drop.'

Matt looked around. He couldn't wait a minute longer than was necessary and only one other detective had arrived as yet.

'I'll be with you shortly,' he said pacing out of the room.

Rob Wallace was waiting at the entrance to the lab when Matt got there, his red hair and long sideburns like a beacon against the white sterile background. The two men shook hands warmly and Rob passed a large brown envelope to Matt.

'Thanks, mate. I owe you one,' Matt called out, spinning round to leave.

And with that he was on his way. His squad car was parked directly outside, with its blue magnetic light still flashing crazily to one side. He climbed back in and took off, sounding the two tone horns and navigating his way through the swiftly parting traffic. The River Thames sparkled in the early light as Matt crossed Lambeth Bridge, with the Houses of Parliament and Big Ben to his right. The traffic was heavy but he made good progress, swinging past Horseferry Road Magistrates' Court and through some of the back streets, until he emerged on to Victoria Street.

New Scotland Yard stood directly in front of him, its twin towers dwarfed by the surrounding office buildings. Concrete blocks had been erected along its frontage, bland and ugly but necessary in the fight against terrorism. The metal prism bearing its name rotated slowly, the printed words moving from dark to light alternately, as its surface met the rays of sun. Matt walked briskly, stopping only briefly to allow his warrant card to be checked by security. The eternal flame burned discreetly on its stone pedestal as he walked past. It already seemed like a lifetime had passed since he'd buried his son and lit the two candles.

He passed the envelope across to the fingerprints technician explaining the urgency and providing Vanessa Barnes' details to be crossmatched against. He couldn't bear to leave the room. He had to get the result the second it was available. Pacing up and down he ran over and over the case in his mind. Had they missed something or made the wrong assumptions? His boss's words kept repeating in his head.

'We've got a match,' the technician shouted suddenly. Matt was at his shoulder in an instant. 'Do you want the good news or the bad news?'

'I don't mind. Just give me the result,' Matt gasped breathlessly.

'Well, the bad news is the prints do not match your suspect Vanessa Barnes.' Matt felt a wave of disappointment wash over him. 'But the good news is they are an exact match for a male by the name of Julian Reynolds.'

'Thanks,' he mumbled, heading for the door. As he made for his car he phoned the office, explaining the new development to his boss. By the time he arrived back at Lambeth HQ he wanted everything possible known about Julian Reynolds ready and waiting. They would be paying him a visit at the earliest possible moment.

The office was tense with anticipation by the time he arrived back. The word had got around that they had another good suspect and the whole squad wanted a part of the action. DI Blandford had spoken with Superintendent Graves and taken charge, delegating tasks to the various teams. The Police National Computer had been checked for convictions and details, the criminal intelligence system was being scanned for any reports relating to Julian Reynolds or his address and a full risk assessment was being carried out. A specialist firearms unit was to be on standby in case the suspect armed himself and a dog unit to prevent his escape. There was no way they were going to cock this up in the full glare of the media.

Ernie Watling had been tasked with getting a warrant from the magistrates' court to search the address, which wasn't necessary if Reynolds was there but essential should no one be at home. They would need to conduct a full search of the premises with or without their suspect being arrested. They couldn't risk losing any evidence that might be present.

They had a limited time to get everything set up. A car had already been dispatched to keep observation on their suspect's home address. It appeared empty at present but they were to watch for their suspect's return and report in immediately. Matt wanted to be ready the moment that time came.

In the meantime he needed to get the whole operation up and running and ready to brief his troops. Tom and Alison had compiled much of the intelligence and Matt set about getting it in order. By the time the briefing was ready to be given an air of impatient excitement seemed to be crackling around every corridor and room in Lambeth HQ. Matt glanced out of the window as he made his way to DI Blandford's office to tell him he was all set. The number of press had doubled from the normal contingent and more were still arriving. Word had obviously gone round about the increased activity at the station. With any luck no details would have been leaked. From previous operations he knew the squad kept specifics tight. The HQ would know another arrest was imminent but whose, they would have to guess.

Roger Blandford was ready for him when he got to his door.

He looked slightly more relaxed than on his last encounter. As if reading his mind he nodded his head towards the jostling group.

'Bloody press. They're the last thing we need turning up at the venue.' He grimaced towards Matt. 'All set?'

Matt nodded back and the two men walked silently towards the briefing room. As they entered heads turned expectantly and a hush fell. Pens and notebooks twitched in readiness and every face was turned towards them. DI Blandford addressed them first as Matt set up the projector.

'Ladies and gents, thank you for all arriving so promptly. We have a second suspect identified from fingerprints found on the plate. The suspect has been named as Julian Reynolds, and today's operation is to arrest him and carry out a full search of his home address for any other physical evidence to connect him to our series of murders.' He paused and then added. 'Vanessa Barnes remains as our main suspect but while she's kept in hospital we have a duty to continue following every lead that comes to light. This new suspect may turn out to be connected in some way to her, but he may be totally separate. We'll have to wait and see. Anyway, Matt will be briefing you all and I'll pass over to him now.'

Matt stepped forward.

'Good afternoon, everyone. As the guvnor's just said, the aim of today's operation is to arrest a male by the name of Julian Reynolds on suspicion of the murder of Tunde Oshodi. His fingerprints have been found on a plate left at the murder scene. At the moment he's only to be arrested for Tunde Oshodi's murder, but in due course he may well be further arrested for the linked murders of Ray Barnes and Jeffrey Bamfo.'

He flicked to the first slide. A man's face and shoulders flashed on to the screen. His cheeks were hollow and his eyes bulged, the creamy white pool of his irises appearing to swallow the pupils so that they were only the size of pin pricks. His fair hair was long and lank and fell across his face, curtaining the oval shape of his head. Both ears were pierced and he wore large clear stone stud earrings in both ears. His expression was both challenging and submissive, his eyes cast downwards but his brow furrowed in anger.

'This is Julian Reynolds. He is a white male, with a date of birth of 12th December 1979. He is about 5ft 9" in height and thin build. He has come to notice on several previous occasions, most notably through Operation Ore, which in case you don't know was the operation set up to catch persons downloading pornographic images of children from the Internet. He is on the sex offenders' register for this offence. He has also one previous conviction for GBH, a bottling after a pub brawl which left his victim needing forty-three stitches to his face. He also has a few other minor theft convictions thrown in. We're obviously very interested in the fact he's got convictions for sexual offences and violence.'

He switched to a different slide, showing a photograph of the front of a small block of maisonettes. Stairs wound up the sides of the buildings to the upper residences, while the front doors to the lower level faced the street. Two large trees in the front gardens and a hedgerow down the centre of the building partially obscured the view to and from the front doors to the lower maisonettes.

'The address we will be attending is number 5 Park Terrace, SW12, off Weir Road. That address is the one with the blue front door, on the left in the picture.' He pointed to the door. 'It is a wooden door, hinged to the left, with a single Yale lock. It does not appear to be particularly secure.

'In view of Reynolds's history of violence, Lambeth South Task Force will be conducting a rapid entry and we will be containing him fast and hard if necessary. I have arranged to have armed Trojan units on hand should he try to arm himself, in which case back off and let them do their thing.

'Once contained an arrest team led by myself will move in and arrest him. No one else is shown on the voters' register as living there and there is no intelligence to suggest any other persons or dogs on premises, but if someone else is there they are to be detained and DI Blandford will make a decision as to whether they should be arrested or not.

'Once the premises are secure, search teams and forensics will move in and scour the place for evidence. I have a full list of property for them to look for. Finds will be photographed in situ and bagged up at the scene. We have a warrant to do the address should Reynolds not show but I want to give him time. There's directed surveillance set up at his address but at the moment we don't think he's there. There has been no movement and no sign of life.'

He paused and checked his watch. 'I propose to wait until they contact me to say he is housed then get him inside the premises if possible. If he hasn't arrived home by midnight we'll go in anyway to secure any possible forensic evidence.

'The entry squad and search team, can you both stay and I'll brief you individually on what to expect and what to look for. The rest of you, wait in the canteen or make sure you can be contacted to move as soon as we get the word he's there.'

He looked up. 'Otherwise, are there any questions?'

The room stayed quiet. 'Needless to say,' Matt added, 'this operation is likely to be conducted in full view of the press, so don't cock up and be professional at all times. Julian Reynolds is a good suspect and I want him ready for interview as soon as possible.'

He turned to his boss who was still standing close by. 'And if we can find some link between him and Vanessa Barnes, so much the better!' he said quietly.

It was several long nervous hours before the phone call came.

'A male fitting the description of our suspect has just entered the venue. He's inside now.'

'Is he on his own?'

'Yes.'

There was no need for any further words; Matt gave the thumbs up to DI Blandford and the word spread like wild fire throughout the headquarters. Teams were mobilized and within minutes officers were pouring out into the rear yard. When everyone was ready they set off, Lambeth South Task Force leading the way, followed by Matt, Alison, Tom and DI Blandford in another vehicle and a convoy including search teams, an armed response unit and a dog van. As they streamed out a bevy of press vehicles tagged on following the procession in a winding animated tail.

They stopped just around the corner from the venue in a forward rendezvous point while Matt made one final phone call to the observation van to confirm the situation was unchanged.

Nothing had changed. He grimaced at the other three. 'Here we go,' he whispered into the gloom of their vehicle.

Pushing the button on his radio he spoke clearly and precisely. 'All units. Go, go, go.'

The van carrying the entry team raced forward, followed

swiftly by Tom. They jumped out of their vehicle behind the van and watched as eight fully kitted, helmeted officers ran towards the address. The street became bathed in the sounds of loud, shouted commands and the splintering of wood as the front door to the premises gave way under the weight of the heavy red enforcer and the entry squad ran through the premises searching for its occupant.

Matt waited at the front door until the all clear was given, then he was shown to the back room. It was a functional room, with bookcases floor to ceiling, filled with a variety of books, videos and DVDs. A TV rested on a coffee table in the corner, opposite a slightly stained threadbare beige suite. A computer desk surrounded by further shelves of DVDs was positioned along one wall of the room and to the right of this stood Julian Reynolds, his hands securely handcuffed behind his back, his head facing downwards. Two uniformed police officers, one on each side, had hold of each of his arms, periodically pulling them back so that he was forced to stand more upright. He was visibly shaking. Matt glanced towards the computer monitor as he walked across the room and saw an image of a young, naked boy sitting in a bath. The boy had his head thrown back laughing, a picture of childhood innocence that reminded Matt forcefully of their own family bath times. He glanced at Reynolds and noticed at once his clothing was in disarray, his trousers unzipped, his belt unbuckled.

'We caught this sick bastard at the computer, sarge,' one of the officers growled, pulling his suspect's arm back so that his head jerked upwards.

Matt swallowed the urge to punch him forcefully in the stomach, reminding himself of the need to keep the bastard sweet. He needed his suspect to trust him, to talk to him, to tell him everything. He stepped up in front of the man.

'Julian Reynolds?' he asked, staring into his bulging eyes.

The man drew his gaze up so that he was staring directly into his own and nodded. 'It's not what it looks like,' he stammered. 'I was just getting ready to go out and was looking at some photos a friend sent.' He paused. 'Honestly.' He let his gaze slide back down to the floor.

'Julian Reynolds. I'm arresting you on suspicion of the murder of Tunde Oshodi. You do not have to say anything unless . . .' Matt's voice was monotone. He had taken an instant dislike to the sniffling man in front of him.

The man's face shot up, his expression unreadable in a mix of conflicting emotions. Relief, puzzlement, annoyance and anger in turn flicking across his features.

'I don't know what you're talking about,' he said. 'I thought you'd come because of the . . .' His voice tailed out as he glanced towards the laughing boy on the computer monitor.

He looked back towards Matt, a slight smile playing on his lips.

'Cover that up,' Matt instructed, motioning towards the screen. 'And get him out of here.'

SIXTEEN

Julian Reynolds shifted his body on the plastic mattress and waited. While he waited he thought of how much younger policemen looked these days. Then he thought of an eight-year-old boy as a policeman. Then he imagined the eight-year-old policeman gradually stripping his uniform off in front of him. He liked the thought. He liked it a lot. He liked it so much that he didn't notice the sound of the key in the lock and footsteps entering his space as the heavy cell door swung open. A young constable stood at the door to the cell. He only looked to be about nineteen years old. A little bit too old for his predilections, but maybe he could make an exception. He normally preferred them younger, more pliable, more suggestible. So far he had mainly only lusted after images on his computer, but things were changing. He'd made contact with a group of younger boys on an Internet chat room and was gradually gaining their trust. It was exciting becoming friendlier with them. Thoughts of what might follow were beginning to take control of his mind. He couldn't stop thinking about them. Now the shock of his arrest was over, he was more confident, cocky even, about his ability to deflect any charges.

'Follow me,' the young policeman was saying. 'Your solicitor's here and you'll be interviewed soon.'

Julian stood up and stretched, readjusted his trousers and sauntered after his teenage gaoler, noting how pert his arse was in his uniform trousers and how his collar length and smartly groomed hair gave him the appearance of a child in school attire. The constable disappeared behind the custody desk, forcing him to avert his gaze back up to a small, waiting group. The policeman who had arrested him was in the group and he spoke first.

'Julian, this is Miss Khan. She's a duty solicitor. She will be acting for you during interview and she wants to have a consultation with you before we start.'

Julian swivelled his eyes towards her without moving his head, allowing the pupils to disappear almost totally into the corner of his eye sockets so that the whites appeared even more globular. It was a trick he'd learned in school and one that he'd recently discovered worked well in the company of children. The sight of his huge, bulbous frog-like eyes shocked them into wanting to see more and he could manipulate them to stay with him for longer.

He could see the solicitor baulk slightly at the sight of him. He was glad. He didn't like her; she was smart and female and would no doubt be overtly judgemental of his previous conviction. He turned his head towards her allowing his eyes to readjust and fixed them straight at her. She was an Asian woman, about thirty-two, he estimated, slim and pretty, with long, black hair swept high on to her head in a tight bun. She wore dark rimmed oblong spectacles and a smart, dark brown suit. She was everything he despised about a society that he believed had left him on the scrap heap, uneducated and unable to fit in. It was only since realizing that he had to take love wherever he could find it that his life had improved and if it happened to be against the law, then so be it. He couldn't stop now, even if he wanted to. And he didn't.

He followed the solicitor into an interview room and slumped down in a seat in the corner, rolling his eyeballs dispassionately. He watched amused as she flinched away from directly addressing him, preferring to stare at a folder on which half a page of notes were scribbled.

'You've been arrested on suspicion of the murder of Tunde Oshodi,' she started.

He interrupted her almost immediately, jerking forward in his chair so his face was just a few inches from her own. She jumped momentarily and he grinned at her discomfiture. 'That's complete and utter bollocks. I have never met the man, if it is a man, and I have never murdered anyone.' He leant back, keeping his eyes fixed on her. 'Though sometimes I wish I could.'

She smiled nervously towards him and coughed. 'I have been given disclosure on the evidence the police have and there is forensic evidence that links you to the murder scene.'

'That's bollocks too. How could they? I wasn't bleedin' well there and I don't know nothin' about no murder. What evidence anyway?'

'They wouldn't say exactly what. I asked them to reveal the details but they refused.'

'Some solicitor you are then. You should have made them tell you.'

She glanced up at him clearly annoyed. He was amused.

'They don't actually have to tell me the specifics. It's enough for them to tell me there is forensic evidence. Are you sure you can think of no reason why your DNA or fingerprints should be at the scene of a murder?'

It was his turn to get annoyed now. Bleeding woman. Why didn't she just fuck off and leave him to his own thoughts and dreams. They had been quite pleasant until she'd interrupted them. He swivelled his eyes in their sockets again, watching for the look of distaste to reappear across her pinched, irritated face.

'Don't you believe me?' he queried malevolently. 'I've already said twice I don't know nothin' about no murder. How many more times do I have to repeat myself before you get it into that pretty, dumb head of yours that I'm not bleedin' guilty.'

'Mr Reynolds, I do not appreciate being spoken to like that and if you don't want to go back to your cell for another few hours while you wait for another duty solicitor, I suggest you start treating me with a little more respect.'

She stared quickly back down to her notepad and started to scribble on it again. Julian Reynolds sat silent for a few seconds, thinking. He couldn't make his mind up whether to continue with this dopey bitch or go back to his cell and wait for another brief who might with any luck be a young male counterpart. He sighed, coming to a swift decision. Much as he would like a different gendered solicitor, the chances were pretty remote that he would strike lucky.

'Alright, lady,' he drawled. 'There is no reason I can think of for how my DNA or fingerprints or any other bleedin' thing of mine could be at a murder scene, unless they are trying to set me up for some reason. They were pretty rough when I was nicked and I don't think that DS Arnold particularly took a shine to me either.'

She ignored the final sentence. 'In that case I will be advising you to make no comment to every question. That way they will have to bring out the exact nature of the forensic evidence and it'll give us time to think about what your answer is going to be for the next interview.'

He nodded. Maybe she wasn't as dumb as he'd thought. That

made sense. Play them at their own game. If the cops were going to withhold information so could they.

Matt was raring to get stuck into Julian Reynolds.

Things were finally looking up. A cursory search of Reynolds's address had revealed a small pile of the same type of plate as had been used in the murder and a roll of garden twine that also appeared to be of the same sort as that used to bind the victims. Added to that Reynolds had longish blond hair. Was it possible that the murder suspect was indeed him all along and they had mistaken the suspect as a female simply because of the hairstyle? He didn't know. Even when they had pulled out the working copies of the CCTV tapes and rechecked, it was still unclear. The images were too grainy and blurred to make any identification conclusive. But he had to admit now that it was a distinct possibility. Reynolds also seemed to have a predisposition for males and male pornography, that was quite obvious from his viewing choice at the time of arrest, and this also corresponded with the images found on his computer when he was convicted previously. All in all Reynolds was now shaping up to be a better suspect than he had at first thought.

DI Blandford would be sitting in with him for this interview. He wondered fleetingly whether this was due to their previous conversation about keeping an open mind to other lines of enquiry. He dismissed the thought. Matt's decisive action in arresting Reynolds had seen to that. Besides he'd sat in on many previous interviews and this case was obviously worrying him more than most.

He still secretly hoped that there would be something to link Vanessa Barnes and Julian Reynolds but as yet nothing had come to light.

The door to the interview room swung open and Miss Khan appeared at the entrance.

'We're ready,' she stated simply.

As they entered the small room, Julian Reynolds folded his arms and leant back in his chair. Matt surveyed the man as his boss seated himself and made ready. He really was quite ugly and knowing what he knew about the man's preferences Matt found it hard to see anything good in him. His hair appeared even more lank and greasy in the bright light and his cheeks, more sunken and cadaverous. The eye sockets were deep-set, making the pupils bulge even more starkly and his skin was pockmarked and pitted.

In spite of his small frame and gaunt features his stance appeared confident and confrontational, all the stumbling reticence gone. The potential for violence pulsated from behind his tightly folded arms and thin lips and there was a tension between him and his solicitor that even Matt could sense.

Matt smiled at his suspect in spite of his desire to punch his lights out for the way he was. It wouldn't help to alienate him. Paedophiles were frequently receptive to friendship and there was nothing to be gained from an antagonistic approach.

'How are you?' he asked conversationally.

Reynolds said nothing. His solicitor intervened. 'My client is anxious to get this over with. He denies any knowledge of the murder for which he has been arrested and has maintained his innocence to me of any other wrong doing. Due to the fact that we have not been made party to all your evidence, I have advised him to make no comment to any questions you may wish to put to him, at least until I get a chance to consult with him over the details.'

Matt sighed. So that was the way they would be playing it. He had half expected that course of action. She would know that further interviews would be likely. Why show their hand until she'd forced the police to show theirs.

It was irritating but he would try to engage him as best as he could and at least put to him the basis for his arrest. A jury in the future might wonder why he'd refused to answer any questions if he was not guilty, rather than answer honestly and proclaim his innocence. It was worth a try anyway.

He settled himself, spending more time than was usual to get prepared, while at the same time appearing relaxed and unaffected by Reynolds's obvious irritation. When he was ready, he ran through the preliminaries, taking care to ensure his interviewee was fit, feeling well and was perfectly ready to answer questions. He wanted to see if he could provoke a response by being slow and methodical. By the time he actually started asking any pertinent questions, Reynolds's impatience had been ratcheted up several more levels. He looked as if he was barely able to control his temper.

Matt started with general questions and conversation about what made Reynolds tick, but he wouldn't be drawn.

He continued by delving into his movements on the evening of Tunde Oshodi's murder.

'What were you doing on the night of Sunday 17th June?'

'No comment.'

'Were you with anyone that night who can verify what you were doing?'

'No comment.'

'Do you own a car?'

'No comment.'

'Or do you have access to anyone else's?'

'No comment.'

'A body was found on Monday 18th June in Brockwell Park. Do you know anything about that?'

'No comment.'

'Did you go to Brockwell Park that night or have you been there before?'

'No comment.'

'The body was that of Tunde Oshodi, a young married man with a small child. Do you know him?'

'No comment.'

'Have you ever met him before?'

'No comment.'

Matt watched Reynolds carefully as he spoke, watching for any betrayal in his expression that he knew more than he was letting on. His face was a mask of impatience. He decided the time was ready to drop their forensic evidence into the conversation.

'Are you aware of the series of murders currently in the news?'

'No comment.'

'Three men have been murdered and their bodies dumped in wooded areas. You seem to have a preference for males?'

His lip curled slightly. 'No comment.'

'Tunde Oshodi is the third body in that series to be found.'

'No comment.'

'I presume you realize the implication of being arrested for *one* of these murders?'

Reynolds shuffled slightly in his seat, his interest rekindled. He rolled his eyes towards Matt so that he was staring straight into his face.

'No comment.'

'Some green garden twine was found at your home. Where did you get it from?'

'No comment.'

'Tunde Oshodi had been mutilated before he died and asphyxiated. His hands were bound in green garden twine, of the same type that has been found in your home.'

'No comment.'

Reynolds appeared to relax slightly as if he thought for a moment that was the piece of forensic evidence that linked him to the killing. Matt pounced.

'Some of the victim's body parts were put on a plate at the murder scene. Can you tell me how come your fingerprints were also on the plate?'

His eyes bulged slightly and he blinked, preventing the glimmer of panic and confusion that flicked across his face taking hold. He kept his voice even. 'No comment.'

'What explanation can there be for their presence, except that you were the person who carried the plate to the scene and consequently you must be implicated in the murder?'

Reynolds frowned. A bead of sweat prickled on his forehead and he wiped at it with the back of his hand.

'No comment,' he said eventually.

Matt was pleased at the reaction. His cool had been broken and the man was showing his guilt, even though he was sticking to the script. He continued in a similar vein.

'The same brand of plain, white plates has been found at your house.'

Reynolds's frown deepened, then he sat bolt upright and his stare intensified. 'The plates wouldn't happen to come from Ikea, would they?'

It was Matt's turn to look slightly confused. 'Yes they do,' he answered, not quite knowing where the question was leading.

The solicitor had rested her hand on Reynolds's shoulder in an obvious attempt to stop him talking. Reynolds shrugged it off and leaned across the table so that Matt could smell his stale breath on his face.

'You stupid, fucking bastard,' he sneered. 'I work at Ikea and if you'd done your homework properly you should have known that. Those plates are for sale in the kitchen section that I work in. I stack them on the shelves day in and day out. That's obviously how my fingerprints got to be on them.'

*   *   *

DI Blandford sucked on another cigarette at an open window in his office as he went over the events of the interview. It was nearly midnight and he was beyond exhaustion. He blew the smoke out fiercely trying to concentrate on their next move and trying hard to ignore the growing buzz of news reporters camped out by the main gates awaiting news of the latest suspect.

He closed his eyes and frowned. What suspect? This one was destined to go down the pan like all the other leads they had followed. Maybe Matt was right and Vanessa Barnes was their murderer. He hoped so. It would certainly put an end to the niggling worry that was keeping him from sleep.

He lit another fag and drew deeply on the nicotine; running back over the farce into which the interview had dissolved. Reynolds had a realistic excuse for why his prints were on the plate. Leaving fingerprints on so obvious an item was sloppy and the murderer was anything but sloppy. It was possible, of course, that the killer was becoming careless and Reynolds could indeed be their murderer, but he didn't think so.

He'd dealt with enough criminals to know when the truth was being told and Reynolds was not nearly clever enough to conceive and carry out such well-planned and meticulous murders. The man was too volatile and reckless and his obsession was with boys, not grown men.

After his outburst Reynolds had started talking freely, recapping on the previous questions and studiously ignoring the pleas of his solicitor. The garden twine he'd bought at a local DIY store. There was no reason to disbelieve this and their enquiries had already shown this store to be one of the many retailers who sold this particular brand. The sample found at his home address would be compared against the twine found at the scene to check whether it came from the same batch. Only if it was, would any relevance be attached to it.

Reynolds had also provided an alibi of sorts. He'd stated he had been on a chatline speaking with several other users. He could not provide exact identities for his compatriots, only email addresses and user names but at least his computer could be interrogated and a record of times and names retrieved. The man lived alone and although it was possible he could have allowed a friend to use his computer during the relevant times, it was unlikely. He appeared to be somewhat of a loner with few friends, other than work colleagues with whom he chose not to socialize.

His computer had obviously been seized and Roger Blandford expected its contents to provide adequate evidence for a raft of pornography charges. Tom was checking Reynolds's employment record to confirm that he did work at Ikea, although whether he *should* work there with the number of children who passed through on a weekly basis was a different question. Maybe an off-the-record word in the manager's ear wouldn't go amiss.

All in all Julian Reynolds, while initially appearing to be a credible suspect for murder, was turning out to be nothing more than his record indicated: a sick bastard, with low intellect, low competence and low self-control. A sad but possibly dangerous paedophile left unchecked in a community ignorant of his presence.

Reynolds would be kept in custody at Lambeth HQ pending the results of the enquiries. There was still enough on him, until actually proven otherwise, to prevent his early release. Matt was due at court the following day to see Andrei Kachan charged with causing the death of his son by dangerous driving. Hopefully his sergeant would be back before Reynolds's custody clock had expired, to re-interview the man and after that . . . He'd probably be released back into the community on bail. Great!

DI Blandford took one last drag on his cigarette before throwing the dog-end out of the window. He watched its glowing free fall as it sped steadily towards the ground.

The investigation would shift back towards Vanessa Barnes. He only hoped she was their suspect or else the murderer would be free to strike again. Sunday was only a couple of days away and he was worried they'd missed something obvious. Maybe they should be concentrating more on what was linking the three victims together, rather than what was linking the suspects they did have to the victims.

The niggling fear rose up in his head again. He watched as the tiny glow from the dog-end faded out completely and he turned silently to return home for another night's insomnia.

SEVENTEEN

Inner London Crown Court imposed itself on the area of Newington Causeway, South London. Its entrance comprised two large creamy stone arches supporting four high metal gates each bearing the coat of arms of London County Council.

The actual site had housed a judicial building since 1794, becoming The Sessions House in 1917 and replacing the Middlesex Sessions House by 1921. It was not until 1971 however that the building was designated as a Crown Court and extended to provide ten courts. It had spread out even further now into nearby Swan Street, unable to cope with the rising number of cases whose defendants requested trial by jury.

Matt stood staring up at its creamy stone frontage with its central flight of steps leading up into its bowels. He could almost hear the crack of the hammer and the shout of 'take him down' echoing across the courtyard. He hoped the sentiment would be repeated in his case and Andrei Kachan would receive a long, deserved custodial sentence.

The car park was just beginning to fill. There were still two hours until the main business of court began at ten thirty but Gary Fellowes had requested his early attendance in order to confer with Crown prosecution lawyers about the further charge of causing death by dangerous driving. He'd arranged to meet Jo outside the gates at about 10 a.m., half an hour before court was due to sit. She was still not keen on attending, arguing that justice would never bring Ben back. It would never make up for Matt's loss either, but it would go some way to achieving some sort of closure.

He felt a hand on his shoulder and heard a familiar voice. Gary Fellowes was extending an arm towards him.

'How're you doing, Matt? Glad you could make it so early.'

Matt swung round towards him and offered his hand too. The two men shook each other's warmly.

'Good to see you too, Gary. What time is the meeting scheduled for?'

Gary Fellowes checked his watch. 'In about five minutes. We'd better go in.'

They climbed the steps and pushed the revolving doors, stepping into the high, stone entrance hall. Wood panelling on either end of the hall and narrow arched windows imbued the room with an air of gravitas, further enhanced by uniformed security guards and metal detectors. The heavy wooden entrance doors to the main two courts led from the hall and the marble stone flooring threw the sound of their footsteps up into the staid atmosphere. Matt and Gary showed their warrant cards and were granted entry, walking purposefully towards the offices of the Crown Prosecution Service. They knocked smartly on the door and it was opened by a tall, slightly scruffy barrister. He eyed them up and down before nodding a greeting.

Matt sized the barrister up too. His hair, combed over to one side, was black and heavy, standing thickly on top of a rough, ruddy scalp. His nose was bulbous with large, open pores visible to the naked eye and his voice was loud, booming out from a lopsided mouth.

'Good morning, I'm James Wentworth. You must be DS Matthew Arnold and PC Gary Fellowes? I'm the only QC here at the moment and I don't imagine there are too many police officers here as early as this without a good reason.'

Matt nodded and offered his hand. 'I'm Matt Arnold and this is Gary Fellowes.'

'You'd better come straight through.'

He turned and walked back inside and they settled themselves around a table in a small wood panelled office. James Wentworth stared down at several boxes of paperwork. He pulled a file from the top and opened it, flicking through to a précis of the case.

'I'll come straight to the point,' he said, pulling a few pages up in front of him and adding a statement from the pile. 'We haven't enough to further charge the defendant with causing death by dangerous driving.'

The strain of the last few weeks burst inside his head. Matt sat bolt upright, his eyes immediately challenging as a surge of white hot anger ran through him. He tried to keep his voice under control.

'What do you mean we haven't enough to further charge

him? My son is dead as a result of the manner of the defendant's driving, what more do you need?'

The barrister fidgeted uncomfortably, pulling a statement to the front of the small pile. He let his eyes run over it.

'According to the statement from the doctor at the hospital, your son died as a result of heart failure, brought on by an acute temperature and infection—'

'But who put him into hospital in the first place?' Matt interrupted.

'I know and I completely sympathize but I can only go by previous stated cases. In your son's circumstances, we cannot prove that he actually died as a result of the injuries inflicted in the accident. As far as I can see, he had stabilized after his initial trauma and was in fact gradually improving in a separate rehabilitation unit. If it hadn't been for the infection, who knows whether he would have continued to improve enough to achieve a reasonable quality of life?'

'A reasonable quality of life! Stuck in a hospital bed unable to walk or talk or hardly even communicate. You call that a reasonable quality of life? If it hadn't been for the defendant's reckless driving in the first place he would never have been in that condition. Andrei Kachan caused my son's death. His driving caused his death. You must see that?'

The barrister sighed heavily. 'You and I know that. The judge will no doubt realize that, but unless we can prove that he died as a direct result of his injuries and not as a result of an infection six months later, we can't further charge him. And we can't prove it. The medical evidence just does not support the case. It would be thrown straight out.'

'But isn't it worth a try at least? My son's dead and Kachan is going to get away with it.' He turned towards Gary Fellowes. 'If it hadn't been for the persistence of Gary here and my own good luck, he wouldn't even have got this far.' He threw his hands across his face, drawing them down over his mouth to try to control his words. 'That bastard sent my little boy flying through the air and then just drove off, leaving him lying in the road like an animal. Worse than that he even got out and looked back and still did nothing. He didn't try and help, he didn't move him out of the road in case he got hit again, he didn't even call an ambulance. He just left him to die and drove off laughing. And then he reported his car stolen to try and worm out of it.'

Matt turned away with his backs to them. 'And now he's going to fuckin' walk.'

Gary Fellowes put a hand on his shoulder. 'He won't walk. He'll get sent down for something. Don't forget he's up for perverting the course of justice as well.' His voice tailed off as he turned towards the barrister questioningly.

James Wentworth cleared his throat. 'Perverting the course of justice carries a maximum life imprisonment, although of course he's not likely to get anywhere near that, especially now he's pleading to it. The offence of driving dangerously carries a two-year term of imprisonment on indictment, failing to stop after an accident also carries a term of six months imprisonment. He will also be disqualified from driving and may also receive a fairly hefty fine—'

'That'll make it all worth while then,' Matt interrupted sarcastically.

The barrister continued. 'I will obviously refer to the case of *R v Wagstaff* in 2000 with regards to asking the judge to consider the aggravating factors in this case, when deciding on a sentence.'

'The most he can get for killing my boy is two and a half years then, even if he's given the maximum sentence and it runs consecutively. Plus a little more possibly for lying.' Matt couldn't even bear to turn round and look at his legal rep.

The barrister coughed uncomfortably. 'He's not likely to get the maximum. He's pleading guilty now so he'll get time off in recognition of his plea.'

'Great!' Matt said with even more sarcasm. 'By the time he also gets time off for good behaviour and early parole it'll hardly be worth him going inside.'

'I'm really sorry, but that's the law. There is precious little consideration given to the consequences of dangerous driving. Two years imprisonment does not adequately compensate a family left with a seriously disabled child or parent.'

'Or a family left with a dead child.' Matt's voice was as dead as his sentence. He walked towards the exit, turning just briefly at the door.

'Kachan will only be banged up for about a year, two at most. That's not justice. Two years for a child's life.' He paused, before finally pulling the door open. 'I could have left him to die in his burning car.' He walked through into the solemnity of the entrance hall and glimpsed the figure of Andrei Kachan conferring with his barrister.

'I wish to God I had now,' he said quietly.

It was ten forty-five when Gary Fellowes joined Matt outside. His friend had hardly uttered a word since getting the news and Gary didn't know quite what to say to breach the impasse. He couldn't begin to imagine his own despair if he were in the same position.

The morning was balmy and small groups of people were clustered together, smoking and discussing the case in which they were involved. Traffic droned past, constant but not too heavy in the outskirts of the congestion zone.

He sauntered across towards his colleague. Matt was standing alone, puffing on a cigarette, deep in thought. As Gary drew close, he turned slightly.

'She's not coming,' he said dully. He guessed to whom Matt was referring.

'Who, Jo?'

Matt nodded. 'She was supposed to be here an hour ago. I've tried to phone her at home and on her mobile but there's no answer. She's switched them off.'

'Maybe she's just delayed on public transport or something.'

'She was driving. Besides there's no reason why her mobile's going straight to answer phone or why she hasn't returned my calls.'

'Give her time. She might still be on her way.'

Matt laughed quietly under his breath and Gary acknowledged the truth. She wasn't coming. Matt knew she wasn't coming. She had never wanted to be there, preferring to stay at her son's bedside rather than seeking the justice that Matt or Gary, as policemen and fathers, so desperately craved.

He waited while Matt finished the cigarette, feeling the silence between them deepen again.

'We'd better go in,' he said eventually, checking the time. 'Our case is due on in a few minutes.'

Matt nodded and followed him silently. As they entered the building, Gary noticed Matt turn one last time and survey the main gates and roadway, scanning the streets outside for the familiar figure of his wife. It wasn't there.

Court two was one of the oldest courts in the building. Oak

panelling and heavy wooden tables and furniture afforded it due formality and grandeur. A raised wooden dock now surrounded by toughened glass held the defendant or defendants, usually with a couple of uniformed warders who fought, in the thickening warmth of each day, to stay awake and alert. The witness box stood to one side of the judge and the jury to the other.

The court was almost ready to proceed when they entered. James Wentworth was positioned in the prosecution benches, wearing a wig that struggled to stay perched on top of the mass of thick dark hair. A wiry, grey-faced barrister held court on the defence benches, keeping his team rapt in an increasingly loud rendition of a well-worn and well-received story.

There was no jury sitting. There was no need. Andrei Kachan would be pleading guilty and the judge would be told only the parts of the story that the prosecution and defence thought relevant.

They sat down quietly and waited and Gary found himself replaying all the hours spent gathering the evidence that Kachan now accepted was overwhelming. Only he and Matt would know the true consequences of that one night of drunken revelry: the grief and despair that had replaced the loving core of one family's life. He vaguely heard the usher as he entered a side door at the front of the court.

'Court rise,' he ordered as the judge strode to his seat.

They stood up when required and sat back down when required and Gary watched the flicker of despair settle permanently across Matt's rugged features. The defendant was ushered to the dock and the clerk of the court read out the indictments.

Andrei Kachan was well presented, dressed smartly in a dark two-piece suit, his dark hair tamed, the expression across his face one of contrition. He had obviously been schooled well. Gary remembered only too vividly the contemptuous way in which the man had attempted to lie and deceive his way out of blame, finally treating his fiancé with such disdain that she had betrayed his whereabouts to them. She was not at court for him either, both the defendant and victim deserted by the women in their lives. He wondered vaguely whether justice and vengeance was the prerogative of the male sex.

James Wentworth was on his feet addressing the court. Gary listened as he spoke eloquently outlining the way in which the defendant had driven an uninsured, untaxed motor vehicle at speed, on the wrong side of the road, hitting five-year-old Ben Arnold. How he had got out to look at the boy briefly before laughing and speeding away to set fire to the vehicle subsequently. How he had lied and manipulated his loyal fiancé into reporting the vehicle stolen, until finally attempting to flee back to his native Russia when the net was closing in.

Gary nodded to himself. Their barrister had done well. Kachan had been shown as the uncaring, callous monster that he was, although it had been heartbreaking hearing how the crime had impacted so hard on his friend and friend's family.

He waited for the defence, watching as the grey-faced barrister stood slowly and adjusted his wig.

This rendition was completely different. Kachan was painted as the victim, a man lurching from one crisis to another, his actions dismissed as the behaviour of a person in fear for their life. Gary listened as his impoverished background was recounted, how he had moved to England to better the lives of himself and his family, working and sending back money to his destitute mother. He listened to Kachan's recollection of the events of the night, how he had been encouraged to drive dangerously by his friends, who were also the ones who had persuaded him to leave his victim lying for dead in the road. How he had panicked at what he had done, setting fire to the car and reporting it stolen in a desperate attempt to cast the blame on someone else and thereby allay his fear of being deported back to a country that held no promise of financial or personal reward. How his actions had been dominated by his love for his fiancé and the fear of losing her and how finally he had not been trying to flee from justice, but instead was attempting to have a few weeks away in which to face up to the realities of his situation.

Gary couldn't believe what he was hearing. He turned to Andrei Kachan and noticed the trace of a smile playing on his lips as he sat, head bowed, trying to appear contrite. He looked at Matt, whose eyes were fixed on Kachan and knew that he too was reading the contempt. He saw Matt's hands clenched tightly into fists, the spark of despair flaring into righteous anger. Kachan was not remorseful in the slightest, but he was playing the game well.

The grey-faced barrister was continuing. 'Your Honour, as

a result of this one tragic day, Andrei Kachan has lost everything. His fiancé has left him, the home he once shared with her has been sold and he has lost all his honour and pride. He does still work and to that end is willing to pay fines or costs at your discretion. The fact that the young child has died weighs heavily on him too and he is devastated by this news. He offers the family his sincere and honest sympathy in their loss and to try to minimize their suffering has now taken full responsibility for the manner of his driving on that fateful day. Your Honour, I would ask you to give him credit for this plea and take into consideration his remorse. The child's death, although tragic, cannot be directly attributed to him, a fact to which my learned friend has concurred.

'I would therefore ask you to take into account these facts and his willingness to make amends in whatever way he can and ask you to consider some form of community service, coupled with a financial penalty. As far as a custodial sentence is concerned, I would ask that you think long and hard about imposing imprisonment. He is gainfully employed at present, a situation that would be squandered, should he receive custody. He has lost much by his recklessness and he is the first to admit that. I ask that you seriously consider whether there is anything to be gained should he lose his liberty too.'

The barrister kept his eyes fixed on the judge for several seconds before sitting slowly down. There was complete silence within the room as each occupant waited for the sentence. The judge rose and gathered his papers together. Gary watched as Matt, too, rose and strode angrily from the court.

'He's going to get away with it,' Matt was incensed. 'Did you see the way he was smiling as his barrister spoke? He's not remorseful. He doesn't give a fuck. All he cares about is himself.' He paced up and down outside the building in the bright sunshine. The midday temperature was high and within seconds beads of sweat were pricking at his forehead. He wiped the sweat away with the sleeve of his shirt, throwing his discarded jacket over a railing. 'And that barrister's no fuckin' better. "He's lost much by his recklessness",' he mimicked. 'What about what we've lost? What about our loss? He might have been kicked out by his girlfriend, but so what. We've lost our son.'

The words hung heavily in the air.

'Doesn't that count for anything, these days?' he continued, quietly. 'That bastard can say what he wants and we can't challenge any of it. Even now he's pleading guilty he's still not taking responsibility. He's blaming his friends, he's blaming his fiancé, he's even blaming the government, of sorts, for the threat of deportation. Well he *should* be chucked out of this country. Only people who abide by our laws should be allowed to live here. He lost his right to stay the minute he mowed Ben down and left him for dead.'

Sweat was trickling down his forehead. He tried to calm himself.

'Come on, let's go back inside. At least it's cooler in there.' Gary gently took his arm to lead him back to the courthouse.

Matt swung his jacket over his shoulder and took the steps two at a time, nearly bumping headlong into the figure of Andrei Kachan as he descended. He stopped, tensing immediately at the sight of his adversary. He was so close he could smell his aftershave, so close he could hear the sharp intake of breath through nervous lips, so close he could easily plant a fist directly into his smug, sneering face. How he wanted to. Gary gave him a slight push from behind.

'Come on, mate. Let's wait and see what happens before you're tempted to take the law into your own hands.'

He waited for Kachan to avert his gaze first before continuing up into the entrance hall. The hall was cooler. They sat on a wooden bench to one side. Gary tried to strike up a conversation but it was too difficult. There were so many subjects that were off limits, too painful to mention. Eventually the subject of the murder enquiry came up. Matt told him some of the details. Gary was particularly interested in the suspect's vehicle.

'You say that you believe the vehicle was on false plates?' he asked.

Matt nodded. 'The bona fide vehicle was in the registered owner's driveway. It was examined and everything checked out. All we have been able to confirm is that the L registered plate would be one of several correct prefixes for that year's model.'

'And you're aware of how easy it is to alter registration numbers?' Matt nodded again as Gary carried on. 'It's extremely common at the moment. By changing even one digit you can avoid getting caught by a whole raft of cameras. It's been particularly prevalent since the congestion zone was brought in. There are too many cameras and people don't want to pay up.'

'Or else they just don't register their vehicle,' Matt agreed.

'What's the registration number of your vehicle?'

Matt took out a small pad from his inside jacket pocket and scribbled the number down, before handing it across to Gary.

'There you go. L889EGB. I see it in my dreams.' He grimaced.

Gary stared at the piece of paper and shook his head. 'Shit! You've got a job on your hands here by the look of it. Most of the digits can be altered with minimum effort.' He pointed to the number eight. 'With a small piece of black electrical tape, a number three can be converted to a number eight quite easily. Likewise an F can be changed to an E, a C can be changed to a G and the P can be changed to a B. Your number could be totally different.'

'That's the trouble,' Matt responded. 'There could be hundreds of combinations and even then the number has to relate to a dark-coloured VW Golf with a registered owner.'

'Would you like me to have a look at them and see what I can come up with? All our traffic cars have registration plate readers, these days. If I found any combinations that fit the bill I could have the numbers uploaded into the machine and then with a bit of luck, the suspect vehicle might drive past. At least we could stop it then and see if it could be your vehicle.'

Matt was interested. 'That would be great. It's got to be better than just hoping some copper somewhere actually remembers what index number we have and looks for it. It's still a long shot though. The whole number could be false.'

Gary tucked the slip of paper into his warrant card.

'Thanks though,' Matt said. He paused and turned towards his friend. 'For everything.'

Gary nodded grimly. Nothing more needed to be said.

They made their way back to the courtroom. Andrei Kachan was already in the dock, chatting amiably with his barrister. He appeared to be taking the whole procedure in his stride. Matt stared at his swarthy opponent bitterly. Now he was no longer facing the more serious charge, the man could afford to relax. The punishment was almost certainly not going to fit the crime.

By the time the judge started speaking, Matt's mind was

numb. He could hear snippets of words but his brain couldn't adequately take them in.

The judge was going through the whole incident again, picking out points that he considered salient. He tried to concentrate.

'I have listened to what you have both said,' the judge was concluding. 'And considered carefully what has been asked of me.' He directed his words towards the dock. 'Stand up.' Andrei Kachan rose to his feet. 'It seems that a term of imprisonment is both necessary and inescapable. Your manner of driving was patently dangerous and reckless in the extreme and the consequences fatal. In addition, you were neither a qualified driver, nor covered by a certificate of insurance, a fact that no doubt had a bearing on your ability to drive safely and your indifferent reaction after the accident.

'I am disappointed not to be able to sentence you for the more serious charge of causing death by dangerous driving. This, as admitted previously by the Crown, cannot be proved and I therefore have my hands tied to the maximum term of two years for the lesser offence. It is for yourself to judge, however, whether that five-year-old boy would be alive today, were it not for your recklessness. Your action in failing to stop after the accident I consider to be utterly callous, having a total disregard for the child's injuries. I take exception to your excuse that you panicked and were coached in what to do by your friends and find, by your continued lies, that you were a very willing participant, if not the creator of the deceit that was then perpetrated.

'Your attempt to cast the blame on to fictional car thieves and so pervert the course of justice, I regard as extremely serious and have sentenced you accordingly. I am bound by regulations to give you credit for your guilty plea at court today, whether or not it was forthcoming during the investigation and I take account of your background poverty and situation you now find yourself in.

'My judgement is as follows.'

Matt felt his breath coming in short nervous rasps. The judge seemed to have taken the case seriously.

'I am sentencing you to a term of eighteen months' imprisonment for the offence of dangerous driving. You will also be disqualified from driving for three years. In addition I am sentencing you to six months' imprisonment for failing to stop after an accident to run concurrently and your licence will be endorsed.'

His heart was pounding so hard he could almost hear it in his skull. He looked across at Andrei Kachan, who was staring impassively in front of him. He thought he saw a slight twitch at the corner of his mouth, a momentary betrayal that he feared what was to come.

'And finally, for the offence of perverting the course of justice I am sentencing you to one year's imprisonment, to run consecutively. The public has got to know that they will be dealt with extremely severely if they attempt to evade punishment by making false allegations and casting the blame elsewhere.'

He got up to leave. All around was the sound of people coming to their feet and the general hubbub of court. Matt stayed seated, mentally tallying up the punishment. "The public has got to know that they will be dealt with extremely severely." Two and a half years imprisonment, with six months running concurrently. With good behaviour he'd be out within eighteen months. And that was dealing with him *extremely severely*. Less than two years for killing a child and covering his blame with a web of lies. Less than two years for attempting to leave the country and evade justice totally.

He looked across at the dock. Andrei Kachan was talking with his barrister and smiling. He glanced up and Matt held him in his stare. He couldn't take his eyes off the man who had killed his child, the man whose own life he had saved, the man who would now be spending just eighteen months locked up away from society. How cheap Ben's life was in comparison.

A prison guard sidled up next to Kachan and took hold of his arm. Kachan held Matt's gaze for a second or two longer, allowing his lips to turn up slightly into a sneer, then turning abruptly, winked towards him and followed the guard down the stairs and out of sight.

EIGHTEEN

'That bastard only got two and a half years.'

Alison Richards put an arm around Matt's shoulder. 'He'll be out in eighteen months. Eighteen months,' he almost shouted. 'He should have got at least eight years for what he did, ten even and that would still not have been long enough. A life for a life, that's what it should be! It would be fucking laughable if it wasn't so appalling.'

Alison was shocked at his vitriol. He was normally so calm but she could feel his whole body taut, quivering with rage. The tension transferred to her body. He was staring straight at her.

'That bastard was laughing when he got sent down. He even winked at me as he left the court room.' He spun round, turning his head away from hers. 'And I could do nothing to stop it happening. Nothing.' His voice was barely audible. 'How do you think that made me feel?'

She couldn't answer the question. He turned slowly around so that he was facing her again. She could feel the warmth of his breath against her cheeks.

'I can't begin to imagine how I'd feel . . .' Her voice petered out. He was so close. 'Oh Matt. I'm so sorry . . .'

His mouth folded over hers, stopping any further speech. The kiss was long and urgent. She responded to his touch, pressing her body against his and feeling the strength of his anger. It felt good to be held by a man who was passionate. So good, even if it was wrong. She could feel his hands circling her back, pulling her harder and harder against him. She could feel his erection hard against her too. He manoeuvred her against the wall, lifting her body slightly so she fitted against him. Her head was muzzy with desire. She wanted him so much. She probably always had and yet the timing was all wrong.

She felt his hands moving across her body, encircling her waist, moving upwards until they cupped her breasts. A white hot tingle of desire ran up her spine, throwing her body towards him. God how she wanted him. The tingle ran up through her neck, exploding in her head. She opened her eyes. They were in his office. She heard voices in the background, laughing, talking, the sounds of the squad moving about.

She pulled his hands away, holding them tightly. She had to stop them moving over her body or else she wouldn't be able to say no. Her head took over. Nothing could happen now, not here, not when he was so vulnerable, not when they could be caught. Not when it might mean nothing.

'Matt, stop,' she whispered, pulling her lips away from his. 'You shouldn't be here.' Her voice came out huskily and she realized how much she didn't want to stop the moment. But she had to. 'You should go home.'

She felt his body tense again.

He snorted with derision and let her go. 'What for? To watch Jo laugh at my disappointment. She couldn't even be bothered to turn up at the court. I've been trying to phone her all morning but she's switched off her phone. She still doesn't know what happened and she doesn't care.' He gave a bitter little laugh. 'So much for supporting each other.'

Alison couldn't bear to see the defeat that suddenly swept through him.

'I'm sorry,' she murmured impotently.

He looked at her then and she knew that he'd read her need. She knew that he'd read her genuine care, her longing. And she also knew that he felt the same. She could see it in his eyes.

'We shouldn't be doing this now,' she murmured, touching his arm and feeling the same shiver of excitement run through her fingers.

He put his hand over hers, gripping her fingers tightly. 'I know. I'm sorry,' he whispered back.

He let her hand go and she turned towards the door, feeling immediately bereft. 'Another time though,' he said, stronger now as she opened the door.

'Another time,' she replied and smiled back.

'I'm not going home in case you ask,' Matt said tersely. 'Thanks for your sentiments but I'd rather just get on with it. Jo couldn't be bothered to come to the court case so I can't be bothered to go home and tell her the result. She obviously doesn't want to know.'

DI Blandford held up his hands in mock surrender. 'OK Matt, just a thought.'

'Anyway,' Matt said finally, 'there's nothing I can do to change the result now so I may as well get on with work. How's it going with Julian Reynolds?'

His boss sighed and shook his head. 'Well, quite enlightening really, although not so much help as far as the murder enquiry goes. Here, have a read!'

He pushed the file across to Matt who read the interim lab report on the contents of Reynolds's computer. Hundreds of photos of young boys had been found, although none were overtly pornographic; mostly the sort of stuff usually found in family albums, images of holidays, bath times, swimwear. It repulsed Matt to think of Reynolds using the innocent childhood photos to feed his perverted desires.

He flipped a page. The lab had been able to establish that the computer had been in use at the time of Tunde Oshodi's death, although it didn't necessarily prove that it was Reynolds who was using it. It seemed that the user was in contact with children and the conversation pointed to the user, if it was Reynolds, using a pseudonym and purporting to be the same age as the children on line.

'I presume this means we could do Reynolds for sexual grooming of a minor?' Matt queried.

DI Blandford nodded. 'Yes, it does and we can introduce bad character from his last conviction.'

Matt was thoughtful. 'That might be a useful lever when he's re-interviewed. I know his alibi, as far as the fingerprints go, does appear to check out but I'm sure he knows more than he's letting on. He's an evil bastard. Who's to say he's not involved in some way?'

The interview was nearly at a conclusion when Matt dropped the bombshell on Julian Reynolds.

Swift to deny any knowledge of the murders, Julian knew he was set to be walking from the police station a free man. It had been easy. The old bill had nothing on him except a few fingerprints, that he had effortlessly batted away and a roll of garden twine that most of the gardeners in South London were also likely to possess. His precautions in never saving any of the more interesting images had worked too. He wanked over them and then he deleted them. Simple. He got his thrills without the risks.

'Your computer records have been checked and it appears that the computer *was* in use at the time of Tunde Oshodi's murder,' the dark-haired police man was saying.

'I told you that before, didn't I?'

'Who was using the computer?'

'I was. That's why I couldn't have been the killer.' The stupid bastard wasn't listening.

'And you were on your own?'

'Yes, I was on my own.'

'So you are "metal maniac", are you then?'

The question took him off guard. How did they know the name he used? He stalled. 'I don't know what you mean.'

'I think you do.' The copper was looking straight into his face. 'You say that it was you on your own using the computer. The person conducting a conversation on line used the name "metal maniac". That must be you then?'

He flinched at the assertion but swallowed hard. Shit. He dropped his voice. 'It might be.'

'Well, is it?'

'I said it might be. What does it matter anyway?'

'If it's not you, then someone else was using your computer and your alibi is blown out.'

He was trapped into the admission. 'Yes,' he said slowly. 'It is me.'

'So it's you that is purporting to be a sixteen-year-old teenager and is chatting to a couple of young boys?'

He made no reply.

'Well is it?'

'What if it is? There's no law against chatting to other people.'

'There is if one of the participants is a Registered Sex Offender and is deliberately attempting to sexually groom minors.'

His face reddened and he frowned at his momentary lack of composure. He turned towards his brief, alarmed at the situation he had been talked into, swivelling his pupils through bulging eyes. Miss Khan shrunk back slightly at his gaze and he felt the flush rise in his cheeks again. Bloody woman was supposed to be acting on his behalf and she'd sat back and let him crucify himself. The copper was talking again.

'We've got transcriptions of what was said in several of your conversations and it appears that as well as pretending to be a much younger man, you've been offering to meet up with the boys and take them to a gig. If you've actually met up with them you would be committing a further offence. We'll be looking into that. I can have every conversation you've had for the last six months transcribed if I want to, so I suggest you think very hard about that possibility.'

'What do you want me to say?' He was boxed in and struggling to find an out.

DS Arnold leant forward towards him, fixing him with another cold stare. 'I want to know every little scrap of information you might have about the murders because your fingerprints, your description and your sexual preferences fit the bill, not to mention the careful way in which you make arrangements to meet your likely victims. There are a lot of similarities. If you're not willing to assist police in any way you can with their enquiries, the CPS will shortly be receiving a file recommending an interim charge of sexual grooming, while further investigations are continued with regard to the murders.' The copper leant back, smiling. 'And of course we'll be asking for you to be kept in custody for the duration of this process.'

He could feel the pulse throbbing in his temples. He couldn't risk another term inside. He needed to find a means to end the interview.

'The plates have only been in stock for a couple of months and your killer must have bought them from my branch for them to have my prints on them. How about I tell you who I think your suspect really is?'

'So Reynolds reckons he can point us to our murder suspect, does he? Why's he being so helpful now then?' Tom's voice sounded gruff over the phone line.

'Because he's trying to get out of being charged with sexual grooming of a minor. We've had to offer him a deal. It's more important in the grand scheme of things.'

'And why should we believe him?'

Tom's question was pretty valid as far as Matt was concerned.

'Well, if he's not telling the truth he'll have another charge added to his list, of wasting police time. He seems quite genuine though.'

'I can't bear to be anywhere near the fucking nonce. He makes my skin crawl.'

'Me too but we've got to try. He reckons he remembers some small dark-haired bloke, clean shaven and early twenties coming into Ikea a couple of months ago. Says he thought he was strange because he was wearing surgical gloves and appeared nervous. He says his voice was strange too, as if he was trying to disguise it. He thinks he only bought our dinner plates, no other crockery.'

'I thought we were looking for a female?' Tom sounded unimpressed.

'We are but we have to keep an open mind.' Matt was irritated at Tom's intransigence. 'Maybe our killer has an accomplice or maybe this male is a partner who may or may not know what's going on. He might be nothing to do with the case but it is a bit fucking strange wandering around Ikea in a pair of surgical gloves, don't you think? If we can identify this man maybe he'll lead us to our murderer.'

'Yeah, if we can. But the description's not much to go on.'

'I know it's not great but apparently there are CCTV cameras everywhere at Ikea. Reckons you can't even scratch your arse without someone commenting later. There can't be many blokes walking around with those gloves on? Anyway I need you to get down there and seize as many CCTV tapes as you can. Reynolds can pretty much time the date to within a couple of days when he returned from being off sick. This could be our first chance of a proper breakthrough.'

'Even if we have to let Reynolds off?' Tom's voice was still surly.

'Yeah, Tom. Even if we do, until next time. Once a pervert, always a pervert.'

NINETEEN

Matt stared at the screen, squinting at the image. It wasn't anyone he'd had dealings with in the past. He was sure of that. The man was quite insignificant as a murder suspect. Small proportioned with very short, almost black hair combed over into a side parting and cut sharply over his ears. He wore a diamond stud earring in both ears and was clean shaven. His eyebrows and lashes were dark and he appeared to be aged in his early to mid-twenties. There was nothing particularly startling about him other than his thin, almost skeletal body. He wore black trousers, low slung with a plain white T-shirt, tight against his skin and fashionably sparse. And surgical gloves.

'I don't recognize him,' Matt said, after he'd taken in the picture. 'Did he pay by cheque or credit card by any chance?'

'You'd be lucky,' Tom smiled back. 'He paid cash, of course.'

'I thought that'd be the case,' DI Blandford chipped in. 'What about a car? Can you see him getting into a vehicle in the car park?'

'No, 'fraid not. He comes in and only buys the plates; nothing else at all in the whole store. You can see him leaving the store and walking across the car park but then he just keeps going on foot until he walks out of the camera shot. If he had a vehicle with him, he parked it well away from the store. We've got a good likeness of him but nothing to actually identify him. I'll get the best image enlarged and see if anyone can come up with a name.'

'Let's hope someone can,' Matt added. 'He's obviously not the suspect in our murder shots but it would be great if someone can ID him and see if he's linked in some way to one of our suspects.'

'We could even send the photo up to Crimewatch if we can't put a name to him,' DI Blandford said, absently running his hand over his hair. 'I've always fancied appearing on TV myself.'

Tom and Matt burst out laughing simultaneously, making their boss frown towards them in mock indignation. 'And what, may I ask, are you two laughing at?' he raised an eyebrow. 'I hope you're not trying to insinuate I don't look the part.'

'Of course not, guv,' Matt sniggered. 'But you must agree you look more like one of the bleeding suspects in your current state than a commanding officer.'

'You can talk,' DI Blandford responded.

Matt grimaced down at himself. He had to agree he also looked like shit. He felt like shit too after spending the evening with Roger Blandford at their local. Too many beers and too many shots on their return to the office meant that both had spent a few uncomfortable hours propped against the back of their chairs, attempting to sleep off hangovers from hell. He hadn't returned home, in fact he hadn't even spoken to Jo since the verdict. Nor had she attempted to call him. She obviously didn't care what had happened and he wasn't going to be the first to make the call. He looked at his boss and perked up.

'OK, OK. You might have something there,' he agreed, smiling. The *Mission Impossible* theme rang out over his boss's mobile. DI Blandford picked the mobile phone up shrugging an apology through his grin. His expression changed within seconds. Matt and Tom stopped laughing and strained to listen but the call was ended abruptly.

'Sussex police have just found another body,' DI Blandford said. 'It's been in situ for about four weeks and bears all the hallmarks of the same murderer. They want us to go to the scene and liaise with them. It sounds like we've got the fourth body we were waiting for.'

The location of the murder scene was, without doubt, even more secluded than the others. Its access was from a small country lane, through a closed but unlocked gate and along a narrow farm track. It was a track that would have been used only by the farmer who owned the land and it was no wonder the body had remained undiscovered for so long.

After donning the obligatory white forensics suits, Matt, Tom, DI Blandford and Alison were walked directly to the scene by DI Scott Newton, a tall, blond, handsome man whose smile was serious and handshake strong.

A multicoloured patchwork quilt of fields and bordering hedgerows shimmered hazily in the warm air and the bird song from within the nearby trees and bushes sounded melodic and harmonious. Walking along the rutted path from the road next to Alison, Matt could feel the baking rays from the hot June sun beating against his head and shoulders. If it hadn't been for the purpose of their visit, he could have quite enjoyed the short sortie into the Sussex countryside.

Scott Newton spoke as they walked. 'We've identified the victim as a single white male, aged thirty-nine years old. His name is Edward Piper and he lives in a small bedsit on his own. He wasn't reported as missing, we found ID on him.' He paused to explain. 'Brighton houses a lot of single males. It's allegedly the gay capital of Europe. There are a high proportion of large houses converted into bedsits whose residents are quite transient. Nobody really knows their neighbours. Consequently, it was only when we started knocking on doors this morning, after the body was found, that some of the other residents realized they hadn't seen him for several weeks.'

'Can you put a date on the last time he was seen?' DI Blandford asked.

'We think so. The man in the room next door can remember having trouble with him on his pay day in May. He apparently had a few mates round for drinks and Piper banged on the wall to complain that they were making too much noise. That was on Saturday 26th May. He hasn't been seen since that night. There's a Sunday paper in his room dated the 27th May and that's the last thing we can find. There's post from after that date still unopened downstairs in the hallway.'

Matt ran through the dates in his head. 'That would make this body the first in the series for definite then, with Jeffrey Bamfo's the second, Ray Barnes third and Tunde Oshodi the fourth.'

'And after each death the suspect's getting more confident,' DI Blandford added. 'As this was her first, she was probably nervous and wanted to make absolutely sure she wouldn't be disturbed. That's why she chose somewhere so remote. I wonder if she realizes this one's been found yet?' He scratched his head. 'She'll probably be pleased as punch if the papers have got hold of it.'

Scott Newton nodded. 'They've been sniffing around already.'

DI Blandford grimaced. 'Shit. More pressure and I'm going to have to let Julian Reynolds go imminently, unless there's something here to tie him to this murder.'

'What?' Tom was appalled.

'I know, it's a pisser, but I was discussing it earlier. I really don't want to lose him, especially with it being Sunday tomorrow, but I'm arranging to have him kept under surveillance. I can't risk letting one of our suspects out on bail to kill again and not keep an eye on them.'

'We shouldn't be letting him out at all, ever.' Tom's voice was angry.

'I agree. But we haven't enough to keep him in at the moment.' He turned to Scott Newton. 'I presume there was a Bible passage with the body?'

The DI pulled out a notepad from his back pocket. 'It was difficult to make out the words as the paper was pretty dirty but we think it says: "This is what the Lord declares: The dead bodies of men will lie like refuse on the open field, like cut grain behind the reaper, with no one to gather them. Jeremiah 9, verses 21-23."'

'Sounds like a warning about what she was about to begin,' Matt chipped in.

'It also said, "One for every year of suffering".'

'That's what really worries me.' DI Blandford frowned. 'We still have no idea how many more years of suffering there might be.'

'And, how many more bodies,' murmured Scott Newton.

'Quite,' Matt added. 'At the moment she's committed a murder every Sunday for the last four weeks and it's Sunday tomorrow. We actually need to make sure this body hits the news tonight. If she only wanted to do four I don't want her feeling she has to do another, just because this one hadn't been found. I just hope to God we've got the right two suspects. I don't want to be walking to another murder scene on Monday.'

They continued for another few minutes deep in thought before Scott Newton pointed to a clump of trees.

'It's in there,' he said impassively.

Matt felt his innards churn at the thought of the body. It was a sight and smell he could well do without on a delicate stomach.

The actual scene bore the same marked similarities as the others. Hidden within the undergrowth in a copse at the inter-section of several fields the body was secured in the same manner as the latter ones. The warm June weather and wild animals had disposed of much of its flesh and what remained

sat tilted to one side, held upright by the same green garden
twine as the others, most of which had disappeared from view
inside the decomposing skin around the neck. From the state
of the clothing and remains of dry blood around the base of
the body, it was obvious the same mutilation had occurred but
the plate, on which the severed genitals had on latter occasions
been spread, was empty, its contents no doubt eaten by the
woodland creatures.

They didn't stay long, there was no need. Once they'd
confirmed it as having the hallmarks of the same killer, they
left.

The drive to the victim's address took about fifteen minutes
taking in a slow cruise along the sea front with its central pier
jutting out into a calm sea. Matt sat in the rear of the car with
Alison. He let his leg rest against hers wondering whether she
would move it. She didn't and he was glad of the contact. He
caught her eye and they both smiled. His fear that he'd over-
stepped the mark was obviously unfounded. He looked out of
the window. Small groups of tourists and holidaymakers sat on
the shingle beach, making the most of the warm weather and
ice-cream vendors drove sporadically from position to position,
the tinny bars of their music enticing the youngsters to point
and plead. They continued past the rows of bright seafront
hotels and turned into the side streets to their rear, slowly moving
up the narrow lanes away from the beach. The neighbourhood
was greyer here, dingy in comparison with the garish lights of
the tourist sector. Eventually they pulled up outside a large
Victorian house with paint peeling off window sills and a garden
alive with weeds. The front door had several small broken panes
of glass and numerous bell pushes down the right-hand side.

Scott Newton pushed the door open and climbed the stairs
to the second floor. Four rooms led off the bare landing, one
of which had a uniformed police officer standing sentry. The
inspector nodded towards the officer and beckoned the others
forward.

'Forensics are positive he was killed in the location he was
found so we're not treating his room as a proper crime scene.
We're just searching it for any evidence that might help. Come
on in and take a look.'

Matt stepped into the room first and was immediately taken

aback by its musty aroma. It smelt as unkempt as it looked. Posters and photographs of naked men and women adorned the walls, stuck up carelessly in random positions. Magazines lay abandoned across furniture parading the same naked poses of both sexes, engaged in sexual acts. A CD case with traces of white powder lay casually on the bedside table, with a razor blade set to one side. Ashtrays spilled over and discarded cans dotted the floor. A chest of drawers stood to one side of the room, its drawers hanging open revealing assorted dildos, hand-cuffs and sex toys. The air was heavy with dirt and grime and its general disarray proffered an image of sad sleaziness to its deceased resident.

'Bloody hell! He seemed a bit obsessed with sex,' Matt commented.

'And not particularly choosy about whether he gets it from men or women judging by the stuff on the walls,' Tom added.

'We've found diaries and notepads with descriptions of his sexual exploits,' Scott Newton agreed. 'He certainly seemed a busy boy, boasting of pulling both men and women on the same night. It appears that he was a very promiscuous bisexual. The neighbours say that he entertained a large number of young men and women who came and went at all times of the night. From the contents of his diary it doesn't appear that he told any of them he was HIV.'

'Was he now.' Matt was interested.

'Yep,' Scott Newton continued. 'He's apparently been HIV positive for some years according to some of his correspon-dence. And worse still, he boasts about rarely using a condom. He seems to take a perverted pleasure in passing on what he calls his "gift".'

'Some gift.' Matt was appalled. 'What sort of sick bastard would get pleasure passing on that death sentence? How long exactly has he had it?'

'Well, he was diagnosed right back in 1998 according to his medical records. I've contacted his doctor who was fine about disclosing that information. He needed us to be aware of any possible risks touching or transporting the body.'

'Wish his patient had been that responsible too,' DI Blandford commented. 'At least Piper's behaviour deserves punishment. What the hell could link our victims though? I know we can link two of them but there must be a connection that we're missing. What would a teacher, a lawyer, an immigrant carpenter and now a down-and-out, HIV-carrying sex addict have in common?'

'They're all willing to pay for sex or have done in the past?' Alison questioned.

'Could be," DI Blandford said quietly.

'Yes, that's it,' Matt almost shouted. 'And, Vanessa Barnes could be the prostitute. We know from her past that her ex made her do sexual favours; that was one of her reasons for killing him.' Matt was thinking fast. He turned to the Sussex inspector. 'Did Piper have any links with London?'

'I'm pretty sure he has had addresses in London. He moved around a lot. He's got correspondence with addresses from all over the place.'

'So all our victims used to live or still live in London. I need to get copies of Piper's diary and any address books he might have lying around. Likewise with the other victims. There must be a phone number or address that all four have and if we can link it to Vanessa . . .'

He paused before turning to his boss. 'I'm going to spend all night if necessary going through their contact lists.'

TWENTY

'Is that DS Matt Arnold?' a female voice asked. The voice sounded panicky and he couldn't immediately put a name to it. He checked his watch. 7.30 a.m. He opened his eyes and focussed hazily on his cluttered desk.

'Yes, it is. Who's speaking?'

'It's Evelyn Johnson. Sorry to phone this early but I needed to speak with you urgently.'

'No problem. What's the matter?'

'I got three silent phone calls during the night. I think they were from Vanessa Barnes. They were like the other ones I got before Ray was . . .' She faded out and Matt recalled the rather plain, dumpy caller whose affair with their station's first victim had been the catalyst for Vanessa Barnes' arrest.

'They can't be,' he said, a little too quickly. 'She's still in the mental hospital and I'm sure she wouldn't be allowed access to a phone during the night.'

'But they were just like before. I tried to get the number but it was withheld. I don't know who else it could be.'

'Well, I wouldn't worry too much. The hospital promised to let us know if she was going to be released and we've heard nothing. I'm sure she's still safe and secure in one of their wards. It's probably just a crank call.'

'But what if she's escaped?' She didn't sound at all reassured.

'They would have told us.' Matt paused and closed his eyes. This was all he needed. 'I'll phone the hospital and confirm she's still there, if it'll help. Give me an hour or so and I'll ring you back.'

'Thanks. I'd really appreciate that. We're both at our wits' end. We haven't slept a wink all night.'

'OK, I'll be in touch.' He rubbed his eyes. He'd had precious little sleep for two days himself and he desperately needed a change of clothes and a chance to freshen up. Evelyn Johnson was wrong. In any case he wouldn't be able to get an answer from the hospital until at least 9 a.m. Just time to pop home and collect some stuff.

As he was leaving he bumped into Alison.

'Looking good,' she smiled, reaching up and rubbing her hand against his stubble.

He grinned apologetically. 'Yeah, sexy eh?'

'Where are you off to?'

'Don't ask! I'm just popping home to get some stuff. That's if Jo hasn't changed the locks.'

Alison smiled sympathetically. 'Have you spoken since the court case?'

'No, not yet and with any luck she'll be out now. I don't really want to explain it all when she obviously doesn't care.' He shook his head sadly. 'Not that I imagine she'll even ask.'

Alison smiled sympathetically. 'How did it go last night?'

Matt was glad to change the subject. 'Well, I spent most of the night going through Piper's address book but everything's so random. There are names all over the place, some just first names, some street names, none that I recognized and none by the name of Vanessa. Although that doesn't mean she wasn't using another name. There are loads of names and addresses in London, but some don't even have names, just the service they offered.'

'Nice.' Alison grimaced.

'You should have a read of the diary if you think that's bad. Piper was disgusting. He thought nothing of having several sexual partners over the course of a weekend, or at the same time for that matter and he never used a condom. God knows how many people he might have infected with HIV. I think he got what he deserved in the end.'

He raised his eyebrows. 'Right I'd better be off, I suppose. Could you phone the hospital for me? Evelyn Johnson thinks Vanessa Barnes has been making phone calls to her and is worried that she's been let out.' He started to walk away, shrugging his shoulders.

'There's no way she can be though.'

As soon as he opened his front door, he knew that a quick, affable visit would be out of the question. His wife's anger at being left without a word of his whereabouts was as strong as his own at her failure to attend their court case.

'Thanks for letting me know where you were,' she said sarcastically, coming to the hallway.

'I didn't think you'd care where I was,' he countered. 'And since you've started it, thanks for turning up at court on Friday.'

'You know what I thought about that,' she hissed back. 'I never wanted to be there. It doesn't matter to me what happens to that man. Whatever he got will never bring Ben back and that's all that matters. He's gone.'

'Don't you think I know that? But I can't believe you don't care about the sentence.'

'Well I don't.' Her voice was rising. 'And don't even try to tell me because I don't want to know. It's irrelevant to me.'

'How can you call it irrelevant? That man killed our son. It's his fault that Ben's gone. That's not irrelevant. It's important he pays for what he's done.' Matt was incensed by her attitude.

'Well that's news to me. I thought you said it was my fault before.' She left the accusation hanging in the air between them.

Matt turned away angrily. 'Don't start that again. You know as well as I do that I didn't mean that.'

'Didn't you, because I think you did mean it. I think you still do. You still blame me for what happened.'

Matt could feel his control slipping. 'For fuck's sake, Jo. Will you just listen to me? I don't blame you. I never did. Ben was five years old. He wanted to run and you did everything you could to keep him safe. I would have done exactly the same.' He dropped his voice. 'Andrei Kachan was to blame. If he hadn't been speeding and on the wrong side of the road, Ben would still be here today. It's his fault.'

He turned back round and was surprised to see that Jo was crying. He felt his stomach lurch. It had been so long since they'd touched properly that he didn't know what to do. He took a few steps towards her and stopped, unable to decide.

'He got two and a half years.'

She threw her hands up to her ears. 'Stop! I don't want to know.'

He carried on. He could hear Chloe's plaintive cries from her bedroom, but he couldn't stop. She had to know. He couldn't let her get away with not knowing the result. It was eating at him and he suddenly needed for it to devour her too. Then they would be the same, feel the same, know the same grief. 'Eighteen months for the accident and one year for perverting the course of justice. That's all. That's all that Ben's life was worth to them.'

'No.' The scream was pitiful. She pulled her hands from her

ears and stared straight at him, with tears streaming down her face.

'Don't tell me that. Don't tell me any more. Why do you think I didn't want to know? Because I knew this would happen. I knew that man wouldn't get what he deserved. But you –' she spat the words at him – 'you had to go and see, you had to get your precious justice and for what?' She pushed past him and started to climb the stairs. 'So that you'd feel better? So that you'd be seen to do the right thing? So that you could be the big man at the station? Or was it . . .' She paused a few seconds as if deciding on whether to go ahead. 'Or was it so that you could play the wounded victim again?'

Matt stood stock still. He could hear her scrambling about in the bedroom while she screamed out her venom. She had wounded him with her words. He felt paralysed, numbed by the full extent of her vitriol.

She came to the top of the stairs looking down at him, with an envelope in her outstretched hand.

'I suppose you've got to get back to your beloved job again in a minute or do you want me to cook you some breakfast, or wash your clothes, or make you a packed lunch?' Her voice was heavy with sarcasm.

He shook his head.

'You'd better read this if you want to know more about justice. It arrived a couple of weeks ago. I didn't want you to know before, in case it destroyed you. But seeing as you don't care if you destroy me, read it.' She threw the envelope down the stairs towards him. 'Read it and then tell me whether you still believe in your precious justice.' She disappeared into Chloe's bedroom and he could hear the same voice, this time speaking gently, soothingly, lovingly, as she'd once spoken to him.

Bending down he picked up the envelope and opened its torn edges, pulling out the official letter from the Home Office and reading the words slowly. He knew what they were going to say even before he read them, but they still chilled him to the bone.

Dear Mr and Mrs Arnold
This letter is to inform you that the parole hearing of William Mortimer was heard on 30th May 2007 and at the conclusion the panel ruled to uphold his application for parole.

His release date has therefore been set for Friday 22nd
June 2007.

He couldn't get over the irony of the date. On the same day
as his son's killer was being sent to prison, his father's murderer
was being released. The man who had destroyed his childhood
was now free to make a life for himself, just as the man who
had ended his son's childhood had started his own meagre
sentence. His father and his son, two of the most important
people in his life had been taken from him and the men responsible had got away with murder. Maybe Jo had been right all
along. Maybe there was no justice.

He felt his own tears spilling out on to his cheeks as he
listened to her voice. Tears of frustration and anger, but above
all, tears of sadness at the way they were.

It wasn't long before he was back in familiar territory.
Nothing more had been said between he and Jo and the
silence had been unbearable. He was glad to be back at his
desk. He turned back to the address books. Each number
had to be painstakingly compared against the others but the
work was easy and thoughtless. It took his mind off William
Mortimer and his freedom. It took his mind off Jo and their
continuing battles. It took his mind off everything except the
job in hand. He'd decided to check through the address book
of Tunde Oshodi. There were less numbers to check against
than Piper's. He could find no initial reference to Vanessa
Barnes or Barrington or Julian Reynolds and was just cross-
referencing any matching details between the two victims
when Alison burst in.

'They've only bloody well let her go,' she almost shouted.

'What do you mean?' Matt looked up, astonished.

'The hospital. They discharged Vanessa Barnes on Friday
afternoon.'

'And they didn't let us know?'

'No, not a word.'

'Christ! How could that have happened? We asked them
explicitly to tell us even if they were considering it.'

'I know. Someone down there's well and truly in the shit.
I've just come from the ward. Apparently there was some cock-
up between departments and both thought the other had phoned

us, but it turns out neither did. She's been out for a bleedin' day and a half and we didn't even know.'

'Shit! We'd better get round to her address and bring her in before she's able to strike again.'

'Already done and she's nowhere to be found. All the post from the last week was still in the hallway and it didn't look as if anyone had disturbed it.'

'Did you go in?'

'Yes, the door didn't take much of a kicking. She's not there and it doesn't look as if she has been. We checked every room. Nothing's disturbed.'

'So where the hell is she?'

'No idea and nor has the hospital. She gave no clue as to where she was heading. The hospital presumed she would be coming straight back to her normal address. Apart from that they've got nothing.'

Matt slammed his fists down hard on the desk. 'Shit, shit, shit. So we have no idea where our prime suspect is?'

'No.' Alison shook her head.

'And it's Sunday. Bloody great! That's all we need. If there's another murder tonight the news will be splashed across the front page of all the papers. They won't see the incompetence of the hospital. It'll just be another monumental police fuck-up. We'll look totally incompetent especially if we have to admit we have no idea where she is.'

The thought stopped them momentarily. Matt racked his brains trying to recall any small detail about their suspect that might assist in their search. He remembered her desperation to see her husband's body.

'Check with the funeral company that's looking after Ray Barnes' body. She was desperate to visit him for one last time. See if they've had any visits or phone calls.'

'Will do.'

'Shit.' Matt stood up quickly and paced to the window. 'And Evelyn Johnson was probably right. Those crank calls were more than likely from Vanessa. Maybe Vanessa's sizing them up to be her next victims. All the other victims have had calls. I know the others have all been male but Evelyn would certainly fit the category of "sinner" as far as Vanessa's concerned and Ian might be targeted for doing nothing to stop her liaisons with Ray.'

'Do you want me to give her a call to warn her?'

'No, I'll do that, but we'll have to set up some immediate protection for them. We have a duty of care now that we suspect they might be targets. I'd like her, if she'll agree, to stay at the house so that she can answer the phone if Vanessa rings again, but we'll have to arrange for a couple of officers to be in the house with her and others to keep observation all around the outside. Get a street plan of her road and we'll start sorting that out, straight away. And get every available person in today so start phoning around anyone who is off. We've got to locate Vanessa Barnes, keep Reynolds in our sights and be ready for any other eventuality.'

Alison nodded and ran out. Matt sat down heavily at his desk exasperated. How could Vanessa Barnes have been freed without their knowledge? It was so bloody frustrating.

He picked up the phone and dialled Evelyn Johnson's number, idly running his eyes over Tunde Oshodi's address books as he waited. A number caught his eye. He thought he'd seen it before but didn't recognize the name written against it.

The line clicked in. 'Hello,' a female voice said timidly. 'Who is it?'

'Evelyn, it's Matt Arnold.'

'Oh, thank goodness. I was hoping you'd phone back soon.'

'I don't know whether you'll be so pleased when you hear my news. Vanessa Barnes was released on Friday. The hospital were supposed to let us know but failed to inform us.'

'But you can pick her up, can't you?'

Matt winced. 'I'd love to but unfortunately at the moment we don't know where she is. She hasn't returned to her home address.'

'Oh, my God! So it was her on the phone. I knew it. She's coming to get us.' Evelyn started to cry loudly, staccato sobs punctuating her words. 'We've got to get out. Now. Oh my God!'

'Evelyn, stay exactly where you are. You'll be safer there. We'll make sure nothing happens to you.'

But she wasn't listening. He could hear her husband in the background, scrabbling about shouting for her to help him pack. Cursing, Matt threw the phone down and headed for the door. They couldn't afford to lose track of their victims as well as their suspect.

TWENTY-ONE

Bambi poured herself a glass of vodka and smiled lazily. It was almost time. She was amazed at how peaceful and right it felt. How a deep tranquillity had replaced the torment deeply rooted in her mind and how calmness had suffused her tortured body providing a serenity she hadn't known since that time in Westminster Abbey, five years previously.

How her life had changed since then, but now she was ready to finish the work and fulfil the promise made to God all that time ago. He did indeed work in mysterious ways but who was she to argue.

She lifted the glass to her lips and swallowed down a mouthful of strong clear vodka letting the coolness of the liquid inflame her desire to do His bidding. Theirs had been the perfect plan. Kill the sinners who had sinned against them. A modern day Sodom and Gomorrah. A chance to right the wrongs of the past.

She felt the fluid seeping through her, arousing her anger. Men had to take responsibility for their actions, instead of blaming their weakness on the female sex. How she hated men and their bodies and their feebleness. How she loathed all men and everything about them. She was righting a million wrongs.

She rolled over to read more of her Bible, allowing her blonde hair to fall over the pages. God had left instructions and she had followed, killing her victims and removing the offending genitals that motivated men's desires and that – specifically – spread the HIV infection. And He was pleased. She knew that. Each time. From the initial warning that the bodies of men would lie like refuse across the open fields, to the verse she was preparing now. Staring down she read the small print dedicated to her last victim in Hosea chapter 4, verses 13-15.

> I will not punish your daughters when they turn to prostitution, nor your daughters-in-law when they commit

adultery, because the men themselves consort with harlots
and sacrifice with shrine prostitutes – a people without
understanding will come to ruin!

She smiled as she remembered them. The men had come to
ruin. Even their wives and children had been forced to suffer
as a result of their disgusting behaviour.

The next one was different though, more challenging. She'd
had to be extra careful in the arrangements. Her next victim
would almost certainly be more cautious than the others.

Very soon she would strike again for the last time, dispatching
and killing in the hours of darkness and even though death
would come to her shortly afterwards, the world would see that
it was her victims who had sinned and it was they who deserved
to die.

Evelyn Johnson was hauling a large suitcase towards her car
when Matt pulled up. She stared towards him, appalled.

'What do you want? You're not going to stop us leaving.
We've got to get out before she kills us too.' She'd known the
phone calls had been Vanessa immediately. She also knew
without a doubt that she'd never be safe while the mad bitch
was out there. She and Ian were getting out and they wouldn't
be coming back until the woman was safely locked away. There
was no doubt about it, she'd seen the madness in Vanessa's
eyes all those years before and she'd believed all the rumours
of how she'd tried to knife her previous partner to death. The
woman was a psycho. She'd murdered Ray in the most grotesque
manner, just to teach him a lesson for his betrayal. And now
she'd got a liking for blood, who knows who would be next.
Maybe she'd start with Ian. He'd upset her in the past and she
seemed to like killing men. But maybe it would be her. What
the hell might she do to her?

The hand on her arm startled her and she jumped, dropping
the case. DS Arnold was standing right next to her.

'Evelyn, come inside. I need to talk to you and Ian urgently.'

But she wanted to leave. She bent down towards the suitcase but his fingers were already around the handle, lifting it
back towards the front door.

'I promise you, you'll both be quite safe. Come back inside.'

She wasn't convinced, but couldn't do much about it. She

followed him up the pathway and back into their small ordered house. The familiar homely smell hit her as she entered the hallway; vanilla essence, her favourite. She started to cry. She didn't really want to leave, she didn't know whether they'd ever get back but they couldn't stay either. It was too dangerous.

Ian walked towards them when they entered. He glanced ferociously towards the policeman and put a protective arm around her shoulder. It made her cry more. He still didn't know the full details about her and Ray. She hadn't plucked up the courage to tell him the whole story but she thought he'd probably guessed and was obviously willing to forgive. She buried her head into his shoulder and cried, as much out of shame at her betrayal as gratitude for his steadfastness. He was so dependable and she'd been stupid to risk losing that, in pursuance of teenage nostalgia. Ray had rejuvenated her life at a time when boredom was setting in and she'd jumped at the chance to feel attractive and desirable again, but the cost had been huge.

'What do you want?' her husband asked Matt gruffly. 'Haven't you done enough?' He paused. 'Or should I say, have you? How could you let her get out? And not warn us. She could have got to us last night and we'd never even known we were in danger.'

'I'm really sorry about that. The hospital were supposed to be informing us if they were considering her release, but there was a breakdown in communication and we were never told. We're doing everything we can to catch up with her again now.'

'Well, it's obviously not good enough if you haven't caught her yet.'

'That's why I'm here. We need your help.'

'In what way?' She wiped her eyes and looked at the policeman. He seemed to be genuinely sorry. It wasn't often she'd heard police officers apologize for anything.

'I'd like you to stay, so that if Vanessa phones again, she'll recognize you and know that you're still here.'

'Yeah, right,' Ian was saying. 'And let her come round here and throttle me or knife me or whatever she likes to do. I don't think so.'

'No, of course not. Well, at least, we obviously wouldn't let that bit happen, but we would like to lure her here. I'd have an armed police officer here in your house with you and several other officers round the outside. If we could make her believe you're here on your own, she might turn up. What do you think? Would you be prepared to help us?'

'I'm not sure if I could do it,' Evelyn said quietly. 'She scares the life out of me.' Her thoughts spun to Ray's body lying in the woodland, all his life and passion gone. She took a deep breath. She had to do something. Turning to her husband she brushed her fingers lightly across his cheek and dropped her voice still further so it was barely a whisper. 'But for Ray's sake, I'm willing to give it a go.'

Matt got to work immediately. DI Blandford was to be in overall charge of the operation but DS Ernie Watling and his team were dealing with the practicalities, arranging armed cover and overseeing all the other tactical considerations that had surfaced. Nothing could be left in doubt; every eventuality had to be covered. Matt would take over from him later.

Vanessa Barnes was still their prime suspect and had to be recaptured as a matter of urgency. They couldn't risk another death.

Julian Reynolds was also under observation, his every movement watched by Sergeant Mark Lewis and his team. If their man left his house, he too was to be tailed and his every movement logged. So far he had remained holed up and Matt hoped that he would remain so, for the evening at least. Running two separate operations at the same time could lead to confusion and he had an uneasy premonition of trouble ahead. The day so far had not boded well.

He returned to Lambeth HQ just in time to catch DI Blandford striding ashen-faced across the car park.

'Bloody guvnors,' he exploded on seeing Matt. 'I've just been hauled over the bloody coals for *allowing* Vanessa Barnes to get out. As if it's our fault. That wanker, Superintendent Graves has apparently come in especially to oversee the operation to catch her. Doesn't trust me apparently. If you ask me, he seemed more concerned about missing his bleedin' Sunday roast than catching the mad bitch. Anyway, I'd avoid him if I was you and warn Ernie Watling to be ready for him sticking his nose into things.'

He shot a disparaging look towards the superintendent's office. 'I'm getting out of here. I've got things to do.'

'Do you need a hand with anything?' Matt enquired.

His boss paused briefly as if he was making his mind up whether to invite Matt along. Then he turned away. 'No, don't worry, Matt. I think I need to do this by myself and you must have a million other things to get on with. If you need to get hold of me, you can get me on my mobile.'

And with that he was gone, climbing into an unmarked police vehicle and accelerating out, leaving Matt slightly puzzled at his boss's words but with plenty of work to keep him safely out of the superintendent's way.

TWENTY-TWO

It was time to go now. Bambi stood at the door and allowed herself the time to say goodbye. The room was full of so many memories, both good and bad; times when she had known love and acceptance, times when she had felt rejected and disconsolate. It was a room that had witnessed a momentous change in her outlook, both in the way she looked and the way she behaved. She felt strange as she stood gazing around at the gloomy interior.

Two photographs stood peering silently out. She hardly recognized herself in one of them. It had been taken five years before and she didn't like it but she wanted it with her anyhow. She walked over and picked the other frame up, tucking it underneath her arm. This was her favourite. It captured her essence, the way she wanted to be remembered, laughing on holiday in Brighton, carefree and careless. It was the one that showed the world who she really was. She would take this one with her to her death.

Bending down she picked up the small holdall containing her tools and the Bible. She wasn't going to bother with gloves tonight. This would be her last and she had nothing to hide. She would allow the warm blood of her last victim to run through her fingers, knowing that her mission was complete and the last of the culprits was dispatched. She was looking forward to watching the sticky scarlet liquid congeal on her smooth hands. The sight would be symbolic; an eloquent sign to denote the final part of their plan. The victim's blood spilt to right a wrong.

She walked over to the bed, smoothing the tired bedspread and glancing down at the letter she had written. It was her suicide note, written to explain her motivations and the reason why she couldn't go on living. It was in an envelope propped up against the diaries, the larger print Bible and the plastic bag containing her make-up. She picked them up, placing them into a separate bag with a small bunch of fresh flowers and a vase and swung it up over her shoulder. With a last lingering look she walked decisively out of the door. Her way was forward now, she couldn't go back. Everything was gone and she would meet the challenge of the next few hours, calm in her belief in what God had promised.

She closed the door quietly behind her and stepped out on to the landing, treading over the bare floorboards, confident and calm. She listened to the creak of the stairs and the clink of the knife against the plain white plate and the noise seemed dull and distant. She was God's priest, about to do his bidding, but first she had to seek His mercy and strength for the coming night. Stepping through the communal door, she felt the warmth of the day swarming in, surrounding her head with the buzz of life. It made her light-headed.

The car was waiting in the gloom of the underground parking area, hidden behind a peeling metallic garage door. She placed the bags on the ground and swung the door up and over, manoeuvring carefully down one side to open it. Clumps of dried earth crunched under her feet, the lush woodland clods fallen from the tyre treads crushed into small piles of fertile soil on the concrete. She opened the driver's door. In the small interior light she could make out brownish, red smears on the offside carpet and front passenger seat, remnants of the last few Sundays' activities. She climbed into the seat and fired up the engine, manoeuvring it forward out of the garage a few yards before switching the engine back off. The noise was loud in the confines of the concrete garage area, each engine rev reverberating around the walls. She climbed back out and lifted the bag on to the front seat, checking its contents a last time. It was all there: the knife, the plate, the Bible passage, the garden twine, the gag, stiff and putrid from the stale saliva of her other victims, and the syringe.

She folded the edge over, hiding the contents and placed her Bible on the top. There was one last thing she had to do before she left. She couldn't risk the car being recognized. Bending down, she picked away some of the black electrical tape she had so carefully stuck on to the front registration number, changing several of the letters and numbers back to their originals. It had been far easier than swapping the whole plates and had allowed her the chance to change the identity of the vehicle if she'd wished. It hadn't been necessary in the end, the car had remained tucked away in the garage out of sight along with her grisly reminders. Moving round to the rear she peeled away the tape from the same digits, being careful not to break her fingernails. She'd painted them during the day so that they were at their best and the brilliant red veneer was still perfect. She checked them scrupulously, searching for cracks or splits and she was glad that they would be totally intact on her death.

Wiping her hands on an old napkin at the back of the garage she squeezed along the side of the car and climbed in again. This time when she started the engine, she wouldn't be going back.

Evelyn Johnson was nervous. She didn't trust the police to keep her safe. They'd let her down already and it was more by luck than judgement that she was still alive.

Her husband had cooked dinner, anxious to make things as normal as possible, but it wasn't normal to have two burly policemen, one of whom was complete with ballistic jacket, two firearms and a taser sitting in your dining room. The unarmed officer had introduced himself as Sergeant Ernie Watling; the other seemed to be speechless. She'd met Ernie before and he'd seemed friendly enough although slightly inefficient, but that, she told herself, was just her initial impression. He might be totally different in practise. She certainly hoped he was.

The small kitchen/diner seemed cramped with the extra bodies. It wasn't big anyway, just a reasonably sized kitchen separated from a small dining area by a breakfast bar that jutted across at an angle. She glanced across at them from where she sat on the kitchen side of the breakfast bar, pushing the food aimlessly around her plate. After a cursory search in which they'd absently rattled windows and doors and checked the view to and from the seating areas, they had positioned themselves at either end of the settee and seemed perfectly at ease watching TV. She hadn't expected them to be so relaxed. She wanted them both up, pacing the ground floor, watching and listening for any unexpected movement or noise, not enthralled in Sunday evening TV. Her husband Ian walked through and motioned with raised eyebrows his discomfort at the policemen's laid-back attitude.

'Glad to see they've made themselves at home,' he said sarcastically.

Evelyn nodded her agreement, dropping her voice conspiratorially. 'They'd better not muck this up. I don't know why I let myself be talked into this.'

'Don't worry. I'll see that nothing happens to us,' Ian said, picking up a large kitchen knife, wrapping it in kitchen roll and tucking it up his sleeve.

The sight made a fresh ripple of fear run down her spine. She checked the time, just gone seven thirty. It was still light outside, although the sun was getting lower in the sky, wearily throwing out its last weak rays into the balmy air. Within a couple of hours it would be gone and the darkness would set in, increasing her fears and bringing with it shady figures that slunk about in the shadows malevolently. While she could still see outside, she could keep her panic at bay, but with her vision impaired she would feel vulnerable. She knew she would. It was a fear she'd carried with her since childhood, irrational but enduring, of monsters and demons and death.

She wiped her forehead on a paper tissue noticing the whiteness of the clean surface turn a murky grey. She was sweating. The windows and doors were all closed and locked and the house suddenly felt like a prison, strangely alien and unfamiliar, her exit barricaded by locks and an armed guard. It was muggy and claustrophobic and she needed to escape. She walked to the French windows and stared out through the ageing frames, across the garden, hoping the sight of her freedom would calm her nerves, but a movement in the trees at the end just served to make her panic still further. A man came into view and she realized immediately it was one of their guards, but the knowledge heightened her fear still further. They were bait, as simple as that, and the realization prickled, like electricity through her head. She threw her hands up in front of her against the glass and tried to imagine a strong barrier protection but the doors rattled ominously and she could see the panes shaking at her touch.

Her panic was beginning to intensify when strong arms enfolded her and she felt herself pulled against her husband's body. She turned against him, leaning her head into his chest and became aware of the rhythmic pounding of his heart. It was strong and steady, slower than hers and she allowed herself to relax slightly.

'Ian, I'm so sorry,' she whispered into his chest.

'I know you are. Let's just get through this and then we'll

talk.' His voice was low and husky, cracking with emotion and she understood instantly that he knew everything.

'I'm sorry,' she repeated, but he just pulled her against him harder, turning his head away from her so that she couldn't see his face. She sensed a change in the beat of his heart and a slight shudder from within his chest and she knew that he was crying. It was an emotion he rarely displayed. Ian had always been strong and robust, practical in his outlook, even when they'd dealt with the victims of domestic violence at the centre. His way to solve each dilemma had been to offer strength and support but also to allow every woman the empowerment to make her own decisions. She had wounded him by her actions, she knew that without doubt. Had she damaged him and their relationship beyond repair? Only time would tell. Tears of regret flowed down her cheeks, wetting the cotton crispness of his shirt. If only she had stopped to think what damage she and Ray would provoke. Her lover was dead, her husband wounded and her opponent was seemingly now intent on murderous revenge and all, she believed, as a result of her selfishness.

The phone started to ring, its shrillness direct and startling. Ernie Watling was on his feet, beckoning towards her but her legs felt shaky and leaden, unwilling to do her bidding. Everything seemed to be in slow motion, each movement clumsy and stilted.

'Remember to try and keep her talking for as long as you can,' the sergeant was saying. She remembered the instructions. *Engage her in conversation,* she'd been told, *keep her talking and give us a chance to establish the location from where the call is made.* She took a deep breath and tried to stop her hands from shaking.

She heard the policeman radioing his colleagues. He nodded towards her.

Reaching out she took hold of the handset and lifted it unsteadily to her ear.

Matt Arnold was on edge. There was something not quite right and he couldn't put a finger on it. He kept running back through the events of the day, trying to remember what could have triggered his sense of unease. There were too many things that could go wrong and the pressure from the media to get a result was now so intense that it was clouding his thoughts.

He wished he'd had a chance to run through the details of the operations with his boss but DI Blandford had still not surfaced and Matt reckoned he would be gone for some time. Rarely had he seen him so stressed and angry. The pressure was getting to them all.

The plans had been made and a briefing held. Vanessa Barnes was to be target one with her intended victim Evelyn Johnson's house, venue one. Julian Reynolds was target two and his home address venue two. In light of the phone calls, Matt had arranged to have specialist phone engineers on hand to track the origin of any call, with council CCTV staff also engaged to help with any possible sightings. Police units would be standing by, ready to blue light it to any location traced. He wanted to pick up the caller at their chosen site, rather than leave them the chance to gain the advantage. If they could be intercepted before they had the chance to strike, so much the better. If his officers weren't able to get to the location quick enough, Tom would be monitoring the radios and controlling the situation and would transmit any sightings and instructions to the surveillance officers. On the face of it, all should run smoothly.

Still, Matt could not shake the fear that he had missed something.

The radio crackled into life and he immediately recognized Ernie Watling's voice.

'Control, from venue one.'

'Go ahead,' Tom instructed.

'We've got a call. We're about to answer it and we'll try to keep the line open as long as we can.'

'Received,' Tom replied. 'All units, a call has been received. Standby for a location shortly.'

Matt indicated to the technicians monitoring Evelyn Johnson's phone line. They nodded back and flicked a switch waiting for their computer screens to start churning through the data.

Matt could feel the sweat start to gather across the small of his back. The senior technician, a bespectacled middle-aged man who had introduced himself simply as Bill, gave him a thumbs-up sign and he could see the data screens beginning to run.

The seconds sped past and he held his breath hoping for a result.

'There's no speech,' Ernie Watling crackled across. 'Evelyn's trying to get her to talk. We believe it is target one. She's still on the line but I don't think she'll stay for much longer.'

Matt could hardly breathe.

'She's rung off.' Ernie's voice came across the air waves again.

Matt was at Bill's shoulder. The screens were still flicking manically.

'Any joy?' Matt hardly dared to ask. He already knew the answer.

'Sorry mate. Not this time. Not quite long enough.'

Matt closed his eyes and grimaced. He couldn't disguise his disappointment. 'Shit. And I thought we had her.'

The nave of Westminster Abbey drew her back in. She liked the cool tranquillity, the fragrance of the incense, the feeling of inclusion it instilled. It was a place that had become her spiritual home, a place where she frequently retired to consider the fragility of life. All around her the statues and coffins slumbered peacefully, their occupants long since dead. Ashes to ashes, dust to dust. Dead but not forgotten, their mortality forever encapsulated in their sleeping forms.

Bambi knew every crevice, every memorial, every one of the six hundred monuments and statues and felt the ghostly presence of the 3,300 dead, whose bodies lay buried in its midst. At times she wished she could become one of them, forever surrounded by pomp and grandeur, her name immortalized in stone, honoured for her mission to vanquish sin. She'd read the literature. The abbey had become, for several centuries, the place where the nation commemorated its great and good, the men and women who had achieved notoriety for literature, science, music, religion or politics. She belonged there.

She picked up the bag containing her tools. It was heavy tonight but she wouldn't be going back to her car. It was too risky. She couldn't be caught before she'd completed the task. The bishop had his tools of the trade, the sceptre, the wine chalice, the Bible. She had her own apparatus, shocking maybe to some people but just as valid. She breathed in deeply, letting the incense fill her nostrils with its pungent perfume. It was beautiful. The evening service had concluded and some of the congregation were still lingering, unwilling to leave the peacefulness of the nave. Echoes of the organ and hymns still hung in the air providing her with a lasting image of the beauty and power of the music. It brought back memories of Thursday 26th April 2002, the date when life had changed and the count-down had been set in motion. It brought back pain and sorrow and fragments of deep, enduring joy.

She wandered further into the nave standing to stare up in awe at the characteristic Gothic features, the pointed arches, ribbed vaulting and rose windows. Rainbow colours slanted in from the majestic stained glass windows, brilliant ruby and sapphire colours which mixed with the elaborately designed wall paintings and art work. She wandered further into the abbey, drawn towards the great shrine of King Edward the Confessor. She knew nothing about him, other than it was he who had built the first church at the site in the 1040s. Walking quietly past the High Altar she stood silently before the magnifi-cent tomb, hearing at once the choral incantations from centuries gone by. The sound filled her head, obliterating any other thoughts. She concentrated on her last mission; longing for the moment when it would be done and she too would become a distant memory.

Her victim was where she wanted. She would go shortly to meet them and then retribution would be hers. Reaching out she stroked the smooth cold surface of the tomb. The souls of the dead reared up inside her. She smiled at the thought of doing His will, of committing her last victim to the chill of the journey into death and then of allowing her own body to leap across the void into union with her God and those that had gone before her.

She mouthed a small prayer. Opening her eyes, she watched as a shaft of light glinted against the Confessor's dark suit of armour, making it appear steely grey and dangerous. She remem-bered her knife, wrapped and ready, its blade hard and cold, prised to cut through the soft flesh of her victim. It was a thought that excited her. The wages of sin were death and she was ready to collect.

TWENTY-THREE

'We've got another call coming in,' Ernie's distinctive voice said. 'Standby for us to answer. We'll try and keep the caller on line longer this time, if we can.'

It was just over an hour since the last call had been made and the tension was unbearable. Matt was on the verge of leaving to take over from Ernie. He had been looking forward to it. There was nothing worse than listening to the action and not being part of it. All coppers liked to be in the thick of it and he was no exception.

The room stilled, every occupant straining to hear the radio. Bill nodded his readiness and Matt watched as once again the data screens started to whisk across the monitors.

Tom transmitted the information to all the waiting units and the room returned to silence, the only noise coming from buttons being pressed on the computer keyboards.

'It's a silent call again,' Ernie called back through. 'We believe it's target one again. She's still on the line. Evelyn's trying to keep her there.'

Matt ran his hands through his hair, pushing the unruly strands back off his eyes. Evelyn was doing well. If she could only keep their suspect on line for a little bit longer. He strode round behind the phone technicians and stared at the rotating screens.

'OK, we've got a location,' Bill shouted out excitedly. 'The call's been made from a call box in Streatham High Road, junction with Gleneagle Road.'

Tom was straight on the radio again, selecting the team closest to the location.

'Lima Sierra four five, get yourselves to Streatham High Road, junction with Gleneagle Road. That's the location the call is being made from. It's believed to be from target one and she's still on the line at present.'

'On way.'

'And CCTV can you monitor the location too?'

'Received.'

The response was immediate and Matt was pleased. The sense of urgency had infected them all. He just hoped they could get there in time. He paced across the room, hoping against hope that Vanessa Barnes would still be in the call box on their arrival.

'The caller's rung off,' Ernie said.

'Shit,' Matt said out loud. 'Can CCTV assist?'

'CCTV from control,' Tom spoke calmly. 'Can you see anybody at the phone kiosks fitting the description of target one?'

'There's one female who's just left the kiosk nearest to the junction. She's crossing the road towards a bus stop on the other side of the road. Long, blonde hair, slim, wearing jeans and a white T-shirt.'

'Lima Sierra four-five. How far off are you?' Tom asked.

'About two minutes.'

'CCTV from control. Where is the female now?'

'She's out of view at the moment, behind a bus that's just arrived at the bus stop.'

'Received,' Tom replied. 'Keep us updated as soon as she comes into view again. All units, all units, start making your way to the location.'

Each second seemed to expand into minutes as Matt waited for an update. He was sweating profusely now.

'Control, control from units at venue two, target two has just left his home address and is walking east down Rampling Street.'

'Shit,' Matt exploded. 'Not Julian Reynolds too. I can't believe it. Not now.'

'Received,' Tom replied shaking his head in exasperation. 'Keep us updated of his location.'

The CCTV operator came back on the radio. 'The bus has moved off heading south and there's no trace of her at the stop. She must have got on it.'

'Target two now turning right into Seddon Avenue. DC McGovern has the eye on him.'

Within seconds Lima Sierra four-five called backup.

'On scene, control. We can't see target one at the bus stop either. Do you want us to go after the bus?'

'Yes, yes. It's heading towards Norbury. Lima Sierra four-six, make your way to the bus stop and search the vicinity.'

Units were converging on the area from all directions. It was only a matter of time before she was picked up. The officers on Lima Sierra four-five had the bus stopped further down the High Road. Matt waited for the message that she'd been arrested but it didn't come.

'Target two going into newsagent shop at junction with Alsop Road.'

'She's not on it,' the radio operator said, after a couple more minutes had passed. 'We've done both decks and she's definitely not here. According to the driver and several other passengers, no one fitting the description of our suspect got on the bus.'

'Tell them to double check,' Matt shouted to Tom. 'She must be on it.'

'Target two leaving the newsagent shop now and heading back along Seddon Avenue.'

'Lima Sierra four-five, go back and double check the bus. All other units go to the vicinity of the bus stop and search the area. She must still be near by.'

Matt could hold his frustration no longer. 'For fuck's sake. We can't lose her now.' He grabbed his jacket. 'Come on, Tom. Let's go. We'll have a look ourselves and then go and take over from Ernie.'

Tom stood up and his relieving officer immediately took over on the radio.

'All units to clarify. Target two still in sight walking west along Seddon Avenue. Target one temporarily lost in vicinity of Streatham High Road, near the junction with Gleneagle Road.'

They sprinted out of the room and took the stairs two or three at a time. By the time they'd reached their vehicle, however, further information was filtering through. The bus stop was immediately outside a public house. Enquiries with some of the regulars had revealed that a female fitting the description of Vanessa Barnes had walked straight through the bar some minutes earlier and out through the back door into the pub garden. She had then been seen getting into a waiting minicab, described as a Silver Renault Espace people carrier with minicab style aerials and the vehicle was driven away, turning out from the road at the back of the pub out on to the main road and past the arriving police vehicles. The CCTV operators were in the process of going back over the footage and obtaining a registration number for the vehicle, but until then nothing more could be done. Vanessa Barnes had in essence been allowed to walk away unhindered while Julian Reynolds had returned to his home address, his sortie out to the newsagent proving to have produced nothing more than a bag of shopping and several minutes of worthless confusion.

Matt threw his head into his hands and groaned. 'What a fucking disaster. How could we lose her when she was right there?'

'Well, at least we know she's in the area and it was her that made the call,' Tom reasoned. 'We now know we were right to think she might be targeting Evelyn Johnson or her husband.'

'Yes, I know, but if she's got any sense she'll lie low for tonight and try another night now. She must have seen us all down there. And –' he shook his head disconsolately – 'we still have no idea where she is.'

'True, but she's just mad enough to go ahead with whatever plans she's made and don't forget, all the other murders have happened on consecutive Sundays. She's obviously got a routine now that seems to work for her. Maybe she'll just carry on whatever. The murders have been getting successively more careless.'

'Maybe she wants to be caught,' Matt added, allowing the disappointment to drain away. 'And if she does I want to be the one to catch her.'

'Best we get round to Evelyn's house and take over then,' said Tom. 'Or else we might let Ernie have the pleasure.'

He turned the car round and started to head in the direction of Evelyn Johnson's. The light was gone now and the warmth of the day was declining sharply. Headlights flashed towards them, their beams ricocheting around the interior of their car, like spotlights trying to find their target. It made Matt all too aware that their own target was as yet still operating in the wings, their shadowy intentions not yet known or under surveillance.

The more he thought about it on the journey, the more he became convinced that tonight would be their night. Tom was right. Sunday was the day it happened. It always had and there was no reason to think she would want a change. He'd read up on serial killers a bit. They followed the same pattern, the same routine. It was what made it so easy to link their crimes. They needed to be able to concentrate almost solely on their feelings of power or sexual dominance and the physical stimulation they got in carrying out the act. To that end they developed a process or method that they used time and time again. It was a process that became so ingrained that they barely needed to think about the practicalities.

'Control from CCTV. We have a registration number for the people carrier the suspect is believed to have got into. It's LG03KRC.'

'All received. We'll make some enquiries on it straightaway. In the meantime, all units be on the lookout for a silver Renault Espace, LG03KRC, believed to be still in the area.'

The traffic was heavier than he'd hoped with late Sunday evening excursionists clogging up the main roads into central London. Matt found himself more exasperated than he'd expected waiting in the queues.

'Control from venue one,' Ernie Watling's voice came back across the radio. 'Have you any knowledge of a pizza being ordered from this location? We have a delivery driver knocking at the front door.'

'Standby,' came back the instruction. 'I'll make some enquiries. Do you have the name of the pizza company?'

'Negative,' Ernie Watling replied. 'The delivery has obviously been brought by bike because the rider's wearing a full face crash helmet but I can't see the bike itself.

'Are there any other units that can move up and look for the bike? I need a registration number and a company name if possible so that we can make enquiries this end?'

Matt Arnold didn't like what he was hearing. 'Get a move on,' he shouted towards Tom. 'I don't like the sound of this.'

Ernie Watling peered out at the figure standing on the doorstep. The outside light was not working, a fact that he had overlooked and was now cursing, as he strained to make out the features of the silhouette. It was bulked out with motorcycle leathers and a helmet and he couldn't tell what size or sex they were. The figure leant forward and pushed the bell again, before receding into the shadows and looking back and forth in the gloom. The lights of the house were on, so the person would no doubt expect an occupier to be in and wait longer, but would they be willing to stay long enough for the bike to be found and its details transmitted for enquiries to be made.

He'd instructed Evelyn and her husband to wait in the back room, out of the way, while he dealt with their visitor. He didn't like it though. None of them had phoned for a pizza delivery and he was anxious about whether to tackle the delivery rider and risk identifying themselves as police officers and jeopardizing the operation. Word got round quickly in this area about police operations and the order might have been made specifically to test whether this was the case. Their suspect might be awaiting the result of the call nearby and decide to abort their mission on the basis of his action and then all their time and effort would be wasted. More disturbingly, the figure standing on the doorstep might be their suspect. He was unable to make out the facial features at all.

He heard one of the officers from the rear garden call up to state a pizza delivery bike was parked in the roadway several doors away and the details of the pizza company and registration number were given. Hopefully it wouldn't be too much longer before they got an answer.

The figure leant forward and banged on the door several times with its fists and then moved further backwards into the darkness again to stare up at the house. The armed officer stepped up behind Ernie as he waited and motioned towards the figure.

'Any information as yet?' he whispered. 'I'm in touch with my control for instructions.'

Ernie shook his head. 'Not as yet. They're just making enquiries.'

The radio crackled back into life. 'All units, from control. Be aware. Target one could well be nearby. The phone order received by the pizza company was from a call box in Streatham, further down the High Road from where target one was seen. The registration number for the Renault Espace comes back to a minicab firm in SW16. We've contacted them and it's been verified that the female, who hired the car, made calls from both the relevant telephone kiosks.'

Ernie was concentrating fully now. 'Did they say where they dropped her off?'

'Yes they did. She was apparently dropped off two roads down from you in Braxted Avenue.'

'Shit,' Ernie muttered to the armed officer. 'This is it.'

He peered out past the curtains at the figure outside, moving about impatiently now. Their suspect had ordered the pizza and also phoned to check that their victim was in. Would she not be suspicious if Evelyn or her husband did not even answer the door to see who was there? Would she suspect that something was going on? Might she be watching who answered the door? Might the figure standing outside be Vanessa Barnes? The questions were endless.

He instructed the armed officer to keep watch on the figure and ran through to the back room.

'Ian, we need you to speak to the pizza delivery rider. My officer will be right behind you, as will I, and I'll make sure the other officers outside move up in case of trouble. The pizza's been ordered by Vanessa Barnes and she might be watching what happens. If either of us answers she won't come.'

Ian nodded his head slowly. 'OK. What do you want me to do?' His voice was firm, but the shaking of his hands betrayed his fear. Ernie noticed his trembling.

'I must warn you, Ian, there's also a possibility it might be her, because we can't see behind the crash helmet.'

Evelyn grabbed her husband's arm in panic. 'Don't do it, Ian,' she begged. 'Let's just get out of here.'

'It's too late for that now,' Ernie said seriously. 'If it's not her outside, then she's somewhere nearby. You try and get out of here and you'd be in the open. You could be playing straight into her hands.'

'But you could protect us?'

'Yes, we might be able to, but not nearly as easily as we can while you're safely contained here. She has to come to us if she wants to get you.'

'And it looks as if she has,' Ian said grimly. He shrugged Evelyn's hand off his arm and turned to face Ernie. Ernie could clearly see the terror etched across every line in his features as he repeated his question. 'Tell me what I have to do.'

The figure was walking down the path away from the house when he opened the door. It carried on walking oblivious to the sound of the lock clicking back into place. Everywhere was danger. It was living and breathing and surrounding him. She was out there but he didn't know where. The small green conifers on either side of the front door stood silently on guard, shielding his view, concealing his enemies. They barely moved

in the warmth of the evening and their inactivity only heightened his suspense. It seemed as if everything was in slow motion.
His breathing was heavy and loud, each breath laboured and
rasping. He heard himself calling out to the figure, but the
figure carried on moving away from him. He stepped out into
the night and a great wave of vulnerability washed over him.
His head was swimming in fear. He shouted out again and saw
the figure turn and start back towards him.

It was walking fast and purposefully. Too fast for his liking.
He couldn't see the face. The figure was opening the visor and
he stared into the open blackness. The street lightning was
behind it and its shape was a silhouette. He remembered what
to say but the words came out limp and meaningless.

'Could you take your helmet off, please, so I can see you
properly?'

The gap between them was narrowing and the figure was
even now advancing towards him, its identity still as yet
unknown. It was unzipping a large red pizza bag and reaching
inside.

His stomach seemed to contract at the sight. He stumbled
backwards into the door way, falling against the door frame.
The figure lurched forward, reaching out towards him. Then
his head was filled with noise. He was thrown sideways into
one of the conifer trees as the two burly police officers pushed
past him, out of the door. As he crashed to the ground, he saw
the flash of metal and the sight of a gun being levelled at the
figure that was by now falling towards the hard concrete paving
slabs. From every angle in front of him he saw figures looming
out of the darkness of the tree line, watching the action and
waiting, waiting. The figure was crying out, lying prone on the
ground. The armed police officer was shouting instructions, his
gun still pointing at the body of the figure and Ernie was moving
towards him. He could see him bending towards the crash
helmet, pulling at it. The shouts of the armed officer were still
ringing around the front garden and somewhere in the back of
his head he heard the sound of glass smashing.

Evelyn Johnson had stayed rooted to the spot as the shadow
approached along the edge of the garden. She had always
wondered what she would do in this type of situation. Years
before, when she'd helped in the abused women's refuge, she'd

been sent on job training, to teach her self-defence in case of attacks from abusive or violent ex-partners. The course leader had counselled them about their reactions and she'd always remembered his words. They were coming back to her now vividly. *Fear was their saviour, but panic was their nemesis.* It was good and healthy to feel fear. Everyone felt it occasionally. There was nothing wrong with being afraid. It was what you did to control it that mattered. Fear, channelled in the right direction, could save you. It was in the split second when the emotion hit and provoked the body to produce the surge of adrenalin that your ability to stay calm mattered. Control the surge and your body would automatically react, causing the fight or flight response and the means to deal with the terror. Panic and you froze.

Evelyn had stayed rooted to the spot as the shadow had morphed into her worst nightmare. *Stay calm and be prepared,* she remembered the words. *Leave several courses of action open to you and always have a plan.* As the shape ran across the garden towards the rear patio doors, she had not been prepared. Up until now she hadn't had to be. The police were there and Ian was there and they were all the protection she needed. But they were in a different place, dealing with the other danger. She could hear the shouting from the front garden, but the words were far away and muffled and the scream inside her head had got louder with every step the shape had advanced towards her. She had seen the wildness of its eyes, the hatred gleaming in the light reflected from the fragile safety of her home and she had realized with absolute certainty that nothing was going to stop its progress.

It was only when the patio doors crashed open, unable to hold firm against the body weight of the shape, that she had even been able to breathe. Panic had gripped her heart like an icy hand paralysing its rhythmic beating, freezing it solid and stopping it from pumping. The muscles in her whole body had been rendered heavy and useless. Glass flew across the room towards her, displaced like bullets from the shattered rotten frames. A shard caught her on the cheek and the sharp pain stirred her into action. Clasping her face, she stopped the warm fluid trickling down her cheek and saw the bright intensity of the blood against the back of her hand as she sought to shield herself from more flying glass.

The shape was even now changing, solidifying into flesh and blood; the flesh and blood of Vanessa Barnes. And in her right hand raised above her head was the blade of a large hunting knife, its razor edge slicing through the air as it cut a path towards her. The room filled with a high-pitched, disembodied scream which both petrified her and stimulated a response. Panic would be her nemesis unless she could find the strength to conquer it. She had to move or she would die.

'You bitch,' Vanessa Barnes was screaming. 'You stole my husband and you deserve to die.'

Evelyn swung round, searching for an escape route but there was none. Vanessa was swiftly cutting off any possible exits. Evelyn was pinned against the kitchen sink with nowhere to go. She felt the panic rising in her throat again but swallowed it whole. Grabbing a large saucepan and frying pan from the draining board she spun round to face the wrath of her lover's wife. They didn't afford much protection but it was all she had. Swinging them high she heard the clash of metal on metal as the knife struck her temporary shield time and time again. And all the time, the scream reverberated around the room, mixing with the shouts from the front garden and the sentence had been shortened until all she could hear were the words 'die, die, die' repeated again and again.

Tom screeched to a halt in the street outside. Matt was out and running even before the vehicle had come to a halt. Radio messages were coming thick and fast. The words were unimportant. It was the way in which they were said that mattered to him and he hadn't failed to notice the increasingly chaotic spasms of speech. As he ran up the garden path his brain was taking in the scene. All the team appeared to be there, crowded around the figure of a pizza delivery boy, who still laid spread-eagled on the ground, a crash helmet to one side, his face white with terror and dark hair slicked back against his damp forehead. Instructions were being shouted towards the boy from every direction as each officer tried to establish his authority.

Through the shouting he heard the distant smash of glass and knew immediately what was happening. The pizza delivery was a decoy, designed to divert their attention from the main action and they had fallen for it, every single officer wanting a bit of the action, a bit of kudos from the arrest of a serial killer.

He could hear Tom behind him, his footfall heavy and fast. Turning round towards his partner he pointed to the armed officer, still standing over the terrified pizza boy and shouted, 'Get him and follow me.'

He cannoned through into the rear garden of the house, his adrenalin powering him through the wooden gate to the side alley. The back room was lit up against the darkness of the garden. He could see the patio doors smashed and open, a carpet of diamond glass twinkling in the stage lights. The scene that opened up was the finale in an old-fashioned horror movie. *Pyscho*, *The Shining*, *Nightmare on Elm Street*, all mixed together, in black and white. His victim was cornered in the kitchen cowed and clearly exhausted, while his suspect slashed and stabbed, blows raining down in a frenzy. Blood was splashed against the kitchen units, its primary colour, bright and conspicuous against the monotone.

He ran towards the mayhem, sliding on the glass mat on to the stage and shouting at the top of his voice. 'Vanessa, stop.'

Vanessa Barnes wheeled round towards him, her rabid eyes boring into his own. The pause button had been pressed, if only momentarily. Her lips twisted in an insane sneer, victory lighting up the pale blue irises to piercing sapphire lasers.

'So, you've come to watch me slay the whore,' she taunted, her voice calm and melodic. She raised her arm upwards and Matt could clearly see the knife, clasped tightly in her fist, its blade spotted with blood.

'Vanessa, don't do it. I can help you.'

She let out a shrill laugh. 'You want to help me. You want to help me.' Her voice was growing to a crescendo. 'You don't care about me. You wouldn't even let me go and visit Ray. You just want me locked away.' She turned back towards Evelyn. 'Well, just you watch me now. I'll give you something to lock me up for.'

Raising her arm, she stretched up as high as she could, ready to bear down on her prey. Evelyn shrank low against the sink, the frying pan and saucepan held vainly up in front of her in a last ditch effort to defend herself. Her cheeks and hands were smeared red with her own blood and she had an expression of defeat plastered across her face. Vanessa Barnes opened her mouth but before she could utter any words two long thin cables shot towards her from the doorway, their firing darts burying through her clothing into her flesh. A look of incomprehension flashed across her features for a split second before she dropped heavily to the floor with 50,000 volts pulsing through her veins.

Matt glanced round towards the doorway and saw the armed officer, with arms outstretched, the taser still in his hands, its wires flexing out towards the twitching, paralysed figure of Vanessa Barnes.

He indicated to Matt that it was safe to approach and Matt ran across to her crumpled body, kicking the knife along the floor away from her and applying a set of handcuffs to her shaking limbs. Turning swiftly to Evelyn Johnson he pulled her from her crouched position, lifting her easily over the body of her attacker and setting her down on the settee. She was deep in shock, her whole body trembling, her skin pale and clammy. Blood flowed from deep lacerations to her hands and around her wrists, injuries sustained during her determined defence but she was still very much alive, a fact that Matt recognized could so easily have been different.

He cradled her against him, trying to calm her shattered nerves. He knew she'd been lucky. They'd let her down.

'Sorry, we took so long,' he whispered down at her.

She looked up at him and he suddenly understood what Ray Barnes had recognized, beyond her mousy plainness. The fusion of vulnerability, calm determination and common sense made her an attractive proposition. Compared to the beautiful volatility of his wife she would be the eye of the tornado, the stillness at the crest of a wave, the second of silence before the thundering avalanche.

'You got here in the end,' she said and smiled gratefully. 'That's all that matters.'

TWENTY-FOUR

The ambulance lights were retreating down the road when Matt strode back to his car. He watched as the blue lights lit up a path, the revolving eye prying into every hidden crevice that it passed. Evelyn was inside the eye, being whisked to the hospital to have her wounds dressed and stitched; no doubt gazing out at the world from which she could so easily have been severed. Her husband was accompanying her, a fact that had caused Matt to breathe a sigh of relief. His reaction, fired up by the sight of his wife's blood spread throughout the kitchen, had not been as accommodating as hers and the words delivered at the spectacle of his bleeding wife cocooned within the arms of the man he held responsible for the debacle had been choice to say the least. Staccato, brief, raging, and delivered with an equal combination of derision and relief, they had cut straight to the point. Irrespective of the end result Matt knew he was right. Evelyn could so easily have been killed, had it not been for her reaction in grabbing the pans and her dogged defence. His officers had taken their eye off the ball and the ensuing chaos had almost yielded another body to add to the count.

Lady Luck had smiled on them tonight and he was indebted to her benevolence. A hand came down heavily on his shoulder and he swung round to see Tom, standing to his side, his hand held out towards him.

'Well done, mate,' he enthused. 'You did well.'

Matt nodded, declining the outstretched arm. 'It doesn't feel like it, looking at all the blood in here. We should never have let that happen. If we hadn't got here when we did, Evelyn would have been dead. We were lucky, bloody lucky. We cocked up good and proper.'

He looked across to where the pizza delivery boy stood. He appeared remarkably composed considering his recent view down the barrel of a gun. Vanessa Barnes, now sufficiently recovered from the use of the taser, was being walked out to a waiting police van. Her hands were manacled behind her back and tears streamed down her cheeks, small pink tributaries weaving through the splashes of her victim's blood. She looked pathetic now, every hint of malice concealed behind bloodshot fixed pupils. Matt watched as the stationary group of detectives followed her every step, out along the garden path and into the rear of the van until its disappearance signalled the start of celebrations. Officers who had previously looked on ashen-faced at the outpouring of blood were now transformed, slapping shoulders, shaking hands and generally congratulating each other. Their success in apprehending their suspect was tangible, a job well done.

Matt turned away from it, in disgust. 'Give one of them a crime scene log and then let's get out of here,' he said disparagingly. 'I don't really feel like celebrating at the moment.'

His arrival back at Lambeth HQ was met with similar praise. Superintendent Graves complimented him on a successful operation that would do wonders for his career and promised him the waiting press would be updated with the good news as soon as a press release could be worded. Matt smiled his appreciation of the praise but festering within his mind was the knowledge that their arrest had been achieved more by luck than judgement.

He climbed the stairs and walked towards his boss's office to apprise him of all the details, but DI Blandford was not there. A sense of disappointment washed over him at the sight of the empty seat and smokeless atmosphere. He had rather hoped to share his forebodings with his colleague. He pulled out his mobile to dial his boss's number but as he was about to enter the number, the light lit up and it started to ring. It was Gary Fellowes, his traffic colleague.

'Gary,' he queried. 'It's Sunday evening. What the hell are you doing on duty?'

'Very funny,' Gary replied, laughing at the tone of the words. 'People do have accidents at night, you know! Anyway you owe me a pint. I've been doing your job for you, like I said I would.'

'And what might that be, considering we've just this minute nicked our prime suspect down in Streatham?'

There was a pause as if he was weighing up whether to continue.

'What did you want me for?' Matt prompted at last.

'Well, it's probably not so important now, if you've nicked your suspect, but hopefully it'll help.'

'What's that then?' Matt was intrigued.

'It's that car you asked me to look out for. Well, we've just found it. My mate was on an errand up to Scotland Yard and stumbled across it, literally. The registration number pinged up on the registration reader and as I left my details on the bottom of the report they contacted me. I came straight up and I'm here with it now.'

'Where is it?'

'Just around the corner from the Yard in Tothill Street. It's almost within spitting distance but we really were lucky to find it. It was at the front of an underground garage for some offices and it was only because my mates happened to use the entrance to turn around that they found it. It's in a right state but it looks as if there's a fair bit of evidence in it that you'd be interested in.'

'Stay with it. I'm coming up,' Matt said immediately. 'This just might be what we need to tie everything up.'

Within ten minutes Matt was crossing Westminster Bridge. It was only a short drive from Lambeth HQ and he knew the route well. It was a journey that he usually loved, marvelling at the beauty of the City as it rose up along the banks of the Thames. He admired the strength and ability of the river to cut a gash through the concrete. Tonight, though, he had other concerns; it seemed a strange place for the car to be abandoned and he couldn't quite make sense of it. It was almost as if its occupant wanted it to be found but not immediately; as close to the hub of the Met as was possible but tucked away awaiting the Monday morning office workers to report its presence. It was almost as if it had been left as an explanation, a way of signalling the last time it would be used. Maybe Vanessa Barnes had now completed the mission that had started with the slaying of her husband and lawyer. Maybe hidden within it would be the reason too for her choice of Edward Piper and Tunde Oshodi. Maybe she'd wanted to conclude with the woman who in her mind had ruined the fragile life she'd so carefully and gradually built up for herself. A fitting finale.

He rounded Parliament Square passing the Houses of Parliament and Big Ben to his left, before swinging into Broad Sanctuary and straight ahead past Westminster Abbey towards Victoria Street. As he turned into Tothill Street he heard the bells of the great clock ringing out behind him. He checked the chimes against his own watch. It was ten o'clock, an hour since the incident at Evelyn Johnson's house and too many hours to count since he'd walked from his own house with the condemnation of his wife ringing in his ears. He was tired and it was as if a fresh wave of weariness broke over him with each clang of the bell.

Gary Fellowes was standing in the road ahead. He accelerated up to him and pulled over parallel to where his traffic car was parked. Gary was right. Scotland Yard could be only a few hundred feet away from them.

'It's in here.' Gary indicated, waiting for Matt to grab a torch and then strode towards the entrance to a dirty looking office block, under which a small car park was squeezed. Another traffic car stood within the entrance, its headlights shining directly towards a Black VW Golf, whose registration plate was set slightly at an angle. The lettering on the plate was untidy, the print different from the precision of a normal registration number.

'It's as I thought,' Gary explained, as Matt bent down to examine it closer. 'Several of the letters that can be altered have been. Whoever has done this has used black electrical tape to alter the lettering. It's been changed from L339FCP to L889FCP, but you can see where tape has been removed. It looks as if it was displaying L889EGD until very recently.'

'L889EGB is the car that was used in the Brockwell Park case, Tunde Oshodi's.' Matt recapped excitedly. 'You could clearly see it on the CCTV but when we did enquiries on the number, it came back to a different motor altogether.' He paused. 'And it was a small dark L reg car that was used in the Tewkesbury murder of Jeffrey Bamfo.' He stood back up. 'This is definitely our killer's car. Have you done a check on the correct index yet?'

Gary nodded. 'It's not registered. The last owner told the DVLC about six months ago that he'd sold it.'

'Shit,' Matt cursed. 'I thought that'd be the case.'

'I can arrange for an officer to call on the previous owner, in case they still have details of the new owner. I was just awaiting your authority before I did it.'

'Cheers, Gary. Get that done ASAP. You never know. It would be nice to have a name.'

Gary Fellowes stepped back and started to transmit on the radio, leaving Matt free to take a closer look around the vehicle. It certainly was a mess. Mud was ingrained in each of the tyres, along the base of the doors and wheel arches and sprayed up on to the bonnet and boot areas. As befitted its age, old dents and accident damage bore rust and the paintwork was splintered and cracked. It was untaxed and a small round piece of paper had been Sellotaped to the windscreen in an attempt to make it appear legal. It looked to have been kept in a garage, or certainly under cover, as the roof and bonnet was covered with a thin layer of dust whose existence would almost certainly have been washed away had the vehicle been left out to the elements.

Matt moved around to the driver's door and shone his torch into the interior. This appeared to be in a similar state, with dirt and mud smeared across the seating and carpet areas. Several pairs of surgical gloves lay discarded in the floor well in front of the passenger seat, stained and discoloured, with fingers pulled inside out in a grotesque misshapen pile. It didn't take much imagination to work out what fluid had caused the dark brown blemishes spread across them. Small pieces of garden twine were dotted about the passenger seat and a number of syringes lay discarded in the floor well, their needles caught on the carpet, preventing them shifting with the motion of the car. He pointed the beam of light down into the floor well of the driver's seat, noting the abundance of stains on the matting and carpet area. Forensics would have a field day with the vehicle and Matt was certain that DNA samples would be found matching some, if not all, of their victims.

'What do you make of the stuff in the back?' Gary asked, as he moved across next to Matt.

'I don't know yet. I haven't got that far,' Matt responded, immediately swinging the torch light into the rear.

The beam lit up the back seat, on which pages from a Bible, hymn sheets and orders of worship were scattered randomly.

'That fits. The killer's left Bible passages with all her victims; quite extreme ones, too. An eye for an eye and all that. She'd have done well in the Crusades.'

'Or he would.'

Matt grimaced. 'Sorry, Gary, what are you going on about?'

Gary pulled a torch out from his own belt and shone it on to the carpet just behind the front seat. Matt peered down, squinting into the shadows behind the driver. He could just make out what appeared to be a large clump of blonde hair sticking out from underneath the seat.

'If I'm not mistaken,' Gary said, 'that looks like a blonde wig to me.'

'Tom, Alison, come over here. I need to sound you out on a few things.' Matt was still ill at ease. Something just didn't fit. It was as if the case was a jigsaw puzzle, the pieces of which were present but hovering just out of his reach. Parts of the jigsaw fitted, building up sections that tallied and matched, providing chunks of the picture that came together in harmony. The forensics obtained from the scenes, the CCTV footage, the profile and background of the killer and now the vehicle all fitted. They provided the edges of the picture, straight and conclusive, the frame into which everything else jostled.

But it was the inside of the puzzle that was causing the problems. Vanessa Barnes made up a section. She could be the figure captured on CCTV, she had the motive and the means and she was closely linked to two of the victims, not to mention her violent assault on Evelyn. She made up a complete chunk, perfectly formed, but what Matt didn't have was the means to connect her to the framework of the crime.

And then there was Julian Reynolds, a sexual predator. His history, his personality, his previous convictions all confirmed that basic premise. Plus his forensics were the only physical evidence that linked any one person to the crime. He was a smaller piece of the jigsaw and could be linked by forensics to the frame but nothing else about him fitted. It was still so frustrating.

The vehicle would no doubt provide the answer but analysis of DNA samples would take time and that's what he didn't have.

Matt needed the identification now. All his senses were telling him that he had missed something and it was this missing piece of the puzzle which would allow the connections to be made.

He sat down heavily at his desk and leant back on his chair. Tom and Alison pulled up seats opposite.

'I'm not happy with things as they stand. It doesn't feel right,' he said unhappily.

'In what way?' queried Tom.

'Well, I always believed it was Vanessa Barnes but now I'm not so sure. There are too many inconsistencies.'

'Such as?' Tom asked again.

'Well, where did Vanessa keep the car, if it was hers and why couldn't we find any evidence of its existence when we searched her house?'

'It's not hard to hide a key,' Alison chipped in. 'That's all she would have needed. She didn't need to keep hold of anything else. And she's devious enough to keep the car hidden quite easily. She kept her new name from us for long enough.'

'True, but why leave the car so far away?'

'I don't know, but there must be a reason,' Alison continued. 'Don't forget, she did come by taxi so that would still fit. Maybe, like you said earlier, she wanted it to be found tomorrow but not until she'd finished off Evelyn?'

Matt shook his head. 'And that's another thing! Her attempt on Evelyn's life. It was a very different sort of attack.'

'It was always going to be different,' Tom smirked. 'For the basic reason that Evelyn Johnson hasn't got a cock or balls.' He grinned again. 'Plus she knew we would be on to her. She probably even saw us all in the High Road running around like headless chickens trying to catch her. My guess is that she'd planned Evelyn would be the last and the most difficult. She had to just go for it in whatever way she could.'

Tom did make sense in that the whole situation was different this time but Matt had seen the attack. Vanessa was frenzied and uncontrolled. Not the calm efficient killer who'd planned and carried out the other murders. He had also witnessed her mental decline. He frowned.

'What about the wig? Why the hell would Vanessa have a blonde wig when she's got blonde hair herself?'

Tom shrugged.

Alison shook her head too. 'No idea really, although she is quite switched on forensically. Maybe she thought by covering her own hair it would minimize the chance of some of her own being left at the scene?'

'But you'd think she would try and look different, not the same.' Matt pushed a space between the piles of discarded address books and rested his chin on his hand. 'I don't know what to think. I just wish we could have the forensic results from the car right now to clear everything up one way or another.'

His eyes came to rest on Tunde Oshodi's spider handwriting and he flipped the address book open absently at the page he'd last checked, reading out the bottom name aloud.

'Tina (Hair and beauty salon.) Ring for appointment on 07783 292232.'

He'd almost missed it, but the number had rung a bell and he thought he'd seen it before. It was similar to a friend's number and as such stood out in his memory. He opened Edward Piper's address book and ran his finger down through the lists of names and numbers. There it was again or at least the number was the same.

07783 292232, but this time the name next to it was labelled 'Tammy, blow jobs £10. Fucks £25'.

He double checked the number to make sure he was right, shouting out eagerly at Tom and Alison and pointing at the entries.

'Shit, look you two. I was checking through these earlier. I thought I recognized a number but then I was called away. The same number is in both books.' He reached over and pulled up Ray Barnes' address book. 'Please let it be in this one. While I'm doing that can you ring the guvnor and let him know about the match. We're going to need authorization for a subscriber's check to be done on it ASAP.'

Tom nodded and pulled out his mobile, keying in DI Blandford's number. Alison bent down next to Matt as he started running his finger down the lists of acquaintances. It was easier now he was checking specifically for one particular number. At the bottom of a page, just over halfway through the book, he stopped abruptly. He couldn't believe his eyes.

'It's only bloody well here,' he almost shouted.

'Where?' Alison lent further in and looked down at the identical number, her expression as animated as Matt's.

This time the name next to it read simply 'Dick'. Matt almost laughed out loud. 'For Christ's sake, look at the name. If Edward Piper's diary is anything to go by, the number obviously relates to a call girl. That's an amusing way for Ray Barnes to remind himself who the number relates to.'

'Yeah,' Alison agreed laughing. 'I don't blame him though. If your wife was as neurotic as Vanessa, would you risk labelling her correctly? Poor guy's even afraid to have her in his address book as a female.' She paused for a few seconds as they let the full implication sink in. 'I wonder if it's in Jeffrey Bamfo's.'

'I can't check that at the moment. His addresses are all on computer but three out of four all with the same number; that's got to be the link.'

'So what does that mean then? That we've got it all wrong?' Tom asked carefully.

Matt knew that Tom was putting into words the awful uncertainty that had been troubling him all day. It was a doubt which, if well founded could potentially lead to yet another mutilated corpse being found in the morning.

'Let's hope not. Let's hope that the subscriber's check comes back to Vanessa Barnes, but I have an awful premonition that it won't.'

The admission hung in the air between them, like a guillotine, poised to fall. If they'd jumped to the wrong conclusions what hope would there be for an end to the killings.

'I can't get through to the guvnor.' Tom's words cut through the tension. He turned and strode out followed quickly by Alison. 'I'll go and find the superintendent and get his authority straight away.'

Matt could feel the blood draining from his face as he watched them leave. How could he potentially have got it so badly wrong?

'The subscriber's check comes back to a female by the name of Tina Stewart. I've done some digging on the name and there's one on our records. It's got to be her,' Tom explained.

He threw a raft of paper down on the desk in front of Matt and continued. 'She's got several convictions for loitering for the purposes of prostitution, possession of Class A drugs and various theft type offences. There are also a few intelligence reports from years before when she was regularly coming to notice as a juvenile. Had a pretty chaotic childhood by the look of it.'

Matt flicked through the police records, noting that the

convictions had virtually died out in the last few years. Her last conviction for prostitution was five years beforehand in 2003 and since then she had only come to notice a few times for drunken and abusive behaviour, for which she had received warnings. All in all the record told a depressingly familiar tale.

'I've spoken to the Tewkesbury squad and they've verified the mobile number was in Jeffrey Bamfo's computer records too,' Matt added, only too aware that with those words he was admitting his misjudgement. 'That's all four now and this Tina seems to be the missing link. Have we got an address?'

'29 Renwood Court, SW16. She's shown as having lived there at least until a couple of years ago.'

'Get a team ready. We need to get down there before she kills again.'

'I've already told Ernie and he's assembling one now. He's anxious to make amends for the cock-up with Vanessa Barnes.'

'We'll head on down there straight away and keep an eye on it until they're ready.' Matt checked his watch. It was just gone 2243 hours and he was painfully aware that Tunde Oshodi's death had occurred between 0012 and 0214. 'Let's go. We haven't got any time to waste.'

By the time they reached the block of flats, Ernie had radioed up to say they too were on their way. The block was set back off the main road and a light shimmered out from a chink in the curtains, casting a weak beam across the maze of garages and car ports below.

The block was divided into various size flats ranging from three-bedroom family flats to studio apartments and bedsits. Tina Stewart's abode was one of the latter: a tiny living space nestled between larger flats, seemingly making use of a neglected area of floor. It was reached through a communal door, the lock of which had been broken many months before and never repaired.

Matt and Tom crept around the edge of the block, gazing up at the small window of her bedsit, watching and hoping for a shadow to darken the curtain, but it seemed all quiet. They moved round to the entrance to the block, creeping silently up the stairs and listening outside the door. They could hear noises, thudding between paper thin walls but they couldn't tell exactly from which flat they were coming. The backup arrived and

Matt slid back down to the roadway to brief the waiting officers of the layout of the flats. Within minutes the quiet turned to shouts of warning as the door crashed in and Matt ran in, only to stare round at an empty bedsit.

There wasn't really room for anybody to hide but they checked every tiny space just in case. It was Matt who noticed the pieces of cut garden twine lying on the floor next to the sink and counted the used syringes laying in the bin alongside the empty vials, bearing nothing but a clear colourless residue. And it was he who lifted a surgical glove from the floor, next to the bin and saw the stains of dried blood across the fingers.

'Shit,' he exploded, stalking out to the communal hallway angrily. He knocked on the doors of the flats on the same landing and spoke to neighbours who had heard recent movements but knew little of the bedsit's occupants. No one knew and no one cared.

He turned and strode back down the stairway and out into the balmy air. The atmosphere was becoming heavy, with dark swirls of cloud forming, obscuring the night sky and lying ominously above the rooftops. A storm was threatening and the tension was palpable. A coating of sweat prickled up on his back and he ran his hands through his hair gloomily. Their killer was out there, somewhere, brooding and treacherous; ready no doubt to claim her next victim and he still had no idea how to stop her.

The hunted had become the hunter again.

TWENTY-FIVE

A nd now the time was come. Like Babylon, the sinners who had sinned and passed on death would be punished. And the tears fell down her face as Bambi stood and stared down at the mound.

And she knew that when the plan was concluded, she would be taken up to heaven to be with Him and all her loved ones and there would be celebration and rejoicing.

She laid out the diaries across the grass, reverently placing the large print Bible against the small wooden cross. Then she filled the vase with water from the bottle and arranged the flowers, spreading the blooms evenly and precisely.

Standing back she surveyed her work. It was good. She left the letter in her bag for later. It would explain everything when she'd gone.

Then she turned and walked slowly away. She didn't turn back, nor did she falter in her footsteps. She had a mission to fulfil, a plan to complete and then it would be over. She hoisted the holdall up on her shoulders, listening to the muffled chink of the knife against the plate and smiled with anticipation.

Streatham High Road spread out in front of them, a highway to the City. It was now imperative that all local stations be briefed about Tina Stewart, her name, her intentions, her description. She was out there somewhere and time was running out. If, as Matt now believed, her intention was to kill again, her victim would almost certainly be in her sights. The last photograph they had of her was old but it was all they had. She looked rough, ravaged by the drugs she took, her appearance that of a woman twice her age but the likeness with the grainy CCTV stills of their suspect was unmistakeable. She had the same blonde hair and skeletal body.

Matt cursed to himself as he re-ran the investigation through his head. Was there any little thing that would point to who would be her next victim or the location to which she would take them? A dull pain was thumping in his head, fatigue and stress getting in the way of lucid thought.

Tom was quiet too and Matt knew that he would be equally as appalled at the situation as he. They turned off the High Road, barrelling down a quieter road to avoid the monotony of traffic lights. The road took them alongside Tooting Bec Common, an area well known for prostitutes. A lone figure sat on a bench bathed in the darkness of the trees. Matt squinted at the figure, willing it to be Tina Stewart but instead he recognized the gaunt figure of Carol Pritchard.

'Pull over Tom; I'm going to have a word with Tricks.'

The prostitute looked up as he approached, swigging thirstily on a can of Strongbow. Her eyes were unfocussed and bloodshot and her torso swayed from side to side as she strained her head towards him. 'You can't take me in. I ain't doing nothin'. I'm just having a tinnie.'

'I'm not going to take you in, Carol. I just wanted a word.'

'Another one,' she shrieked crazily, her blackened teeth grinning through rouged lips. 'I'm going to have to start charging you for all these chats.' She turned away from him facing the opposite direction.

Matt dug in his pockets and pulled out a fiver, waving it in the air in front of her eyes.

'Get yourself a cup of strong black coffee and a sandwich.'

She swung round grabbing it greedily and stuffed it directly into her cleavage. Grinning she said, 'What do you want to know then?'

Matt came straight to the point. 'What do you know about Tina Stewart?'

Carol Pritchard stopped swaying and straightened up. 'Why do you want to know about Tina?'

'Because I think she might be able to help us with our investigations,' he replied vaguely. 'Have you seen her recently?'

She burst into laughter, rolling backwards so far on the bench that she almost tumbled off the rear of it.

'I'd be a bleedin' psychic if I saw her now.' She continued to laugh. 'And so would you. I don't think she'll be helping you much with your enquiries again.'

Matt was confused and the prostitute's laughter only served to irritate him further. 'What the hell are you talking about, Tricks?' he said abruptly, his expression turning to anger.

'She's dead,' the prostitute said flatly. 'Snuffed it about two months ago and if you don't believe me, go and see for yourself. She's buried at St Leonard's.'

The graveyard was only a short distance away, standing at the rear of St Leonard's church, an old, square-towered minster set on a central junction in the High Road. It wasn't worth driving the short distance so they walked, striding out, their footsteps loud against the stillness of the trees. Crossing the road they turned into the street at the side of the church, passing the terrace of council houses knocked into one large sprawling maze of bedsits and corridors.

The sound of shouting from an open window pierced the street, staccato and sporadic, the tempo rising to a crescendo as they passed. They walked on, turning at the end of the row into the church grounds. Here the air was stagnant, unmoving, at peace with its deathly charges. They stepped carefully, torches in hand, scanning the tombstones for the name of their quarry. He couldn't quite believe what Tricks had said. It didn't fit with what they'd got, but they needed to rule out her information.

The graveyard was in a state of disrepair, its tombstones cracked and askew, its grass overgrown with empty cans and bottles a testament to the itinerant drinkers whose presence each day had gradually driven away the Sunday worshippers. After a few minutes Matt heard Tom call across from the rear of the graveyard. Following what paths he could find, Matt made his way over.

The area in which Tom now waited could not be more different from the rest of the cemetery. Here the grass was cut short and a mound of pitted brown soil was patted down as smooth as melted chocolate. A vase of fresh flowers stood to the side of a rough wooden cross, the blooms still fragrant and perfect.

Matt pushed his finger down into the vase.

'Shit,' he cursed. 'The water's still cold. It's colder than the air temperature. We must have just missed whoever left these.'

He bent towards the cross and saw a small plaque upon which was engraved the words: 'Tina Stewart, 13th July 1979 to 17th April 2008'. A large Bible was positioned carefully at the foot of the cross.

Realizing the significance of the Bible Matt donned a pair
of gloves and lifted it, carefully scrolling through the pages.
The Bible fell open at several pages with snippets of verse cut
out from the large print text.

'It looks like the Bible that our suspect used,' he muttered
almost to himself. 'But I thought our suspect was Tina and she
appears to have been buried right underneath where we're
standing.'

He reached over to a pile of books and flicked them open
reading the thoughts and feelings of the girl whose body they
were now standing over. From an initial look the words conveyed
a life filled with desperation and disappointment, a life cut off
before it had time to start. He read the days when the writer
hadn't enough energy to get out of bed, the days when the
awful blackness of illness filled her with hate and anger. The
name of the illness was never mentioned, it was as if she couldn't
bear even to write its name. He flicked across from day to
month to year picking out days when the vacuum of her life
was filled with despair but also days when joy seemed to trickle
through the blackness. And throughout the diary a name
repeated, time and time again, a nickname whose identity was
not exposed, a name that sounded cute and childlike and cuddly
but one that he now suspected belonged to the person for whom
they were searching.

'Who the hell is Bambi?' Matt voiced his frustration.

'Bambi?'

'Yes Bambi, as in the little deer. It's repeated all through the
diaries.'

Tom looked puzzled.

'I think that Bambi is who we're looking for now but your
guess is as good as mine as to who Bambi is!'

He turned to the last diary and read the dying words of Tina
Stewart. The fight had gone and all that was left was a bitter
acceptance of what life had become. It was as if she'd always
known that an early death would be her fate. Her entries ended
a couple of weeks before the date of her death, but further ones
continued in a different style of handwriting. Matt scanned
through some of the later entries, reading the expressions of
hate and grief that now littered the narrative. Peppered amongst
them were verses from the Bible, quotations from the scrip-
tures that coincided with the author's desire for retribution.

The writer seemed to be almost demented with grief, but the misery had almost certainly been the catalyst for murder. Out of the anguish had come the plan, the start of a desperate attempt to eradicate all who had done wrong to Tina.

Matt scrolled down to the date of the first murder. The name of Edward Piper was written boldly alongside his phone number and the chosen Bible passage. He flicked forward to the following Sunday and Jeffrey Bamfo's name, number and Bible passage was clearly visible. The same was the case for the following two Sundays, the names of Ray Barnes and Tunde Oshodi were inscribed along with the words of warning from the Bible.

'Shit, Tom. This gives the names and numbers of all our victims and what days they were murdered on.'

'Is there a name written down for today?'

Matt was already turning the pages forward to Sunday 24th June 2008.

'There's a first name written down, but no surname. The rest is the same. There's a mobile phone number and a Bible passage.'

'What does it say this time?'

Matt read out the verson carefully. '"I will not punish your daughters when they turn to prostitution, nor your daughters-in-law when they commit adultery, because the men themselves consort with harlots and sacrifice with shrine prostitutes – a people without understanding will come to ruin. Hosea chapter 4, verses thirteen to fifteen."'

'So Tina Stewart is the prostitute and all our victims are no doubt her clients and Bambi is the person who's carrying out God's punishments.'

'But who the hell is Bambi?' Matt was at his wits end. 'For Christ's sake, Tom, we're still no further forward. The suspect we thought we had is dead and we haven't a clue who this Bambi is.' He grimaced. 'But what we do know is that he or she is out there now, probably playing with this last guy whose name is written here, as we speak.'

'Do you think we ought to ring the number and warn him?' Tom was verbalizing the exact thought that was running through Matt's head.

'I think we've got no choice.' He checked his watch. 'It's quarter to twelve. Tunde Oshodi was taken to the park just after midnight and he'd already been drugged up by that time. If we don't phone now, it'll be too late.'

He took out his mobile and keyed in the number that was in the diary, taking care to ensure that every digit was correct. The screen paused for a long second before a name flashed up against the number. Matt stared at the name before him, open-mouthed.

'Oh, shit, Tom. Look.'

TWENTY-SIX

His back was covered in a layer of stickiness as he waited. The evening had cooled considerably from the early highs but sweat now prickled over his whole body. He took a swig from a bottle of water lodged in the door pocket, draining the last few drops from its base. Impatiently he threw the empty bottle over his shoulder and listened as it clattered off the rear seat in to the floor well behind him.

He wound down the top of the window. The darkening air was still, waiting motionless and static, nevertheless it was anything but tranquil. Silent maelstroms pulsed against his ears and their stormy cores vibrated throughout his whole body, sending shock waves of nervous energy thumping against his rib cage. The trees at the side of the common stood immobile too; even the birds hidden within their leafy branches were hushed. Gradually the lights from the houses opposite were extinguished, each loss of luminosity casting the surroundings further into darkness and ratcheting up his sense of foreboding. Each minute dragged and every pore bled sweat.

He checked his watch again. There was still twenty-five minutes to go before the promised meeting that would reveal the information he so desperately needed to solve the case. It was only right. He'd spent a lifetime trying to get credit for his work and he badly wanted the one mistake that had blighted his career to be negated in the kudos of arresting the serial killer. It was his due and he'd take great pleasure in wiping the smug, patronizing expression from the youthful face of his superintendent. The bastard had all but said that he was useless in their last encounter. But what did he know in his fucking ivory tower. Two years on the street, then the rest spent in an office, busying himself self-importantly with targets and flow charts, rather than proper police work. He had no idea what it was really like to deal with the crap.

He wiped his shirtsleeve along his forehead and looked down at the dirty smudge of sweat that now dampened the cuff. He was sweating like a pig and he was starting to smell like one too. He wrinkled his nose at the thought, leaning forward to reach into the glove compartment to pull out the spare bottle of spray deodorant that was always on hand to mask the residual smells of surveillance operations. The radio handset fell out as he pulled out the small can, bouncing on its wire like a deranged bungee jumper. He lifted it back up, stuffing it back into the tiny amount of existing space and jamming the door shut against it. He saw the light of the radio blink on as the lock clicked into place but it didn't matter if it was heard. His informer knew he was old bill. That was the whole reason for getting in touch.

He tried to remember the voice from the calls. It was male, of that he was sure, and it wasn't one that he recognized, but then he'd had the distinct impression the caller was disguising their speech. The sweat prickled on his back again at the memory and he felt a bead trickle down his spine. He knew he shouldn't be there. It was against all the rules and if it went wrong he'd be deep in the shit. There were strict regulations in place to deal with snouts, rules that were made to safeguard both the informer and the police officer, but in this case it was worth the risk. When he'd received the offer to name their killer, the opportunity had been too great to miss. That's why so far that evening he'd been ignoring his phone calls. He didn't want to be dissuaded from this course of action. If it all went to plan the press and public gratitude would ensure his forthcoming retirement in a few short years would yield the rewards to which he was owed. He'd almost let on about the arranged meeting to his colleague, almost faltered and asked for company in case of problems, but the damning words of his boss had stopped any prevarications. This was going to be his victory and his alone. He was going to show that prick once and for all.

He caught a slight glimpse of movement in the wing mirror before he was startled by a knock on his window. He hadn't seen the man coming. Automatically he wound down the window. The man was smiling. He asked for directions. He was too early to be his informer and he didn't seem to be any threat. He relaxed and wound the window fully down. He paused to think of the answer to the query. The sharp scratch on the top of his arm took him by surprise. He stared up at the man to remonstrate with him but the man was grinning now and he didn't know why. There was something familiar about the small, emaciated build, the black hair swept into a side parting and cut high over diamond studded ears but he couldn't think what it was. His head was feeling dull and his limbs heavy. His phone started to ring but he couldn't get to it in his pocket. He tried to wind the window back up but the man put his hand on the top edge. There was a syringe gripped in his hand and his nails were painted a brilliant red. And then he knew where he'd seen the man before and the awful realization of his predicament washed over him. As his mind went blank the memory of a small insignificant customer with low slung black trousers and a tight white T-shirt walking through Ikea with a pile of white plates in his hands filtered starkly into his mind.

Matt redialled the number and listened impatiently at the dull ring tones as it rang and rang before aborting to voice mail.

'Pick up the phone,' he shouted into it, before trying twice more with the same result. 'For Christ's sake,' he muttered to Tom. 'The bloody idiot! Why didn't he say something? I thought the number was familiar when I dialled it but I never thought the Roger in the diary would be our bloody guvnor.'

'That's why he hasn't been answering our calls,' Tom added.

Matt broke into a run as they made their way back to their vehicle. He'd taken possession of the diaries and Bible and Tom had made arrangements for some of his team to get straight to the graveyard to cordon off the area around the grave. It wasn't the best practise to remove the items but Matt couldn't wait a second longer than necessary to leave the scene and he couldn't risk them going missing. Tom jogged alongside him.

'Where the hell can he be?' Tom's voice was flat.

'I wish to God, I knew the answer to that. He could be anywhere. We can get his mobile phone cell-sited to see if it'll tie him down to a smaller area but that'll take time.'

'And that's just what we haven't got.' Tom was opening the car doors.

Matt jumped into the car and pulled the door shut. His breath was coming fast and shallow. He inhaled deeply trying to formulate some sort of plan.

'We need to find Carol Pritchard again. She knew Tina well. She'll probably know who Bambi is? Even if we've got records at the nick they're not likely to tell us as much as she'll probably be able to.'

Tom nodded. There was no sign of her on the bench. He swung the car around accelerating up towards the High Road without speaking. Parking outside the nearest all-night off-licence Matt saw the recognizable shape of Tricks standing beside the counter, hand on hip, open can of beer to her mouth. He ran from the car into the shop, grabbing hold of her by the arm and propelling her bodily from the store.

'Hey, you arsehole,' Carol swore. 'What the fuck are you doing?'

'I thought I might find you here. You're supposed to be buying food with the money I gave you, not more beer. I need to speak to you again and this time you've got to tell me absolutely everything you know. Someone's life might depend on it.'

'No crap,' the prostitute said, allowing Matt to steer her towards the waiting car. She lurched into the rear seat and Matt squeezed in next to her. Her breath stunk of beer and her clothes were dishevelled and musty. He wound the window down slightly as she leant towards him. 'Give us a fag and I'll tell you everything I know,' she slurred.

Matt reached into his pocket and pulled out a packet watching impatiently as she drew on the filter.

'Carol, who's Bambi?' he asked coming straight to the point.

Carol Pritchard exhaled the smoke into the interior of the car, swinging round to look Matt directly in the eyes.

'Bambi is the creep that always used to hang around Tina. She's a headcase, totally fucked up. Or at least I say she, but she's really a he. His name was Trevor but soon after arriving on the scene he changed his name to Bambi and started wearing women's clothes. Got quite nasty if you called him by his old name. Fucking pervert if you ask me.'

'Have you seen him tonight?'

'No, I ain't. The last time I saw him, proper like, was a couple of weeks ago and he was even more bloody weird. Started crying for no reason. When I asked him what was wrong, he just said that he missed Tina so bad. I didn't know quite what to say so I changed the subject. Told him his nice new blonde wig suited him. He cheered up then but what he said really fuckin' freaked me out. He said that the wig was made from Tina's hair, that when she'd died he'd had it cut off and made into a wig so he would have something to remember her with. I just got the hell away from him. He made my skin crawl.'

'Why didn't you tell us this before?'

'You never bleedin' asked.'

She turned away, clearly irritated, dragging hard on the cigarette. Matt watched its tip glow a bright red in the gloom.

'Tell me everything you know about him and Tina.'

She spat the smoke out. 'He turned up about five years ago with Tina. I remember cause I'd just had my third kid. He was a bit of a religious freak, would suddenly start quoting stuff from the Bible at you for no bleedin' reason. Tina said she'd met him up town but she never said exactly where. I presumed it was in some drop-in centre, there's always a few of them religious nuts in those places. I thought he was a headcase then, spoke in a weird voice, had a thing about always having perfectly polished nails and plastered his face with too much make-up. He was a fucking control freak. Liked to know exactly where she was all the time. Then he started to wear her clothes and got himself a wig and from then on started to call himself Bambi. They both did.'

'What did Tina see in him?'

'Fuck knows! But Tina seemed to like him, always spoke nicely about him or should I say her. She always referred to him as a girl. I asked her quite a few times what she saw in him but she couldn't really say. Just said that Bambi was her soul mate and they needed each other. That it was destined, whatever that means.' She took another drag on her cigarette before flicking the dog end out through the open window. 'I'll tell you one thing though. Tina changed when he arrived. She stopped working the streets and got clean from the crack. That part of it was good. I think he helped her do that. But then again he didn't like her going with men. Fucking hated men with a vengeance. That's what I mean by totally fucked up. Something must have happened to turn him off men when he was a kid. That's not natural like, is it?'

She leant across towards Matt, smiling with yellow, broken teeth and he felt the pressure of her hand on the inside of his thigh. Pulling it away he changed the subject.

'What did Tina die from?'

Carol lifted her hand out of his lazily and scratched her head, pulling at a tangle with grubby fingers.

'I don't know but they did like the booze. Maybe it was something to do with that. I often saw them together, pissed up, holding on to each other.' She snorted. 'Our sort,' she said in resignation, 'we never get properly clean. There's always something else to keep us from ourselves.' She smiled a sad little smile. 'They sort of got hooked up on each other and the booze.'

'Where did this Bambi live?'

'At Tina's place most of the time. Towards the end they were never apart.'

'Is there anywhere around here that he liked to hang out? Anywhere at all?'

'Why are you so keen to get hold of him anyway?' Carol Pritchard looked puzzled. 'The guy's just a pathetic freak. What's he done that's so fuckin' important?'

Matt frowned. He didn't want to let on that Bambi was almost certainly their serial killer. However he couldn't risk antagonizing her into silence by being reticent.

'Well, who do you think we're all trying to catch at the moment?' he said at last.

The prostitute took a few seconds but then her face became animated. 'You don't think he's the fuckin' person who's going round popping all those blokes, do you? I thought the papers said it was a woman.'

Matt nodded his head silently. 'Well he almost was, wasn't he? That's why it's important you tell us everything.'

Carol Pritchard stared at him, obviously taking in the severity of the situation. 'Oh, my God,' she said falteringly. 'When I last saw him he grabbed my hand. Said he wouldn't see me again. Said that the last five years with Tina had been the best in his life and that he couldn't live without her. He was freaking me out again. I didn't like him touching me and I told him so. He got really fuckin' angry and started muttering about how he hated men and how Tina and I had been tainted by them. The last thing I heard him say before I was well away from him was that God was pleased with him and that everyone in the world would see him flying with God and the angels.'

She stopped and Matt could see her visibly shaking. 'It was the night before you stopped me in the street that last time. I never thought it could be him or I would have told you. I'm sorry. I never realized.'

*　　*　　*

Bambi climbed into the driver's seat of the police car and smiled to herself. It had been so easy, so very easy. She looked across at the unconscious form of Roger Blandford, the cop, slumped into the passenger seat to which she'd just hauled him. She'd thought that this one might be more difficult but he'd fallen for her ploy just as simply and easily as the others.

She slammed the door shut with a flourish. Offer the right enticement and a man's ego would respond. It just depended on knowing a bit about your victim and his lifestyle. Without exception, though, they all had an Achilles' heel, a weakness, a fault line at which she could pick and wheedle and destroy. With Edward Piper it had been sex, pure and simple. Jeffrey Bamfo had responded to blackmail, the threat of exposing his seedy double-life and destroying his successful career and marriage too much to risk for a brokered deal. Ray Barnes had been slightly harder to call but Tina had mentioned his previous work at the domestic violence hostel. An appeal for his gallant assistance from an imaginary abused female victim and he'd fallen for her rather high, sing-song voice. She smirked knowingly at the thought. Charity had its roots entwined with the greed for recognition and the foolish man had responded as she'd hoped. Tunde Oshodi was just starting out, making a new life for himself, his wife and with a new baby in tow. His was a male ego fragile enough to be proud at the knowledge he'd fathered a baby yet callous enough to reject its existence for a few measly pounds cash.

Adjusting the seat, her arm rubbed against the outstretched leg of the unconscious cop. She'd wondered what his weakness would be, but as time had gone on and there had been no knock at her door she'd realized exactly where his weak spot would be. And she was right. He'd jumped at the chance for information, the opportunity to shine, the possibility of single-handedly solving the crime that held the public in its thrall.

She thought of them all as she put the car into gear and pulled away. They were all thoughtless, uncaring bastards who were guilty of using Tina for their own sordid pleasures while at the same time ignoring her right to be protected. These were her most regular clients back then before they had met, before she had prised her friend from the lifestyle that had caused her death. Any one of these men could be her murderer, any one of them could have been the one to pass on the death sentence and all of them demanded punishment for their sins.

She drove slowly at first enjoying the sight of the headlights disappearing into the foliage at the side of the common. She liked the grass and trees and shrubs; they'd offered protection and seclusion and the chance to bleed her victims slowly and painfully to death, just as they'd afforded her beautiful Tina a protracted and undignified exit. The woodland wasn't dark and menacing to her, it was her friend and it had offered anonymity just as she'd planned. Oh, she'd been careful to mask her identity; she'd taped over the registration plates, kept her head bowed low, used public kiosks out of sight of interfering cameras and been exceptionally vigilant in her preparations. She'd had to be. Theirs was a plan that required completion and that's why she'd chosen to kill in the open air. Just as the wooded copses afforded seclusion so they also offered an environment notoriously difficult to obtain forensic evidence from. It hadn't escaped her attention from the numerous unsolved murders in the past, just how hard it was to obtain DNA or fingerprint evidence from the mud and dirt of the great outdoors.

She turned on to the High Road, heading towards the centre of town. This time the knowledge that they were passing across the vision of countless CCTV cameras heartened her. She was invincible and the immobile body of her captive next to her made her strangely excited. She gazed across at his expression, calm and peaceful, sleeping soundly in the eyes of any other road users. Little did they know that hidden underneath a light cotton scarf were layers of garden twine securing his neck to the head rest. Little could they see the way his hands and feet were bound together to prevent his escape. He was still unconscious and therefore unable to shout out but Bambi knew that gradually, as they neared her chosen destination the stupid cop would come round and slowly become aware of the predicament in which he found himself. A smile of satisfaction played on her lips. By then it would be too late and he would be unable to respond, unable to save himself from the fate which awaited, the gory details of which he would be only too well aware.

She felt a stirring in her own groin and bit down hard on her lip, willing the pain to take away her growing erection. A shudder of repulsion rose up her spine reminding her of the hated appendage attached to her body. How she abhorred being male when every waking moment was spent dreaming of being a woman, every dream, every fantasy involved her body changing, morphing, transforming to a beautiful female form. Tina had understood this. She was the only one to allow his desires to become real and who'd accepted her for how she was. Never had there ever been any attempt to force her back into her maleness. Trevor Bayliss had become Bambi; he had become she and the knowledge that she was really a man was repressed behind the joy of acceptance. They'd needed each other in a way that she'd never been needed before and as their lives had gradually become further entwined so they'd dreamed their dreams. Hers had been to be fully accepted as a woman and Tina's in return was to have retribution against the men who had taken her life. They'd dreamed up the plan together, lived it, fantasized over it, and her friend's death had triggered its beginning.

She relaxed again as the hated genitals came back under her control. The cop stirred slightly against the seat and she smiled sadly at the irony of it all. She had the God-given power to sever what she so desired to have removed from her own body. Her life had been blighted from childhood by the medical profession's refusal to operate and she'd had to live a lie, loathing every single male hormone that pulsed through her body.

She watched the call girls plying their trade down Brixton Hill and saw the look of desperation on their faces and the shadowy figures of their pimps waiting violently in the shadows. It was how the world worked and she was powerless to change it. All she could do, with God's help, was to obtain justice for the woman that she'd loved and who had, in turn, loved her selflessly and unconditionally.

Matt's mobile rang as he was on his way back to Lambeth HQ. It was Gary Fellowes.

'No joy with the registered keeper enquiry, I'm afraid. I thought we'd got something because the previous owner remembered the person who'd bought it from them. It was apparently a guy dressed up as a woman. You wouldn't forget that, I suppose. Anyway as they'd got the cash out of their wallet they passed across an old gym membership card by accident. The name on it was a Trevor Bayliss with an address in Camberwell. The sellers didn't say anything and kept it in case they got any tickets for the car from its new owner.'

'And the address is?' Matt could barely contain himself.

'Empty, I'm afraid. We've already been there. It doesn't look as if anyone's lived there for ages.'

'That's because Trevor Bayliss has been living at his dead friend's bedsit instead. Shit! I thought for one minute then . . .' He sighed heavily. 'When the hell is our luck going to change? Thanks anyway, Gary. Could you ring in all the details to HQ so they can do some checks. I'll be in touch.'

He ended the call not waiting to hear his friend's response. His head was throbbing. All that kept running through his head was the memory of a mutilated body and his boss's head superimposed on top of the neck. He remembered how Roger Blandford had been strangely preoccupied in the last few days and he was torturing himself as to whether he should have realized what was going on. The more he thought about it, the more he feared that he should have checked, but Ben's funeral and his obsession with Vanessa Barnes had consumed his every thought. As he watched the buildings flash past him he was almost overwhelmed with a great wave of fear, fear that he had failed almost everyone around him.

'If only I hadn't concentrated so much on Vanessa Barnes,' he said miserably.

'Mate, you weren't to know,' Tom chipped in. 'We all thought she was a good suspect.'

'But I should have seen it,' Matt repeated. 'The guvnor warned me not to get too focussed on one person but I didn't listen. I thought it was her right up until she'd almost killed Evelyn.' He paused. 'Evelyn could be dead because of my mistakes, so could Vanessa, for that matter, if the armed officer hadn't decided to use a taser. I dread to think what the press would have said if either had been killed, especially when they found out that Vanessa was a victim all along. I feel bad enough about it myself now, the way I've treated her.'

Tom didn't answer.

'And now,' Matt persisted, 'the guvnor might end up dead and all because of my obsession with that one woman.'

'That's not fair,' Tom replied evenly. 'It's not just your mistake. It's all of ours. Even the guvnor must have thought it was Vanessa or he'd never have gone off, knowing that there might be another suspect on the loose.'

The sentence hung between them in the air. Maybe it was

true. Maybe it was the joint failure of them all. It didn't solve the problem of where Bambi had taken his boss and whether they were already too late.

The ranks of press outside headquarters had swelled since his last visit and Matt felt his stomach contract. He didn't want to be the one to admit they'd failed, that he'd failed. The crowd parted as Tom swung the car through to the car park. Flash bulbs went off in his face.

He climbed out of the car and stood silently looking up at the glass fascia of his boss's office. He would have done anything to see the thin trail of smoke drifting out from an open window, or to watch the figure of his friend shuffling about behind the glass, but the room appeared still and silent. He was aware of members of his team gathering around him, their speech bringing the results to enquiries, negative voices giving negative results. He was trying to focus on an idea that was drifting just out of his reach; a memory of something that had just come to him and would surely help.

The superintendent's voice reached him over the crescendo of different voices. 'Perhaps you'd like to explain what the hell is going on,' it said. 'Come up and see me in my office now.'

And suddenly the memory that Matt was so desperately trying to reach, drifted down within his grasp and he grabbed it and held it tightly and it was a memory of Roger Blandford in the same car park, angrily bemoaning the same bland command and it was a memory of tyres squealing on an unmarked police vehicle as it exited the yard. And everything suddenly made sense. Bambi's car had been found abandoned so, in contrast to the other murders, Roger Blandford was not being transported in the killer's vehicle. Matt continued the thread. It was therefore more than likely that this time Bambi was inside his victim's car. But this time it was a police car and a police car which was fitted with a mobile data transmitter, a type of radio used to download calls, a type of radio with which to send messages but most importantly, a type of radio that was equipped with a GPS satellite navigation system that could pinpoint exactly where in London that vehicle happened to be at any time.

If only the radio was switched on!

TWENTY-SEVEN

B ambi couldn't help a last drive past. It always looked so beautiful at night with its illuminations switched on, lighting up the sculptured stonework and grim gargoyles. The stained glass windows were dark and brooding from the outside, their vivid colours splashed by the outside lamp light against the natural mosaics of the abbey interior.

She remembered their first meeting, Tina distraught and enraged, her anger apparent to all, her indifference to the judgemental glances obvious. She remembered so acutely how curious her alter ego Trevor Bayliss had been at the sight of the distressed prostitute. She'd still been clothed as a man then, unsure of how to act or dress or deal with an alien body that did not match her sexuality. But she had recognized immediately that this was another lost soul, another human being whose whole reason for existence had been called into question. She could see it in the girl's eyes, her manner, her hopelessness and she, Bambi, had responded to the cry for help. It was, after all, a calling, ratified by their location. It was meant to be and as she'd edged along the pew that day, five years before, the girl had turned towards her and smiled. It had been the start of a friendship that had deepened to love, but not the normal love of a man and a woman. It was a desire to provide protection, acceptance and friendship without any sexual distractions, an asexual relationship without fear of rejection.

She swung round past the front of the abbey, watching as it became smaller and more distant. Her thoughts returned to Tina and the first time they had walked from the abbey together, as a couple of society's misfits destined to be inseparable in both life and death. It was then he had first learned the reason for her distress and understood the news that had started the count-down. For Tina, the knowledge that she had been diagnosed HIV positive had been toxic, like a poison that had spread almost immediately through every cell of her body. It was a deadly force inflicting both disease and death for the way in which she had been forced to live, passed on to her by one of her clients without caution or care.

Bambi knew as she drove away from the place their spirits had united that she had done all she could to help. It had been she who had masterminded her friend's departure from hard drugs, she who had been her crutch and support for the days when she'd been unable to rise from her bed or had lain in sheets wet with sweat, shaking with the cramps of withdrawal. She had tried to persuade Tina to return to the clinic and be prescribed with the drugs that could have lengthened her life, but she understood her friend's refusal. It had been Tina's sole decision to allow the disease to run its course and her decision to stay away from the medical profession and its false promises. Bambi understood the reasons only too well. It was the only time in her life her friend had ever had the power to control her destiny.

Bambi crossed Westminster Bridge skirting along the banks of the Thames as she made her way to St Thomas's Hospital. She had thought long and hard about where she wanted to complete the plan and knew she wanted the end to happen where it had all begun for Tina. The final corpse did not require hiding in woodland. The circle of life and death would be complete.

The hospital came into view, its nameplate bright and garish against the dark backdrop of the river. She pulled into the site entrance, passing the ramp to the accident and emergency department. Roger Blandford remained immobile, his eyes closed as if in sleep, his limbs just beginning to twitch with the first signs of consciousness. Patients and paramedics alike hovered by the entrance doors oblivious to their movements, ignorant to the nature of their journey. She continued through unchallenged, wending her way along the hospital driveway until she reached a small junction, on the right of which was a smaller track signposted for site vehicles only. She turned into the track following it past silent outbuildings and deserted office blocks until she found a quiet spot shielded between trees and a tall brick wall. She looked across at her passenger. His eyelids were flickering slightly now and it wouldn't be long before he awoke. She couldn't wait to see the expression of terror on his face at the reality of his situation.

She could feel her breathing quicken at the thought. She switched the lights off and allowed her pupils to acclimatize to the gloom. There was enough light to allow her to make her preparations but shelter enough to mask her from prying eyes. She leant back and pulled the holdall from the rear seat, unzipping it and pulling her precious cargo out. The twine was already in use but it reminded her of the need to tighten the pieces already keeping her victim in place. Stretching over she removed the scarf from around the cop's neck, pulling the cord tighter against the back of the seat so there was less room for him to fidget. It looked dark against his pale skin and its thickness left no possibility of escape. She glanced down at the rest of the twine checking its strength on his wrists and ankles and torso. It had been necessary to tie him to the back of the passenger seat, once she'd hauled him bodily across from the driver's position, to keep him upright on the journey through London. His skin was warm to the touch as she examined the twine and she could feel a pulse throbbing against the skin of his neck and wrists. His eyes flickered again. She knew it wouldn't be much longer. Reaching down into the holdall she pulled out the other items, looping the gag around his head and tying it tightly around his mouth. The plate she placed on the top of the dashboard with the Bible passage ready for its macabre contents, and the knife she placed in the driver's door pocket, easily available yet out of obvious view.

The cop was trying to move his limbs slightly, although still semi-conscious. Extracting the make-up bag from the holdall she lifted out the wig, her new wig fashioned from Tina's hair. Stroking it lovingly against her cheek she breathed in the lingering aroma of her friend. Only a slight scent still remained but it was all that was needed to bring the pain flooding back. She felt tears springing up and dabbed them away with the hair before pulling it tightly over her head into position. Checking in the centre mirror she relaxed at the sight. Everything made sense now. She felt right. She pulled out the two photographs and stared at them again, discarding the one from years before in which she was still predominantly male. She hated the image but it served to highlight just how much her life had changed since meeting Tina.

She stared at the second photo. Tina's face beamed out, her head held close to her own and their cheeks ruddy from the bracing sea breezes of Brighton. Tina was too young to die; she should have had a whole lifetime ahead of her, years to grow old together, years in which they would have shown the world the depth of their love and friendship.

The cop's eyes flicked open and his head turned slightly. Bambi quickly tucked the picture into the door pocket making it readily available for her final journey.

Reaching towards the Bible she turned to the page she had selected and read aloud, slowly and carefully. "'I will not punish your daughters when they turn to prostitution, nor your daughters-in-law when they commit adultery, because the men themselves consort with harlots and sacrifice with shrine prostitutes – a people without understanding will come to ruin!'"

She looked around at the cop. She knew his name and she knew where he worked. It had been a source of great amusement to her that he, Roger Blandford, would be trying to catch her just as surely as she was trying to ensnare him. Tina had told her all about him and the way he would ring when he was alone, for company he would say. She had laughed about him, ridiculed him for his inability to ask for what he fantasized about. Straight sex was all he wanted, but the hard-nosed detective had packaged it up with endless talk about his relationship failures. Tina had thought him pathetic, a wretched little man who was unable to either hold down a marriage or succeed at work and Bambi thought the same. Nevertheless out of her friend's five most regular clients he was the only one towards whom Tina had felt even the slightest warmth. Roger had been the only one to show her any kind of pity or support, having been generous with his payments, bringing additional supplies of food for her and ensuring she had enough money to pay for the rental of the room.

Bambi hadn't been taken in by his generosity however. It was just a cynical ploy to keep her friend where he wanted her and prevent her breaking her silence. After all, the policeman was slowly climbing the promotion ladder and his progress would have been immediately halted had his misdemeanours come to light.

She stared down at his body. He was male and he had used Tina for his own selfish pleasures and that was enough for Bambi. She'd shared her opinion with her friend and in time Tina too had come to realize that the policeman was more culpable, for making her think he cared. But he hadn't cared. After the first few occasions he too had used no protection and he too was just as capable of having infected her as the others. For that reason he had to die.

She could hear him groaning now, gagging against the thick wad of cloth around his mouth. She pulled the hair back from her face and watched his eyes flitting around the inside of the car, sensing his desperation to find an escape route, but there was none. He was hers now. She had waited five years for this. The panic in his face excited her. She wanted to kill him now. The knife was calling out to her and she grasped its handle, lifting it into a weak shaft of tremulous light so that it seemed to be throbbing with a life of its own.

The cop made a high-pitched whining noise and tried to move across in the seat, but the twine prevented any movement. Bambi rocked backwards and forwards in the seat. She liked this bit too much and she wanted it to last longer. She closed her eyes as the words of her favourite Bible passage came roaring into her head. *The wages of sin is death. The wages of sin is death. The wages of sin is death.* And as they came to her she opened her mouth and repeated them into the heady atmosphere, louder and louder and louder, until they were all that mattered. And the words calmed her and she knew exactly what she had to do.

Roger Blandford didn't know where he was or the identity of the person armed with a knife sitting rocking next to him but he knew instinctively that he had cocked up big style. Of all the things he had done in his life, or not done, this was by far the worst.

As his surroundings came into focus he strained to move his aching limbs, to ease his discomfiture but they remained static, bound tightly to the seat into which he was restrained. He tried speaking but his mouth wouldn't move and a thick wad of foul tasting cloth was making breathing difficult. He couldn't take his eyes off the knife and the thick mane of blonde hair that masked the face of his captor, but a vague glimpse of a dark-haired man with manicured fingernails danced into his memory. What he did know, without doubt, was that he was sitting next to the very same serial killer he had so recently been attempting to identify.

He swore inwardly at his own crass stupidity. How could he have allowed himself to be lured into this situation? He had ignored every twinge of unease, every rule, every regulation designed to provide him with protection. Through the rapidly clearing fog in his brain he immediately recognized the answer. It was greed, pure and simple; a last desperate grab at the notoriety afforded for capturing a serial killer. Now, by his actions, he was destined to be known as the maniac's last gullible victim, a kind of infamy in its own right.

His head still hadn't cleared sufficiently for him to formulate a plan of escape. There wasn't one as far as he could see. His hands and legs were bound, his body was tied to the seat and a thin but strong layer of twine was bound around his neck. If he tried to move, even slightly, it tightened, cutting into his neck and putting pressure on his wind pipe. He knew what it was for and he knew it would not tighten and take away the pain until he'd been forced to suffer the excruciating agony that would soon follow. He glanced across at his captor and tried to work out who they could be. The voice was unrecognizable, chanting in a high sing-song pitch that he had never heard before but the words were familiar, building as they were to a crescendo in time with the sway of the hair that still obscured the face. They struck fear into him. His gaze fell towards the knife held low in the lap of the driver and he saw bright red fingernails wrapped round the shaft of the blade, perfectly manicured nails that he now realized he had seen before on the hands of the man who'd asked for directions; the very same man he'd seen purchasing plates in Ikea. But who was he? And why would he be dressing up as a female tonight? And more importantly, how the hell was he going to escape the clutches of this maniac?

A violent shudder swept through his body and he started to tremble at the thought of the forthcoming expected mutilation. He couldn't lift his eyes away from the hard, cold metal of the knife. Bile rose up in his throat and he swallowed hard, gagging at its burning taste. He coughed as it filled his throat, choking against the wad of cloth. He couldn't breathe. As his face felt as if it was about to explode he was aware of fingers fumbling behind his neck and the gag was pulled away.

'Say a word and it'll be straight back on, Roger,' the voice said menacingly.

He nodded, swallowing back the bile, shocked for some reason at the sound of his name. It was too personal coming from a stranger but it brought with it the knowledge his abductor knew him and had selected him for a reason. At the same time he also realized that his only chance of escape might be to try to persuade his captor to free him but knowing his captor's record so well, he didn't hold out too much hope of success.

'Who are you?' he asked eventually. 'Do I know you?'

The man turned towards him, pushing back the hair from his face and laughing. His mouth was twisted into a sneer and his eyes, blackened now with eye shadow and mascara, were cold and determined.

'My name is Bambi, remember that name. It'll be the last name you ever say.' He pulled the hair back around his face and thrust forward so that the blonde mane surrounded Roger.

'Smell it, feel it, look at it. Do you remember it? Do you remember where you last saw it, whose beautiful head it used to adorn?'

Roger closed his eyes as the hair pushed against his pupils. It had a musty scent, a hint of abandonment, a smell he recognized from entering neglected premises in which people with little hope lived, drug dens, crack houses, rundown bedsits in large multi-occupancy premises whose landlords cared only for the rent each tenant brought with them. It brought back the memory of a time in his life that he had chosen to forget, a time when depression at the break-up of his marriage and the failure of his career had sent him crawling into the barren sheets of a call girl by the name of Tina. He pushed the thought away, as he had chosen to do ever since she had stopped answering his calls. It had been a mistake anyway, a huge error of judgement that could have precipitated a shameful downfall. He had been glad the temptation had been taken away, glad that after several months of unanswered messages he had moved on, glad that on a few rare occasions when their paths had crossed she had completely ignored him and the memory of their sordid liaisons.

The man was getting angrier now, pushing the hair against Roger's cheeks so that his head was driven against the back of the seat. 'You don't remember, do you? You don't remember her. You don't care. You're just like all the others.'

But he couldn't work out who this person was and why he was asking these questions and he didn't want to admit the thought that was taking shape inside his head. Vanessa Barnes had been their suspect. She was linked to at least two of the bodies. She was the one whom they had all suspected. Matt had been sure and he too had thought the same, but had he allowed himself to be persuaded, while he'd permitted a seed of doubt to fester at the back of his mind. Had he always really known?

The man pulled backwards a little leaving their faces still close. Roger could see the cold intensity of the man's rage in his blank pupils. He didn't know whether to say the name that was screaming within his brain or keep quiet. If he got it wrong he would be paying with his life for sure. He decided to risk it.

'Was it Tina's?' he whispered into the small space between them.

His captor seemed taken aback at the mention of the name and he knew immediately he'd got it right. Sensing a chance to keep the conversation going, he continued.

'Tina Stewart. I remember Tina very well. We were friends for some time.'

'Friends!' the man snorted loudly. 'That's a nice way of putting it.'

'She helped me a lot when I was going through a bad time.'

'And what did you do in return?' His eyes were angry, accusatory.

'I tried to help her,' Roger stammered. 'I did try. I brought her money and food and tried to make sure she had a roof over her head.'

'Only so you could use her. Only so you had somewhere you could go to abuse her. You make me sick, Roger. You took advantage of her desperation. You didn't care any more than the others.' He turned away and started to rock backwards and forwards again.

'Bambi . . .' Roger tried a direct appeal. He knew he couldn't let the man psyche himself up any more. He kept his voice subdued and quiet. 'I know you don't believe me but I did try to help and if it's any consolation to you I have felt bad about the way I treated her ever since.'

The man turned round, scrutinizing his face and frowned.

'Not bad enough to try to save her though. Not bad enough to care what happened to her once you'd finished. You deserve everything you get.' The knife danced back into view as Bambi lifted it up, running his manicured finger along the blade.

'Tell me about Tina.' Roger was desperate to keep him talking. 'You obviously knew her well.'

Bambi let his hand drop back down on to his lap at the repeat of her name.

'She was my best friend,' he said simply. 'She was just a mixed-up kid who didn't deserve the life she was given.' He stared searchingly at Roger. 'She had a bad childhood, parents who didn't give a toss and just gave up on her. She was left to find her own way and instead she found drugs. They screwed her life up good and proper. She said they were the only thing that made her forget the shit. But they cost and to pay for the habit she had to sell her body to any bastard that wanted a bit of it. And that's where you come in, you bastard, as if you didn't know.'

Bambi stopped talking and rounded on him.

'And where do you come in?' Roger tried to fend off the accusation. He had to try to keep the man calm but instead the question seemed to provoke an angry response.

'What do you mean by that?' his captor's voice was louder. 'If you think I would stoop to your level you're wrong. You real men just think with your dicks. You make me fucking sick. I actually helped Tina. When I met her I turned her life around, I helped get her off the game and get clean.' He calmed a bit. 'Yeah we had a few drinks together at times but we had a good life. Tina and I was good together.'

'So what did you get out of it?'

'Why do you people always think I had to get something out of it? I got nothing like you'd be thinking. I looked after her and she let me be me. She showed me I could be myself, have respect. She treated me like the woman I wanted to be. And so will you. I looked after her until the end. We loved each other in a way that you bleedin' macho men will never know.'

'What happened to Tina?'

'She's dead and it's all because of you,' Bambi said dully. 'You killed her. You took her away from me and God will punish you for your sins.' He started rocking again, closing his eyes and chanting the same chilling words. Roger tensed at the phrase, straining hard at his ties but there was nothing he could do to loosen them. The more he pulled at the twine, the more it cut into his flesh until he could feel drops of blood seeping from the wounds.

Bambi suddenly became still. Pulling the Bible from the dashboard he opened it and pressed it to his chest, breathing deeply, his eyes still tightly closed.

'I thought you might be more difficult to capture,' he said, opening his eyes and staring out into the darkness. 'But God has delivered you to me without hesitation and now I am ready to do God's will.'

Roger felt his chest constrict. After all the talking he had hoped the man would change his mind. He had hoped someone would arrive to save him but, in that instant, he realized with awful clarity there was no one. He hadn't told anyone where he was going or who he was meeting. No one would even know he was missing until he was found dead and mutilated in the morning by some random stranger walking through the hospital grounds.

'But God wouldn't want you to kill me,' he whispered tentatively. 'God would want *you* to forgive me, just as He would.' He couldn't hide the tremor in his voice as it cut through the stillness.

'My God wants to punish,' Bambi intoned loudly. '"Vengeance is mine sayeth the Lord". Ever since I was a child God has guided me. He is the One who took me to Westminster Abbey at the exact time that Tina needed me. He is the One who helped us think of our plan and He is the One who has guided me every step of the way. My God is a God of Righteousness and justice will only be complete when the last of the sinners is slain.'

The scream that came from Roger Blandford's mouth took him by surprise almost as much as Bambi. He felt his captor's hand clamp down firmly against his lips and saw him reaching for the gag. Tears of impotence squeezed out of his eyes and sobs shuddered up inside his chest.

'I'm sorry. I'm so sorry,' he stammered as the thick wad of material was pushed back into his mouth.

Bambi hesitated momentarily, reaching out and wiping a tear from his victim's cheek. He paused and for a fraction of a second Roger Blandford thought he might be spared.

'It's too late now. The time has come,' the sing-song voice chanted eventually. '"The wages of sin is death".' And as Bambi leant across towards him and slowly, ever so slowly, unbuckled his belt and undid the zip fastening of his trousers he smelled the odour of the dead call girl's hair.

TWENTY-EIGHT

All thoughts of lethargy had disappeared as Matt stared at the bright lights of the hospital. St Thomas's was a large sprawling mass of wards and outbuildings and somewhere in its grounds, his boss was to be found alive or dead. He didn't know which at the moment and the thought made the search even more frantic than anticipated. The irony of the location wasn't lost on him either. The hospital, instead of being a place to save life, had on this occasion become the setting for Trevor 'Bambi' Bayliss to take his boss's life. He shook his head.

Thank God Roger Blandford had thought to put the radio on; at least he'd had the foresight to allow his vehicle to be tracked. The GPS system had worked brilliantly so far for him and Tom but now he needed it to pinpoint the exact location of the police car.

As if on cue the radio crackled into action.

'Go into the main entrance and take a left turn. Follow the road as it heads around the rear of the main building. The car is shown as stationary in that vicinity.'

What the voice didn't say was whether they would be too late for Roger Blandford. What it also was unable to add was whether his boss would even be in the vehicle at all or whether the vehicle would be found abandoned, its precious cargo decanted to another unknown vehicle or location.

'All received,' he answered back, hoping against hope that the forthcoming answer would be the one option that they all wanted.

Tom navigated their car to the darkened area at the rear. Here a high wall shielded them not only from a view of the Thames but also from the strong winds that regularly whipped up the river funnel. It was airless tonight, with no breeze at all and the trees, heavy with leaves and blossom, appeared cast in stone, so still were they. The clouds which had been gathering as the evening progressed were stationary above them, swelling in strength and colour, like an angry crowd awaiting the chance to riot. Everything about the atmosphere spelt danger. Matt could hardly breathe.

The headlights of the car swept the area slowly, poking and prying into every darkened crevice. With each empty cul-de-sac or car park, the pressure was ratcheted up to an almost unbearable level so that Matt thought that the sound of his heart thudding hard against his ribcage would soon be loud enough to be heard by his colleague. They continued along the back road searching for the dark grey Mondeo police vehicle in which they'd last seen Roger Blandford. A small crossroads lay ahead of them with access on the right only to site vehicles. The road ahead and to their left neared the front of the hospital and was better lit and populated. The track to the right became darker.

'Turn right,' Matt instructed, although there was no need as the front wheels were already angled in that direction. Tom drove slowly, allowing Matt the opportunity to stare into the gloom, scanning behind every tree, every small outbuilding watching for the glint of a tail light, the flicker of a small internal light, anything to show the presence of a car. They were on their own, unwilling to wait a second longer than necessary, while other units mobilized. Matt wished fervently there were more units now to spread out and help identify their quarry.

A glint of light flicked out of a secluded area but disappeared as quickly as it had come. He stared into the void and thought he saw a slight movement. The glint came again, sudden, small, barely noticeable but nonetheless there. It came from a dark vehicle secreted between some trees, a dark vehicle he recognized immediately and one which he hoped would now provide the answer to their prayers.

The cop's trousers lay open, his genitals exposed, his terror absolute. The guy had pissed himself and was sitting in his wet clothing, crying and shaking uncontrollably. Bambi supposed it was because he knew exactly what was to come. She liked this thought. It was a proper punishment; a life for a life and a passage to death just as agonizing and slow as Tina's had been.

She had to give the cop credit for trying to persuade her otherwise but it wasn't washing with her. The guy was lying. He cared no more for Tina than any of the others, despite his protestations to the contrary. She had been no more than a means to satisfy his urges and now she was dead as a result. The cop in front of him was guilty of murder. It had been fitting to hear his scream, good to realize that he was suffering, but it was too late. The five years Bambi had been granted with Tina were over and her fifth and final victim was gagged and impotent. She had heard enough.

Gripping the knife in her hand she leant across, placing the plate into position on the floor beneath her victim. The cop stiffened in his seat, pulling against the ties, trying in vain to move away from her rummaging fingers. She laughed at the useless gesture and switched the interior light on to better see what she was doing. Her pupils recoiled at the intensity and she flicked the switch again to return to darkness but the radiance remained, shining brightly in her eyes. She brought her hand up to her eyes and squinted out from behind the blade, confused. Then she saw the man shining the torch beam straight at her face. His features were difficult to make out but his stance was that of a cop. He was walking towards her slowly, shouting at her. She pushed the door lock, listening as the bolts shot into place. He shouted again and this time she could make out the name he was calling. It was her name. He knew who she was but he couldn't stop what she was about to do. He was shouting at her again and there was another shadow advancing towards her from the other side.

She wound down the window, angry at the intrusion.

'Get back,' she screamed. 'Or I'll kill him.'

The cop put his hands up in a gesture of surrender. He looked familiar and she wondered briefly where she had seen him before. The cop on the other side stopped advancing.

'Bambi, don't do it. You don't have to do it.'

'I do have to and you can't stop me,' she screamed back. Nobody was going to stop her now. She had been waiting for this moment to finish the plan.

'Bambi, my name's Matt. Listen to me. I know about Tina,' the cop said bluntly. 'I know that she was your friend and she died and for some reason you blame these men.'

Bambi stared out at the cop named Matt. He didn't have a clue. He had no knowledge what this was all about.

'Do you know why I blame these men?' she said carefully. 'Do you have any idea what they did to Tina?'

The cop looked puzzled. He paused before speaking slowly, cautiously. 'I know they were Tina's clients and they paid for sexual favours, but it was her life. She chose to live the way she did.'

'But she didn't choose to die the way she did, did she?'

The cop was quiet. 'I don't know exactly what she died of. I thought she died because of her drinking.'

Bambi snorted out loud. 'Drinking! You stupid fucking bastard. She hardly drunk until the last year or so and that was just to make her feel better. It sort of dulled the pain.' She lifted the knife up and scraped it along the top of the window, watching as the cop's eyes were drawn to the movement. 'Tina died from AIDS. One of her clients gave her HIV. One of these bastards as good as killed her. For five years she tried to ignore it and live her life but she kept getting weaker and weaker, until it was as much as she could do to get up in the morning.'

'I'm sorry, I didn't know,' the cop said and suddenly she was cross that he didn't know and she wanted the world to understand why the men had to die. She looked down at her last victim and felt no pity, just pure hatred for the man who had taken her best friend. Turning the ignition switch she jammed the car into gear and slewed the vehicle backwards. Glass sprayed across the interior as the cop tried to stop the car moving, smashing the rear screen with his asp. She saw him pulling at the passenger door but it was locked and wouldn't open. The other cop was at her window trying to reach the ignition key. She thrust downwards with the blade, catching him across the arm and slicing into his bare flesh. Blood spouted from the wound, splashing its warmth on to her hand and the cop shouted out in surprise, pulling his hand back and pressing it against his chest. Revving hard she slammed the car into first gear and rocketed away towards the exit, leaving the two cops running back towards their own patrol car. Her last journey would be short and very sweet.

Matt got to the driver's side first and jumped in. He didn't want to lose sight of Bambi and his prey if he could help it. Tom climbed in beside him and slumped against the back of the seat, groaning. His arm was still pumping blood and even the T-shirt he had wrapped around it was failing to stop the flow. With wheels screeching Matt aimed his vehicle after the disappearing tail lights.

Tom pulled the handset from its seating, informing control they were in pursuit and Matt heard unit after unit responding to the call. There was no way Bambi would escape. There were too many vehicles after him now and in case he was lost temporarily they still had the GPS system to fall back on. Roger Blandford was still alive at least, although in imminent danger, if the brief conversation he'd had with Trevor Bayliss was anything to go by. The man was on the edge and one wrong move would mean the knife he'd so easily wielded could be plunged into his boss's manacled chest.

They swung out of the hospital grounds, turning left. Matt accelerated hard, gaining slightly on the other vehicle. He pulled the magnetic blue light out and slapped it on to the roof, driving hard down the centre of the traffic as a path appeared. Westminster Bridge opened up to their left and he followed his quarry on to the bridge and then, just as soon as it had started, it ended. The grey Mondeo was stationary, stopped in the centre of the bridge at a slight angle, its engine off and its occupants still. Matt pulled up behind it, instructing Tom to remain inside and coordinate the other units. Sirens could be heard echoing across the London streets from all around and he didn't want the man spooked.

He approached the vehicle slowly; his hands open in front of him letting the driver see he held no threat. Bambi opened the window, gesticulating with the knife towards him.

'Don't come any closer and tell the others to back off or he dies.'

Matt nodded, swinging round to see car after car, their blue lights flashing, approaching. He edged back to his car and spoke to control, instructing all units to remove themselves from the actual bridge and cordon off the entrances and exits. Standing by the side of the car he watched as the sea of lights backed away, lining up along the periphery and trapping them in on the short, stubby roadway. He paced carefully back towards Bambi, his hands outstretched and open. Behind him he heard Tom exiting their car and was aware of him moving round to the other side of their suspect's vehicle. Bambi swung round towards the movement.

'And get him out of here too. I'll only speak to you.'

Matt motioned to Tom to back off but he remained firm clearly unwilling to leave. Matt didn't want him to go either but one look at his friend's pale face and bloody T-shirt was enough to convince him that he needed to go for his own sake. As if to press the point, Bambi waved the knife out of the window, cutting through the air in wild, slashing motions.

'Get out of here, Tom. You need help. I'll see you later.'

He watched, as his friend backed away, slowly walking towards the sea of blue lights at the edge of the bridge and for a few minutes Matt felt totally alone. The life of his boss was solely in his hands now and the responsibility weighed heavily.

He sighed out loud as the sound of Big Ben reverberated across the blackness of the Thames. The river looked particularly threatening tonight, its waters mirroring the clouds, menacing and sinister, its hidden depths waiting to suck the flotsam and jetsam of the waterways deep into its belly. A spot of rain splashed on to his forehead and he watched as the surface of the water began to writhe and dance unwillingly to the beat of the shower. Glancing up at the illuminated face of Big Ben he saw its huge hand notch forward to just past quarter to one. It had been over seventeen hours since he'd risen, seventeen hours since his last blistering argument with Jo and a long day in which the whole direction of the investigation had changed. Vanessa Barnes was back in custody, Trevor 'Bambi' Bayliss had been identified and located as the Ikea suspect put up by the pathetic Julian Reynolds and the reason for their new suspect's killing spree, Tina Stewart, was dead.

As if on cue his mobile phone vibrated into action. Automatically he pulled it out looking to see Jo's name flashing up on the rain-flecked screen. He wanted to let it ring out but the noise suddenly became too intense. He needed to stop it.

'Jo, I can't talk now,' he whispered a bit too sharply.

He didn't get a reply immediately but somehow he couldn't end the call.

'I'm sorry,' he said quietly.

'We need to talk,' Jo's voice came back low and intense. 'Very soon,' she added.

Matt's mind lurched back to their parting. He couldn't tell whether her voice was conciliatory or defeated, whether she was holding out the olive branch or admitting it was all over. The fear of not knowing was sudden and almost overwhelming.

'I promise I'll phone back,' he whispered, 'and I promise

we'll talk about things, however hard.' He thought of Ben and his last journey came into his mind, carrying his son's small coffin to its final resting place.

A splash of rain caught him on his forehead. He reached up and wiped its wetness from his brow.

'I've got to go now,' he said finally, ending the call and switching the phone off. As the rain became heavier his mind flashed back to the small mound of earth that had covered his son's grave, so similar to Tina's, and it suddenly struck him how comparable the lives of both Vanessa and Tina had become and how they had been altered forever by the actions of those men who had sought to use them. And he was struck by how his own life had been affected by two men whose actions had inflicted such a heavy toll on his family.

'So, you've stayed to watch the final judgement have you?' Bambi's voice was heavy with malice.

Matt's reverie was broken and, startled briefly, he looked into the rabid eyes of his suspect and suddenly the whole reason for the man's actions fell into place.

'But you don't need to kill him,' he said more forcefully.

'You've already said that but you haven't listened to me, have you?' Bambi's mouth curled into a sneer. 'He is responsible for Tina's death and therefore he must die. And he must die now.'

Turning towards his victim, he pulled at the opening to his trousers. Matt watched horrified as Roger Blandford's eyes lit up in terror.

'He isn't responsible for Tina's death,' he said quietly, forcing himself to remain calm. 'If Tina died of AIDS like you say she did, then Roger Blandford did not kill her. Edward Piper, your first victim did.'

He held his breath as Trevor Bayliss paused, the knife still gripped above the exposed groin of his boss.

'Bambi, let him go. I promise you it wasn't him. I've been to Edward Piper's bedsit and it was littered with drugs for HIV. I've checked his medical records and he was diagnosed with it years ago. He's the one who infected Tina, not the others and not Roger.'

The words stopped her in her tracks. They were not what she

wanted to hear. She was so sure she was doing the right thing, that the possible truth of the words confused her.

Bambi rounded on the cop, her eyebrows furrowed in anger. She needed proof.

'How do I know you're telling the truth? How do I know you're not just saying that to save your precious boss?'

'You don't, but you'll just have to trust me. Jeffrey Bamfo, Ray Barnes and Tunde Oshodi all had full post-mortems and I would have known if any of them had tested positive. They were all negative. Edward Piper was the one. Surely Tina told you what he was like. His room was full of porn. He didn't care what he did and he didn't care who he did it with.'.

The last sentence struck home. He didn't care. He didn't care. Nobody had cared for Tina except Bambi. Not her family, not her so-called friends, not the men she took to bed or fucked on the streets. No one except her. Bambi spun round again to face the man who was to be her last victim and the memory of Tina's words came back to her. *At least he looked after me; he made sure I had food and enough money to pay the rent.* And she remembered his apologetic words. None of the others had said that. None of the others had shown any remorse. They had all come wanting, more money, more sex, an immunity from responsibility. All had had their pound of flesh and all had wanted more. Even Roger Blandford had come for his own reasons.

She pulled out the photograph of her and Tina together and stared into her friend's eyes willing her to communicate the course of action she should take. The memories came flooding back and she didn't know what to do. Raising the knife above her victim's head she waited for an answer. It came in the voice of the cop outside the car.

'Don't do it, Bambi. Tina wouldn't have wanted it and God doesn't want it. You've punished the murderer. Let this man go.'

She relaxed her arm and let the knife fall to the back of his neck. She felt the man tense but she knew what she wanted to do. Slipping it underneath the gag she cut through the wad of material, letting it fall into his lap, across his open trousers.

'Say you're sorry for what you did to Tina,' she instructed. 'I want to hear it again and I want your friend to hear it.'

Roger Blandford's voice came out strangulated and broken.

He licked his lips trying to replace the moisture that the gag had removed.

'I'm sorry for what I did,' he stammered quietly.

'Say it louder so we can both hear it. Apologize for using her. Say sorry for the way you treated her.'

'I'm sorry. I'm so sorry,' he said again, this time louder and she could tell that he meant it. He looked a broken man and she was satisfied. But there was still one thing left to be done.

Pulling the photograph to her body, she slipped the door open and stood up next to the side of the car, gripping the knife in front of her. Nobody was going to stop her taking the last step of her journey. She glanced up at the sky, from which a constant stream of warm rain was falling and breathed in deeply. This was where she belonged, between the abbey and the hospital, the two places that had changed her friend's life forever. This was where they had stood when the illness was too much to bear and spoken of the dreams that would never happen. This was where she had promised to come, after completing the plan, to rejoin the woman she loved.

She moved backwards keeping the river behind her, checking that the cop didn't come too close, until she was leaning against the wall at the edge of the bridge.

'Bambi, stop,' Matt was saying to her. 'I can explain what you've done. I can help.'

But she knew there was nothing he could do. She was doing this for the woman she loved, as she had all along. People wouldn't understand her motives. They wouldn't comprehend the need to sever the offending parts and display them to her God. Hers were actions motivated by love, a deep and debilitating grief and a desire for justice for the woman who had been so grievously wronged.

'You can't help me now. It's too late,' she replied in the high sing-song voice.

She pulled herself up on to the wall, perching on the top and letting the rain soak into her clothing and hair. As the wig grew wetter she could smell Tina's scent, giving her the sense that her friend was with her. She looked down one last time at the photograph allowing her memories to range free. Closing her eyes she concentrated on the past, knowing she was set to rejoin it. The toll of Big Ben resonated again, this time ringing in the hour. She let the sound wash over, preparing for the final boom

of the hour. As the sound of the great bell rang out across the
city, Bambi slid her legs round and leant soundlessly out into
the void.

Matt's grip held firm as he strained over the wall. He looked
down into Bambi's startled face, the eyes wide with confusion.
So engrossed in his thoughts had Trevor Bayliss been, that Matt
had been able to approach him in the last few seconds without
being noticed. The knife had fallen from his grip, spiralling
down beneath his flailing legs into the murky waters below.
Bambi swung beneath him, the photograph still clutched to his
chest with one arm, the other held by the wrist against the dirty
brickwork of the bridge.

Matt could feel the man's dead weight pulling against every
sinew of his body but he was determined to hang on. He could
hear the shouts of his colleagues in the distance and knew they
would be on the way to his assistance. If only his grip would
hold.

The rain was splashing down on his suspect's face, spreading
the dark rings of mascara across his cheeks. His eyes, wide
and frightened, flicked around him wildly, panicking as he
dangled helpless in the stormy air. Pain seared up Matt's arm
as he sought to maintain his hold and he grimaced in agony
with the effort.

Bambi was crying now, as he stared upwards but then a
strange expression flashed across his features. He appeared to
be puzzled, thinking, concentrating on a thought.

Matt grimaced again as his fingers struggled to stay locked
around the thin wrist.

'I know you, don't I?' Bambi said calmly. 'I remember seeing
you on television once before. You said your son was ill.'

Matt went to shake his head but then a brief memory returned
to him of a fleeting instance when a reporter had thrust a mike
into his face and asked him a question as he left headquarters,
a painful recollection of the moment when he'd heard his son
was dangerously ill. He hesitated as the transitory memory
flashed before him but Bambi's eyes had become more
animated.

Matt could feel him locking straight into his eyes, concentrating on him as if trying to read his hidden thoughts.

'Have you ever watched someone you love die right in front

of you?' he said quietly, his voice fading out to a whisper. *And not been able to do anything to stop it happening.* Matt filled in the end of the sentence in his head.

He could hear the shouts getting closer now, the sound of radio transmissions, of footsteps heavy on the soaking pavement and suddenly he understood exactly what Bambi was asking. A raft of memories flooded into his head. The vision of his son flying through the air and landing heavily on a freezing road, the sound of silence as the heart monitor was stopped, the sneer on the face of Andrei Kachan as he was given just two and a half years imprisonment, the letter announcing the release of William Mortimer, his father's murderer.

'Please let me go. Let me be with her.' Bambi was pleading.

And as the footsteps closed in and the rain ran down his arms and hands, mixing with Bambi's tears, Matt felt his own tears falling. And he knew that Bambi had sought justice just as he had done. And even though his method had been different, his motive had been the same.

As the first officer neared him Matt knew what he had to do. He let his fingers relax and felt his grip weaken and he watched as Trevor Bayliss, still gripping his prized photograph, slipped from his grasp and flew backwards through the air into the belly of the river. And as the reinforcements arrived on the scene he gazed down into the vacuum, watching as a blonde wig bubbled up to the surface and floated alone on the dark river. He watched as the ripples spread out from the spot where Bambi had disappeared and wondered how long the repercussions would last. Finally, as he was joined by Alison, an arm placed protectively around his shoulder, he imagined what it must be like to be reunited with the person you had loved and lost.